THE CONSTANTINE AFFLICTION

THE CONSTANTINE AFFLICTION

A PIMM AND SKYE ADVENTURE

T. Aaron Payton

NIGHT SHADE BOOKS
SAN FRANCISCO

The Constantine Affliction © 2012 by T. Aaron Payton
This edition of *The Constantine Affliction*
© 2012 by Night Shade Books

Jacket Illustration by Mark Nelson
Jacket design by Jason Snair
Interior layout and design by Amy Popovich

Edited by Ross E. Lockhart

First Edition

ISBN: 978-1-59780-400-4

Night Shade Books
http://www.nightshadebooks.com

For Tim Powers, teacher and inspiration.

Acts of Love

H e called himself Adam, and all he wanted was love.

     The man who was not quite a man walked across his laboratory, moving awkwardly on a leg still stiff from his accident in the Arctic long years before. His basement workspace was low, cramped, and crowded with shelves, tables, and the myriad tools of his myriad trades, but the unlovely setting only enhanced the luminous beauty of the woman on his examination table. Her hair was the color of a blackbird's wing, her skin pale as snowy alpine peaks, her flesh still cold from the shards of ice she'd arrived packed in. There were no marks on her throat, which meant she had probably been smothered, or possibly poisoned. No matter. The chemical preparation he'd used to replace her blood had flushed away any toxins or disease she'd suffered in life.

Adam attached the hand-woven filaments of wire to her brow, and inserted a metal probe into a tiny bloodless incision over her heart. The wires ran back to a tall wooden shelf that held row upon row of earthenware jars, bubbling with caustic chemicals that combined to produce that modern marvel, captive electricity.

Others who'd attempted similar courses of scientific inquiry had been forced to rely on lightning strikes or tanks of electrified eels and fish to provide the necessary electricity, but science—that bloodless maiden, that haughty mistress, that fecund mother—had advanced since those dark

1

days. Adam himself had perfected these batteries, which stored electricity in greater quantity and dispersed it in more controlled voltage than other designs generally available. He could easily have become wealthy by selling the innovation—the craze for electricity was still growing—but his researches were adequately funded by his patron, and beyond those needs, money did not interest him.

Truth did. Life did. Love did.

After double-checking the thick leather straps that held the slender woman to the operating table, he limped over to a pitted wooden lever fixed to the wall, at the nexus of a dozen wires. He pulled the handle down, and the room filled with a hum that tasted of lemons and a scent that sounded like chimes. Since his misadventures and near death in the Arctic sixty-five years ago, something had changed in him, and Adam's senses were no longer like those of other men. Sound bled into taste and scent into sound, the result of strange cross-connections deep in the structure of his brain. Those changes were indicative of damage, perhaps, but he'd since lived a normal human span without suffering any further deterioration, and on balance, he considered his textured perceptions a blessing. He felt sorry for the mass of men, with their sequestered senses, seeing only the reflections of light, hearing only the vibrations of air—their experience of the world must be like listening to a single lonesome flute, while to Adam, the world was a symphony.

The woman on the table moved, limbs jerking, back arching as best it could against the bondage of the straps, but that movement alone meant nothing—a current passing through the corpse of a frog would make the beast jerk, muscles jumping and tightening, but such movement had nothing to do with *life*, no more than a dead branch that waved in the wind did.

After the appropriate interval, the seconds counted off in Adam's metronomically accurate mind, he shut off the current, and the woman went limp on the table. Adam carefully removed the wires from her body and pressed his ear against her chest, between her breasts, and listened.

Her heart was beating again—the sound tasted like the brine of the sea—which meant this was, at least, not *that* kind of failure. Perhaps half the time, his experiments never even made it this far, the bodies of his subjects too damaged in subtle internal ways to be revived, and they simply remained dead on the table—later to be chopped up as food for the *other* kind of failure, or at least, the ones he kept.

He leaned forward, looking into the woman's face, so tranquil and composed. "Arise," he whispered, a ritual with no scientific basis, but one he indulged in nonetheless.

The woman opened her eyes. Her pupils were enormous, black chasms squeezing the irises into thin bands of impossible-to-ascertain color, but that didn't necessarily mean she was—

"Unggaahhh!" she said, and though the pitch and timbre of her voice were individual, the quality of the moan was familiar, and brought a taste of ash and bile to his mouth. That moan was a sound of hunger, and of desperate, senseless need. She jerked her head toward him and snapped her teeth together hard enough to chip one of her own incisors, but Adam was still far faster than ordinary men, and her bite missed closing on the flesh of his cheek. She jerked her head from side to side and strained against the straps—the restraints creaked, but they held. The woman was far stronger now than she had been before her death and resurrection, using her muscles to their full potential without being troubled by pain or strain or soreness, but she was not Adam's first subject, or even his twentieth, and the straps were strong enough, and held.

Another failure. They were all failures, so far, but love was enriched by struggle, was it not? A love that came easily might be lost easily as well, after all. Adam noted the results of the experiment in his journal, using a cipher of his own invention, then pondered. She was lovely, and it would be marvelous to keep her for his honor guard. His researches were ongoing, and if he kept her, he might someday be able to give her a truer resurrection… but no. She was *too* lovely, and it had been a while since Adam had sent his patron a woman who could work. His associates would not continue to bring him these poor dead girls if he did not occasionally give them some profit in return.

Adam tore off a half-sheet of paper and scratched out a brief note in a more accessible code, one that would have seemed like a meaningless and dull personal note to any reader but its intended recipient. He made his way upstairs to the ground floor of his narrow house, squeezed among warehouses not far from the widely-shunned walled area that included most of what had once been Whitechapel. He donned his hooded cloak, slipped on the plain white mask that hid his features, and cracked open the door.

Outside it was early evening on a squalid London street. The sky was already lit by the strange lights—the newspapers called them the "aurora anglais"—that had appeared a month before, and that some blamed on the Queen's new lover and his rumored atmospheric experiments. Adam did not care about the lights, or their cause, in more than an abstract way. His concerns were far more earthbound.

He called out, "You, boy," to no one in particular, and a dirty-faced urchin emerged from a shadow, saying "Sir?" but not coming close enough to touch. Adam was careful to take his special deliveries only late at night and through the tunnels beneath his house, but even so he was the subject of wild rumors—that he was a vivisectionist, that he'd been horribly scarred in an experiment (hence the mask), that he was a Peer afflicted with the Constantine Affliction (also hence the mask), and other such speculations. But despite their misgivings, a few of the urchins who squatted nearby had learned he was good for the occasional coin, and he usually found one brave enough to approach him. "Do you know the sweet shop on Hay Street?"

The boy nodded.

"Give this letter to the shopkeeper." He held out the sheet, and the boy quickly snatched it, darting in and out of seizing range as fast as he could. Foolish boy. Adam could catch him in a flicker if he wished. Before injuring his leg, Adam had been fast enough to run down wild deer and boar without becoming winded, and when the situation required, he could ignore the pain of old wounds and reach nearly those speeds again.

Adam tossed the boy a coin—a pittance, by Adam's standards, but enough to make the boy a little king for a day, or else a target of those who preferred theft to running errands. "Be quick now."

"Want I should bring word back?" This boy was bolder, or perhaps merely more desperate for money, than most of his fellows.

"No. There will be no reply." None was necessary. The arrangements were now routine. The man at the sweet shop would send word to his employer, who would in turn send men in the dark of night to collect the latest failed experiment and—Adam hoped—drop off another subject. There were always dead young women to be found in London, especially in the taverns and gambling halls of Southwark, the narrow lanes of Alsatia, in the lamplit alleys of Limehouse, in all the myriad brothels of the East End—at least, those portions that had not been walled off to save the city from the seething chemical reactions and ever-burning fires inside.

Adam returned to his front hall, already weary at the thought of the labors that lay before him. He would feed the woman some meat—he had no human flesh to hand just now, and in the absence of spare corpses, he fed the mindless reanimated ones offal, because it was cheap: kidneys, lungs, brains. After she was fed, he would etherize her into unconsciousness. Fortunately, her kind still breathed, and ether still had its effect. To feed a living person and then anesthetize them was dangerous, an invitation to vomit and subsequent aspiration, but the dead had iron stomachs.

When she was unconscious, he would cut off her hair (reserving it to be fashioned into a wig by other hands and then sold—his associates had so many ways to profit), remove the top of her skull, and make the necessary changes in her brain. The device he would implant there took advantage of recent advances in magnetic technology, and had a most striking effect on behavior. The ravenous, inhumanly strong creature he'd created would awaken biddable, docile, and capable of following simple instructions. Despite the semblance of obedient life, she would remain empty of self and incapable of thought or true emotion. Even so, Adam did not like to think long on the uses to which she would be put by his associates— placed in one of the lowliest of the now-illegal brothels and passed off as a living girl, albeit one heavily drugged... He shuddered.

Adam twitched aside the curtain by his door and looked into the empty street, brooding on the city beyond, his thoughts turned from love toward the filth of humanity. London, victim of three Great Fires and innumerable smaller ones, the eternal Phoenix rebuilt every time, even after the alchemical blaze of 1829. Parts of that fire still flickered greenishly, and might burn forever as far as anyone knew, in the walled-off section of the city. People who slept too near the contained area reportedly suffered horrible dreams and, sometimes, miraculous healing, but Adam put little stock in such anecdotes.

Despite their city's repeated immolations, the people of London still breathed, mated, gambled, wrote, composed music, drank laudanum, smoked opium, stabbed one another, studied the great poets, built houses, danced at parties, delivered unto him their beautiful dead... and eternally disappointed him. There were times when he missed the long years he'd spent essentially hibernating in the Arctic, brooding and waiting for a death that never came.

The city, he mused, seemed almost to be a vast experimental chamber, with Adam as its subject.

And its aim, to discover how long it would take for his desire for love to curdle into something altogether darker.

The Marriage of Two Minds

P embroke "Pimm" Halliday woke with an abominable pain in his head, a throat as dry as week-old bread, and last night's final regurgitation perfuming his breath. He rang for his valet—the ringing of the bell almost enough to make his skull shatter, he fancied—but the cursed man did not appear in the doorway with a cup of tea and a solicitous smile, or even at all.

Pimm struggled into his Oriental silk robe—it was a bit like wrestling an ape, which Pimm had done once, though not while sober—and walked with great care into the front room of his apartment. He called "Ransome, are you here?" in a uselessly soft voice, but a louder cry would only have invited further cranial cataclysm.

"Ransome has given his notice," Freddy said. Pimm's oldest friend and dearest confidant sat in a bright corner of the room, reading a newspaper, at ease in a chair placed regrettably beneath an unshaded window that faced east. "Have you seen the latest *Argus*? Well, of course not, you've been abed. This article by Mr. E. Skye, about the so-called river monsters purportedly seen in the Thames, with each witness drunker than the last? It's marvelous. Though I'd wager none of the witnesses were drunker than you last night, dear—you wouldn't have noticed a river monster if it swam

7

through your bathtub. Mr. Skye's story strikes just the right tone of mordant hilarity without edging quite into disrespect, quoting liberally from the river men and letting their own words do the job. His talents are really wasted on journalism, he should—"

Pimm's mind slowly began operating at something approaching its usual level of efficiency. "Ransome is gone? He's left our service? Why the devil would he do that?" Pimm sat down in another chair, as far from the light as possible. He squinted; Freddy didn't appear to be wearing much in the way of clothing, and if not for the backlighting, shocking amounts of flesh would likely be on display. "Lord, man, cover yourself! How often have I told you I have no desire to gaze upon your flesh?"

"So avert your eyes." Unperturbed, Freddy sipped tea, somehow deftly managing cup, newspaper, and cigarette all at once. "If you had to wear a corset every time you went outside, you'd relish these unconfined moments as much as I do. As for Ransome, he said he simply couldn't abide the prospect of cleaning out another basin of your vomit, and so he gave his regrets. I told him I quite understood, and paid him through the end of the month. I promised him a glowing reference, though I gather he already has another offer."

"I hope you weren't dressed like this during that conversation." Pimm squirmed down in the chair and pulled the front of his robe up over his head to cover his eyes. Ah, blissful dimness. "Or should I say undressed."

"If I'd been dressed like this, he would certainly have stayed, don't you think? He probably would have pledged himself to my service—he was always scandalized that I don't have a ladies' maid."

"Not as scandalized as any ladies' maid who came to serve you would be," Pimm said. "Couldn't you have tried to change his mind? Ransome made a good cup of tea, and an even better brandy and soda. I could use one of those now. Either one, really. Both, for preference." He briefly peeked out of the robe. "That was a hint."

"There's a kettle in the kitchen. Help yourself."

"You know I'm terrified of that stove. In my day we cooked over fire, not bottled lightning. Well. *One* cooked. I did not cook."

"You're a child, Pimm. We live in an age of wonders, the world transformed by electricity, magnetism, alchemical innovations—"

"And what's it used for, hmm?" Pimm uncovered his head and gave

Freddy his most cutting glare. "New ways to murder people and the fab-rication of clockwork prostitutes."

"Clockwork prostitutes could have come a little sooner, by my prefer-ence," Freddy said frostily.

Pimm winced. "Quite, of course, I didn't mean... I apologize." Dur-ing the early days of their current arrangement Freddy had descended fairly often into black moods that sometimes lasted for days, sullen storms punctuated by furious flashes of unreasoning anger, but in the past year things had settled down as Freddy grew accustomed to the new status quo, and had been positively chipper on the whole. It was impressive, really. Freddy had been through a rough few years, a victim of illness and society and family all at once. Pimm wasn't sure he'd have adapted half so well.

When Freddy rose and walked across the room, Pimm couldn't help himself. He peeked. An instant later he turned his eyes away from the creamy flash of breasts, the shapely line of leg, the smooth muscle of thigh. "Cover up, please, I can't bear it!"

"You're a beast," Freddy said, amused, and stood sorting through a pile of paper on the table by the door. "It's a good thing I'm not *really* your wife, or such an outcry might bruise my feelings."

"Tell that to the Church of England," Pimm said. "They certainly con-sider us well and truly wed."

"Except that legally I'm still a *man*, which tends to invalidate your argument."

"What the Church doesn't know..." Pimm muttered. Victims trans-formed by the Constantine Affliction were, legally speaking, considered to be the same sex they'd been at birth—otherwise you could have a daughter transforming into a firstborn son and inheriting her father's estate over her younger brothers. In practice, though, most victims of the Affliction went into hiding, or tried to pass as their original sex, or—like Freddy—simply changed their identities and began a new life. The women transformed into men preferred that latter path, especially, as it tended to open up all sorts of new possibilities for them.

"Never has there been a more inconvenient marriage of convenience, eh?" the lady of the house said. "Fine, I'll dress." Freddy went into the bedroom, not bothering to shut the door, and called out. "I'm going to a salon later today. Christina Rosetti may be there. Her recent poetry isn't up to the standards of her *Goblin Market*, but still, she's very interesting." Freddy emerged, walking and gazing into a hand mirror at the same time.

"You modern women and your intellectual pursuits. Between your tinkering with inventions downstairs and your writing of poetry upstairs, you constitute a one-person society of arts and sciences." Pimm risked a glance at his friend, then winced and looked away. "You were hideous when you were a man, Freddy, with a face like a frog, and ankles like a stork's. How is it that after the fever you became so, so...."

Freddy put the mirror down on a side table and stepped in front of Pimm's chair, hands on hips. He—she—Curse it. Pimm tried, in private, to avoid the use of pronouns in relation to this person who was technically his spouse, though to most eyes, Freddy was indeed female, and was more generally known by the *nom de* what-have-you of "Winifred Halliday née Sandoval," or more properly "Lady Pembroke." Calling Freddy "she" and "her" seemed more and more natural every day, which made public appearances less fraught with opportunity for confusion, but also seemed in some way a betrayal of the man who had been Pimm's friend for so long.

Freddy now wore a partially-unbuttoned and fortunately oversized man's shirt and, it seemed, nothing else. Her hair was a golden cloud, her nose adorably snub, her lips plump and currently frowning. "If I were uglier, I'd be wearing a false mustache and binding down my breasts with strips of cloth and passing for male like some of the *other* bastards, who were luckier in their transformations." Freddy sighed. "Though I suppose I'm lucky too—I didn't die, or get stuck halfway through the change, like some." The Constantine Affliction was unpredictable and cruel in its course, though many expressed the opinion that being transformed into a woman must surely be a fate worse than death. Spoken like someone who had never died, Pimm always thought.

"And you spared me the horrors of marrying someone else," Pimm said. "Someone of whom my relatives might have *approved*." Pimm's marriage to the mysterious Winifred Sandoval—a person of no particularly notable family connection—hadn't delighted his aunts and uncles or his elder brother the Marquess, but he'd made an impassioned speech about true love and they'd eventually agreed to go along with things, mostly just to stop him quoting love poetry. The wise old heads of the family were happy to see him married to *someone*, anyway, and hoped he would stop embarrassing his illustrious older brother and the rest of the Halliday line now that he'd settled down with a good woman.

He had, alas, disappointed them. They didn't mind the drinking and the gambling and the *bon vivant* lifestyle, really—every well-established family had its dissolute spendthrifts. It was… the other thing. His hobby. The one thing he did well *other* than drinking and playing whist. The thing that got his name in the papers.

"Mmm," Freddy said. "It's good to know I saved some poor woman from a life of misery at your side. Oh, a letter came for you. It's by the door—I had intended to place it in your hands, out of deference to the headache you clearly have, but then you insulted my physique and demanded I cover myself up."

"Your physique is fine. That's the problem." Pimm rose, groaning, and went to the table by the door while Freddy sashayed away back to her bedroom. His spouse had been practicing a feminine carriage, but took too many lessons from women of the wrong class. Pimm sorted through the post until he found the letter Freddy meant. He tore it open and read the few lines while standing by the door, then crushed the paper in his fist. "Damnation. Freddy!" he shouted. "What time is your salon?"

"I have a few hours yet, though I thought I'd do some shopping beforehand." Freddy emerged, still underdressed. "Why do you ask?"

"Abel Value wants to meet with me."

"Oh, my." Freddy looked at the ceiling for a moment, humming a bit. "When?"

"He proposes to meet for lunch."

"Drat. And we had a scientist coming to the salon today, an expert on certain fish who sometimes change their sex. He has some interesting ideas about the causes of the Constantine Affliction. Something about pollution in the water supply, I think."

"Better than the ministers who say the transformations are judgments from God, because men have become too feminine and women too much like men, though to be honest I'm not fit to judge either argument on its merits, being as ignorant of biology as I am of theology. I suppose I can handle things with Value myself…"

"Pish," Freddy said. "Where will you meet him? The Luna Club?"

"I wouldn't want to be seen with him in my club, and he knows it. No, he proposes to meet here."

Freddy nodded, thoughtful. "Hmm. The closet in your bedroom shares a wall with this room, and at midday that side of the room is fairly well shadowed. I can drill two small holes, one to look through, the other to press the barrel of the air-pistol against. Just make sure Mr. Value sits in *that* chair, facing the window, so the sun is in his eyes, and so I can get a clear shot at him, if need be."

"He'll probably bring one of his men," Pimm said. "Who will, doubtless, loiter by the door unless called upon."

"Three holes, then," Freddy said. "And I'll prepare both pistols."

"You're the best wife a man could hope for," Pimm said.

Freddy grinned wolfishly, and that, at least, had not changed a bit with his transformation from man to woman. "In certain respects, at least," Freddy agreed.

Scandal and Poppycock

Eleanor Irene Skyler, called Ellie by her friends (though her byline ran as "E. Skye," with the extra "e" at the end because her editor felt it added a touch of sophistication), stepped off the self-propelled streetcar and directly into a heap of horse manure. She did not curse aloud, because though she was of necessity more independently-minded than most women in the city, she could not entirely forsake her upbringing. After scraping off her shoe as best she could on a cobblestone, she stepped around another heap of horse leavings and made her way toward the offices of the *London Argus*, not far from Printing House Square.

The streets of London were still very much contested territory, with the new electrified carts rumbling along their pre-ordained routes while more traditional folk tried to prevent their horses from being run over. And, of course, most everyone was far too poor for horse *or* electric cart, and made their way on foot. There had been a few noteworthy crashes involving the electrical omnibuses, some of which she'd covered for the paper, and so she rode the bright red "devil carts" as often as she could in hopes of being a firsthand witness to another such disaster. Even most Londoners who could spare the fare didn't bother with the carts, both for fear the things would crash and because they didn't go much faster than a brisk walk anyway—though the latter problem tended to mitigate the severity of the former. The omnibuses were part of Sir Bertram's brave new vision for the future for London, though, and so the Queen insisted they keep running. Perhaps they'd vanish into the background of the city's life in time, and cease to be a novelty. After all, even the railroads had seemed dangerous and shocking once upon a time.

The city—the world—had changed immeasurably since Ellie's girlhood. Just over a dozen years ago the Great Exhibition at the Crystal Palace had trumpeted the coming of a new world of scientific advancement and industry, and that conceptual world had come into being even more swiftly than she'd ever imagined. Parts of central London were electrified, with night never seeming to truly fall; swiftly whirring calculating engines made greater and greater feats of engineering possible, including the tunnel beneath the English Channel first proposed by George Ward Hunt, with excavations recently commenced; and medical advances like magnetic field manipulators and Pasteur's controversial germ theory had improved life for everyone—why, without Pasteur's innovations, the Prince Consort would surely have died of Typhoid fever. (Not that staying alive had done Prince Albert much good, ultimately—he probably wished he *was* dead, now.)

There were more advances rumored every day, from flying machines that could go faster than the swiftest airships, to expeditions into the depths of the Earth, to high mountain telescopes so powerful they could reportedly glimpse the contours of vast alien cities on the moons of Jupiter. And now Bertram Oswald was preparing his own Great Exposition to be held in Hyde Park, a spectacle devoted to showcasing the newest technological wonders created in England—mostly, it was worth noting, developed by Oswald himself, the greatest mind of their age, as he never tired of reminding anyone who would listen. The worst part was, he was almost certainly right.

Of course, there were darker sides to progress, too—the depraved uses of advanced automatons, the terrible new engines of war, the Constantine Affliction and its high-profile victims. (The objectively meaningless term "The Constantine Affliction" was itself a printer's error from a rival newspaper—"The Constantinopolitan Affliction" had proven too difficult to for the typesetter to manage, and the simplified form had stuck in the public consciousness, to the dismay of grammarians and historians both.)

For good and for ill it was a cracking good time to be a journalist—disasters made better stories than glorious successes, but even the brighter side of progress would fill column inches and draw the reader's eye. If she could only get away from covering society galas and the weddings of the rich, delightful as the food usually was at both. Her editor Cooper had finally given in to her complaints and sent her to interview the river men and the tide-wives and mud-larks about the monsters seen in the Thames, thinking that such rough company would dissuade her from requesting more interesting assignments, but he'd been disappointed. He'd cut the portions of her article that featured more sensible and reasonable voices admitting to seeing strange things in the river, but she didn't blame him—they'd run short of space, and the more buffoonish quotes made for better reading. Ellie had seen no monsters in the river herself… but she'd spoken to people who genuinely believed they had.

The newsroom today was the usual buzz of activity, shouting voices, and the smell of ink, and she wove through the desks and knots of her colleagues with the grace of a dancer before ducking into the editor-in-chief's office without bothering to knock.

"Oh, good, you got my message." Cooper looked up from the wreckage that was his desk. "You'll take passage at week's end, then?"

"No, I will not." There was no chair on this side of the desk—Cooper didn't like to encourage his reporters to dawdle and chat—so she leaned over it, pressing her hands down on two unyielding piles of newsprint for balance. "I have no interest in reporting on the latest French fashions."

"Contrary woman." Cooper puffed at his pipe, dispersing clouds of foul-smelling spiced tobacco. "You demanded I send you abroad, and now you refuse a trip to Paris—"

"Send me to Mexico to cover the war. That's the kind of travel I meant."

"Mexico? I hardly think so. Do you even speak Spanish?"

She was prepared for objections based on her safety or the weakness of her sex—she had been arguing against both lines of argument for most of her twenty-five years of life, it sometimes seemed—but this tactic gave her pause. "Well, no, I don't—"

"But you *do* speak fluent French?"

"Yes, of course, but—no! I have no interest in fashion, Cooper."

"That much has long been apparent," Cooper said, still infuriatingly calm. She had a sudden urge to tell him his mustache and whiskers looked ridiculous, but refrained. Mustaches and elaborate Dundreary whiskers were the current craze among men—proof they hadn't contracted the Constantine Affliction and tried to conceal it, she supposed, though fake mustaches were no doubt readily available to those who *had* transformed, and wished to put up a masculine pretense. Cooper's nasal undergrowth was, she decided, no more foolish than most, for what little that was worth.

"Please," she said, trying for sweetness. "Perhaps I could do something closer to home and spare you the expense of a trans-Atlantic crossing. Send me to Paris when the tunnel is done, and I'll report on both the novelty of the journey *and* the dresses I see on the other side. In the meantime, I have something else in mind, and I have already written the first lines." She opened her journal, annoyed as usual at the graceful looping curves of her handwriting, which did not match the crispness and seriousness she attempted to convey—she much preferred to see her prose in neatly typeset lines. She put the journal on the desk before Cooper, and he sighed and began to read. The lines were fresh in her mind, and she could almost follow along as his eyes tracked the page:

> It is a great irony that no rich or influential man will ever admit to entering a clockwork pleasure house—when only rich and influential men are *permitted* through those elegant and well-guarded doors. We at the *Argus* are pleased to give you vicarious entree, and provide a rare opportunity to glimpse the velvet-lined rooms in these houses of—

"Oh merciful heaven." Cooper slammed the journal shut. "You can't seriously propose an investigation like this! You know I believe you write as well as most men, but you are *not* a man, and no woman would ever be permitted inside one of those, those—"

"Clockwork brothels? Temples of mechanical immorality? Gear-driven bordellos?"

"Yes. *Those.* How do you expect to get inside?"

"Deception, of course. I can pitch my voice low—" she demonstrated "—and disguise myself as a man. Such disguises aren't hard to come by, and at the risk of sounding crude, I am well aware that my figure is better suited than *some* to such a ruse. It's not as if I would need to consummate a liaison with a clockwork courtesan in order to write about them."

"Nor would we print such details—we aren't the *Lantern*, after all, we have depths beyond which we will not descend." He shook his head. "But, no. I cannot permit this."

"Ah, but if I go on my own, despite the lack of permission—would you be interested in the resulting story? Or should I sell it instead to the *Lantern*?"

He sighed. "Ellie… if I were your father, or your brother…"

"You are neither." Nor was anyone else. She had no living near relations, which made living by her pen a necessity as well as a choice. Cooper had been a friend of her family—Ellie sometimes wondered if he'd wooed her mother, once upon a time—and had initially given her work out of pity, before coming to count on her for dependable prose delivered in a timely fashion. He sometimes still treated her like a sort of honorary younger sister, but not as often as he once had.

"It would have to be published anonymously," Cooper said after a long moment of contemplation.

"'E. Skye' is already a pen name, and everyone assumes it's a man's name, besides. Yet you see the need for greater subterfuge?"

"The men who run these establishments are unsavory characters, and it is better if they cannot easily identify the source of such an article. The truth behind a pen name can be uncovered. Better to have no name attached at all. If you write it—which I wish you would not—we will simply credit it to 'A Gentleman.' Let me reiterate, I strongly object to—"

"So noted," Ellie said.

"But of course you won't heed my advice. Why should today depart from the norm?" He sighed. "When do you propose to undertake this invasion?"

"Oh, not until later tonight. I doubt such establishments are open before nightfall."

Cooper tapped the end of his pen against the desktop. "First you report on monsters in the river, and now you propose to expose the prurience of the city's elite. You do go from poppycock to scandal, Ellie."

"If you don't like it, send me to be a war correspondent." She dropped an ironic curtsey and strolled out of the office, visions of mustaches and trousers dancing in her head.

A Meeting with Value

In the end, they decided to be more cautious, and hung a not-very-good Chinese tapestry over the two holes drilled for the pistol barrels, leaving only one hole unobstructed and unhidden, for Freddy to peer through. The rounds fired by the air-pistols would not be impeded by the tapestry's cloth. Pimm sincerely hoped all these preparations would prove unnecessary—even paranoiac—but from what he knew of Abel Value, it was wise to take precautions. The man was in the sort of business where the occasional murder was necessary to keep things running smoothly, and while Pimm did not expect to be assassinated in his own home, it never hurt to be careful.

When the knock came at the door, Pimm was largely over his headache and taking his ease in the chair under the window where Freddy had been lounging that morning. He waited a moment, then remembered their one servant had quit that morning, and frowned. Another knock, more peremptory, and he said, "Let yourself in!"

The door swung open, though Value did not enter first. A man roughly the size of a river barge came in, ducking his head to avoid bumping it on the doorframe, and scanned the room. He then stood against the wall by the door, clasping gloved hands together, and looked at Pimm impassively.

"Big Ben, isn't it?" Pimm said.

The man scowled. He clearly didn't like the idea of someone like Pimm knowing his name. "Yes, sir."

Abel Value entered the room, but Pimm didn't pay him any attention yet, still talking to the bodyguard. "Do they call you that after the prize-fighter, Benjamin Caunt? You're at least as big as he is. Or, ha, after the bell in the clock tower?"

"They call me that, sir, because I am of large stature, sir, and because my given name is Benjamin." His voice was calm, his diction clear, his tone dry as chalk, and Pimm mused that it was foolish to assume a man the size of a plow horse would be no smarter than one.

"I find that eminently logical."

"They call you 'Pimm,' don't they, sir?" Big Ben asked, his tone deferential, his expression anything but.

"Some do," he acknowledged.

"Why is that, if I may ask, sir?"

"I assume because my own given name is Pembroke, and because I'm a notorious drunkard, Benjamin. Pimm's Cup isn't my libation of choice, but it's still a good enough joke, by the standards of my usual drinking companions."

Pimm turned his attention to Abel Value, who was either the most notorious criminal or the most prosperous businessman in London, de-pending on whom you asked, and on what sort of people were within earshot when you did the asking. Value was dressed in a suit that was certainly more expensive than Pimm's own, and he had iron-gray hair, an unfashionably clean-shaven face, and a nose that had been broken at least once. He didn't bother to hide his smirk, and he patted his bodyguard on the arm when he passed by.

"Good day, sir," Pimm said. "To what do I owe the pleasure?" He ges-tured at the only other empty chair in the room, the other seats having been removed earlier by Freddy to make sure Value arranged himself properly.

"Necessity," Value said, and Ben shut the door behind him. Value looked at the empty chair for a moment, as if assessing whether or not it might be a trap, then sat down, crossing one leg over the other and lacing his fingers across his knee. "I need your help, Halliday. And you need to help me."

"Ah," Pimm said. "I confess a measure of surprise. I had assumed you wished to speak to me regarding Mr. Martinson."

Abel frowned. "I can't imagine what you mean. It was a terrible tragedy, of course, that the blackguard could not be brought to justice, but his unfortunate demise has nothing to do with me."

"Really. I was under the impression that my investigation into his business had displeased you."

Abel shrugged. "Martinson was an old friend. I was, naturally, reluctant to believe the allegations of criminal behavior against him, and assumed you were acting on false information—or else in bad faith—when you made your report to the police. But since Martinson took his own life, I can only conclude he suffered from a guilty conscience. A shame. He was a good man, but weak."

Pimm limited himself to a nod. Martinson had been the headmaster of a prestigious public school, but he had also been selling his students illegal alchemical stimulants, and a handful of the children had died from over-indulgence—including the nephew of one of Pimm's old school chums, who'd asked him to investigate. Proving Martinson's guilt had been easy, but Pimm had hoped to use him as a stepping-stone to incriminate the seemingly untouchable Value, who had certainly supplied the illicit substances. Instead… well. Martinson's death had been ruled suicide—death before dishonor and all that—but Pimm had his doubts.

"I am here now," Value said, "to retain your services as a consulting detective."

Pimm could not have been more surprised if Value had proposed marriage. "I think you misunderstand my, ah, situation. That is, I have occasionally intervened on behalf of certain friends, or assisted the police, making what poor efforts I could to aid their inquiries. But I have always operated on a purely informal basis. Though I have a certain amateur interest in matters of criminology, I am hardly a detective, and I regret that my services, such as they may be, are not actually for hire." He chuckled self-deprecatingly. "My family wouldn't stand for it, I'm afraid, if I adopted such a vocation. It would hardly strike them as a gentlemanly pursuit."

"He does use a lot of words to say 'no,' doesn't he, Ben?" Value said.

"Some might say that's the sign of an educated man," Big Ben opined.

"Listen, *Lord* Pembroke," Value said, leaning forward. "Someone is murdering my whores, and I need to find out who."

Womanly Arts

Ellie numbered among her acquaintances a certain tailor on Savile Row who, in addition to his other business, also catered to those men who'd been transformed by the Constantine Affliction—and hoped to hide that fact. Though Mr. James had the usual distrust for the press (a stance that was, if anything, amplified by the necessarily confidential nature of his back-room business), he'd been fond of Ellie ever since her engagement to his nephew David, and tolerated her inquisitiveness. David had worked for the British East India Company, and had sadly perished in 1858 during the Indian uprising, crushed by one of the Steel Raja's terrible steam elephants. For Ellie, his death had been the end of her hopes for a traditional life as a wife and mother, and her dabbling in writing for women's periodicals had blossomed—both due to passion and from financial necessity—into a life's work as a journalist.

Mr. James greeted her warmly, taking her by the hand and directing his assistant to watch the store while he led her through the workroom at the back and into a small office, where he had a gas ring and a kettle, and busied himself preparing tea. "Such a pleasure to see you, Eleanor," he said, setting out cups and spoons and sugar with the same sort of precise movements he used when taking measurements for a new suit. "How are you keeping yourself?"

"Very well, thank you."

"Still wielding your ferocious pen?"

"Indeed, uncle," she said, using a term of affection they had settled on long ago. "Your assistance on the article I wrote last year was a great boon to my career." Mr. James had put her in touch with a few of his clients, who were willing to speak about their experience of the Constantine Affliction on the condition of anonymity. Ellie had also spoken to the close relations—mothers, fathers, children, husbands, wives—of the afflicted. The resulting article had been a great sensation, and a source of great surprise for Ellie personally. She'd known there were some highly-placed figures who'd succumbed to the affliction—everyone knew about Prince Albert, who now languished in the Tower of London as punishment for his infidelity, and no one had much sympathy for him—but she'd spoken with two members of parliament, an Oxford don, and a judge who'd all successfully hidden their transformations. She was not surprised at their subterfuge—their bodies had not become as obviously womanly as some, and Mr. James's skill was equal to hiding those changes—but at the knowledge that all those men of fine reputation had at some point engaged the services of a prostitute who carried the affliction. That was the beginning of a certain cynicism that had served her well in her chosen career, though it also sometimes made her sad.

The genesis of the disease had been tentatively traced to an English-born gentleman named Orlando, onetime resident of Constantinople—most assumed the disease had its origin there, possibly developing somehow among the eunuchs, hence "the Constantinopolitan Affliction"—and a frequent visitor to one of the city's more exclusive brothels, where he had infected several employees. From there, the disease had spread through surprising heights of society. Orlando had fled the country long ago, which was a shame. What an interview *that* would be.

"I wonder if you might work your art upon me, uncle?" Ellie said, putting her teacup aside. "Could you make me into a man?"

He frowned. "Eleanor, I am willing to help conceal perversions of nature, but what you're asking is simply deceit—why would you want me to do such a thing?"

"It's for a story," she said, choosing her words carefully. Her uncle would not approve of an undercover excursion into a clockwork brothel. "I need to enter a certain gentleman's club without being noticed."

"You're not out to ruin any reputations, are you?"

"No, uncle. And none of your… special customers… are involved." That much was probably true. She stood and twirled around. "What do you think? Can you make a man out of me?"

He grunted. "I suppose. There are, ah, certain cloth bindings we can use for your…" He gestured vaguely at his own chest. "Your hips are fairly slim. I have some trousers that would fit you, and a shirt and waistcoat—it's fortunate the fashion lately is for clothes of a looser fit. A false mustache… but the hair, Eleanor." He shook his head. "My special customers cut their hair in a man's style, of course, but you…"

Eleanor touched her hair, which was, at the moment, pulled back and done up in a tight bun. When unconfined, her hair fell past her shoulders. "I'll cut it, then," she said after a moment's thought. "I can wear a wig until it grows back, and I have a fanchon bonnet that covers most of the back of my head anyway."

"The story is that important to you, dear?"

"It is, uncle, and I would be forever in your debt."

"You said that last time I helped you with an article."

"Then make it twice forever," Ellie said, and he laughed.

Gazing at herself in the mirror, Ellie could scarcely credit the change. "You've made me into the very vision of a respectable businessman, uncle." She wore a black frock coat and a matching waistcoat beneath, with a white shirt and an elaborate cravat. Her trousers were crisply pressed and high-waisted, and the polished shoes fit well enough once Mr. James shoved some paper into the toes. He had lopped off her hair, not without sighs and lamentations, and what remained was slicked back with pomade. Ellie's head felt several pounds lighter, a peculiar but not unpleasant sensation.

"Now for a mustache. If I had time enough, I'd create one especially for you from your own hair, but it's the work of many hours, and I gather you're in a hurry, so we must make do with a readymade, though it pains me." Mr. James fetched a black velvet display tray that held a score of mustaches of assorted colors and textures, pinned like the specimens of a butterfly collector, a sight Ellie found rather dreamlike. He held up several mustaches against her face, shaking his head each time, until saying, "Ah ha. This will do."

Ellie eyed the item with suspicion. "It's… a bit large, uncle." Elaborate facial hair was in vogue since the Affliction began to spread, but Ellie feared such an impressive follicular display might appear ridiculous on her.

He grunted. "The Hungarian style, yes. It has certain advantages, in that it will conceal more of your face—which is a lovely face," he hastened to add, "though that beauty is no benefit in these circumstances. More importantly, however, it matches your natural hair color better than any other option." Mr. James allowed himself a small smile. "It is a rather… *forceful* mustache, and will draw attention away from your other features."

"I'll pass for a man, then?"

"You will, at the very least, pass for a victim of the Constantine Affliction *attempting* to pass for a man. Which, in polite society, is usually good enough."

Hmm. That wasn't quite good enough for *her* purposes. Men who'd transformed into women after sleeping with prostitutes were probably not chief among the clientele for a brothel, staffed with clockwork women or not. But with the right hat and enough confidence, perhaps… "Thank you, uncle. How is it to be affixed?"

Mr. James applied a sticky, slightly sweet-smelling substance to her upper lip and carefully pressed on the mustache, holding it in place for a few moments. Ellie felt as if a rodent were attempting to nest on her face, but there was no help for it. "Thank you, uncle."

"You can thank me best by bringing these items back, unstained and whole, at your earliest convenience. You're off straight away to your mysterious meeting, then?"

"Not for an hour or two yet." She was unsure of the protocols, but assumed visiting a brothel after the dinner hour might be more reasonable.

"What will you do in the meantime?" he asked.

Ellie favored him with a smile, though she wondered how much of it was visible beneath the abominable mustache. "I believe I'll walk a bit and find out what life is like for a man. There could be an article in *that*, too."

"And a scandal as well."

"Nothing better when it comes to selling papers, uncle."

An Offer One Cannot, In Good Conscience, Refuse

He means to shock me, Pimm thought, and did not allow the shock he did in fact feel to show. "*Your* whores, Mr. Value?" Prostitution, long tolerated as a necessary evil, had been made illegal by a special act of Parliament once the full impact of the disease known as the Constantine Affliction, and its most common means of transmission, came to be understood. The clockwork brothels which had sprung up to at least partly replace the need for human prostitutes currently operated in a legal shadow land—officially they were classed as "amusement arcades," no different from bagatelle parlors and penny-admission showcases of automatons, though they were rather more expensive, and had a more limited clientele—but by admitting to employing human prostitutes, Value was confessing to a serious crime.

"I think we're past the need for discretion, aren't we, Halliday? You aren't a police inspector, though I'm told you drink as much as most of the constables do. I could confess to the murder of an Archbishop in your presence and it wouldn't matter. It would merely set my word against yours, and I've been accused of worse crimes by better men. So, yes: *my* whores. There are still independent operators, of course, women who have no other options making personal arrangements with men who have no

25

better sense, but I've been organizing, and plenty of the whores in London pay a certain percentage to me. In exchange for their contributions, I offer them safe places to ply their trade, plus protection from the police—and even more unsavory characters." He leaned forward, clutching the silver head of a cane he certainly didn't need to help him walk. "But now the situation has become unbalanced. Those ladies are no longer getting good value for their money. Someone is killing them."

"Murder is a matter for Scotland Yard," Pimm said.

"Old Bill is no good to me. The police don't even know these crimes have been committed."

Pimm frowned, interested despite himself. "How so?"

"The corpses are left on my doorstep. Figuratively, anyway. They appear laid before the thresholds of my more... exclusive establishments. The legal ones. I've chosen not to involve the police. That kind of attention is bad for business, in so many ways."

"Exclusive establishments? The ones with the clockwork courtesans?" Pimm suppressed a shudder at the thought of such creations. He loved women, or at least, had loved *certain* women, though the one he'd loved most was nearly a dozen years dead. The thought of having intimate relations with what was, essentially, an enormous *doll* was comical at best, and horrifying at worst.

"Yes." Value sighed. "I do miss the old times, Halliday, when real girls could live off the farms of their bodies without worrying about being persecuted by the police, or getting sick and turning into *men*. The clockwork whores are expensive to produce, too—they don't just wander into the city seeking their fortunes like ordinary girls do. Admittedly, once they've been built, the only costs are cleaning and maintenance, and the clockwork girls never complain, get pregnant, or catch the pox. I'm not saying they aren't profitable—they are. But even though my clockwork girls are guaranteed clean, plenty of men refuse to achieve release with an automaton, no matter how cunningly contrived it might be. More often, we get men who come once, for the novelty, to see what it's like, and then never return." He tapped his cane a few times on the polished floor. "Even with all the... changes... we've seen in recent years, most men are conservative. We haven't gotten to the point where human whores are entirely replaceable. Yet."

"And so you still have real women working, out on the streets," Pimm said.

"Of course. Men are men, Lord Pembroke, and they will do what men will do, despite the disapproval of Parliament and the threat of the Affliction. But business on the street has declined terribly as well, recently. There's a rumor that some men who were transformed into women have turned to whoring, trying to spread the Affliction out of spite, and anyone who's reasonably sober is being unusually cautious. Of course, plenty of whores were diseased *before*, but risking a weeping sore on your cock is apparently preferable to having your cock disappear entirely." Value laughed, a sound like a razor rasping over stubble. "Time was, a man paid his penny and took his chances, but the pennies are getting thin on the ground. The last thing I need is someone killing the few women I *do* have out there earning me money."

"Hmm," Pimm said, choosing to ignore, for the moment, the essential vileness of Value's character, and to focus on the crimes at hand. "Killing human prostitutes and leaving them outside houses full of artificial women? It seems like a statement of some kind, wouldn't you say? Though I confess, the exact nature of the commentary eludes me…"

"The killer's motives do not interest me. Only his actions. Find out who he is, and bring me his name, and my men will stop him."

Pimm shook his head. "I don't deny it's an interesting problem, and it may even have diverting psychological elements, but I simply cannot work for you, sir. I don't 'work' at all—my family frowns on my hobby as it is, and if they thought I was taking up detection as a vocation…" He spread his hands.

"That's fine, Halliday. Our arrangement will be a secret. No need for your family's venerable feathers to be ruffled."

"You mocked me before, sir, for using too many words to say 'no.' I acknowledge my tendency to excessive circumspection, and will endeavor to overcome it, thus: No."

Value sighed. "Ah, well. It's a shame, Lord Pembroke, but I won't try to tell your mind. Still, it's an ill wind that blows no good. At least your decision will make my friend at the *Lantern* happy. He's been losing circulation to the *Argus*, but an exclusive scandal like this should sell a few more papers, I wager."

"I'm afraid I've lost the thread, Mr. Value."

"Hmm? Oh, I just think the editor there will be quite interested to hear about your marriage to Lady Pembroke, who was once Miss Sandoval. She had another name before that, though, didn't she? Frederick... something, wasn't it?"

Pimm rose to his full height, which was easily four inches taller than Value, and amounted to rather more as the criminal remained seated. "You dare insult my darling Winifred? I cannot imagine how you think such a slight would aid your case—"

"Use some of that vaunted mental skill, would you, Halliday?" Value said. "I *own the whores.* I know which of my women were unaffected carriers of the Constantine Affliction. I know which men *slept* with them. Some of those men died, some of them went into disgrace following their transformations, and some of them are passing for the men they once were, even now. But only a few of the men simply *disappeared*—it was mostly women who chose that direction. One of the men who vanished was your old chum Freddy Banks. And shortly after he disappeared, you took up with a woman named *Wini*fred. You should have named her something else, Halliday. Rebecca. Caroline. Anything, really."

"Freddy took a trip to America," Pimm said stiffly. He was half-tensed, waiting for the short crack of an air pistol. If Freddy felt threatened, Value would certainly fall, even though Freddy was ostensibly armed only in case he needed to save Pimm's life. Pimm had certain resources and connections, and the police wouldn't expend much effort apprehending the killer of scum like Value, but it was a bloody ugly business, and Pimm had never been a party to murder before. He didn't much want to start, especially since Freddy would have to kill Big Ben, too. That man was no angel, but he certainly didn't deserve to die. "Freddy is in New York, last I heard. I've even had a few letters from him, you can compare the handwriting if you like—"

"I'd rather compare your wife's handwriting to Freddy's," Value said. "That would, I think, be more illuminating. Sit down, man. I have no desire to disgrace you."

Pimm did sit, as he'd felt like a bit of an ass standing up like that, but he kept his spine stiff. "Who would believe such allegations from you anyway?"

"You know the latest forensic advancements, Halliday. The new applications for the alchemical law of similarity can achieve remarkable things."

Pimm frowned. The police alchemists had indeed recently made great strides. They could place a bit of skin or blood or hair from a crime scene in an alchemical bath, along with similar samples from criminal suspects, and if the samples came from the same man, they would attract one another like iron filings to a magnet, drawn inexorably together by the law of similarity that joined like to like. The technique was excellent for proving the presence of criminals at crime scenes or linking the skin fragments under a victim's fingernails to the killer, but—

"Nonsense," Pimm said. "Why, there's no reason to believe that test would even work with victims of the Affliction. Their bodies change so utterly that even if you had samples of Freddy's flesh—"

"We do," Value murmured.

"—and a sample of my wife's, what makes you think they would be drawn together, even if your outrageous claims are true?"

"It's been tested, Pimm."

Pimm noted, with distress, Value's use of his nickname, rather than his surname or courtesy title. He felt it showed far too much confidence.

"Not by the police," Value went on, "but by my own specialists. They are rather more advanced—it's important for those in my business to exceed the capabilities of the civil authorities whenever possible. It's true, the tissue taken from men before and after the change do not draw together so strongly… but they are attracted. They pull at one another well enough to detect. You know what that means, hmm?"

Pimm did. Samples from siblings, or from father and son, or other close relations, also displayed that sort of reaction, the familial connection revealed by the movement of flesh or hair in a dish.

"So if I put a bit of Winifred's hair in a dish with a bit of Freddy's, will it show that they're brother and sister, I wonder? Of course, Freddy doesn't *have* a sister. At the very least, questions would be asked. You know as well as I that you don't need *proof* to create a scandal. There's never been a bit of proof that I've engaged in any illegal activity, after all, but everyone knows I'm a whoremaster and a thief. The difference is, I don't have a reputation to ruin—unlike you. And when I put one of those eager young journalists on the scent, especially from a muckraking rag like the *Lantern*, and point them in your direction… Well. When they find out Mrs. Halliday—forgive me, Lady Pembroke—has no history beyond, oh, two years ago? That will make for quite a story. You'll be accused of perpetrating a fraud, at the very least, though there will be inevitable whispers of perversion."

"I am not as concerned with my own respectability as you might believe," Pimm said coldly. "While I hate to disappoint my family, I daresay they have grown used to disappointment by now. You are a fool if you think threatening me—"

"Then think of Freddy," Value said softly. "Think of how *she* will be hounded, ridiculed, caricatured in the press, perhaps brought up on criminal charges—I'm sure she's breaking *some* law, probably more than one. Let alone what the Church will say when they realize your marriage is a sham. The peaceful quiet life you've made for her will be overturned."

Shoot him, Pimm thought, with uncharacteristic bloodthirstiness, but Freddy didn't pull either trigger.

Which meant, Pimm supposed, he would have to go about this the other way. He took a deep breath. "There's no need for unpleasantness between us, Mr. Value. As a man of conscience, I am, of course, eager to see a killer brought to justice."

"Good," Value said, smirking.

"But if I am to investigate, I'll need… access."

"Access to what?"

"Wherever the investigation leads me."

"You'll be accommodated. Don't get any clever ideas about building a criminal case against me while pretending to serve me, Pimm. I float above all this sordid business like a cloud above a dung heap. I have no direct ties to anything unsavory. You could disrupt my business, true, but I would still be at home, living my life as always. Except I would be exceedingly wroth with you."

"I'll need to see the bodies," Pimm said.

"Yes, of course," Value said, rising. "We don't have *all* of them, but they've all been examined, and I think my consultant still has the most recent on hand. Ben, give him our man's address, would you? I'll let him know to expect you—when?"

Pimm considered. "I'll try to call on him this evening, or failing that, tomorrow morning."

Value inclined his head in agreement. "I look forward to your report."

Ben passed over a slip of paper, which Pimm didn't bother to examine before stuffing it into the pocket of his jacket. Value sauntered out, with Ben following, and Pimm locked the door behind them. He pressed his forehead against the wood.

"Bugger," he said at length.

Freddy appeared, wearing an entirely respectable dress, and fastening on a hat at the very height of the current style—or so Pimm assumed. Freddy paid more attention to such things than Pimm did, and always had. "That went well," Freddy said.

"I thought you'd shoot him."

Freddy shrugged. "A dead master criminal in the sitting room would have caused more problems than it would have solved. This way, you can find his killer, and then he'll leave us alone."

"And if he continues to exert pressure on us? To threaten to ruin us?"

"If you're worried about him exposing my little secret, simply begin putting aside enough money that we can live a life of leisure even if your family disowns you. But don't fret now. If Value oversteps, we can deal with him then."

"He has *already* overstepped!"

"Oh, please. I know you, Pimm. 'No doubt with diverting psychological elements.' You *want* to investigate this killer. If Inspector Whistler of Scotland Yard had come asking for your help to investigate these murders, instead of Abel Value, you'd already be looking over the scene of the crime."

"Just because I'm being led somewhere interesting doesn't mean I don't resent the leash, Freddy."

Freddy patted his cheek. "You get to look at corpses later. Take heart." Freddy paused. "I don't mean that literally. Leave the hearts where they are. I'm off to my salon. That little tete-a-tete didn't take nearly as long as I'd feared." Freddy gave a little wave and departed.

Pimm poured himself a drink, emptying a bottle. He'd need to send Ransome out for more brandy—damn. He needed a new valet. A twinge of guilt passed through him. His little problems hardly seemed worth mentioning when desperate women were being murdered.

Pimm looked at the address written on the slip of paper Ben had given him.

That part of the city.

He started looking for another bottle.

Modern Advances in Scientific Pleasure

"**I**'m a friend of Mr. Addison's." Ellie pitched her voice lower than usual, though not comically so; she made a man of rather slight stature, she knew, and it would be incongruous for a bullfrog rumble to emerge from such a form.

The butler who'd answered the door of this stately old townhouse transformed from severely frowning guardian to smiling affable doorman at the mention of Mr. Addison's name. Ellie knew there was no actual Mr. Addison, but she'd been told by one of her sources that his was the name to give this week. "Come in, come in," the keeper of the door said. Ellie stepped inside, and the butler shut the door after her. "I'll let the lady of the house know you're here. Do you have an account with us?"

"Ah—no, I... It's my first visit."

"Of course, sir. Just a moment." He slipped away, and Ellie allowed herself a long exhalation. She had passed the first barrier, at least. Ellie had spent all afternoon playing at being a man, having a drink in a pub and stopping at a tobacconists and strolling about in a park, and no one had pointed and whispered or shouted "Imposter!" She glanced around the foyer, trying out adjectives in her mind: elegant, restrained, spare... but it was just a rather dull foyer, really, with too much chintz for her taste.

The butler returned and led her down a hallway. She glanced into one room as she passed, and saw three men playing cards around a small table. Though she didn't dare pause for a better look, Ellie thought one of the men was an ex-prizefighter named Crippen—"Crippler" Crippen, who'd been involved in a scandal regarding bouts deliberately lost to enrich corrupt bettors. The man had withdrawn from the sport, though it was rumored he still worked for the man suspected of orchestrating the illegal wagers—the gentleman criminal Abel Value. So she might surmise this was one of Value's houses, then. Crippen caught her eye, gave her a gap-toothed grin, and winked. Unsure how to return such a gesture appropriately, Ellie just kept walking.

The butler directed her to a parlor that was *actually* furnished elegantly. She took a seat on a velvet-upholstered chair, endeavoring to sit like a man, spine straight, hat resting on her knees. A moment later a woman appeared in the doorway, and Ellie went tense again. Men she could fool, she knew that, but would another woman sense her essential femininity?

Not that this woman was terribly feminine. Ellie had expected the hostess at a brothel to be flamboyant as a peacock, all ruffled silks and feathers, but this woman had the severe features of a teetotaller and the fashion sense of a schoolmistress, wearing a black dress of conservative cut. She was perhaps fifteen or twenty years Ellie's senior, and something about her precise movements and perfunctory smile made Ellie think she surely excelled at running a house and keeping accounts. "I'm Mrs. Hadley," she said, frowning, and Ellie abruptly stood up—good lord, she was a *man*, that meant she should rise when a woman entered the room!

"I'm, ah, that is…"

"We'll call you Mr. Smythe, hmm?" she said. "For convenience." She sat down in a chair, perched well forward, alert as a hunter on the scent of a fox, and Ellie sat, too.

"Of course, yes, Mr. Smythe. Forgive me. I must be a bit nervous." *Don't talk so much,* Ellie thought. *Every syllable risks giving you away.*

"It is your first visit? I'm afraid, then, that we must broach the matter of payment. Are you familiar with our schedule of fees?"

"Not specifically…"

She named a sum. Ellie had enough on hand to cover it, though only just. Cooper would reimburse her, eventually, though she'd have to economize until he got around to putting in her chit.

"Payable in advance," Mrs. Hadley said.

Interesting. "And if I'm not, ah, satisfied?"

"You are paying for time, a room, and the opportunity to examine one of our fascinating scientific devices in private, Mr. Smythe. What you do with that time is entirely up to you. The payment does not vary according to your satisfaction, or lack thereof. Ordinary wear and tear is accounted for in the fee, though you may be charged extra for any… unusual damage."

Ellie blinked. "I can't imagine there will be any damage at all!"

"That is reassuring," Mrs. Hadley said. "For those who *expect* to cause damage, we offer specialized devices at an increased rate. Now, I have here some etchings, and a few other details. Please peruse these documents, let me know which model interests you, and I will direct you to the appropriate room. All right?" Mrs. Hadley passed over a thin roll of papers, tied with a red ribbon.

Ellie opened the roll. The first sheet featured a rather good drawing of a buxom bare-chested woman with great expanses of curly hair and big doe eyes, and some neatly handwritten cursive lines of description: "Matilda's skin is pale as milk, her hair as yellow as sunshine, and her lips soft as ripe berries—" From there, it described other assets in a mix of high and low language that Ellie found profoundly embarrassing, and more than a little unprofessional. Why hadn't they hired a writer as skilled as their artist? Though she supposed men were more interested in the pictures. "These are all… clockwork, then?"

"Of course," Mrs. Hadley said. "It would be inappropriate for a gentleman such as yourself to spend time alone with an unchaperoned young woman, would it not? And any display of affection with such a young lady could be cause for concern, given the prevalence of… certain maladies." She shifted on the chair, her crinoline rustling. "But rest assured, Mr. Smythe. Our devices are as realistic as any living woman. They breathe, they have heartbeats, they are warm, and they are… welcoming… to a man's touch. Each is crafted from the finest materials known to science, in a perfect imitation of life, and every one is carefully cleaned and prepared before entertaining a new gentleman caller. Admittedly, they are not accomplished conversationalists, but they have certain vocal capabilities some men find pleasing." She softened her tone, voice becoming soothing. "Men have urges. We understand. We help to fulfill those needs, with no danger to anyone involved—men *or* women."

"How marvelous," Ellie said, and looked back down at the sheets of paper. More drawings of women, some of them slim, some voluptuous, some with straight hair or curls, a few done in "exotic" styles—Nubian, Oriental, Odalisque.

For Ellie's purposes, the precise model didn't much matter, so she chose one at random. "Here. I find her… most fetching."

"Delilah. Very good." Mrs. Hadley rose, and Ellie followed her to a staircase and up to the second floor, to a hall lined by doors labeled with brass number plates. Mrs. Hadley directed her to room number four, opened the door, and said, "Our standard period is one hour, but you may have an extra half hour, free of charge, to acquaint yourself with the device, as this is your first time. When you are done, and decently attired, pull the bell cord inside, and someone will show you out."

"Does she need to be… wound up, or anything?"

"She is entirely ready for your company, sir," Mrs. Hadley said.

"In I go, then," Ellie said, and stepped through the door.

The bedroom was the lavish land of velvet Ellie had expected, with a great canopied four-poster bed the clear centerpiece of the room. Mirrors hung all over the walls, making the room into a miniature Versailles, and a large sea chest stood at the foot of the bed, lid just cracked open. The windows were heavily obscured by curtains, and one of the new alchemical lights stood on a dresser and provided illumination, its blown-glass bulb filled with a shining luminous gas. Some said the alchemical devices were safer than gas jets, less likely to start fires, though Ellie was unconvinced. Certainly the light was steadier than that provided by gas, and warmer (and far cheaper) than the new electric lights that had lately been exhibited, but there was something eerie about the glow, making her think of tales she'd read about will-o'-the-wisps and St. Elmo's Fire. Ellie glanced at the figure atop the covers. She (or rather it) seemed to be nothing more or less than a sleeping woman, chest rising and falling slowly. Ellie was not *quite* ready to examine her, so she went to the chest at the foot of the bed, wondering what it might contain.

There were frilly underthings inside—including, shockingly, some garments in bright scarlet—and a small whip, and a riding crop, and bits of leather and metal of uncertain utility, and deeper layers of folded cloth she didn't investigate too closely. Ellie clucked her tongue. Cooper wouldn't let her describe most of these things, alas. If she did, half the readership would swoon, and though the other half would be secretly titillated, Cooper would err on the side of caution. Perhaps she could do an unexpurgated article for the *Lantern*; they would print anything...

She hadn't dared bring a notebook or a pencil, afraid she might be searched and recognized as a journalist, so she couldn't take down any notes, but she doubted she would forget anything important. The time had come to study the thing itself —the love-doll, the clockwork courtesan, the automatic trollop.

Ellie circled the bed, examining the woman—well, the woman-like thing—from all angles before finally giving in to the inevitable and climbing atop the covers. This model, Delilah, had wavy auburn hair and blue eyes and lovely creamy skin, and her—its—body was dressed in a black silk robe with short sleeves and a shorter hemline. The thing was too life-like to seem a doll, but though the chest moved with artificial breath, it did not seem *alive*: there were none of the small shiftings and movements that characterized the living. No, this was more like a corpse on a slab, despite the perfectly even and regular breaths, and Ellie could not imagine how any man could lay down with this and pretend it was a real woman. Most men must have far better imaginations than she'd realized. Ellie reached out a hand to touch the flesh of the thing's arm—

—and the clockwork courtesan came more fully to life, half-turning its head toward her, eyelids fluttering, mouth parting, a warm and sultry "Mmm" sound emerging from its throat. Ellie jerked back, surprised as much by the warmth of its flesh as by its sudden movement. The skin was not exactly like that of a real woman's, but it was soft, yielding, and pliant. She'd expected something like the gutta percha rubber used to make the dolls she'd played with as a child, but this flesh was far more... flesh-like. It seemed almost real, though the smell was wrong—too neutral, too in-human—and the movements were somehow indefinably artificial.

Ellie reached out and placed her palm between the automaton's small breasts, and yes, there was a heartbeat there, and little eager-sounding moans emerged from the courtesan's throat with each exhalation.

You are a journalist, Ellie thought, and opened the thing's robe.

The clockwork courtesan's skin was not perfectly unblemished, as Ellie had expected—there was a mole drawn on below one breast, and a few dark hairs leading down from its belly button to the fuller thatch at its crotch. Leaning in close, Ellie could see where the hairs emerged from the skin, each one hand-sewn with great care. Running her fingertips through the hair between the courtesan's legs, curious whether the hair was human or animal—it seemed human—she was shocked to touch warm wetness, and her fingers came away moist. She smelled her fingertips, and there was, perhaps, the faintest scent of some pure, neutral oil. Had the butler or some other functionary hurried up here and... *lubricated* the thing, after Ellie chose this model? But, of course, that would be necessary, wouldn't it? "Welcoming to a man's touch" indeed.

Ellie shuddered and wiped her hand on the comforter. She and her fiancé had shared kisses and a few more intimate moments before his dispatch to India, but as they never married, they never had the opportunity to explore one another any further. She understood how these things worked, of course, but it was a bit disconcerting to be with this doll, something built so obviously for that purpose and no other. Was this *really* what men wanted? Something with the shape of a woman, but with no mind, no will, no personality? Surely they'd prefer the company of a real woman, if it weren't for the danger of contracting the Affliction and *becoming* one.

She rolled the courtesan over, and was surprised when it moved on its own, getting first on all fours, then lowering its arms and head to the mattress, leaving its bottom tilted provocatively up in the air. This *was* a sophisticated machine. Ellie had seen an exhibition, years before, of famous automatons, including geese that laid eggs, boys who cast fishing lines, and women playing lutes, but those devices were both smaller and obviously unreal. This machine was of a different order altogether. From a distance—even quite a close distance—something like this would be indistinguishable from a human. Ellie smiled to herself. A few of the sleepier members of the House of Lords should consider commissioning clockwork imitations of themselves to sit in their places during sessions of Parliament, freeing themselves up to play cards or go shooting. If the engineers here could make a clockwork woman put her bottom in the air, surely they could make a clockwork old man capable of shouting "Hear hear!"

Ellie pressed her ear to the automaton's back and could hear, faintly, the whirring of some engine. They weren't steam-powered, obviously—perhaps they ran on some electrical or alchemical battery? If only she had tools... though she couldn't see where the thing would come apart. She would have to examine it as best she could anyway.

Ellie carefully tested the movement of its joints, and touched its hand—the fingers closed on hers and began gently tugging in a disturbingly rhythmic fashion until Ellie pulled away. She brushed her hand against the thing's cheek, marveling at the smoothness of its skin—and then the automaton turned its head and parted its moist and shapely lips. It sucked at her fingers like a piglet at a teat, moist tongue undulating, and Ellie pulled her fingers out, which necessitated further disgusted wiping of lubricant on the coverlet. Ellie considered exploring the courtesan's capabilities more thoroughly, but the idea was repugnant to her. Who knew how it would react if she pressed a finger into... or even into... No matter. Cooper wouldn't print the details even if she found out.

She'd discovered all she could, and certainly had enough for a memorable article. A glance at the case clock on the dresser told her she had another forty-five minutes with this creature. Should she pull the bell cord, then, and declare herself done early? Would such behavior be suspicious?

Ellie opened the door and glanced down the hallway. No sign of anyone, mechanical or otherwise. If she could only get her hands on those drawings of the models—that would be a great coup, and a boon to circulation, if reproduced in the paper. Perhaps she could find an unattended sheaf of the materials and slip them into her pocket.

If nothing else, she could creep across the hall and get a look at another model. She tiptoed to the door across the way, number five, and listened at the keyhole. There was the faint sound of grunting and squeaking springs, and she hurriedly moved away. Door number seven was quite silent, however, and when she touched the doorknob, it turned. Did she dare? If caught, she could always claim she'd stepped out for a moment, gotten confused, and returned to the wrong room. Her article would benefit from descriptions of more than one of the amorous devices.

With a last glance down the hall, she pushed open the door, and stepped through.

Inside, she discovered a man wearing a set of complexly-lensed goggles, holding a long screwdriver, and poking around in the exposed mechanical guts of the naked creature on the bed.

"Oh, I'm terribly sorry!" Ellie said—squeaked, really. Clearing her throat and roughening her voice, she said, "Wrong room, my mistake, I…"

She stared. She *knew* this man. Not personally. But he had a very recognizable face.

He pushed the goggles up to his forehead. The eyes that looked at her were bright and curious, but not particularly kind. "The door should have been locked, the madam must not have—" He stopped speaking and cocked his head. "Oh, dear," he said. "I see you recognize me."

"I—I don't know what you mean, sir—"

Sir Bertram Oswald, noted scientist, leading expert on pneumatic alchemy, famed experimentalist, head of the Royal Alchemical Society, and close confidant (and rumored lover) of Queen Victoria, sighed and reached over to pull the bell rope dangling by the bed. "I do hope you aren't anyone terribly important," he said, almost apologetically.

Interviews with Horrible Men

P imm took a hansom cab as close to the address as he could. None of the electric omnibuses serviced *this* route, and horses generally refused to get closer than seven hundred yards or so from the walls that enclosed the remnants of Whitechapel (and a small bite of Mile End), so he had to walk the last mile or so. He strolled along the largely deserted street, past shuttered shops and sagging warehouses, aware of the eyes watching him from alleyways and empty windows, and from behind the safety of rubbish heaps. He kept to the center of the street, and frequently paused to glance behind him, to make sure no one was attempting to take him by surprise. He was dressed entirely too well for this vicinity, and though daylight robbery was rare even in this wretched part of London, twilight was near, and it was best to be vigilant. He was more worried about the walk back, when it would surely be full dark. The West End and parts of central London had electric lights now, but streets in the East End were still lit only by gas lamps, and only intermittently by those.

Pimm grasped his walking stick—black, heavy, four feet long, topped with a silver ball, and specially modified by Freddy to serve as something more useful than a mere bludgeon—and strode along, doing his best to look confident and untouchable. Such a pose would have been easier if he hadn't tossed back quite so many drinks before coming this way. He'd only intended to have a single drink to fortify himself around teatime, but one drink had turned into two and then into four, as sometimes happened. He was not *drunk*—it took a certain concentrated effort over the best part of an evening for him to get drunk, at this point—but his reflexes were not all they could be.

Hideous yellow fog steamed out of the vents of the dome that covered the devastated area in Whitechapel, just a few streets to the north. Proposals had been made to seal the dome more tightly, to keep in the noxious vapors, but some scientists worried the gases from the alchemical fires inside would build up enough pressure to cause a more air-tight structure to explode. Yellow smoke was considered preferable to a rain of poisoned dome-fragments.

Finding the address proved difficult, as most of the houses hereabouts didn't have numbers, but he was in luck: one house *did*, and it was the house he sought, the address spelled out in brass and affixed to the front door. Pimm's destination was a tall and narrow structure of old stones and timbers with a steeply peaked roof, pressed in on by long low warehouses on either side. Something about the house seemed vaguely Germanic, or perhaps it just looked like something that belonged in a fairy tale—the residence of a witch, or a more-than-usually genteel ogre.

Pimm rapped on the door with the head of his cane. After a few moments, a dolorous voice on the other side said, "Well?"

"Is this Mr. Adams? My name is Pembroke Halliday. A… mutual acquaintance suggested I speak with you."

"Ah, yes. Please, enter." The door swung open soundlessly, and Pimm removed his hat before stepping into the gloomy entryway. As his eyes adjusted to the dimness, he blinked, because this appeared to be an impossibly vast space—how could the house be bigger on the inside than the outside?

After another moment, he understood. The interior walls had been torn down, except for the supporting pillars, opening the house up on either side to merge seamlessly with the warehouses that flanked the structure. What appeared to be three properties from the street was in fact a single voluminous space. Shrouded shapes—scientific equipment? old furniture?—hulked at irregular intervals, and filthy rooftop windows let in a thin trickle of attenuated light. The floors were made of great unvarnished slabs of quarried stone, covered here and there with carpets that seemed woefully small in all this space, and lent little warmth.

Mr. Adams was even stranger than his home. Though he stood hunched over, the man was still taller than anyone Pimm had seen outside of a carnival, towering over Pimm by at least a foot and a half. He wore dark robes of the sort a scholar might affect for a ceremonial occasion, but stained and threadbare, along with dark leather gloves. Strangest of all, a smooth white mask covered his face, giving him a terrifyingly blank affect—but his eyes were alive and watchful. "You are the detective?" His voice was raspy, as if Mr. Adams had damaged his throat. Perhaps he'd been in a fire—burned skin would explain the mask, and inhalation of smoke the rasp.

Pimm made a point of treating everyone, from tradesman to villain to beggar, with the same geniality, so he merely chuckled. "Oh, heavens no. I have some interest in criminology, that's all, and I offered our mutual friend my assistance."

Mr. Adams didn't move. "I have heard of you. You worked with Scotland Yard on the Constance Trent case, did you not?"

Pimm nodded. "An ugly business. The death of a child…" He shook his head. "Nothing was ever proven, of course, which makes it all the worse. The murderer is still free."

"We all suffer for our sins," Mr. Adams said. "If not in the immediate aftermath, than in the fullness of time."

"Yes, quite." Pimm cleared his throat. "Our mutual friend—"

"You may call him by name." Was Adams amused? With that rasp, it was so hard to tell. "We are both inclined toward confidentiality, I am sure, and thus need keep no secrets between us."

"Mr. Value, then. He says you can show me the bodies of these unfortunate women?"

"One of them, at least. Follow me." He led Pimm deeper into the house, through corridors made of stacked crates, some of them ancient and furred with dust. While this combined house was in truth one great open space punctuated by pillars, someone had created the illusion of rooms and corridors by artfully stacking boxes, hanging tapestries, and erecting tents beneath the high dark ceilings. Soon Adams halted at a seemingly arbitrary point, a narrow cul-de-sac made of stacked crates—those on one side bore markings like Egyptian hieroglyphics, and on the other each crate bore the single, rather ambiguous, word "Materiel." Pimm glanced around the narrow space, and realized where they were going next.

The towering figure crouched—even bent down, his head was level with Pimm's chest—and drew back the corner of a faded Oriental rug, revealing a trap door with an iron ring set on one end.

"I'm afraid your trap door isn't very well hidden," Pimm said apologetically. "The corner of the rug you lifted is more worn than the rest, and the outline of the door is visible if one takes the time to look. If this place should ever be raided by officers of the law, I fear they might discover this door."

Adams nodded. "I suppose so. But the police will never trouble us here—Mr. Value pays well to see I am undisturbed. And while there are certain unsavory elements who might break in and attempt to discover my secrets…" He gestured at the ring. "Try to lift it, Lord Pembroke."

Pimm crouched, seized the cold iron ring in both hands, and heaved. He might as well have been attempting to lift the Tower of London by main force—indeed, he began to suspect he was the butt of a joke. "Is the ring just set in solid stone, then?"

"Not at all." Adams reached down and, with one hand, lifted the trap door open with an air of ease. After it rose halfway, some mechanism was engaged, and the trap door stood open on its own, revealing a set of wooden stairs leading below.

"Is there a trick?" Pimm said, squinting. "A hidden switch of some kind, to release a lock?"

"Perhaps I am just very strong." Adams started down the steps, and after a moment's hesitation, Pimm followed. In for a penny, after all.

Adams threw a switch at the bottom of the short flight of stairs, and the long low room beneath the floor lit up, illuminated by strings of electric lights, the bulbs dangling like strange fruit from wires overhead, and banishing all shadows. The strange giant gestured toward the bulbs. "They are incandescent lights, based on the design of the great magician and passable inventor Jean Eugène Robert-Houdin, though I have made certain improvements to increase their useful life."

"The light is marvelously steady," Pimm said. "Most of the electrics I've seen flicker a bit, but these, they're like suns done in miniature."

"My studies benefit from light."

Pimm looked around the laboratory. There were racks holding rounded vessels of clay, a long table covered in glassware, a wall entirely taken up by a huge apothecary's cabinet, and shelves holding countless books, mixed in with specimen jars full of cloudy fluid and half-glimpsed biological oddities. "You are a natural philosopher, sir?"

"I am principally an anatomist. The human body and its working are my ongoing fascination. Mr. Value is kind enough to send me any dead bodies he discovers, so their misfortunes might at least further the sum of human knowledge." Adams approached a table covered with a sheet, and Pimm braced himself when the giant pulled the covering aside.

He had seen many dead bodies since taking up his criminological hobby, several of them damaged by terrible acts of violence—poor Constance Trent was probably the most harrowing, though he'd also seen men with their heads smashed in by andirons, a handful of slashed throats, and people with their faces convulsed in the final rictus of death by poisoning.

The woman on the table was the least distressing corpse he'd ever seen outside of a coffin. She was young, red-haired, milk-pale, and nude. That final point might have been awkward, but Pimm had long ago learned the trick of looking at the dead clinically—their souls were fled, and their bodies were merely empty vessels, worthy of respect, but no longer in need of the courtesies he would accord them in life. Pimm instinctively took a handkerchief from his pocket to press to his nose, but there was no odor. "How long has she been dead, Mr. Adams?"

"She was found this morning, on the steps of a house on St. James's Street."

Pimm grunted. "My club is on that street. I had no idea Value kept an establishment there."

"I understand the management is most discreet."

"It's quite some distance to transport a dead girl, since she was unlikely to be working in the vicinity. That's a fair bit of effort—the killer is certainly trying to make some kind of point." Pimm peered at the victim. "This girl has been dead the best part of a day, yet there is no sign of decomposition. Does that strike you as odd?"

"Mr. Value's men brought her in a chest of ice. And for my part, I make use of certain... preservative elements," Adams admitted. "They slow decay, which makes my work more pleasant. You don't seem troubled by my occupation, if I may say. Most find it off-putting."

"I had a second cousin who went into the medical profession. He was the despair of the family—until I came along, at least. He told me about his studies, bodies rendered down for their skeletons, cadavers dissected. He explained that the study of the dead could help the living, and ease suffering. It seems a noble enough goal to me, if the poor souls being examined have no families to claim their earthly remains. Not that I expect Mr. Value bothers with such niceties." He glanced at the giant's blank white mask. "And you, I wager, are no member of the teaching staff at St. Bartholomew's?"

"I learned my profession in the old style, as the assistant to a master surgeon, when I was a younger man. I have no formal certificate, nor do I wish for one. I am content to perform my own researches, and my patron finds my work useful enough to fund those studies."

"You are the one who tested the efficacy of tissue sympathy in victims of the Constantine Affliction, I suspect?"

The giant merely inclined his head.

"Quite clever," Pimm said. "I do admire such intellectual accomplishment. Do you know what purpose your patron Mr. Value has found for your discovery?" He could not keep an edge of bitterness from his voice.

"Science is a tool, Lord Pembroke. Sometimes it can be used as a weapon, I know. But its intrinsic moral orientation is entirely neutral. The Steel Raja crushes his enemies with steam-powered automatons in the form of war elephants. Yet the same fundamentals of science power the ships that ply the seas, bringing trade to distant shores, and the digging machines that even now chew at the earth beneath the English Channel to connect this island to the Continent. Steam is not evil. Machines are not evil. But their uses can be."

"An interesting perspective, Mr. Adams. While we are on the subject of evil, let us return to the nature of the murder before us. In your medical opinion, what was the cause of death? The poor girl has not a mark on her."

"Poisoning, this time. Or perhaps inhalation of ether or some other chemical. Sometimes the killer—assuming it is the same killer—suffocates his victims, but in this case, there are no broken blood vessels in the eyes, as one sees in smotherings, and no marks on the throat, such as one finds in cases of throttling." He paused. "The victims—there have been five—

have all been only lightly marked, each more pristine than the last. When Mr. Value's men found the first girl, they thought her heart had simply stopped, though no one understood why she'd strayed so far from her preferred neighborhood, to fall dead on the steps of a clockwork brothel. When another girl was found dead at a different establishment belonging to Mr. Value a week later… well. Coincidence no longer seemed likely."

"Hmm." Pimm gazed into the poor girl's blank blue eyes. "If only she could tell us what she'd seen. The best witness of any murder is always, sadly, beyond the reach of questioning."

"Not necessarily," Mr. Adams said. "If a victim were brought to me within an hour of her death, say, I might compel her to answer a question or two. Any later, and the brain would surely be too damaged to be revived, but…" He shrugged.

Pimm stared at him. *That* explained why Adams had to work for a man like Value; he was mad. "What you describe… it's impossible. Necromancy."

"The body is a machine, Lord Pembroke. I will not address the question of whether humans have *souls*—but they do have brains, and those brains, if nothing else, reveal the pathways and passages favored by the thoughts of those souls. The cells begin to break down and decay soon after death, it is true, but if I could access the brain before decay went too far, who knows what secrets might be recovered?" He shrugged. "The difference between life and death is less clearly delineated than you might suppose. Bring me a fresh dead girl, and she might tell you her secrets."

Pimm shuddered. "Cutting apart these bodies to learn the secrets of life—that is distasteful, Mr. Adams, but I recognize how it serves a greater good. What you describe now is…. One hates to be overdramatic, but I am tempted to call it *blasphemy*. To speak to the dead must surely be an affront to God."

Mr. Adams chuckled behind his impassive mask. "Hadn't you heard, sir? Man has already seized the power of the gods. We have stolen fire, and we bank those fires ever higher. We have eaten of the fruit of knowledge, and been expelled from the Garden, and yet every day we try to claw our way back into that lost Eden." He took a shining scalpel from a tray of instruments. "Bring me a fresh victim, and you may be able to ask her what Heaven looks like personally. Though you might not like the answer."

Pimm turned away before Adams made his first incision.

Escape from a
Mechanical Brothel!

Ellie ran, of course, because she knew a threat when she heard one, no matter how genial the phrasing. She jerked the door shut after her and hurried down the hallway toward the stairs. As she ran, several doors along the hallway swung open… and clockwork courtesans stepped out.

She hadn't realized they could walk, and they probably weren't often called upon to do so, but they walked now, emerging naked or dressed in bits of lingerie, moving two abreast to block her path to the stairs. Men shouted angrily in a couple of the rooms, their mechanical paramours having abandoned them in the midst of carnal acts. (Though technically to be a "carnal" act, Ellie supposed *both* people involved had to be made of flesh.)

Ellie considered just trying to push through the courtesans, but there were half a dozen of the machines standing, blank-faced and patient. What if they seized her? The thought of being touched by such creatures—especially the ones that had so recently been touched by men—was abhorrent. She turned the other way, though there was nothing at that end of the hallway but a velvet curtain. Though she had no idea what waited behind that barrier, it seemed unlikely that it would be *worse* than a small army of mechanical women. Oddly, Sir Bertram didn't emerge from his room to pursue her—perhaps he was afraid someone else would discover his presence here? The man widely believed to be the Queen's unofficial consort—some wags even called Queen Victoria "Mrs. Oswald"—found in a house of extremely ill repute, in the act of tinkering with the mechanical innards of one of the clockwork courtesans... the scandal would be extraordinary!

But there was no time to think of being a reporter now. Ellie dashed for the curtain, pulled it aside, and found a set of stairs. As she rushed upward, she heard human voices shouting in the hall below. Were they merely angry clients, or the rough men who inevitably policed establishments like this? Men like Crippen? The stairs switchbacked, leading up to the third floor, and to another velvet curtain. Ellie peeked around the edge of the flimsy barrier, and saw only another hallway, not unlike the one she'd just escaped. These doors were all closed, except for one on the left at the far end. She raced down the hall and looked into that room. It was furnished in the same style as the other boudoirs, but presently unoccupied by either man or machine. Ellie pulled the door shut behind her and listened intently.

Footsteps pounded up the stairs, and a male voice—not Oswald's—said, "He must be hiding here somewhere. Check the rooms."

Ellie rushed to the window, hoping for a ledge she could stand on, but when she threw back the drapes, there *was* no window; it had been boarded up, and the nails were driven too deep for her to pry them loose. She could hear, faintly, doors opening farther down the hall. They would reach her, soon, and when they did...

She closed her eyes for a moment. They were looking for a man. Well, then. She'd just have to make sure they didn't *find* one.

Ellie tore off her false mustache and stuffed it in her coat pocket, then slipped off the coat, vest, shirt, shoes, and socks, and undid her trousers, finally removing her underwear. She unwrapped the bandages that constricted her breasts—worse than a corset, honestly, and at least unwinding them was a relief—and hurriedly wadded up the clothes and shoved them deep under the bed. Now she could just climb into the bed and try to look like a switched-off machine, with the covers arrayed to hide her modesty—

Her hair. All the models had long hair, of course. She went to the sea chest at the foot of the bed, though it was a futile hope. The courtesan she'd examined hadn't been wearing a wig, after all, the hairs had been sewn into her scalp—

And yet, in the depths of the chest, beneath the frills and bits of leather, she found a blonde wig, a pair of ridiculously oversized high-heeled shoes, and a corset large enough to fit a gorilla. How odd. Clearly none of this clothing was made to fit the clockwork women, so whom—

A door nearby opened with a crash, so Ellie hurriedly pulled the wig over her own head, trying not to think of who might have worn the false hair last. She checked herself in one of the mirrors, adjusting the wig and trying not to notice her own nude body, something she'd certainly never perused in a looking glass before. Ellie was not as *bountiful* in her figure as the Delilah model, but some of the sketches had shown slimmer models, so perhaps she could pass.

After snatching up a flowing silk scarf and draping it around her neck and to cover her breasts, she hurried onto the bed, trying to remember how the courtesan in her room had been arranged. Not *too* lewdly, fortunately—it had been almost demure, like a sleeping woman, and she should pretend to be the same. She stretched on the coverlet, hoping the bedclothes were laundered between sessions but knowing they almost certainly weren't, and rested her head on the pillow. Eyes open, or eyes closed? She settled for a sleepy sort of half-lidded gaze which allowed her to keep an eye on the door. The clockwork women appeared to breathe, and even to move, in imitation of life—now she would have to imitate their imitation. At least the alchemical light on the dresser was relatively dim.

As she awaited capture, she wondered how much of this she could put in her story. Precious little if Cooper insisted on using "A Gentleman" as a byline. He'd sell more papers if he let it be known a woman had done the report, but he would also risk being denounced in Parliament. The story skirted the edge of decency anyway. Perhaps if she wrote it as a fiction...

Keep your head, Eleanor, she scolded herself. In times of extreme stress her mind tended to spin and whirl, addressing everything except the problem at hand. When she'd gotten word of David's death in India, all her thoughts had gone to practical matters: how to assist the family with funeral arrangements, the difficulty of conducting those arrangements when his remains were impossible to recover, making sure his mother and sisters had all the support they needed, and so on. It was weeks after the services before the grief finally caught up with her, a wave of sudden loss that had had made her knees buckle in a millinery shop. The shopgirl had assumed Ellie was swooning. Alas, no. She was entirely conscious the entire time. That was the problem. Those who fainted in the extremity of emotion were lucky. Ellie was awake and aware to experience everything.

The door opened, and Ellie willed herself to lay still. Her concubine hadn't reacted until Ellie touched it, so there was no reason she herself should react to the sudden entry of a lantern-jawed man in an ill-fitting suit—"Crippler" Crippen.

Crippen looked behind the drapes, but paid no more attention to Ellie than he would to an ornamental vase or an ottoman. He crouched and looked under the bed, and Ellie tensed, lest he discover the men's clothing and false mustache and make the connection. But apparently a wad of discarded clothes was no reason for alarm in this establishment, for he rose to his feet and turned toward the door.

Then he paused, and looked down at Ellie, and grunted.

She did her very best not to tense, or to flicker her half-lidded eyes. Crippen leaned over her, openly ogling—and why not? She was a machine; she had no dignity or modesty to protect. That was the *point*. Still, his gaze made her skin crawl, and it was so much worse when he extended a hand toward her bosom—

"Here, now, no time to play with the dollies," said a gruff voice from the hallway. "I checked all the rooms on the other side, and the bloke's nowhere to be found. Must have slipped past the mechanical dollymops before we got upstairs. The old man's going to be furious, he is."

"Who cares if some toff's poking a rubber doll anyway?" Crippen prodded Ellie in the ribs sharply with his forefinger, as if by way of illustration, and she bit the inside of her cheek to keep from crying out.

"What, you don't know? That man with the funny goggles isn't just any old knight of the realm, Crippler. He's got the Queen's ear."

"Ha. Just her ear, then?" Crippen said. "None of her other parts? Maybe he comes here because Vicky doesn't satisfy—"

To Ellie's surprise, the other man stalked over to Crippen and snarled. "Here now, don't go disrespecting our sovereign. She's our mum, ain't she?"

"She's got nine children, but I'm not one of them," Crippen said. "I didn't know you loved her so."

"Just watch what you say," the man said darkly, and stormed out of the room. Crippen chuckled and pulled the door closed after them, leaving Ellie alone.

She'd survived that, at least.

Now what?

"Charles!" Ellie bellowed, slamming open a door, and startling the man inside. He was in his fifties at least, pale as a fluffy cloud, and with a similarly amorphous body shape. He fell off the clockwork woman he'd been riding and landed on the other side of the bed, where he cowered. Ellie stomped on to the next room, brushing a length of blonde hair out of her face. She'd done the best she could, dress-wise, though the most modest thing she'd found to wear in the courtesan's room was a satin evening gown better fitted to a ballroom than a boudoir, and there were a few small stains on the skirts she chose not to contemplate too deeply. Who knew the fantasies of men were so *elaborate*? The dress didn't fit her terribly well, and she had entirely the wrong undergarments, but it would stay on her body, and any disarray would likely be overlooked given her obvious state of agitation.

She flung the next door open. "Charles, I know you're here, you debased animal, you wretched philanderer—"

"Madam!" The man who'd admitted her to the establishment earlier rushed down the hall toward her, and Ellie had a twinge of fear that he would recognize her, but he saw what he was meant to see: a furious woman, looking for her husband.

"I wish to see my husband at *once*," she said icily.

"Madam, I'm terribly sorry, no one by the name Charles is here this evening, I can assure you. If you'd like, I can make sure a message reaches him if he—"

"As if I would trust a message to someone employed in this… this den of iniquity!"

He winced. "Madam, please, I understand your distress, but you are quite correct—this is no appropriate place for a lady."

Ellie made a great show of calming herself and controlling her emotions. "Yes. Fine. I'm sure you are quite correct. I should… Perhaps I should go."

"Please, allow me to escort you out." He took her gently by the arm and led her toward the stairs, which would take her to the first floor and, blessedly, the front door. "If I may ask, madam, how did you obtain entry to the premises?"

"I knocked at the door, and no one answered. I tried the knob, and it opened. I heard shouting upstairs—I gather there was some commotion here?"

He colored. "Yes, madam. One of our guests suffered a mishap. Nothing serious, I assure you."

Ellie said nothing as they proceeded to the front door. The man touched the doorknob, then paused, and Ellie was afraid he'd recognized her after all. But he merely looked at the ceiling, and said in a low, solicitous voice, "I hope madam will forgive me for saying so, as it is hardly my place, but… men have certain needs. Surely it is better for your husband to sate those needs here, in a safe, clean establishment, where he will not suffer any… ill effects… than to seek satisfaction in less salubrious circumstances?"

"I will thank you to keep your opinions about my husband to yourself, sir," Ellie replied in her best icy matron's voice. The man sighed, nodded, and opened the door.

Ellie stepped out, walked in stately dignity toward the nearest alley, and, once she made sure no one was watching, slipped into the shadows and shrugged off the dress. She was wearing the suit Mr. James had provided her underneath, with the jacket tied around her waist by the sleeves. She shoved the dress into a heap of rubbish, along with the wig, though she hesitated over the last; it was good quality, and her hair *had* been cut terribly short. But better to erase any connection between herself and the brothel. She had not re-bound her breasts, and though the cut of the jacket was generous enough to keep her from looking too obviously feminine, she still worried the ruse was unconvincing. Her mustache would not reattach to her face, the adhesive of pine tar and alcohol having lost its efficacy. She pulled her hat low, looked down at her feet, and walked in as straight a line as she could manage in the direction of Mr. James's shop so she could recover her own clothes. She would not tell her dear uncle of her dangerous experience, nor would she tell her editor—at least, not yet.

Ellie had gone in search of a bit of risqué fluff for the newspaper. In the process, she'd stumbled onto a mysterious link between the brothel's apparent owner, the notorious criminal Abel Value, and Bertram Oswald, the Queen's closest confidant. She could scarcely imagine a more unlikely pairing.

Now all she had to do was uncover the nature of that link. Despite her attempt to mimic a masculine stride, she found herself almost skipping as she walked. She should have been afraid, she supposed, but—oh, there was a story here. The spinster Eleanor Skyler might have been afraid… but the writer E. Skye loved nothing better than a good story.

Deductions

"**A** map," Abel Value said, and then puffed his cigar with an air of thoughtfulness. Pimm wasn't thrilled at spending the morning in this man's office, especially given the beastly headache he'd cultivated the night before, but it was better than having the criminal in his own home again. Abel's lair of the moment was a room above a cobbler's shop—cramped and crammed with tottering heaps of paper, except for the surface of the large desk, which was peculiarly clean. That neatness made Pimm wonder what papers had been hurriedly swept aside and hidden in advance of his arrival. Big Ben loomed in one corner, seeming to fill about a third of the room's available space.

"I don't know," Value mused. "Someone could do me harm with that information. It's not the sort of thing one does in my line of work. Drawing a map for a man with connections to the police."

"You sought my assistance," Pimm said. "I cannot help you without adequate information. If I don't know where your... female employees... ply their trade, how can I hope to prevent more of them from being harmed?"

Value grunted, reached behind him, and found a rolled-up map of London. "This is Stanford's map," he said. "You've seen it? Indispensable for men of industry, shows every railway line, and every street." He rolled out the map, which filled most of the table, and Pimm leaned forward, his interest piqued despite himself. At first the map seemed just a riot of lines and letters, but the twisting ribbon of the Thames allowed him to orient himself. "The city looks so much more orderly pinned down on paper, doesn't it, than it does when you're out walking the streets? Still a messy place, though, streets thrown down every which way, the present built on top of the past, and the future just lying in wait for its own turn. I do love it so. I have business interests south of the river, of course, in Southwark. I also have a few girls working in the West End, late—it can get positively raucous around Leicester Square, you know." Pimm, who'd stumbled out of the music halls there with a bellyful of gin to join the merry-making crowds on more than one occasion himself, merely nodded. "None of the women have been killed in those areas, though. The one's who've died have all been north of the river." He tapped the map, indicating a portion of that far-from-respectable region known as Alsatia. Pimm was surprised. He'd heard the area was much improved since the installation of a police station in the vicinity some years previous—but he supposed such improvements were relative.

Value fished a shilling, a penny, and a few florins from his trouser pocket and scattered them on the map, then began arranging them with deliberate care, leaning close to the intricately-detailed map to read the street names. "Molly." He put down a shilling. "Letitia." A florin, perhaps an inch farther away. "Juliet." Another florin. "Abigail, we called her 'sweet Abi,' you'd think she was a choir girl until she put her hands down your trousers." The penny for her. "And the latest, Theodosia, you saw her remains today." The final florin.

"When did the first one die?" Pimm asked.

Value glanced at Ben. The big man said, "Twenty-seven days ago, m'Lord."

"Mr. Value. Five murders in a month? Someone is trying to make a point, and most forcefully."

"I can't say I care what that point might be. I just want the killings stopped. Can you do that?"

"Have you posted men to keep watch in the area?"

"Of course. But the girls go off with men, find a nice alley, and… well, we can't watch all of them, all the time."

"Where have you placed your watchmen?"

"Near the sites of the killings, of course."

"Near the site of the *last* killing?" Pimm said. "Understandable enough, but attempting to stop a crime that has already occurred is a poor substitute for attempting to stop one that will happen in the future. We should place watchmen where the killer will strike *next*."

Value snorted. "And how do we know that? Are you an occultist, too, sir? A gypsy fortune teller?"

"Hardly. But the killer has been proceeding east along the river through Alsatia, traveling approximately half a mile with each murder. I suspect he's moving along just far enough to avoid your ever-expanding sphere of watchmen, sir."

Value leaned forward, frowning. "But how would he know where we're watching?"

"He's obviously familiar with your business," Pimm said. "How else can you explain the fact that, in the course of five murders, he has always managed to kill *your* whores? Not every girl or ponce in that area is in your employ, but only *your* interests have been impacted. He also knew where to find your houses of clockwork pleasure, though their locations are hardly advertised. Most men who know of such establishments know the location of one, or perhaps two, but this fellow knows of *five*—frankly I'm astonished there are so many—which implies a certain degree of intimate knowledge."

"Betrayal," Value murmured.

"Is there anyone in your organization you have reason to distrust?"

"Those who give me *reason* to distrust them do not remain long in my employ." Value sucked at his cigar, brows beetling in a scowl. "My people are at your disposal, Halliday. Tell Ben where you want guards placed, and he'll see that it's done."

"Perhaps you should tell your girls not to work this evening," Pimm said. "For their own safety."

Value shook his head. "If they do not earn me money, Halliday, I do not *care* about their safety."

"You place your own wealth above the lives of these women?"

"Everyone puts personal gain above the interests of such common scum, Halliday." Another puff of smoke. "I just don't bother lying about it."

Pimm tried to restrain his fury. Just talking to this man made him feel filthy. "I have reason to hope such callous views will become the exception, rather than the norm, soon. We are in a new world, Value, a world of progress and scientific advancement that promises a better life for all people—"

Value burst out laughing. "Ben," he said. "Tell the lord about your cousin that worked in one of Sir Bertram Oswald's factories."

"Timothy, sir," Ben said, voice impassive. "Ten years old, he was. Worked making alchemical lamps, you know the ones with the glass globes and the lovely yellow light inside? Timothy was really just helping out, sweeping up broken glass, fetching tools, and the like. Perhaps you don't know, sir, but the substance that lights up those lamps is made of all manner of different chemicals, mixed together in a particular way. The chemical you get at the end isn't so dangerous—you shouldn't drink it, and it stinks a bit, but it can be sopped up with rags and thrown out if you happen to break one of the lamps. But one of the chemicals they use earlier in the process is an acid, terribly strong, and it so happened that one day Timothy was racing through the factory on an errand. It's a dreadful loud place, and even though the man shouted 'Watch out,' Timothy didn't hear him. Crashed right into the legs of a man about to pour a beaker of that acid into a vat, and the acid spilled on Timothy instead. Burned a hole right through his skull, it did. I hate to even think about it. He was a good boy." Ben lapsed into silence.

"Progress is fine for those who get to enjoy its fruits, Halliday," Value said. "Not so fine for those who tend the roots. Those often get their hands mangled by the machines, and their faces burned by the steam, and end up with more holes in their heads than they were born with. But you and I are blessed by God, aren't we? My, but it's good to be rich."

Pimm rose stiffly. "I will attempt to apprehend this killer, Mr. Value," he said. "After that, I wish to have no further involvement with you."

"Then you had best hope I never need your services again," Value replied.

"Call on me at home this afternoon, Benjamin," Pimm said. "We'll make our arrangements then."

"Consider it done, sir," Big Ben said.

Pimm went down the cramped stairs, nodded at the cobbler working at his bench, and stepped out onto the street. He walked briskly along through the warm spring afternoon… and a young woman hurried across the street to intercept him. She wore a dress of severe gray and rather dowdy cut, though her face was younger than her matronly garb would suggest, and she wore a rather fashionable little bonnet on the back of her head, just above a shower of curls. "Excuse me," she said, and Pimm looked around for her escort. She seemed to be a woman on her own, which made her accosting him in the street even stranger.

"Miss? May I be of some assistance?"

"I do hope so, Lord Pembroke. Forgive me, but I recognize you, from the *Argus*, the coverage of the Trent case—"

Pimm nodded and forced a smile. His head still pounded, and meeting with Value had done nothing to improve his mood. "Ah, of course, they put my likeness in the newspaper. Silly, really, I was only assisting Detective Whistler—"

The woman covered her mouth. "Oh, dear me," she said. "I have not made myself clear. I recognized you, not from a likeness, but from your visit to the offices of the *Argus*. My name is Eleanor Skyler. We did not meet on that occasion, but I was in my editor's office, and he pointed you out to me."

Pimm's mind underwent a ferocious reorganization. "You are a journalist, Miss?" She couldn't be more than twenty-five, half a dozen years his junior. Of course women *did* write, Freddy had taken a subscription to the *English Women's Journal* until it ceased circulation earlier in the year, and now had a fondness for the *Alexandra Magazine and English-woman's Journal*. (Freddy, whose interest in women had once been limited to whether they'd overlook his coarse manners in favor of his fortune, had become quite the advocate of women's rights lately.) Pimm hadn't realized the rather staid *Argus* had a woman reporter on the staff. But, wait, Eleanor Skyler—ah, yes. Mr. E. Skye. Mystery Skye? How droll.

"I am indeed a journalist," she said. "Currently investigating a story that, to my surprise, appears to concern you."

Pimm gave his most self-deprecating chuckle. "Miss Skyler, I am of course delighted to assist in any manner that I can, but I'm afraid the Trent case was my last endeavor into criminal matters—"

"Really, sir?" She blinked at him, and he couldn't help but notice her long lashes, her eyes the dark blue of a still Scottish loch on a summer's day, and so what if her nose was a bit long? It suited her face. She cocked her head, a gesture of innocent curiosity, and said, "Then may I ask why you were meeting with the notorious criminal Abel Value just moments ago?"

Pimm's smile froze on his face. "I'm afraid I don't know what you mean…"

"Please, Lord Pembroke. I mean you no harm. If I wished to embarrass you, I would have followed you clandestinely—"

"It seems that is precisely what you've done."

She shook her head. "Not at all. I was watching Mr. Value. Imagine my surprise to see *you*, a man known to be a friend to the police, a man who recovered a baroness's stolen black pearls, a man who proved the ghost of Hodgson Manor was no spirit but actually a madman who'd lived for all those years hidden in the walls of the house—what business does a man like that have with Abel Value?"

Pimm was glad he hadn't allowed himself to drink this morning. Well, he'd had the one, but one hardly counted—it was practically medicinal. He needed his wits about him now. "Miss, I am going to pretend to give you directions, all right? And you should nod and thank me, and then walk away."

"Value has men watching you, then?"

Pimm was impressed. He pointed along the street and gestured with his other hand. "Almost certainly. I don't suppose you really *will* walk away?"

Her face took on a confused expression, and it took a moment for Pimm to realize it was false, for show. She pointed in the opposite direction, tilting her head in a questioning way, and said, "Now that I *know* there's a story? Certainly not. Where and when shall we meet to discuss your situation?"

It was quite sophisticated of her, really, to let the threat remain merely implied, instead of stating it baldly. How crass it would have been if she'd insisted he meet with her, lest a story appear in tomorrow's *Argus* linking Pimm to known criminal figures.

"Meet me in half an hour at St. James' Park, near the Ornithological Society. We'll sit and have a talk."

"And you'll tell me everything then?" Her eyes twinkled. She clearly enjoyed this. Pimm could sympathize—he never felt more alive than when he was on the hunt. But he wasn't terribly pleased to be the hunted.

"I'll tell you what I *can*," he said.

"Oh, so it's *that* direction," Miss Skyler said loudly. "Oh, dear me, whenever I leave the confines of my own kitchen I become so *frightfully* disoriented." She dropped him a curtsey, and then—shockingly—a wink, and went on her way.

Pimm watched her go. Oh dear, oh dear. He had enough on his mind without *this*.

He simply didn't have time to be so intrigued by a woman.

Investigations

Lord Pembroke sat on a bench, watching ducks drift about on the surface of the water. Ellie sat on the bench behind his, so they were positioned back-to-back. She had a fine view of trees and of a slightly frog-faced statue of a man in military dress. "My lord," she murmured. "I'm so pleased you kept our appointment."

He stirred behind her. She couldn't see him now, but when she'd looked at his face in the street, she'd been struck by the shrewdness of his gaze, and the darkness of his eyes, and the faint smile playing around the corners of his mouth. He had a reputation as an ingenious man, but it was hard to separate the real man from the stories—the nobleman detective, younger son of a Marquess, and, according to some rumors, an inveterate drinker who'd married a woman of no particular status for reasons that were unknown, but open to all sorts of speculation.

"Being a journalist is a bit like being a detective, I suppose," Lord Pembroke mused. "Albeit with fewer rules."

"And far less at stake. If I fail, some other paper will run the story, most likely. If a detective fails, the wicked go unpunished, and victims fail to receive justice."

"Miss, Skyler—or shall I say Miss Skye, since you are here in a professional capacity?" Ellie didn't answer, surprised and pleased that he knew her byline. "I have nothing but respect for journalists. As a gesture of that respect, I will be happy to give you an exclusive interview about my… current case… once it is concluded."

"What case is that, sir?"

Lord Pembroke sighed. "In exchange for this interview, I ask only that you leave Mr. Value's name out of any story you run."

"Why would you want to protect him?"

"Ha. Oh, no, Miss Skye. You mistake me. I wish to protect myself, or rather, my family. My dear brother would be apoplectic to see our family name in connection with Mr. Value's."

"Then why *are* you connected with Value? And I repeat—what is the nature of your current case?"

"So many questions. I've never realized how troublesome it is, to be bombarded by inquiries. I now feel sympathy for all those I've interro-gated over the years. Suffice to say that Mr. Value's interests and my own align, temporarily, at this moment. It is an exceedingly rare alignment, akin to an unheard of syzygy of stars and planets, something that might come only once in an epoch. But I can tell you will not be put off without some specifics, so: a person unknown is killing women, Miss Skye. Five have been found so far, all slain within the past month. I mean to stop the killer, and Mr. Value is in possession of information that will enable me to do so. That is the whole reason for our current affiliation."

"I've heard of no rash of murders," she said. "The usual drunken mishaps, of course, but five women killed? Surely that would not go unnoticed."

"Certain forces are making sure they *do* go unnoticed. I should say no more. I must save *something* for that exclusive interview, to be conducted once my investigation is concluded."

"You have piqued my interest," Ellie admitted. "You will contact me?"

"I will. After the killer is apprehended, you will be the first person to hear my story, after the police."

"And when do you expect this business to be concluded?"

"In a few days, I hope—assuming he attempts to strike again. It is an uncomfortable position, to hope a murderer will try to kill again, but it is my best hope for finding him."

"Just don't forget me," Ellie said.

"I do not believe it would be possible to forget you, Miss Skye."

Ellie hesitated. "Lord Pembroke… is there anything I can do? To help?

I am not without connections and contacts, made in the course of my business. If I may be of assistance…"

"I appreciate the offer." Was that a hint of surprise in his voice? Pleasure? And why should Ellie care if he were *pleased*? He was handsome enough, and as interesting a man as she'd ever met, but what did that matter? The moon was lovely, too, but she would never have it on the shelf in her room, so why wish for it? "But I think I have matters well in hand. I will let you know if that changes, however. I trust I can contact you in care of the *Argus*?"

"That would be fine."

"Then may I be excused? Killers to apprehend, and so on."

"Certainly."

He rose and strode off around the pond. Ellie turned on the bench and watched him go. Considering that she'd essentially extorted an interview from him, he'd been remarkably polite. As irritated by her meddling as he must have been, he'd never once called her "girl," or told her journalism was no business for women, or treated her as anything other than a somewhat adversarial equal. That kind of respect was refreshing to the point of intoxication.

Ellie stood and adjusted her hat. The false curls pinned underneath matched her own hair color nicely, but they made the back of her neck itch. It would be months before her hair grew in. Oh well. She'd get a decent article out of it, at least, though she needed to write up the notes she'd hurriedly scribbled the night before into something more formal. But she no longer cared much about writing a bit of fluff about the secret interior of the clockwork brothels. She was on the scent of a *real* story now.

She pondered for a moment, watching the ducks. Lord Pembroke was investigating murders by the river, and Value was helping him, which suggested that the murders somehow intersected with Value's interests, or his territory. She decided to stop by the office and speak to a certain reporter who had close ties to the police. He might be able to point her in the right direction to further her inquiries. Not that Ellie doubted Lord Pembroke's promise to give her an interview, but she could hardly just take *his* word for things…

Pimm shivered in the shadow of a grimy brick building, not far from the stinking breadth of the Thames. The river was the mother of London, but progress had not been kind to her course. The healthy old river stink of Pimm's youth had been replaced by something more acrid and sharp. Portions of the river glowed at night, now, covered by scums of weird luminous algae, and there were rumors among the mud-larks who scavenged along the river about strange creatures dwelling in the depths, occasionally tearing oars from the hands of boatmen, or pulling an unwary tide-waitress from the slimy shore. Miss Skye had written a story about that subject, hadn't she, in the paper recently? Pimm would have to remember to read it, if Freddy hadn't thrown it out. River monsters indeed. But on this particular night, Pimm was on the watch for more mundane threats.

Unfortunately, he couldn't concentrate on keeping his eyes open for a killer. He was thinking about Ellie Skye instead. Policemen generally hated journalists, since they poked their noses in where they didn't belong, interfered in ongoing cases by calling public attention to said cases, and were generally never satisfied with whatever answers they received. Pimm wasn't very fond of journalists as a class, either, because his family was willing to tolerate almost anything from him, as long as he conducted himself *quietly*—they could accept eccentricity, so long as that eccentricity was wed to discretion. But the younger brother of a Marquess dabbling in criminology was the sort of story reporters loved, and Pimm had resigned himself to smiling affably and giving all credit to the police whenever a reporter spoke to him. He wasn't sure such deflection would work with Miss E. Skye. She might not go away satisfied with such platitudes. Worse, he was afraid he wouldn't *want* her to go away. Skyler clearly had a lively mind to go with her lovely face, and if she had more curiosity than was good for her, well, so did Pimm himself. He could hardly fault her for—

"There," Big Ben murmured. "He's a dodgy-looking fellow, isn't he?"

Pimm looked over. A man in a long overcoat scuttled along, keeping close to the shadows, looking around nervously, starting to approach some of the women lingering in doorways and cooing from alleyways, then retreating and hurrying farther along. Pimm shook his head. "No, he's *too* dodgy, that would make any girl nervous and watchful. According to your man Mr. Adams none of the bodies showed any sign of a fight, apart from the marks on the throats of those he choked. Our man is confident, and will surely seem comfortable and experienced. He gets close, and takes control quickly, with a rag doused in ether, or knocks them down before they can cry out and smothers them."

"Sounds a right cold bastard," Ben opined.

"Coldness in a killer can be worse than heat. The hot-blooded killer usually only kills once, in a flash of terrible fury. After the deed is done, the violence flows out of them—just leaks away. Often, the police can take such men without any trouble, and sometimes the killers are already weeping over the damage they've done. But the cold ones…" Pimm shook his head. "They might commit any atrocity you can imagine, and think nothing of it afterward."

"Perhaps you're right about it being an employee, then," Ben said. "Mr. Value does hire some cold bastards."

"Do you count yourself among that number, Ben?"

"Me?" The big man sounded surprised. "No, sir. I'm a victim of circumstance, me, and such crimes as I've committed have always been crimes of heat. I was a respectable lad, once, in service at a great house. My sister was a parlor maid. Pretty, she was… until the young master tried to take a liberty with her, and she resisted. He slashed her across the face with a knife, left a terrible scar, and blinded her in one eye. I was only fifteen, but already fairly big, and I doted on my sister, I did. When I saw what the lord's son had done…" He shrugged. "I didn't kill him. But he will never walk right again. No one could prove I was the one that done it, I made sure of that, but everyone knew anyway, so I had to flee. I came here, and I've worked for a lot of nasty fellows ever since. Mr. Value is no worse than most, I suppose."

"Ben, that's terrible, I—"

"I shouldn't have brought it up," Ben said. "We have a job to do, don't we?"

And so they waited, Pimm doing his best to keep a watchful eye while at the same time *not* watching women disappear into alleyways with men. He liked women as much as anyone, and he'd been to some of the nicer brothels once or twice—though not since his days at Oxford—but what pleasure could there be in rooting in an alleyway? Then again, his working day didn't involve hauling crates or laboring in a factory, and he had more to look forward to at home than stinking rooms filled with children he barely knew and a wife who was probably none too pleased to see him come home. Perhaps a moment of pure, unthinking, convulsive pleasure was the best men such as these could hope for, and attractive enough to overcome the fear of the Affliction. There were only several hundred verified cases over the past few years, though there were surely many more that had never been reported to the medical establishment.

This kind of alley work couldn't be much fun for the women, though. He'd heard there were some girls in this business who genuinely enjoyed the work—or at least found it less objectionable than other forms of labor—but he couldn't imagine any woman going to work for Abel Value in these ugly alleyways with any motivation other than total desperation.

A shrill whistle sounded thrice, and Ben and Pimm raced together in the direction of the sound. Two short blasts, and one long, the agreed-upon signal for catching the murderer in the act. Sound bounced around damnably among the cramped taverns and warehouses in the area, but Ben seemed to know precisely where the sound had come from, so Pimm went along at his heels. Perhaps it was a false alarm—Value's men were on edge—but if not, Pimm dearly hoped he'd be able to prevent Value from killing the murderer. The perpetrator needed to be taken to the police, if only because his victims surely had families, and they deserved to know the killer had been caught. If the man didn't confess, the girls would simply be presumed to have disappeared, gobbled up by the streets of London, and wasn't uncertainty even worse than the knowledge that you'd lost a daughter or sister?

They found the whistle-blower gasping and clutching his forearm, leaning on a wall near the motionless body of a red-haired girl, lying face-down in an alley. "Bastard had a knife, he cut me," Value's man said, removing his hand to reveal an open gash on the meaty part of his bicep.

"Which way did he go?" Pimm said.

The man gestured, and Ben shook his head. "Never catch him, sir. Five steps past the mouth of the alley, there are ten different directions he could go."

Pimm looked the whistle-blower over thoughtfully. "Ben, would you mind checking our friend, to make sure he's... quite well?"

"I get you," Ben said. "All right, Solly, turn out your pockets, there's a good lad." The big man's tone was entirely affable, and Solly frowned, but did as requested. He had nothing on him but a few coins, a bit of string, and a little pen-knife, which Ben passed to Pimm. The detective removed a small alchemical device from his coat pocket, shaped like a pocketwatch, and opened the metal cover. A bright, intense light shone forth from the device, focused through a lens of clear glass. It was impossible to touch the device without thinking of Ben's (alleged) cousin, burned to death by acid in the creation of this little wonder, or one like it. Pimm shone the light on the knife and carefully examined the blade and clasp. Not a spot of blood on the metal or in the crevices, and when Pimm touched the blade with the ball of his thumb, it was nearly dull as a spoon—a thing carried more from habit than utility.

"He has no other weapons?"

Ben shook his head. "I wouldn't even call that a weapon, m'lord, but no."

"It's unlikely he cut himself to lead us astray, then." Pimm folded the knife and passed it to Ben.

The outraged man opened his mouth to protest, but Ben just patted him on the shoulder. "Don't take offense, Solly. He's just doing what Mr. Value asked, suspecting everybody and everything." Ben began grilling the man about the appearance of the killer, while Pimm knelt to examine the body. He turned her over. Pretty girl, surely no more than seventeen, Irish coloration, eyes staring wide. Pimm leaned almost close enough to kiss her, then turned his face away. The smell of ether still clung to her face. He put his head to her chest, and felt for a pulse in her wrist, but there was no heartbeat.

"I didn't think nothing of it," the man was saying. "He walked up to her like anybody, and they chatted real pleasant, almost like old friends, but Margaret there was a friendly soul. I suppose they made an arrangement, and they headed into the alley. I wouldn't have thought anything of it, but..." He trailed off.

"You crept up to the alley to have a look," Ben said. He turned to Pimm. "Solly here's a peeper, sir, everyone knows it."

"Just doing my duty." Solly looked down. "Keeping watch. I saw him pressing her up against the wall, and that looked all right, but he was holding something to her face, and she was going all limp, so I shouted, and ran in. He stepped right up to me, slashing out with this big old knife like, and I got cut. Thought he was going to cut my head off, but he sort of wavered, then turned and ran off. I whistled as hard as I could."

"The ether killed her, I think," Pimm said, putting his hand against the girl's cheek. It was still warm. "It seems likely some of the other women died the same way."

"Think he'll try again tonight?" Ben said.

"It's possible, but I suspect he'll be more cautious than that."

"What happens next?" Ben said.

Pimm sighed. "We'd better get her body to Mr. Adams. And quickly. Within the hour is best."

Ben and Jim exchanged a glance. Ben shrugged. "As you like. We can manage that if we hurry."

"Sometimes I think science has replaced necromancy as the darkest art," Pimm said, looking down at the dead woman, wondering if Adams could possibly accomplish what he'd promised. Wondering if he should be allowed even to try.

"I disagree, sir," Ben said. "Why, the city's never been brighter. You can see everything so much more clearly now, and that's all thanks to science."

"I threw out the alchemical light my missus brought home," Solly said. "I'd never had any idea my house was so *filthy* until she brought that light in there. I could scarcely bring myself to sit in my own chair, t'was so disgusting." This from a man so dirty crops could grow in the creases around his nose.

"No one ever said progress was pretty," Pimm said, and helped them carry the poor woman away.

An Eyewitness,
Sans Eyes

Adam looked up when someone began banging on the door to one of the tunnels. The block beneath the warehouses where he lived and worked were riddled with passageways, some natural, most built by men long ago for purposes forgotten, and a few breaking into even older burial chambers where there were artifacts that did not seem wrought by human hands. Adam had, in his many years here, expanded a number of those tunnels, or caused them to be expanded. Most of the passages were known only to Adam himself, but the steel door currently ringing with knocks was at the end of the tunnel Abel Value's men used to deliver dead women to him.

After slipping his white mask on, Adam pulled on a rope, perfectly balancing counterweights swaying to pull the door open. There were two men beyond the door, in the dark space that had once been a coal cellar of a neighboring house: the one called Big Ben, and the detective who'd visited the day before. They carried a dead woman between them, one of her arms slung over each of their shoulders, her small feet dragging the ground.

"Why, Lord Pembroke," Adam said. "You bring such interesting gifts."

"She's been dead forty minutes, more or less." Halliday was red-faced, and out of breath, but had a look of determination that Adam had seen in the mirror once or twice, before he'd had the good sense to get rid of all the mirrors in his living space. "Died from inhaling too much ether. Can you do what you promised?"

"It is possible, in theory." He paused. "I have only actually accomplished it with dogs, and it's hard to tell how much reason a dog retains after death, as they have precious little to start with. But I am eager to try with a human subject. Even a failure could be instructive. Bring her, and place her on my table." He led the men down the brick-lined corridor to his laboratory, and they wrestled the woman's lifeless body onto the same table where her sister of the streets had been so recently. Adam considered his tools. The bone saw, of course, but it might be better to prepare the nutrient bath first—

"If that's all, gents, I'd best go report to Mr. Value," Big Ben said. "Though I'm not sure *what* I'm reporting."

"Tell him the killer got away, and that Mr. Adams is examining her body for evidence that might reveal the miscreant's identity."

"That is a tale that has the advantage of truth." Adam pulled a leather apron on over his head. "You might wish to step away, gentlemen. Time is of the essence, so I must value haste over neatness."

"I'm on my way then." Big Ben gave Halliday a nod, cast a worried look at Adam, and hurried back down the tunnel. Adam didn't bother to watch him go. Ben had sense enough to make sure the door—disguised as just another filthy bit of wall on the other side—was firmly closed. He'd been here before, carrying other victims, and not just those who'd fallen victim to this new murderer. Adam had been about his researches for a long time, and there were always dead young girls to be found in London.

Halliday stepped back, but didn't turn away, watching with an interest that Adam perceived as more than morbid curiosity. Halliday was a man who sought to understand the world. He was a fool, of course, and ignorant, as all normal men with their pitifully short lives were when compared to Adam or his patron. (How hilarious it was that Halliday thought *Value* was Adam's patron, when in truth Adam and Value both served the same, far greater master.) Still, Adam's reflexive contempt was softened a bit by Halliday's clear-eyed willingness to watch this procedure.

"You seem rather more sober today than you did yesterday, Lord

Pembroke." Adam busied himself preparing the nutrient bath, filling his largest glass vessel with the component fluids.

"I do enjoy a tipple from time to time, Mr. Adams, but when pursuing a murderer, it is best to keep one's mind clear."

"I did not say you seemed *entirely* sober, sir. The alcohol on your breath is merely fainter today." The smell of the brandy appeared, to Adam, the color of pale green grass.

"A drink can give one the courage to pursue a murderer, too." Halliday spoke without apparent shame. "You have a good sense of smell."

"All my senses are highly developed. I was endowed by my creator with *marvelous* gifts."

"Such modesty."

"It is modesty, in fact. My gifts were *given* to me—I am due no credit for them."

"I see. All glory to God, indeed. But surely you were the one who developed those… gifts. With hard work, and study? One does not attain all this"—to his credit, Halliday's voice betrayed not a hint of sarcasm as he gestured at the dank subterranean laboratory—"without sustained and serious effort."

"We are all just machines, Lord Pembroke. Created, presented with a certain set of initial conditions and constraints, and set on our courses, which we follow unerringly."

"Surely you don't believe we have no choice—"

"The brain is a machine, too," Adam murmured, raising his bone saw. "I will have to remove her head now. Do not be alarmed." He cut through her throat and spinal column with his bone saw, careful to decapitate her well below the brain stem. The blood flowed, but didn't spurt, as her heart was no longer pumping. Once the cut was complete, he arranged the straps and clamps on the table to hold the severed head in place for the more delicate work.

"Now I must scalp her. Normally, I would shave the head first. But time is limited. We may already be too late."

"You said an hour. It's only been forty-five minutes now."

Adam began to scalp the woman, much as the savages in the New World were said to do to their enemies, only in reverse, starting in the back of the head and peeling upward. "Yes. That was merely an estimate, however.

I did not expect you to actually bring me a fresh victim, Lord Pembroke. I assumed our conversation was theoretical. But you will note I am proceeding with all due haste, despite my surprise, and I have some hopes for a positive outcome." He peeled the flesh and her lovely red hair away, letting it fall across her face, the scalp attached by a flap of skin at the base of her nose, revealing the bare skull beneath.

Halliday still did not turn away, though Adam sensed a certain level of agitation. Adam took his bone saw and began to cut around the circumference of the dead girl's skull, just above the eyes. "The key now is to cut open the skull without damaging the brain. With a dog or cat, you can cut through the skull with shears, but the human skull is a mighty helm of bone, and requires a strong hand and a sharper blade." Adam did not add that his strength was equal to the task, as that would be readily apparent. His movements were smooth and meticulous. The slip of a fraction of an inch would destroy portions of her brain, and this procedure had only a marginal chance of success under ideal circumstances, which did *not* include inadvertently sawing through her gray matter. "Tell, me, Lord Pembroke. Do you believe in love?"

"Love? You speak of love, at a time like this?"

"What better time? The death of an individual is often the death of love. The victim's love dies with her, and while those who love the victim might experience no diminishment of their own feelings, all reciprocity is lost." Adams was quite capable of paying attention to surgical matters and musing philosophically at the same time. Doing only *two* things at once was almost too easy. "I know it is hard to credit, as I stand here with my sharp knives and my leather apron, but everything I do, I do for love. I seek only the true connection between two beings, individuals who understand one another utterly and instantly—who are as one mind, in two bodies."

"Well," Halladay said, apparently glad of the distraction from Adam's gruesome work. "I'm not sure that's the ideal I'd strive toward, myself. That whole commingling and being as one flesh sort of thing, it's not to my taste. I'd prefer a lover who pushed against my expectations, I think—who surprised me constantly, in delightful ways. You see, in my dabblings in the criminal world, I see a lot of things I *expect* to see, the same petty motivations for the same sad crimes, the same sordid acts played out again and again for the same foolish reasons. But a woman who could *surprise* me, a mystery I could not unravel—that would be a woman worth loving. I knew a girl when I was at school, her name was Adelaide, daughter of a family friend, and she had that effect on me. Alas, she died, oh, more than ten years ago now. But I would say, yes, I believe in love."

"Hmm. This eternal state of congenial surprise—is that the sort of relationship you have with Lady Pembroke?" Adam asked.

Pimm hesitated only a fraction before saying, "Oh, yes, of course," but it was enough of a pause for Adam to know he was lying. So even the rich, the handsome, the intelligent, the ones blessed by all things in life, could fail to find their heart's desire. Adam found that fact simultaneously depressing and heartening.

Once the top of the skull was cut through, he lifted away the cap of bone, gently pulling, tearing loose the slimy connective tissue between gray matter and white skull.

The detective finally turned away. Just as it was becoming interesting. How disappointing.

"We are nearly done." Adam set the skull cap aside and took up one of his knives. "I have only to sever the optic nerves, the pituitary gland, the third and fourth cranial nerves, a few other connections..." He trailed off, absorbed in the work, almost forgetting the detective's presence. Soon he reached in, carefully slipped his fingers around the spongy brain matter, and lifted the organ free. The sound of a brain lifting away from its container is unlike anything else, and the noise sparkled like golden fireflies.

"Now, the true test." Adam carried the brain to his work table, where the vessel of fluid awaited. He attached tubing to the spine, and pressed metal probes trailing wires into sections of the frontal lobe. Once he was satisfied that the connections were tight, he immersed the brain into the nutrient fluid, his oxygen-rich blood substitute. Adam threaded the wires running from the brain through small holes in a circular steel plate. He placed the steel plate carefully, so that it entirely covered the top of the jar, then picked up a rubber-lined lid, which he screwed down tight around the plate.

Halliday was watching again, and had even approached the worktable. "That looks like an oversized Kilner jar."

"It is similar, though I hope to preserve a human mind, not pickled cucumbers or peach preserves."

"The brain *floats*," Halliday said. "That… surprises me, somehow. I'd think it would be heavier."

"Adult human brains tend to weigh a bit over three pounds. But the weight is irrelevant—density is the issue, and my artificial blood is denser than gray matter." Adam connected the wires that emerged from the brain to a complex metal and brass apparatus that took up about a foot square of table space and resembled a half-melted pipe organ. "This is my artificial voice machine. I have canisters of air under pressure, which blow through a series of baffles, flaps, tubes—well. The engineering is rather complex, but it may give this poor girl back her voice. I've never heard this machine make a sound other than a dog's howl, though it renders that accurately enough." Adam checked and double-checked all the connections, strangely reluctant to activate the magnets and try the final test. If he succeeded, it would be a great triumph, the sort of accomplishment Adam's creator could have only dreamed about, and never attained. But if he failed… it would be, after all, just another failure, added to a long ledger of the same.

But one could only delay so long before it *looked* like a delay. Adam flicked a switch, activating the electromagnets arrayed around the jar, which would stimulate the brain, though not to control it, this time—merely to stir it back into life.

He picked up a conical brass tube, like an old woman's ear-horn… which it was, more or less, though now it was wired into a brain bobbing in the dense fluid of a jar. Adam paused and looked at the detective. "Do you know her name?"

"Margaret." The detective stared at the brain in the jar as if he could not believe such a thing could possibly be addressed by name.

Adam cleared his throat, held the speaking horn to his mouth, and said, "Margaret? Can you hear me?"

A sound like a long sigh emerged from the speaking apparatus, and Halliday gasped. Adam did not; the sound was not actually a sigh, but old air being flushed from the system.

The sound that emerged next was toneless, but entirely understandable: "Yes? Where am I, sir? Why is it so very dark here?"

"Merciful God in heaven," Halliday said.

"Merciful God may keep his heaven," Adam replied. "We men have work enough to keep us occupied on Earth."

Pimm found Mr. Adams's company profoundly unsettling, but the man was certainly a genius. Could even Sir Bertram have accomplished such a thing? To allow one to hear a voice from beyond the grave? The woman was dead, yet Pimm could hear her voice—or *a* voice, that seemed to emanate from her mind. As a detective, he should remain suspicious and skeptical, and it was possible this was some elaborate ruse on the part of Mr. Adams, but what would such trickery accomplish? In a world where a sickness could change one's sex, where strange lights lit the night sky and eternal alchemical fires burned in Whitechapel, where lightning could be bottled and used to run an omnibus, where a man could peer through a lens into a drop of water and discover a teeming world of tiny savage organisms living and dying and vying for life, who was Pimm to doubt a brain could be made to speak?

The priests wouldn't like this sort of thing, of course. The woman's soul had surely departed, after all, when her body died, so what was speaking now? Obviously not her immortal essence, which had gone on to its final reward. Perhaps this was something like an echo, then, or a voice record-ing of the sort one could make on wax cylinders with a moving stylus, or… Leave it to the metaphysicians, he decided. Pimm had more worldly concerned. "May I?" He held out his hand for the speaking-horn.

Mr. Adams raised a finger. "Let me explain a few things to the woman first, lest we alarm her." He put the tube to his lips. "Margaret. I am a doctor. You were attacked. Do you remember?"

"I… yes." The voice was eerie, not really masculine or feminine—as if the wind blowing through the branches of a tree began speaking words.

"You were terribly injured, my dear. Do not be afraid. You may yet be saved."

Pimm raised an eyebrow, but Adams was immersed in his task. It was kinder, in a way, to tell the girl she was only hurt—but in another way, it was terribly cruel.

"Have I been blinded, sir? And… I can't seem to feel my arms or legs."

"Your eyesight may also be restored in time," Adams said. "As for the lack of sensation, we have high hopes on that score as well. May I ask… are you frightened?"

Stupid question, Pimm thought. Of *course* she was—

"No." The voice did not hesitate. "As strange as that may seem, I am not afraid."

Adams covered the mouthpiece and turned his head toward Pimm. "Interesting. I have theorized that, if removed from the glandular system, the brain might feel fear less intensely. When the body's myriad systems are not sending messages of fear, after all—"

"May I question her, sir?" Pimm said. "While the memories are fresh?"

The mask on Adams's face made it impossible to read his expression, but Pimm thought he was annoyed. He spoke into the tube. "Margaret. A detective is here to speak with you. He is investigating the terrible crime perpetrated against you. His name is Pembroke Halliday—"

"Lord Pembroke, the toff detective? I have heard of him."

"How wonderful." Adam passed the horn to Pimm.

How peculiar, Pimm thought, and then put the mouthpiece close to his lips. "I am terribly sorry this happened to you, Miss. I will do everything in my power to apprehend the, ah, assailant. Do you think you could provide a description? His height, build, hair color, eye color, distinguishing features—scars, birthmarks, facial peculiarities? Anything at all would help."

A long pause, followed by another susurration of air. "I could describe him, sir, certainly, if you wish. I have seen him many times, after all, and know his face well. But would it be more helpful if I simply told you his name?"

Despite the gruesome circumstances, Pimm couldn't help smiling. "Yes, Margaret. That would be most helpful indeed."

What Follows

Because she was afraid Lord Pembroke might recognize her, and because this particular part of the city wasn't particularly welcoming to women (unless they were women of a particular sort), Ellie donned her disguise again. Mr. James had, reluctantly, agreed to let her keep the clothing and other accouterments for a few days, and had provided her with a small tin of spirit gum to help affix her mustache. She had dressed in her rooms, a small apartment on the ground floor of an establishment near the Charter House inhabited exclusively by unmarried professional women and their widowed landlady. Once dressed in her guise as Mr. Smythe, she'd hurried from her room and out the front door, hoping none of the neighbors would happen to look then and see a strange man emerging from the premises—something like *that* would occasion a great deal of shocked talk, and a visit from the landlady; perhaps even an eviction for whichever tenant she deemed most likely to consort with strange men.

Once Ellie had made it around the corner without any sound of alarm, she walked with more confidence until she was able to catch one of the omnibuses. She swung up onto the cart, delighted at the ease of motion that came with wearing trousers. The omnibus trundled along its predetermined route, with a young-looking driver by the brake who seemed terrified by the very machine he commanded. She got as close to the proper neighborhood as the omnibus would take her, and walked the rest of the way.

Her garb was rather too posh for this part of the city, and she drew a few dark looks from workingmen on the street, but she had no other options when it came to male attire, and anyway, it was hardly unheard of for more professional men to seek illicit pleasures in such parts of the city. She prowled along the streets, smelling the reek of the river, avoiding the throngs trying to sell wares to those who could scarcely afford them, and peering into the smeared windows of taverns as she passed. As the sun began to go down, and there were more shadows for her to hide among, she began to feel less watched and more secure.

Her colleague Barnard at the *Argus* had told her that Abel Value's undisputed territory covered a significant swath of Alsatia, which was no surprise. It seemed reasonable to Ellie that, if someone was killing Value's employees, they must be doing it here—and, in that case, Lord Pembroke was probably here somewhere as well, keeping an eye on things, hoping to catch the killer in the act. Ellie would happily interview him once he concluded his business, but she hadn't become a reporter to take dictation. She wanted to be on the ground, in the thick of things. Cooper had often cautioned her—"*See* the story, don't *be* the story"—and she recognized the wisdom in that. She just wanted to *see* the story from the closest possible vantage.

Unfortunately, she didn't see much of interest. Several women propositioned her, which at least spoke to the efficacy of her disguise, and she always politely declined without getting too close. If Mr. Value had men watching the street, they were good at blending in with all the *other* men, the ones staggering out of taverns, or lounging in shadows watching the ones who staggered with speculative eyes. Of murder or Lord Pembroke, there was no sign.

The hour grew later, the air grew colder, and the terrible strange lights overhead waved and rippled like unnatural ribbons. Ellie was hungry, thirsty, and her feet hurt in the men's shoes that didn't *quite* fit. She resolved to go home and sleep—she needed to finish writing up her article on the visit to the clockwork comfort house in the morning—when a piercing whistle tore through the air. A few people looked up, frowned, and then went about their business, but to Ellie, the noise had the quality of a signal. She started walking, as nonchalantly as possible, toward the sound of the whistle, but after three bursts it didn't sound again, and she was unable to pinpoint the location of its origin. After a moment's hesitation, she started down a narrow alley crowded with splintered crates, the sweet smell of rotten fruit emanating from a pile of refuse. A man rushed down the alley toward her, almost but not quite running. Ellie noted his fine coat—it seemed to be bright green, a rather daring shade, but in the dimness it was hard to tell—and his anxious face. The man pushed past her without slowing down, almost knocking her into a crate, and Ellie caught a distinct whiff of something chemical as he went by. She hesitated. Would she be better off following the running man, or going to investigate what he was running *from*?

Shouting voices echoed from the direction of the running man's origin. Knowing how shortly this alley entered a maze of streets, and deciding the running man was likely already lost among them, Ellie crept toward the other voices. She peered around the corner, just briefly, but long enough to glimpse a body on the cobblestones, and Lord Pembroke crouched over the still form, listening for a heartbeat, and two other men deep in serious conversation.

A chill gripped Ellie's heart, far colder than the clammy air wafting in from the river. The man who'd rushed past her was the murderer. She had no doubt. Would she be able to recognize him again, if the police called on her to do so? She'd barely registered his face, just a pale smear beneath a top hat—he'd been clean-shaven, and his cheeks pockmarked, but beyond that, she would have been hard pressed to come up with any identifying characteristics, though something about him had been faintly familiar. She hesitated over whether to step forward and let Lord Pembroke know she was there. Explaining her garb would be embarrassing at the very least, but she had a duty to see that justice was done, and if she could help apprehend the killer, she would. Then again, the men Lord Pembroke was with were likely Value's employees—hardened criminals!—and they might not appreciate a witness to their involvement with Lord Pembroke. As embarrassing as it would be for Lord Pembroke to have his name linked with a criminal like Value, wouldn't it also damage Value's reputation to be a known associate of the great detective?

Ellie expected Lord Pembroke to send for the police, and considered waiting until an officer arrived before stepping forward, but to her surprise, the detective and the big brute lifted the dead woman between them, the third man hovering about unhelpfully, and began to carry her north, her toes dragging on the ground as they proceeded in the general direction of the devastation that had been Whitechapel.

Now *this* was interesting. Were they attempting to cover up the crime? If so, why? Or was the woman only injured? She certainly appeared dead, but she might simply have fainted, or been rendered unconscious by a blow to the head. Ellie decided to follow them at a discreet distance.

As if she could possibly do anything else. Walk away, now, without knowing the particulars of the situation? She could no more do that than she could sprout wings and fly. Elllie had an excess of curiosity. That quality had caused her trouble, over the years, but not as often as it had shown her wonders and delights.

After a few blocks, the large man barked at the smaller one, who shrugged and hurried off in another direction. Ellie kept following the others, and after a long walk through twisting alleys, they reached a truly atrocious neighborhood, not so much dangerous as abandoned by most sensible folk in the city—sagging warehouses that hadn't been used to store anything in years, broken-roofed houses inhabited by desperate people willing to risk living so close to ruined Whitechapel if it meant a measure of shelter. Lord Pembroke paused by the front door to a par-ticularly narrow house squeezed between two warehouses, then conferred with his companion. They continued on, rounding a corner farther down the street and disappearing from view. Ellie followed as discreetly as she could, though she was aware of eyes watching her from a little knot of children sitting on the steps of crumbling brick structure across the street. She pressed herself against a warehouse wall, crept forward, then peered around the corner just in time to see Pimm, his large associate, and the presumably dead woman vanish into what looked like a cellar door. The entrance was guarded by another man, dressed in rags, but presumably in either Lord Pembroke or Value's employ. Were they hiding the body? The basement of a building this close to Whitechapel was a good enough place to do so, but to what end?

Ellie decided to take up a position in the shadows across the street, to wait for Lord Pembroke to emerge. Or, if the entry to the cellar was at any point left unguarded, she could sneak down and see what waited in the dark for herself. Perhaps whatever she found there would answer some of her questions. Lord Pembroke, Value, Oswald, the clockwork courtesans, murdered girls—how were they all connected?

Ellie had the sense that she'd glimpsed a portion of something far larger than it first appeared—the peak of a mountain breaking through clouds, the jagged top of an iceberg visible on the surface of the sea. She'd followed that sense into big stories before. Cooper called it her "woman's intuition," not without a certain amount of admiration, but Ellie preferred to think of it as reporter's instinct.

She crept across the street, finding a likely-looking doorway to shelter in. The entryway had been clumsily boarded-up, so the rightful inhabitants were unlikely to be along anytime soon. Ellie pressed her back against the boarded door, confident the shadows hid her utterly, and settled in to watch the alley.

After a few minutes, the large man who'd helped Lord Pembroke move the woman's body reappeared, pausing to speak with the guardian of the cellar door, then hurried on his way. Ellie tensed, waiting for Lord Pembroke to emerge, but he didn't. Ten minutes became fifteen, then twenty, then half an hour, then perilously close to an hour. Her feet ached, her left leg kept falling asleep, and the bindings on her breasts itched. She feared that, if things took a dangerous turn and she had to run, she would collapse on her cramping legs. When she could stand to be motionless no longer, she stepped out of the doorway, sidling along close to the building until the alleyway and its guardian were out of sight. She stretched her arms over her head, flexed her knees, and twisted her torso, wincing as she stretched out her protesting muscles. Once she felt less like a half-carved statue and more like a living woman again, she started back toward her doorway. After no more than five steps, something sharp and pointed pricked Ellie in the back, to the right of her spine, just above a kidney. "I didn't think you'd ever come out of that doorway," a man's voice hissed in her ear. "I was beginning to think I'd have to walk up to you bold as brass and demand you tell me your business." The man holding the knife on her whistled, and the vagrant-guardian from the end of the alley soon appeared, and trotted over.

"Who's this, then?" he said.

"Someone spying, but I don't know who or why," the man behind her said. Ellie's stomach lurched as she recognized his voice. It was "Crippler"

Crippen from the clockwork comfort house, perhaps banished to serve as a guard in this filthy neighborhood as punishment for his failure to apprehend Mr. Smythe in the brothel. Now he'd remedied *that*, though Ellie feared his redemption would do her no good. Crippen prodded her with the knife, not hard enough to break the skin, but enough to remind her how easily he could. Ellie hoped the knife hadn't damaged the coat she'd borrowed from Mr. James, and a moment later, realized the hope was a bit ridiculous—the coat, and the person wearing it, would very likely be sunk into the Thames, or perhaps interred in a dark cellar with the body of at least one other woman.

"But we'll find out his business, won't we?" Crippen said. "People are always happy to answer my questions, after they hear how sweetly I ask."

Footsteps sounded on the stones as another man approached from the alleyway. He stopped a few feet away, frowned, and sighed heavily. "Gentlemen," Lord Pembroke said. "May I ask why you're holding a knife on my assistant?"

The Luna Club
Unknowingly Integrates

"**S**orry, my lord." Ellie made her voice as gruff as she could. "They spotted me."

Lord Pembroke nodded. "Yes, well. Subterfuge has never been your specialty, Jenkins. I'm disappointed, of course, but these things happen."

"Wait," the vagrant guard said. "You *know* this fellow?"

Lord Pembroke sighed as only a put-upon son of nobility, forced to deal with the lesser orders, could sigh. "Of course I know him. I am currently doing a bit of work for Mr. Value, but that doesn't mean I *trust* him, any more than he trusts *me*. Jenkins here was meant to follow me at a discreet distance and step in to assist me in the event of any... unpleasantness."

"What's he supposed to do?" the vagrant said. "I've met ten-year-olds bigger than him."

"Jenkins is a master of the mysterious Eastern art known as gongfu," Lord Pembroke said, voice absolutely deadpan. "Though unarmed, he is deadlier than most men who wield swords or pistols."

"Ha," Crippen said. "I'd like to see proof of *that*." The knife pressing against her back was removed, and Ellie let herself fully exhale for the first time in minutes. Well. As fully as she *could* exhale, given the bindings wrapped around her chest. "We'll have to tell Mr. Value you had a confederate skulking around," Crippen said.

"Oh, dear," Lord Pembroke said. "Why, then Mr. Value might learn I believe him capable of low acts of betrayal! How will our relationship ever recover from such a crushing blow?" He snorted. "Come, Jenkins. We have work to do. The night is not so young as it was."

Ellie tipped her hat to the vagrant guard, and started to follow Lord Pembroke. She tried to keep her face averted, but Crippen made a point of circling around and peering at her. His eyes widened. "Halliday," he growled. "This man works for *you*? Always?"

Crippen recognized her, she was sure of it, from the clockwork comfort house. He'd seen her only for a moment, when she passed him playing cards downstairs in the brothel—he'd even winked at her—but that glimpse was enough to doom her now.

Lord Pembroke stopped walking, and frowned. "I do not engage his services at every hour of every day, man. Why do you ask?"

"He has a familiar face. Mostly it's that mustache."

"Mmm," Lord Pembroke said. "It *is* a fairly beastly mustache. Now, if you don't mind, I have business to pursue." He started to walk away, then paused. "Crippen, isn't it? Crippler? I saw your bout against Hamilton in '59. A truly fine example of the pugilistic arts."

The suspicious cast left Crippen's eyes, and he straightened, puffing out his chest. "Hamilton never fought again after that night, you know."

Lord Pembroke smiled, showing a flash of teeth as thin as a knife blade. "I rather doubt he ever ate solid *food* again after that night, Crippler."

"Ha! Too right, m'lord." Crippen tipped his hat, then nodded to his fellow guard. "Back to our posts, mate. Only a few more hours until relief, eh?"

Lord Pembroke walked on, and Ellie hurried after him. They walked silently for some time, the only sound their footsteps and the click of Lord Pembroke's walking stick against the ground. At last he said, "I confess, Miss Skye, I found your earlier attire more fetching. And that mustache *is* beastly."

Ellie laughed. "I wondered if you recognized me. I'm a bit disappointed. I thought the disguise was rather good."

"It is, and at first, I took you for a man, and stepped forward only to prevent the murder of a stranger. But once I got closer… there is no disguising your eyes, Miss Skyler. Not even that mustache can distract me entirely from those. You followed me tonight, then? You're playing a dangerous game."

"This is no game for me, sir. This is my business. My vocation. Indeed, my life."

"I cannot be responsible for your safety."

"And I, Lord Pembroke, cannot be responsible for yours. But… thank you for helping me. Things might have become… awkward."

"You have a remarkable gift for understatement. Did you learn anything interesting while skulking along after me?"

"I am fairly certain I saw the face of the murderer," she said.

Lord Pembroke's footsteps faltered, the rhythm of his step-click-step thrown off, and Ellie allowed herself a small smile.

"That *is* interesting. Of course, I recently learned the killer's name, but still, a description is always helpful, as names can be changed."

Ha. Well, he'd outdone her, then. "Why did you take her body away, Lord Pembroke? I am inclined to think well of you based on your past services to justice, and of course because of your recent more personal intercession on my behalf, but… you must recognize that some of your recent behavior lends itself to… misinterpretation?"

"A gift for understatement *and* diplomacy. You know, I think I'd back you for prime minister."

"Alas, my sex disqualifies me from such office, even if my good sense did not."

Lord Pembroke *hmmmed*. "One might think after three years, the Constantine Affliction would lead to some… flexibility of thinking in terms of men's spheres and women's spheres. But it seems to me the plague has only strengthened the divisions."

"People fight far more desperately to hold on to things they are afraid they might *lose*, Lord Pembroke."

"Understatement, diplomacy, and wisdom. I might be tempted to add 'beauty'—but, well."

"The mustache."

"Quite so," Lord Pembroke said. They rounded a corner and continued walking. Their environs became gradually less atrocious, with alchemical lights replacing the flickering gaslamps, and streets that were quiet because the residents were respectable, rather than lying silently in wait.

"Do most women stop asking you difficult questions once you distract them with flattery?" Ellie said.

"Most women never ask me difficult questions at all. Apart from my wife. Winifred never hesitates."

"She sounds like a woman I would admire. You will need to answer me eventually, sir, or I will have to ask the questions in print, and then everyone *else* will be asking them as well. The promise of an interview is all very well, but the things I've seen tonight… it's hard to construe them as anything but the concealment of a heinous crime. Please do convince me otherwise, Lord Pembroke?" She really hoped he could, and not just because he'd complimented her eyes. Because of the intelligence and humor she saw in his, mainly. She did not want him to be a villain.

Lord Pembroke sighed. "Would you like to have a drink with me at my club, Miss Skye?"

"Which club is that, sir?"

"The Luna Club."

Ellie laughed. "They admit women, now?"

"Of course not, Mr. Jenkins. But why should that concern men such as ourselves?"

They found a carriage for hire and rode toward the West End, conversing in low voices as they went. The dim interior of the cab was curiously intimate, and though they were discussing matters of life and death and crime, it was remarkably like having a chat with an old friend. Ellie told him how she'd seen a fleeing man in the alley, and was apologetic at being unable to provide a better description of the likely killer.

"It's all right," Lord Pembroke said. "It's only in sensational stories that the murderer invariably has an eyepatch, a wooden leg, and a birthmark in the shape of a cello on his cheek. Most people just look like… people. We're not terribly memorable, as a rule."

Ellie was glad he couldn't see her smiling in the dark. *He* was certainly memorable enough. "If you knew a murderer was operating in the area, why not tell the police?"

Lord Pembroke sighed. "Mr. Value insists on handling the situation himself. He believes the killer is trying to embarrass him, or call police attention to some of his other businesses. His concerns are plausible, though I am unconvinced—I think the killer has more complex motivations than annoying Mr. Value, though that's clearly part of it. Men like Value believe the world revolves around them, though."

"That tells me why Value wants the police left out of it. Why do *you*? Why work for him at all?"

"On that, I can say only that life is complicated, and men of conscience must sometimes make uncomfortable alliances in order to serve the greater good. I know such an answer will not satisfy you, Miss Skye, but… let me only say that further secrets are not mine to tell, all right?"

Ellie shifted uncomfortably, aware of how small and dim the interior of the carriage was, how close together they were—practically knee-to-knee. She didn't want to think ill of this man she'd admired. "You are working with Value to protect… someone else?"

The interior of the carriage was dim, but she thought he nodded, imperceptibly. "Mr. Value is not above threats of blackmail, and there are those I… care about… who I would not see harmed." He glanced out the carriage window. "Ah, we're nearly there."

Ellie had to admit a certain degree of excitement at the prospect of entering a gentleman's club. For someone of her sex, such clubs were as mysterious as the distant Orient or the jungles of Africa. It was nearly midnight by the time they pulled up outside the stately brick building on St. James's Street and alighted from the carriage. "Is it truly open so late?" she asked.

"Indeed. The Luna Club has always been open at all hours of the day and night, though it's most trafficked during more sensible hours, of course. Some of the gentlemen play cards until dawn almost every night, but that's about as boisterous as it ever becomes. The new clubs on Pall Mall are more lively and fashionable, but it's a bit quieter here. I come to the club to relax and think, you see, unlike some of the younger set."

"Are you a card player, sir?"

"Oh, a bit, of course, but not a serious one. I am not competitive in that way, nor am I terribly interested in either winning or losing money.

Which is fortunate. A taste for heavy betting would interact in a terribly dangerous way with my *other* vices." He grinned at her, then rapped the knocker on the imposing carved oak door. A moment later the door swung soundlessly open, revealing a middle-aged man with white whiskers. He looked like a perfectly ordinary servant to Ellie, but Lord Pembroke staggered back as if the man had struck him. "Ransome!" he said. "What on Earth are you doing here?"

The man stood ramrod straight, like Dignity personified, and said, "The Luna Club was in need of a night porter, and Lady Pembroke was kind enough to provide a reference."

"Ah. Well done, then." Lord Pembroke seemed a bit lost, and Ellie found the effect rather endearing in a man who was otherwise so confident. "I regret that your, ah, prior situation proved untenable."

"I have only the utmost respect for you, my lord. But this position is simply a better fit for my abilities."

"Quite." Lord Pembroke gestured at Ellie. "This is Mr. Jenkins. He will be my guest tonight."

"Welcome to you, sir." Ransome stood aside to let them in, and once they entered the foyer, took their coats and hats. "A number of gentlemen are playing cards, sir, if you'd like to join them."

"No. I believe we will go and talk in the library. Jenkins and I have much to discuss."

Ransome bowed smoothly, as if he were hinged at the waist, and took their things away.

"Simply a better fit," Lord Pembroke muttered as they continued deeper into the club. "That man was my valet! Really our all-around servant, he did a bit of cooking, too, but he didn't have to stay awake all night when he was in my employ! At least, not regularly. I am *quite* certain I paid him more than the Club possibly could. Can I really be such a dreadful employer?"

Ellie chose not to answer, looking around the club as they walked. She found it disappointingly dull, even stuffy—room after room of dark paneled walls, faded floral carpets, gleaming brass gas lamps (neither alchemy nor electricity here), dead fireplaces, and the occasional framed portrait or landscape or severed animal head on the wall. Lord Pembroke led her into the library, which was the very exemplar of its kind: shelves standing twelve feet high on all the walls, inviting-looking club chairs clustered in the corners, a long library table surrounded by straight-backed chairs. She had no doubt all the furniture was antique, but none of it struck her as particularly beautiful.

"We should have this room to ourselves. Those gentlemen who remain past midnight are not here to read." Lord Pembroke slid the wooden doors shut, closing off the library from the corridor, and Ellie felt a fluttering thrill of the illicit. Of course, she had been alone in rooms with men who were not blood relations before, most recently with Mr. James, but that was… altogether different, somehow. Lord Pembroke was only a bit older than she was, and handsome, and *married*. Ellie's late mother would have been appalled to learn she was alone with him, irrespective of her unusual garb. For that matter, so would Mr. James.

Lord Pembroke gestured for Ellie to take a seat in one of the armchairs, and she sank down gratefully, still sore from her hours of walking and standing. He opened a cabinet and removed two glasses, then poured himself a measure of brandy from a decanter on the small round table between them. "Drink?" he said. "Or are you an advocate of temperance?"

"Few would call me temperate, but no, I seldom imbibe." Ellie tried to smile, but it made her mustache itch. "I will have just a splash, for appearance's sake."

Lord Pembroke poured her a quarter of an inch in a snifter and passed it over. "Drinking for the sake of appearance. What a peculiar notion. I sometimes *abstain* for the sake of appearance, but more often, I do not bother. Appearances are given entirely too much weight, I think." He didn't savor the brandy, as Ellie had expected, but tossed it back, as if taking medicine, and then poured another glass, larger than the first. That one he sipped. After a moment, he leaned forward, rolling the glass between his palms. "I spoke to a dead woman tonight, Miss Skye. She told me the name of her murderer. I don't know if that is the sort of story your editor would print. Or, for that matter, if you even believe me yourself."

"I have met people who claimed they could converse with spirits," Ellie said carefully. "I did not find them… credible."

Lord Pembroke shook his head. "This was no spirit. That place you followed me to is the laboratory of Abel Value's pet scientist. The fellow is a bit odd—that's an understatement—but he's undeniably brilliant. He explained that, because the body was freshly dead, it might be possible to… extract information from her."

"Like that old story about how you can see the last thing a murder victim witnessed by looking at the reflection in her eye?"

"A bit. A bit. But more scientific. There were… strange apparatuses, and a jar of fluid, and delicate wires attached to an organ still warm from life, and when all was said and done… a voice emerged from a horn, and told me the name of the murderer."

Ellie frowned. "It was a hoax, surely? Like the mechanical Turk? Perhaps this scientist bears some grudge against the person named, and set up an elaborate ruse to fool you?"

"The possibility has crossed my mind, Miss Skyler. And yet… the details the voice gave were compelling and personal. And in this age of wonders, where men can be transformed into women, where fires can burn eternally, where strange lights flicker in the sky and bizarre creatures are glimpsed in the waters of the Thames, who can say what might be impossible?"

Ellie tsked. "The existence of one unlikely thing does not necessitate belief in *all* unlikely things. But… it is probably best to proceed with an open mind. I have heard stories of people who seemed to be dead, who were later restored to life—bodies pulled out of icy lakes and laid out on the slab, only to sit up with a gasp once they warmed up. Perhaps a fresh corpse could be made to speak. I could not say."

"It's certainly worth investigating the voice's claims, and I intend to do so, and swiftly. I have asked Mr. Value's scientist not to divulge the name of the accused to his employer until I have had the opportunity to investigate. I did not accuse the scientist of deceit, of course, but simply expressed caution. Even if it *was* the poor woman's voice, she might have been mistaken in her identification, after all. The scientist agreed, but I have no idea whether or not I can trust him to keep silent. He may have sent word to Value already, and if so, the accused may not survive the night."

Ellie shuddered. "Value is truly so savage?"

"He would call his actions pragmatism, not savagery, but they amount to the same thing. I will endeavor to see the killer brought to *proper* justice if he is guilty—not to Value's justice. The reason I am here, drinking, instead of out there, looking for the man, is because I have no way of *finding* him. Normally I would reach out to my police contacts to help me locate someone, but I can't do so in this case—even my closest friend in the police, Inspector Whistler, would ask too many questions. One of the advantages of working with a criminal like Value is access to a network of criminal information—but I can't ask *him*, either, without risking the death of the subject of my investigation, before I can satisfy myself regarding his guilt or innocence. I am at something of a loss as to how to proceed. I find a few drinks and a bit of conversation can help stimulate my mind. So here we are."

Ellie smiled, itchy mustache and all. "You do have one other resource at your disposal, Lord Pembroke. The power of the press. We are adept at locating people."

He grunted, leaning back in the chair. "You're also adept at spreading secrets."

"Lord Pembroke, I will only print this man's name if we determine that he is a murderer."

"We, now, is it?"

Ellie merely shrugged.

Lord Pembroke sighed. "All right. The purported killer's name is Thaddeus Worth."

Ellie blinked at him. "Are you sure?"

"Yes, why? You look as if you've swallowed a ghost." He scowled down at his drink. "Seen a ghost, I mean. Or perhaps swallowed a fly. I—"

"I know him," Ellie interrupted. "I interviewed Thaddeus Worth for an article. His wife was transformed by the Constantine Affliction, and subsequently disappeared, about three years ago. Hers was the first transformation ever reported, in fact, though she was never examined by a doctor, as she fled soon after her change. Her husband was dismissed as a madman at first, raving about how his wife had become a man and abandoned him. The authorities assumed he meant she'd taken up crossdressing, or become enamored of another woman, or some other such behavior. It was only when *others* began to sicken with fever and awake after three days with altered bodies that the authorities understood Mr. Worth was speaking literally, and credibly. Imagine how terrified *Mrs.* Worth must have been? To suffer the pain, the delirium, and awake to find herself *changed*, with no understanding of what had happened..."

"It's no wonder she fled," Lord Pembroke said.

"I do not know for certain, but I always assumed Mr. Worth contracted the disease from a prostitute, but was himself only a passive carrier, transmitting the disease to his wife later, where it manifested in its active form." Could Worth have been the man she saw barreling past her in the alleyway? "It *could* be him," Ellie said. "I'm not certain, but the height was right, and the build. Worth wore a beard when I last spoke to him, and the killer was clean-shaven, but they both had pockmarked cheeks and foreheads."

Lord Pembroke sat back, swirling his brandy, and gazing into his glass. "A man like that might hate prostitutes and blame them for his misfortunes, don't you think? If not for some disease-carrying woman, his wife would never have transformed and abandoned him. A twisted chain of thought, but I can see how it might be compelling... Do you happen to recall Mr. Worth's address?"

A Worthwhile Inquiry

❧

"**H**e lives in a respectable enough neighborhood," Pimm said, peering out the window of the carriage he'd had his ex-valet Ransome summon for them. The streets here, some distance west of the Seven Dials, were lined with electric lamps, making the interior of the carriage bright enough for the passengers to see one another. They still had some distance to go, but at least the streets were relatively empty at this hour. Traffic in the area was atrocious earlier in the day; it was almost better to go on foot. "What is this Mr. Worth's occupation? Is he a barrister? Or does he own a shop?"

"We never spoke about his profession," Miss Skye said. "In truth, he seemed out of place in his own home, and I think he came from rather humble beginnings. I sense he came into his fortune only recently. Mostly we discussed how his wife's transformation and subsequent disappearance had affected him, left him lost and unmoored. He seemed a bit vague, and he wasn't particularly articulate. I assume he was drinking heavily, or taking laudanum. I was unable to use much of our conversation in my article, actually. The best stories are full of particulars, you see, specific details, and he seemed incapable of anything more than generalities."

"He didn't inveigh vociferously against the evils of prostitutes, then?"

"No," Skye said. "But some men are hesitant to broach such subjects when speaking to a woman. I wish I'd obtained this particular disguise earlier in my career—it would have done me much good."

"I don't think your career has suffered. I read your article about the Constantine Affliction's victims, actually. I thought it exceedingly well done."

Pimm, for understandable reasons, had a certain interest in the Affliction. Freddy had enjoyed the article, too, though she'd lamented that her pretense of being a woman born was so complete that no one had tracked *her* down for an interview—"Not that they would have been able to print all the necessary profanities to convey my true feelings," she'd concluded. Freddy had become more accustomed to her situation since then, however—if not quite embracing her new sex, than at least choosing to focus on the inherent interest and novelty of being in a female body. One of the benefits, she said, was how much easier it was to shock someone as a woman. Freddy had always enjoyed shocking people. The drawbacks were the abominable way women were treated as lesser beings. Freddy had grown to particularly admire those women who could circumvent or overcome the stultifying expectations of society, slipping past or leaping over barriers Pimm could not even perceive, let alone truly understand.

Women, he suspected, like Eleanor Skye.

"Thank you," she said, and was she actually blushing? The woman was simply too fetching. Pimm decided he'd best disentangle himself from her before he became entirely smitten. "Your high opinion is appreciated."

"I suppose you're something of an expert on the Affliction, aren't you? How widespread do you think the disease is?"

"I have read estimates that say it has affected one in five thousand in this city," Skye said, though from her tone, she did not believe it. "Some say the Affliction can lie in wait in the blood for months, perhaps even years, before becoming active, and there are some who carry it passively, never sickening themselves at all. Many may be infected without even realizing."

Pimm shook his head. "Still, though, even confining ourselves to active cases, only one in five thousand, in a city of more than three million souls? That's only six hundred cases. No, I'd say that's far too low. Perhaps that many have been *documented*—counting those who died in the transition, and those who sought medical help in the first wave of transformations, before the disease was named and better understood, and people began trying to hide the changes. But how many men simply took new names, or disappeared, or were sent to live in the country by embarrassed relatives, or boarded ships to France, or bought suits like yours and tried to pass? And how many women transformed only to be murdered by their terrified husbands, or to murder their terrified husbands first? Or, to look at things in a rosier light, how many women who changed just went out into the streets and started new lives for themselves as men? The factories are always hiring, and they do not require references."

"The Affliction began among the middle class—and the upper class, try as they might to deny it," Skye said. "Which makes sense, if it originated among the more rarefied class of prostitutes, and was spread by the men to their wives. Men and women of property and stature would find it difficult to shed their old lives without detection, don't you think?"

Pimm waved his hand. "Oh, no, it moved on *swiftly* from the upper classes, and among the poorer of the city, it is far easier to disappear and begin a new life. When the disease can lie dormant for so long, and be passed on by intimate contact, it's simple to see how rapidly it could be transmitted. The first time an unknowingly-infected merchant cornered his shopgirl in the storeroom, and that woman went home to her husband unwilling to speak of her shame, and then he went out whoring, it would spread as swiftly as the French disease—" He stopped abruptly. "I apologize, Miss Skye. It's that beastly mustache of yours. I forget I am talking to a lady. Forgive my indelicacy—"

"The only indelicate thing you said was that you could forget I was a woman," Skye said, her expression impossible to read beneath that great bushy thing under her otherwise adorable nose. How had he ever thought her nose was too long? Though finding her attractive, given her current garb, was almost as disconcerting as finding Freddy beautiful. "I am a journalist, Lord Pembroke. I have interviewed all manner of men and women. I have, I assure you, heard far worse. But, yes, I suspect you're right. I think the disease is far more prevalent than anyone realizes. And it's not as if it's been cured, or its progress even notably arrested. The clockwork courtesans provide a safe release for those men who can afford them, and in general I'm sure men are exerting tremendous force of will and avoiding temptation, but... the Affliction will continue to spread."

"What percentage of the population would the Affliction need to infect to bring about the total breakdown of society, do you think?" Pimm mused. "Before it completely altered our sense of what makes men men, and women women? After all, if you can't tell what sex anyone was *born* with, it becomes increasingly absurd to insist that women are inherently one thing, and men are inherently another. Do our personalities change when our sexes do? Do our minds?"

"Our minds are not wholly divorced from our bodies," Miss Skye said. "Anyone who has ever had a loved one grow sick and suffer, and become dark and angry and sad, knows that—the body affects the mind."

"Fine, then, say *every* individual is different, then," Pimm said. "Drawing lines between men and women, when those lines refer to anything *other* than reproductive capability or, say, the average quantity of ear hair or upper-body strength, strikes me as absurd. A brilliant man who is transformed into a woman is still brilliant, and vice-versa."

"I had no idea you held such radical opinions, Lord Pembroke. You don't agree that the separation of the world into men's spheres and women's spheres is obviously right? That men, being stronger than women, should take the lead in society? Surely that's only natural."

"Cannibalism is natural, too. Infanticide. Murder. Living in trees, going naked, eating grubs. All very natural. While cooking fine meals, playing cricket, drinking brandy, and living in houses with roofs and fireplaces is obviously *unnatural*. Why privilege the natural? We can do so much better than that."

Skye leaned forward, intensely interested now, and Pimm felt a chill at the thought she might quote him. His family would be apoplectic with him if they knew his true opinions. Damned brandy. It always loosened his tongue.

She asked, "Do you see the Constantine Affliction as a path to true equality for the sexes, Lord Pembroke?"

He was taken aback. "I think not. The high mortality rate rather mitigates against viewing the Affliction as an engine for positive social change, Miss Skye. But there are some who might view so many deaths as an acceptable loss, I suppose. Who don't mind if revolutions spill a great deal of blood. For those, this disease might seem... tailor made." That idea had just popped into Pimm's head. Perhaps the medical miracle he'd witnessed earlier in the night had set his mind on this path. If a dead woman could be made to speak, then why not…. "Where do you think the Affliction originated?"

She shrugged. "Some say it was brought to London from Constantinople, hence the name, though how it got started *there* is barely even a subject of speculation. I've heard some blame the smoke pouring out from the factories, or the alchemical refuse dumped into the river. That these substances are seeping into the drinking water, poisoning us, changing us. Some fish and frogs can change their sexes, and I've heard it suggested that the ability was somehow transferred to mankind—though as far as I know none of the Afflicted have ever changed *back*. Surviving the Affliction seems to grant one immunity to further ravages. And, of course, those more religious than myself either see the Affliction as a test from God, or a punishment."

"I wonder if someone released it on purpose," Pimm mused.

Skye looked shocked. "What on Earth do you mean?"

Pimm shrugged. "You were close to Whitechapel tonight. *That* was an experiment gone wrong. You've heard about—written about!—the slimy things in the Thames, which are also rumored to be the result of some scientific exploration gone awry. Don't misunderstand me, I am a great proponent of scientific progress—how many lives has the germ theory saved? And our economy is prospering as never before thanks to our technological progress. Even the poor often have alchemical lights in their houses. But not every experiment is successful, or wise."

"Are you suggesting someone might have created the Constantine Affliction? And released it deliberately?"

"I am merely passing the time in conversation with a lady of my acquaintance, in idle speculation," Pimm said. The carriage lurched to a stop, and the driver rapped on the roof of the carriage. "Here we are," Pimm said brightly. "Shall we wake up a potential murderer, Jenkins?"

"Do you have a strategy in mind?" Ellie asked. Lord Pembroke had told the carriage driver to wait, offering him enough money to make him agree without complaint, and now they stood on the doorstep where Ellie herself had stood alone, in rather different garb, several months earlier.

"No, but I have a belly full of brandy. I find that, combined with a certain amount of improvisation, is usually sufficient to carry the day." Lord Pembroke rapped on the door with the head of his cane, steadily, loudly, and methodically, for more than a full minute.

Finally a hoarse voice shouted from within, and the door opened a crack, revealing the face of Thaddeus Worth, his hair sticking up in all directions.

He'd shaved since Ellie interviewed him, and she had no doubt he was the man who'd pushed past her in the alleyway earlier tonight.

"Mr. Worth?" Lord Pembroke said pleasantly, as if the hour were not past midnight, and this were a friendly social occasion.

"What the devil is the meaning of this? I was sleeping—"

"Were you?" Lord Pembroke said. "How wonderful. I wish I could be in bed. My name is Pembroke Halliday. Perhaps you've heard of me? I occasionally assist the police in their inquiries. I was invited to examine a crime scene tonight. A terrible thing, the murder of a young girl not far from the river."

Worth paled, then appeared to take notice of Ellie for the first time. His eyes widened.

"This is my associate, Mr. Jenkins," Lord Pembroke said. "May we have a few moments to speak to you?"

"The hour is late, and this is nothing to do with me." Worth tried to push the door shut, but Lord Pembroke slipped the end of his cane into the crack.

"Ah, sir, you may have noticed, I asked politely. The police will not be so courteous. Still, I am happy to wait with you while my associate Jenkins goes to Scotland Yard to fetch someone. Or we can clear up matters ourselves."

Quite a bluff, Ellie thought. If Worth *was* the murderer, as seemed likely, would he try to run, or stall for time? Ellie's only experience with criminals was writing about their exploits. She'd never been face-to-face with one in the act of trying to avoid apprehension, not like this.

"I suppose you'd better come in, then," Worth said, easing the door back open. "Though I still don't know what help I can provide." Another flicker of the eyes toward Ellie. Did he recognize her as the man he'd passed in the alley?

"We just have a few questions," Lord Pembroke said. "They will take scarcely a moment." His voice didn't slur at all, every syllable clearly enunciated. He seemed, if anything, *more* sober than he had when he was actually sober. But was it a slightly exaggerated sobriety, an *act* of sobriety?

Ellie hadn't always been an only child. Her brother Robert had fallen in with bad companions, taken far too serious a liking to rotgut whiskey, and died with a bottle in his hand and without a penny in his pocket. The whites of his eyes had turned yellow, a sign that his poor beleaguered liver had given up under the onslaught of poison he daily ingested. But Robert had been quite charming, after a drink or two. It was only after three or four that he became a dark cloud in human form.

"Come in, then," Worth said, stepping back, and ushering them into the foyer. He shut and locked the door after them, then led them to his study, a room dominated by a large wooden desk, its surface devoid of anything but an inkwell, a sand cellar, and an uncut quill pen. The walls were covered in framed drawings of birds, but there were no shelves, and no books. "A drink, gentlemen?" He went to a small bar and began rattling glassware.

Lord Pembroke stepped around and in front of Ellie, clasping his walking stick in both hands. "No, thank you, we won't be here that long. We have a witness who saw you in the vicinity of the murder."

Worth stiffened, his back still turned to them. "What are you suggesting?"

"Hmm? Oh, no." Lord Pembroke chuckled. "My apologies. No, we have no reason to suspect you, sir, we merely wanted to ascertain whether you had, in fact, been in the area, and whether you might have seen any suspicious—"

The killer whirled, a knife in his hand, and lunged toward Lord Pembroke. Ellie gasped and staggered back a step, but Lord Pembroke merely lifted his walking stick and prodded the ruffian in the chest with its head. Ellie expected Worth to bat the stick aside and strike, but instead, there was a peculiar buzzing sound, and Worth gasped, then collapsed, knife falling from his hand. He fell to the carpet and twitched, his body drawn in on itself like a dying spider's. He squirmed and moaned and spasmed.

Lord Pembroke sighed. "It does make it easier when they try to kill you—it's the next best thing to a tearful confession—but I always find it so tiresome when things descend to the level of gross physicality. I imagine he recognized you, and knew you'd seen him fleeing the scene of the crime. He felt the walls closing in, and made a last desperate attempt to break free."

"Did he suffer a heart attack?" Ellie wondered. "Or is he… having some sort of fit?"

"Oh, no, it's my walking stick." Lord Pembroke held up the item, and pointed to the silver ball on top. "My—ah, a friend of mine, made certain modifications for me. There are batteries hidden in the body of the stick, and there is a switch here, you see. I can activate the switch and discharge a potent electric shock through the metal ball at the top. Like going swimming with an electric eel. It tends to end arguments quickly."

Electricity! "Will he recover?"

"Oh, yes, of course. I wouldn't use such a device against the aged or infirm, or someone with a weak heart, but for a healthy adult, the effects are temporary. Convulsive muscle spasms, loss of motor control. It should pass in a few moments." He kicked the knife away from Worth's hand. "Granted, I did not know before I struck whether Mr. Worth had a bad heart, but the fact that he was attempting to stab me made me less concerned for his well being than I might have been otherwise."

"What happens now? Do we send for the police?"

"Oh, eventually," Lord Pembroke said. "But we need to have a conversation with him first. Let's see if we can find something to tie him up with before he recovers, shall we?"

True Confessions

P imm sat patiently in one of Worth's chairs, one leg crossed over the other. His attention kept drifting to the bar along one wall, and the bottles Worth had pretended to fuss with as he'd readied his knife for a desperate lunge. A drink would be a great comfort now, but he didn't think Skye would approve. "Skye"—of course her name was really "Skyler," but her nom de plume seemed a better fit in the current circumstances.

Her writing was truly *her*, he suspected, while in person he had interacted only with her disguises: respectable matron outside Value's office, man with a horrible mustache now. Her piece on the victims of the Affliction had been thoughtful and sensitive without being overly sentimental, the journalistic voice reserved and careful, while she expertly chose and juxtaposed quotes from her subjects to create more emotional effects. He hadn't remembered the byline on the article, but knowing now that it had come from her pen only increased his respect for her. Pimm could write a letter well enough, and he'd dashed off the odd essay at Oxford, but the ability to change minds and moods with the written word was a talent he'd never cultivated, and he admired it.

Spoken words, though, were a different matter. He could sometimes change moods, minds, and even lives with those. He tapped Worth gently on the knee with the wooden end of his walking stick. "Mr. Worth, please.

You awakened almost five minutes ago. Please stop feigning unconsciousness. I've given you time to gather your thoughts, but now, really, we must speak."

Worth lifted his head. He didn't strain against his bonds, which held his ankles to the chair's legs, and his wrists to the chair's arms. Skye had found the rope in one of the other rooms, used to tie up drapes, and Pimm had pressed them into their current service. The chair was more likely to give way than the knots.

Worth stared at Pimm with eyes empty and despairing. "I have been thinking," Worth said, voice dull. "You did not summon the Peelers. You are not working for the police."

Pimm nodded. "Not in this particular instance. We are acting as private individuals. Concerned citizens. We—"

"You work for Value."

That rankled. "Mr. Value did ask for my assistance, yes. He takes a dim view of his employees being murdered."

Worth shook his head. "Only when someone else is doing the murdering."

"You do not deny your actions, then?" Skye said, and Worth flinched, trying to look behind him. Skye sat there, in a corner, in shadow, watching. Observing. Very likely recording, though Pimm dearly hoped none of this would end up in the newspaper.

"That I killed those women?" Worth shook his head. "I did it."

"Because you lost your wife?" Skye said. "Because you blamed them for the disease you brought home, that transformed your beloved?"

"You lot have done your research," Worth said. "Though not quite enough, it seems. No, I don't blame the whores for *that* misfortune. I did not kill them out of some sense of outrage, or for revenge. I know about whores, sir. I was a whoremaster, once, and a successful one."

Ah, Pimm thought. A disgruntled employee, then? One of Value's lieutenants, turning against his master, killing the women who earned Value money in an attempt to hurt his enemy's business? Plausible, though less romantic than the notion that his grief over his wife's transformation had driven him to derangement.

Worth went on. "Those women working the street will have short and unpleasant lives anyway. Their miserable deaths are a foregone conclusion. At least with me they died swiftly, in a cloud of obliterating ether, a loss of breath that lulls them to a sleep and shades into easy death. I had hoped to save them from pointless deaths—to see that their deaths had *meaning*."

Pimm had heard many justifications for homicide. Revenge, fury, whim, compulsion. But to give the lives of the murdered meaning? That was a novelty. "How do you mean? What kind of meaning?"

"I killed them, his whores, and I left them, on the steps of his brothels, because I hoped that would make the police finally investigate him. I thought such murders could not be ignored, especially if they came swiftly, in series, I thought surely they would draw attention to his business."

As if there were no better ways to draw the attention of the police! Though it was true, a series of murders would certainly have more impact than an anonymous letter full of unsupported accusations. Pimm cleared his throat. "I can assure you, the police are well aware of Mr. Value. He is the subject of many ongoing investigations—"

"They suspect *nothing*," Worth said. "They think he is merely a criminal, but he is involved in so much more, crimes that make smuggling and prostitution and theft look like schoolyard japes."

"Enlighten me, then," Pimm said. "I so enjoy learning new things."

The man began to tremble, and squeezed his eyes shut. "Enough of this folly. Go ahead. Kill me."

"I beg your pardon?" Pimm said.

Worth opened first one eye, then the other. "You... Do not toy with me, sir. You have been sent to kill me. Pray, do it, and let my suffering end."

"We are not murderers," Skye said. "We are, ah, detectives. We seek only the truth."

Worth began to laugh. "You are fools. You work for Value. You think you are merely investigators? If you are not assassins yourselves, then you are the assassin's hounds, leading him to his prey. When Value finds out I was the one murdering his whores, I will be fed to the things that live in the Thames, or tossed over the wall into what was Whitechapel. He does that, you know, to *his* most hated enemies. Some of those have survived for days inside, screaming at the walls, until they give in to thirst and try to drink what passes for water there."

Pimm suppressed a shudder. "I have not alerted Value to my findings. I am here on my own. I do not doubt that something terrible will befall you if Value learns your identity, and I cannot stall the man forever. But you have another option open to you."

"What might that be?"

"Confess," Pimm said. "I know men in the police, trustworthy men, incorruptible men—"

"I have heard you called incorruptible, *Lord Pembroke*, and yet you took Value's coin."

Pimm was offended, for an instant, and then he chuckled. "His coin? I neither need nor want his coin, Mr. Worth. My family is not one of those that possess titles and little else. We still have our wealth. Money is... simply not something I need to think about. I agreed to assist Mr. Value in order to stop a murderer. Mr. Value wished to avoid police involvement, and I agreed to his terms because I knew my chances of catching the killer—of catching you—would improve greatly if I had his cooperation, access to the schedules of his women, and the armed assistance of his men. And, indeed, less than a day later, here we are—I have succeeded in my task. From the point of view of those dead girls, and those you would have killed tomorrow, next week, next month, I believe I remain quite pure." He leaned forward. "True, Value wants me to hand you over to him, for his own justice, but I will happily deliver you to the police instead. You can tell *them* what you did, and why."

"They will hang me."

"Surely you deserve to hang?" Pimm said, tone more thoughtful than accusatory. "But perhaps you can buy your life as well. Whatever secret you wished the police to uncover about Abel Value—why not simply *tell* them? I know you'd hoped to draw their attention anonymously, but we're past that now."

"I am a murderer. My word would never be believed."

Pimm shrugged. "What is your alternative? You are a murderer, as you say. I cannot let you escape. I *am* going to summon the police. Now, when they arrive, you could deny everything, and have me arrested for breaking into your house—I've engaged in truly shocking behavior, and not even my friends in the police could overlook the fact that I entered your home under false pretenses, assaulted you with an electrical weapon of dubious legality, and subsequently tied you to a *chair*. But I would tell them everything I know—"

"There are no bodies," Worth said. "Value conceals them, to frustrate my goals. So where is the proof of a crime?"

"Indeed," Pimm say. "It is likely that Jenkins and I will be clapped away in a cell, and the police will apologize to you for the inconvenience, and that will be the end of it—for us. But do you think word of my imprisonment will reach Value? Do you think he will draw... certain conclusions? Do you think he will come for—"

"Enough!" Worth groaned. "I will confess. It will only delay the inevitable. Value will have me dead soon enough—and if he cannot reach me in the cells, he has associates who *can*."

"If you would care to tell me what you suspect about Value's crimes?" Pimm said. "I have no love for the man, you know."

Worth spat. "You are working for him. Perhaps you cannot screw your courage to the point of murdering a bound man, but you are tainted by your association. Why should I tell you what I know? You would only run along and report my words to Value, and I have no desire to reveal the extent of my knowledge to *him*."

"Can you answer one question for me?" Skye said.

"Almost certainly not."

"I will ask all the same. How is Bertram Oswald involved with Mr. Value?"

Pimm frowned. Sir Bertram? What a strange question. Might as well ask how the Prime Minister was involved with Value, or the Queen herself. Surely there was no connection.

Worth tried to twist around in his chair again. "You ask the right questions, at least, Mr. Jenkins."

"And yet you refuse to supply useful answers."

"What do you expect? I am a lowly killer. Now let us find a real detective, Lord Pembroke, so that I might make my confession."

The Living, the Dead, and Others

"This is the bit where you leave, Jenkins," Lord Pembroke said, helping her into her borrowed coat in Worth's foyer. "I can just barely explain my presence here, or come up with some explanation the police won't bother to question, but your presence would make things difficult, especially the way your mustache is wobbling on its foundations."

Ellie tried to hide a yawn behind her hand. "I did see Mr. Worth flee a crime scene. I could be a witness."

"Hardly necessary when he intends to confess. Besides, there is no crime scene any more, as the body has been moved. I may need to do something about that. A crime with no victim is a difficult crime to prosecute… Well. Just because sleep will be a long time coming for me does not mean you should stay awake."

"I am happy to accompany you." She stifled another yawn, less successfully. "This has been quite interesting."

"For me as well. You can make it home all right?"

"At this hour? Alas, my rooming house is firmly shut for the night, and nothing less than the trumpeting of an angel of judgment could compel my landlady to open the door past midnight. But it is no matter. I have a key to the newspaper office. It would not be my first night spent sleeping at my desk."

Lord Pembroke looked horrified at the prospect. "Nonsense! No, you must stay at my home. I have no idea when I will be along, but I will write a letter for you to give to my wife."

"I could never intrude so! To wake your wife—"

"Ha. Winifred keeps owl's hours, Miss—ah, Jenkins, and she loves nothing more than the disruption of routine. Our apartment has a spare bedroom that I daresay would be far more comfortable than your desk."

Ellie groped for further objections, though in truth, the thought of meeting Lord Pembroke's wife intrigued her for reasons she could not specify beyond her usual intense curiosity. What kind of woman would marry a man like *this*? "But, my attire—"

"It is unfortunate," he said. "But our house is relatively secluded, and we have no servants at present, as my valet, who also served as our butler, has moved on to pleasanter prospects, as you heard. I think you can slip in without causing a scandal. And if anyone asks, claim to be Winifred's brother, visiting to see how married life is treating her. No one in London knows her family."

Ellie bowed her head in assent. "You are too kind, Lord Pembroke."

"Please, call me Pimm. After what we've been through tonight, a bit of informality would be welcome, don't you find?"

"Then you must call me Ellie."

"It would be an honor. Here, just let me write a note to my wife, explaining who you are and so forth." While in the midst of scribbling on a bit of paper taken from Worth's desk, he said, in a voice so casual she knew it was anything but: "Why did you ask Mr. Worth about Bertram Oswald?"

"It is… complicated. I did not mention Oswald's name before because it hardly seemed germane to the pursuit of a murderer, which surely took precedence over all other matters. But… I have reason to believe Oswald has some connection with Mr. Value. I am curious to discover the nature and extent of that connection."

Lord Pembroke whistled. "Indeed? You saw them together?"

"I…" She laughed, the very idea of telling him about her visit to a clockwork brothel embarrassing—but also, oddly, titillating. She reined herself in. He was a married man, and she was a spinster. This was business. "When I said it was complicated, I was not exaggerating. Telling the tale would take some time."

"I'd very much like to hear it," Lord Pembroke said. "There are a few reasons a man of Sir Bertram's stature would be involved with someone like Value, and none of them are terribly salubrious. If I were you, I would be *very* sure of my facts before I wrote a story linking two such well-known figures—and even if I were sure of my facts, I would still consider whether drawing the ire of the man rumored to be the Queen's consort would be worth selling a few papers."

"Oh, I wouldn't publish it under my name, fear not." She smiled, to make it light-hearted, but Lord Pembroke's expression remained serious.

"If a man like Oswald wants to find you, Ellie, he will do so. The shield of a pen name would prove insufficient under his attack."

The words chilled her. Crippen had recognized her tonight—in her male guise, at least—and would surely report to Oswald that Lord Pembroke had been seen in the company of the same man who'd discovered him at the brothel. Was Ellie putting Lord Pembroke in danger, too, by keeping that connection to herself? "Perhaps it *would* be best if I told you the whole story," she said, and then yawned, hugely.

Lord Pembroke nodded. "I would be pleased to hear it, as I said. But not tonight. I have much work ahead, and you need sleep. We will talk tomorrow, all right?"

Ten minutes later, Ellie was climbing into the waiting carriage. If the driver was curious about what she and Lord Pembroke had been doing in the house, or why only Ellie was leaving now, he did not show it. She gave him Lord Pembroke's address, and he jostled the reins and set the horse to clip-clopping along the stones.

Despite the terrible things she'd witnessed that night, Ellie allowed herself a small smile beneath her faltering mustache. Her life had certainly taken some unusual turns.

Spending the night at Lord Pembroke's! She wondered if she could squeeze an article from that experience. Or perhaps just write a profile of his mysterious wife. That would certainly be a coup.

Detective Whistler emerged from Worth's study, frowning. "He's confessing to terrible crimes, Pimm. Are you sure he isn't mad?"

Pimm, who sat on a stiff chair with a cup of rapidly cooling tea balanced on his knee, shook his head. "No. Some of my contacts have mentioned rumors of working women disappearing in Alsatia in recent weeks. I was prowling about the area this evening, hoping to catch sight of anything untoward—don't smile at me like that, I'm serious—and happened upon this man in an alley. I smelled ether on him, suspected him of wrongdoing, and confronted him. He fled, but I was able to track him here, where I gained entry to his home and convinced him to confess."

"I see." Whistler's voice was mild. "I sense you have elided over several relevant details in that account, such as how you knew women were disappearing, and how precisely you tracked the man, and how you enticed him to confess."

Pimm sighed. "Jonathan, I have... certain sources in the underworld. You know that. I would rather not have to name them. They might be less willing to talk to me in the future if I involve their names in your inquiries."

Whistler took a seat. "The problem, Pimm, is this: I have no evidence that a crime has occurred, only this man's word."

"You don't believe him?"

"Belief is irrelevant. I require evidence. No bodies have been found. We had a man down at Scotland Yard yesterday who claimed he'd killed the moon, knocked it right out of the sky. *He* believed he was telling the truth. But that didn't make it true. My men are searching this house, looking for some evidence, but apart from a rather large quantity of ether, they've turned up nothing. I'll admit, the ether is suggestive, but it does not constitute proof of murder. I—"

One of the officers appeared in the doorway, holding a carved wooden box perhaps a foot across. "Mr. Whistler, sir, you should take a look at this. Mr. Worth said we should look in a secret compartment in his desk if we didn't believe him, and..." He handed over the box. Whistler opened the lid and looked inside for a long time.

"What is it?" Pimm asked, though he knew quite well, having advised Worth to reveal the box and its contents—which Pimm had provided.

He'd coached Worth extensively after Miss Skye was gone about the best way to confess. Pimm hadn't wanted to reveal the extent of his planning to Miss Skye, lest she think ill of him. Pimm had known ever since speaking to Margaret's brain that he'd need to manufacture evidence to implicate the killer, and he'd taken steps to create a compelling proof of crime. False evidence of a true murder… well, it wasn't strictly ethical, but it would get the job done.

"Rather cheap jewelry, for the most part," Whistler said. "Rings meant to look like silver, necklaces meant to look like gold. A bloody knife wrapped in a handkerchief, and a hank of blonde hair, tied up with a ribbon. There appears to be blood in the hair as well."

"I would say that is more than suggestive," Pimm said.

"And if I find a dead *body* that matches this hair, I will agree that we may have a murderer on our hands. Until we do…" He shrugged.

"Perhaps Worth would be willing to—"

"Lead me to the location of his latest victim's remains, yes, I know my job, Pimm. The man has already offered to do just that. I shall have to investigate, of course, and hope the trip is not a waste of time. But something about this whole affair strikes me as odd. I sense there is much you are not telling me."

"I feel obliged to protect my informants, but I can assure you, none of them are guilty of anything as terrible as this string of murders." Not entirely true. Value had surely done worse things… but he was a target for another day.

"I gather we're bound for a trip down to the river, then. Would you like to join us?"

Pimm considered, then nodded. Best to see this thing through. If Mr. Adams had not done as Pimm requested, some improvisation might be necessary. He hated plans that depended on unreliable people doing him favors. Worth had acquitted himself admirably, at least, salting his true confession with the inventions Pimm had prepared for him, but Adams was an enigmatic fellow. Who knew if he would do as Pimm had asked? The scientist had waved away the offer of money for his service. Pimm would have felt better if he'd believed the man could be bought.

"Let's go then," Whistler said. "There's nothing I like better than tromping through riverfront slums looking for corpses."

"Come now, Jonathan. You love a good crime."

"No, I love a good mystery, and there is no mystery here—everything is laid out neatly before me. At this point, it's all mere police work. Still, it must be done, I suppose."

Adam carried Margaret's corpse over his shoulder as he trudged through the stinking tunnels beneath Alsatia—but the stink did not bother him, for the redolence of nearby sewage brought with it a vision of beautiful swirling gray-green fog, with patterns that fascinated him. He did not whistle as he walked, but he considered whistling, because he had seldom been happier.

Bringing Margaret's brain back to life had been a great triumph. Adam's own creator had been able to reanimate dead flesh, yes, but he had not been able to maintain continuity of mind, and memory, and personality. Whatever thoughts Adam's own brain had possessed in its original life were lost forever, entirely overwritten by his new personality. His creator had brought dead flesh to life; but Adam had brought a *person* back to life.

Of course, he'd ruined her body in the process, something he had not mentioned to Margaret. But he had some ideas about how to correct that situation. Since he had no pressing use for her broken-skulled corpse, he was content to perform the favor Lord Pembroke had asked of him—the detective had brought him a freshly-killed woman, as requested, so Adam owed him a favor in return. He did not understand Halliday's plans, nor did he much care. After Margaret revealed the name of her murderer—her former pimp, Thaddeus Worth—Halliday had asked Adam for a knife, and a hank of Margaret's bloody hair, and for any jewelry or personal effects that remained from the other dead women. Adam kept those few things Value's thugs didn't steal for themselves in a box on a shelf, mostly because he never threw anything away in case he someday needed it, and he handed the cheap rings and necklaces over without comment.

Halliday's final request had been for Adam to deposit Margaret's body in a particular location near the river. Halliday had been very concerned about how Adam might manage to complete that task without alerting the guards, suggesting a series of complex subterfuges, until finally Adam

grew bored enough to say, "Fear not, detective—I have my own methods
for traveling throughout the city unseen. There are… tunnels." Halliday
had looked about him then, peering into the laboratory's darker corners,
clearly unnerved at the thought of secret passageways all around him, and
why not? There were all manner of mysteries beneath the Earth. Adam
himself was one of the least of them.

He reached the end of the tunnel, and peered up toward an exit hatch,
which was hidden beneath a heap of refuse behind a dockside cavern.
Adam gently deposited Margaret's broken-headed form on the ground,
then climbed up the wall, fitting his feet into holes cut into the stone long
before his own creation. At the top, he shoved open the hatch, emerging
to look around and make sure he was unobserved. He descended again,
collected Margaret, and clambered back up. Adam could fault his creator for many things, but at least he had endowed Adam with prodigious
strength.

He closed the hatch, kicked rotted vegetables and broken boards across
it to once again disguise its existence, and made his limping way toward
the riverbank. The bank was built up here, bolstered by crumbling stones,
and he had to step over a low wall and then gently ease himself down a
steep slope toward the muddy, mired edge of the water. As he lowered
poor Margaret's body to the mud, he heard a gasp.

Turning, Adam beheld one of the creatures called tide-waitresses, wom-
en clothed in filthy rags who picked among the refuse along the banks of
the river for anything they could sell, from bits of wire to empty bottles
to pieces of wood. She stared at him, and Adam stared back, and then she
shrieked and ran.

Or tried to run. Ignoring the ache in his leg, Adam surged forward as
quick as he could, and seized her from behind. She was frail as a twig
in his hands, and he squeezed her throat as she beat her hands against
his chest and face helplessly. Finally she went slack, and he continued
to squeeze, because it took longer to cause death than it did to induce
unconsciousness. Once he was convinced the woman was dead, he slung
her body over his shoulder and trudged back up the hill. A shame. He
had hoped to walk back home unburdened. He could always toss her into
the river, but he wasn't one to waste a perfectly good body. She could
become one of Abel Value's mindless whores, perhaps. Or failing that, she

could join Adam's honor guard—or become food for them. He had over a dozen of his own feral, reanimated women now, each one officially a failed experiment, as far as Value knew. Adam did not expect that he would ever have need of their violent services, but when dealing with someone as treacherous as Value, it was good to have protection—and why should Value be the only one with bodyguards? The honor guard was ravenous, though, and he had to keep them fed, or even the magnetic devices he'd implanted in their brains to let him guide their movements would prove insufficient to curb their natural urges. They were not altered into docility like the unliving whores he provided to Value.

His honor guard required flesh, and no matter what, they would feed.

A Body, As Evidence

"**T**here we have it, then." Whistler shone his alchemical torch on the corpse his men had dragged up from the riverbank. "Right where Worth said she would be, and in the state he promised." He shook his head. "Why go to all that trouble to remove a woman's brain? Just to toss it in the river?"

"Who can fathom the behavior of such men?" Pimm said. "I understand his wife was transformed by the Affliction, and disappeared not long after. Presumably Worth was infected by a whore—one of his own, he was a known purveyor, after all—and then brought the infection home to his wife. He may harbor some twisted grudge against such women as a result."

"Motives do interest me," Whistler admitted. "And what you say makes a certain amount of sense. I still don't understand the bit with the brain, though. Worth said it was just a strange impulse, a whim, but good heavens, the effort—the *tools*—required to cut open a skull and—"

"It is a mystery." When Pimm had asked Adams to dispose of the body in this spot, to make it appear Worth had dumped her corpse here, the giant scientist had paused and said, "I will do as you ask, so long as I am permitted to keep her brain. I enjoy having someone to talk to. It is generally very lonely here."

Pimm had assented, having little choice—the mutilated skull would

115

be noticed in any event, even with the brain shoved back into the cavity. Worth had been disgusted when Pimm suggested he tell the police he'd mutilated the body. "I never left a mark on them!" he'd objected, "or took souvenirs, either!" Pimm had apologized but insisted, saying it was the only way to make the police believe his confession. It was the oddest apology he'd ever given.

"Worth says he has information about Abel Value," Whistler said. "But I hesitate to deal with someone who commits acts like *this*."

"It is a terrible crime," Pimm acknowledged. "And Worth is a terrible criminal. But Value's criminality is of a whole other order. Worth commits terrible acts personally, according to some derangement, but Value orchestrates terrible acts coldly, impersonally, and whilst in full possession of his faculties."

"True," Whistler agreed. "No one is actually howling for Worth's head, since the murders have not been publicized—or even noticed, really. If he does have information that might be useful to me, I can save him from the gallows tree, and see him merely imprisoned, or committed to Bedlam. The latter seems appropriate, after seeing what he did to this poor girl's head. You've brought me another long night of work, Halliday. I hope you're pleased with yourself."

"I am always pleased to help the police with their inquiries." Pimm shook Whistler's hand. "Now, sir, I believe I will take my leave. I don't mind staying awake until the sun rises, but I prefer to spend those late hours in more pleasant occupations than this."

He started to turn away, but Whistler put a hand on his shoulder. "Take care, old man. Don't overindulge, eh?"

Pimm smiled. "You know I believe alcohol is the panacea, detective. If one has a triumph, champagne for celebration. If one has a setback, whiskey for comfort."

"As long as you have a *reason* for drinking a whole bottle down," Whistler said. "It's when one starts to empty bottles for no particular cause that I become concerned."

"Ah, but a resourceful man can always find reasons to celebrate, detective—or to seek comfort."

Whistler sighed. "It's none of my business, Pimm. But this work we do… I've seen good colleagues succumb to drink, because they could find no other way to deal with the things they'd witnessed."

"Fortunately I am a mere hobbyist when it comes to being a detective," Pimm said. "My profession is being a bon vivant. Fortunately, I excel at both." He tipped his hat.

"You know, I thought finding a wife would settle you down."

Pimm looked skyward, striking a pose of thoughtfulness. "Winifred? Settle me down? Oh, that's right. I forgot—you've never met her." He grinned wolfishly, and the detective snorted laughter.

"Away with you, then. I may have further questions tomorrow, after I talk to Worth a bit more. I trust you won't tell me any more lies?"

"Not any important ones," Pimm promised.

At least from the outside, Lord Pembroke's home was not as lavish as Ellie had expected. She wasn't sure *what* she'd expected, but surely the younger son of a Marquess could be expected to live in splendor. His home was certainly *nice*, but it was not the palace she had, on some level, anticipated. (Of course, his family's country estates were surely a different matter.)

Lord Pembroke and his wife had a small house near Hanover Square in Mayfair, with a front garden surrounded by an iron fence, and colorful stained glass panes set in the windows. Ellie rapped on the door, well aware of the lateness of the hour, feeling ridiculous and conspicuous.

She had expected a servant to answer the door, remembering only as it swung open that Lord Pembroke's man Ransome had left his employ without notice. Instead of a servant, the open door revealed a woman with long blonde hair, a face that might have been the model for a Greek statue of a nymph, and a body in keeping with that general theme. She wore a robe of Chinese silk in shocking red, patterned with gold dragons, and held an ebony cigarette holder smoldering in one hand. The other hand was hidden behind the door… and Ellie, strangely, wondered if she was hiding a weapon. Lady Pembroke's eyes were blue and merry, and her lips the sort of red that most women required cosmetic assistance to achieve. Ellie felt a certain shifting in her attitude toward Lord Pembroke, a change epitomized by the stray but fully-formed thought: *Ah, so he likes women like* this, *then.*

"May I help you, sir?" She looked Ellie up and down. "Or, rather, madam? Pray do let me know which form of address you prefer—should I refer to you as what you are, or as what you are attempting to appear to be?"

Ellie blinked. She had assumed a woman who looked like this—who answered the door looking like this—would not be particularly perceptive, but she had punctured Ellie's guise readily, and responded with a certain sardonic wit. The sparrow always hopes the peacock is a dullard, Ellie supposed. How unfair that one person should be both bright *and* look as though they'd just stepped off a pedestal in a museum. "Ah, I am Eleanor Skyler. My appearance is… Here. I have a letter from Lord Pembroke."

"Dear old Pimm sends the most peculiar messengers." Lady Pembroke held out her hand, and Ellie passed her the folded sheet of paper. She opened it and scanned the page rapidly, a line appearing on her forehead just between her eyes. The line did little to mar her appearance. Indeed, Ellie suspected most men would find it adorable.

Lady Pembroke lifted her eyes to Ellie. "Did you read this, Miss Skyler?"

"I did not."

"Did Pimm tell you what it said?"

"Ah, just that he would explain who I am, and…."

Lady Pembroke dazzled Ellie with a smile. "It does tell me who you are, and more. Come in, my dear, come in, get changed, have a drink if you like, I'll get the guest room prepared. But I hope you aren't too tired. You must tell me *everything.*" She beckoned, and for the next twenty minutes Ellie found herself caught in a sort of benign whirlwind as Lady Pembroke ("Call me Winnie, dear") poured her a cup of tea laced with a lavish dollop of brandy, helped her remove her false mustache and the sticky spirit gum, exclaimed over her short hair ("Just tell everyone it's the latest Continental style, the height of fashionable rebellion among the young ladies in Paris"), convinced Ellie to wear one of her nightgowns (fortunately quite modest), complimented her writing ("Mr. E. Skye is a woman! You are a credit to our sex!"), and generally never gave Ellie the chance to tell her *everything*, or really much of anything at all.

Only when Ellie was settled to Winnie's satisfaction did the woman of the house curl up in a chair by the window, smile enigmatically over the rim of a steaming cup of tea, and say, "Pimm thinks quite highly of you, it seems. He does not often invite those he's only just met to stay overnight."

"It was a very kind offer," Ellie said. "But if it is any imposition, I—"

"Nonsense, I adore having a captive audience. Tell me, did you see anything terribly shocking while you were out with my husband?"

Ellie considered. She was capable of writing sensational articles, and dramatizing situations to entertain the public, but in this case, she did not have the strength. It had been a long day and a longer night. "I saw a dead woman," Ellie said. "And the murderer brushed past me in an alley. The night began as something of a lark, almost—dressed as a man, sneaking around in the darkness—but…"

"You found the murderer, though. Pimm's note said that much. So all is well. Yes?"

"I suppose so. But the culprit, Mr. Worth, he implied there was some deeper conspiracy involved. We have solved one mystery, but we may have also found the leading edge of another."

"Then you simply must investigate further!" Winnie declared. "A crusading reporter and a dogged detective, fighting crime together. What combination could be better?"

Ellie smiled. She had worried Lady Pembroke would be jealous or suspicious of her—a young unmarried woman, attaching herself so firmly to another woman's husband. But Winnie seemed entirely unbothered by their relationship. Which made sense. Why should a wealthy, beautiful woman possibly worry about Ellie becoming close to her husband?

Still. It would have been nice if she saw Ellie as *something* of a threat. Even if only slightly. Ellie felt more drab with every moment she spent in Winnie's presence. "I am not sure your husband would welcome my further involvement. I am afraid I was rather indelicate when I offered my assistance—"

"Threats of blackmail, hmm?" Winnie struck a lucifer against the surface of a beautiful antique table and lit another cigarette. "You threatened to write a story about him working for Abel Value?"

Ellie stared at the floor. "I… may have implied something of the sort. But later he explained that he needed Value's cooperation to capture the killer, and could not risk involving the police without losing

Value's assistance." She considered mentioning that Pimm was also trying to protect someone he cared about from Value's blackmail, but it was hardly her secret to reveal. And what if that someone was Lady Pembroke? Who knew what secrets *her* past hid?

"Mmm. That *does* explain it," Winnie said. "Pimm is not a bit nefarious, you know. He drinks too much—even more than I do—and he doesn't tend to think much beyond the end of the night, or the end of the week at the latest, but he means well. He almost *pathologically* means well. If there is a mystery, he will find himself compelled to unravel it, and if you can assist him, I believe you should." Winnie leaned forward. "He *likes* you, Ellie. I can tell from the note. He was most unsparing with his adjectives. And Pimm does not like many people. He finds people *interesting*, certainly, but liking them is a whole other proposition." She yawned. "I'd best turn in. I have a busy day of being idle and rich and socially provocative ahead of me tomorrow. Do you need anything else?"

"No, thank you. You've been too kind already."

"Sleep well, then, and I'll see you in the morning. I'll cook eggs. I like to dabble in the kitchen, and I'm getting quite good at it. Last time I made breakfast, hardly any bits of eggshell made it onto the plates."

The house was dark when Pimm arrived home, and he wove with the ease of long practice around the ottomans and tables and chairs until he reached his bedchamber. He'd made that walk successfully in far drunker circumstances than these—indeed, he was abominably sober, having emptied the flask he habitually carried in his jacket long ago. A fresh flask waited in his bedside table, and a last bit of brandy would send him off to sleep nicely, he hoped, banishing the cares and worries of the day before they could transform into dreams of broken skulls or wrathful crime lords.

He sat on the edge of his bed to remove his shoes, not bothering with a light, and very nearly screamed when a quiet voice said, "Good morning, Pimm."

"Freddy! What the deuce are you doing in my bed?"

His best friend levered herself up on her elbow and chuckled. "Keeping up appearances, of course. Unless you're planning to wake up earlier than usual, Miss Skyler might notice if we were sleeping in separate rooms. She might begin to wonder about the health of our marriage, don't you think? Feel free to take a pillow and a bedspread to the floor. That Chinese rug I bought last month is quite thick."

Pimm groaned. "I suppose you're right. It's beastly to make a man sleep on the rug after a night of defying criminals, apprehending killers, and planting evidence."

"And wooing lady reporters?"

Pimm paused with one shoe in his hands. "Wooing? There was no woo. The woman tried to blackmail me. And then, I admit, she became somewhat useful—"

"There was a decidedly admiring tone in your letter."

"I just wanted you to be pleasant toward her."

"Ah, but you usually don't mind if I'm unpleasant. You fancy our Miss Skyler, don't you?"

"For most of the time we have been acquainted, she has worn a false mustache, Freddy. That is a powerful countervailing force when it comes to attraction."

"Ah, but under that mustache, she's adorable, you know. Pretty eyes and cheekbones sharp enough to slice an apple—"

"I am a married man," Pimm said.

"You *know* I think you should take a mistress. They're good for the soul. Why do you think I go to so many salons? That's where you find all the free-thinking girls. Heaven knows I haven't paid a whit of attention to our vows, at least in regards to marital fidelity."

"I rather doubt heaven *approves*, though. And do you think Miss Skye seems like the sort of woman to become someone's mistress?"

"You never know," Freddy said sleepily. "I suppose it all depends on the man."

Thus giving Pimm something else to think about while he lay on the Chinese rug under the second-best bedspread.

Although, in this particular case, he would not have objected if his thoughts had bled over into his dreams.

Housebreaking

reakfast was exceedingly awkward, at least from Ellie's point of view. She dressed in her "Mr. Jenkins" garb, sans mustache, refusing Winnie's offer to loan her a dress, mostly because she didn't like to contemplate how Winnie's clothes would look hanging on her own rather less voluptuous frame—something like a sheet draped over a coatrack, she imagined. She agreed to eat before departing, and Winnie clattered around the kitchen, chattering merrily, and manufactured a pan full of eggs that were simultaneously gritty and flavorless. Given the fact that Winnie was smoking the entire time she cooked, Ellie considered herself lucky there were no ashes in the dish, and swallowed a few bites out of politeness.

Winnie dropped into the chair opposite Ellie's and leaned her elbows on the kitchen table, smiling. "I presume you want to pelt Pimm with questions when he awakes?"

"I *am* curious about how things worked out with Mr. Worth. Did he mention anything when he came in last night?"

"Oh, I was fast asleep, he didn't even wake me when he came to bed. I'm as curious as you are." She glanced at the clock on the wall, which read half past seven. "I wouldn't expect him up for a few hours yet. Pimm is more of an evening person than a morning one. You might be better returning for lunch."

"Oh, I couldn't impose—"

Winnie laughed. "Don't worry, I won't cook again, I'll have a picnic basket packed by one of the shops. We can eat in the park and converse about all manner of nefarious things without fear of being overheard, how does that sound?"

Ellie blinked. She had the impression that Lady Pembroke was not often denied, and though being in her presence made Ellie somewhat uncomfortable—mostly out of guilt for the way her thoughts strayed inevitably to Winnie's husband—the woman's warmth was undeniable, and pleasant. "I… would be delighted."

"Marvelous." Winnie patted her hand. "We'll see you around noon—no, better say one, just to make sure Pimm will be up and around."

Moments later Ellie found herself out onto the steps, where she walked in a sleepy daze onto the street, joining the stream of serious men and buttoned-up women bustling about on their way to whatever occupations filled their days. She joined the throng, caught a passing electric omnibus, and rode without incident to the vicinity of her rooming house. She approached the front door with the stealth of a criminal, slotting her key into the lock and slipping into the foyer and down the hall to her own room without encountering any of the other tenants or the landlady. Once in her small bedroom she stripped off the suit, unwrapped the bindings from her chest, and washed away the day's grime at her basin. After looking longingly at her bed, she decided if she lay down again she might not rise again until nightfall, and so she dressed, choosing one of her best day dresses in green silk, with wide sleeves, a high bodice, and a crinoline skirt. Ellie's corset had never felt so freeing—she didn't know how the men transformed into women by the Affliction and trying to hide their condition could bear being wrapped up with those tight bandages all day long. She affixed her bonnet with the false curls to hide her man's haircut, and was ready to face the world.

She had writing to do before she met with Lord and Lady Pembroke again: her article on the clockwork brothel was written in her head, and needed only to be transferred to the page, and she needed to organize her notes about the events of the day before. Figuring out what she could print, what she could imply, and what she must avoid mentioning entirely would take a bit of thought. She resolved again to tell Pimm about seeing

Bertram Oswald at the clockwork brothel. He had resources she did not, and if she intended to investigate the relationship between Sir Bertram and Abel Value, she would need all the help she could get.

But that was a problem for later. For now, she should visit the paper and check in with Cooper before he gave away the column inches he'd promised her.

Ellie stepped out of her room, and into the presence of a man crouched in the hall, holding a knife. It was Crippen, the prizefighter turned criminal, and his sooty, thuggish presence in Ellie's rooming house was as disconcerting as finding a serpent on one's pillow. She took a step back, and Crippen rushed toward her, knife raised, face twisted in a snarl. "Where is he?" Crippen hissed.

Whom did he mean? Pimm? The murderer Thaddeus Worth? Before Ellie could even try to stammer out an answer, Crippen jabbed the air in front of her with his knife. "Jenkins!" he said. "Where's Jenkins? I saw him come in here, where is he?"

He was looking for Ellie, and he didn't realize it. "I—I don't know who you mean, this is a woman's rooming house, men are not allowed here, you must be mistaken."

"Useless cow," Crippen said, and something in Ellie went cold. She wondered if Pimm's remarkable walking stick with its electric shock capability could be adapted into something suitable for her own use—a parasol, perhaps. A weapon like that would be quite useful now.

Suddenly Ellie's landlady, the widowed Mrs. Reynolds, came shrieking from the kitchen, holding a cast-iron pan aloft like a war club. Crippen actually cried out and staggered back a step, barely moving in time to avoid having his head stove in by the weapon. Mrs. Reynolds struggled to lift her weapon aloft again, and Crippen brandished his knife, eyes wild.

Ellie knew he was acting more on instinct than design, but that didn't change his murderous intent. She snatched up a vase of fresh-cut flowers from a table in the foyer—Mrs. Reynolds made a point of brightening the common areas with blossoms, now available even in winter, thanks to Sir Bertram's wonderful municipal hothouse—and smashed it, flowers and all, into the thug's face. The vase broke, and Ellie suspected Crippen's nose did, too. He shrieked, dropping his knife, and rushed for the front door, his head dripping with water from the vase, and a daisy sticking out of his collar at a jaunty angle.

Mrs. Reynolds picked up her frying pan, looked at Ellie, then looked at the mess on the floor, and sighed. "I'll get the mop," she said. "You step outside and see if you can find a policeman."

Ellie nodded, stepping around the broken fragments on the floor, and found a small crowd already gathering outside, loudly conversing about the bleeding, soaking man who'd fled down the street. A policeman in his distinctive rounded helmet approached, drawn by the commotion like a bee to a flower, and Ellie raised her hand to beckon him, already practicing in her mind the words she would say: A strange man had broken into the rooming house with a knife, shouting incomprehensibly. Her landlady had driven the man off. No, she'd never seen him before, but he looked like a person of low character.

Of course, she *could* identify him by name to the police, but wouldn't that just draw more attention to her? Crippen's employers were looking for a man named Jenkins, with a horrible mustache, not a woman named Eleanor Skyler. Ellie resolved to retire the mustache immediately, and let Jenkins vanish utterly—let Crippen and his fellow thugs search all they liked for a man who didn't exist.

But when Ellie took the policeman in to speak to her landlady, her discretion became irrelevant: "Surely I recognized him," Mrs. Reynolds said. "He was Crippler Crippen, big as life."

"The prizefighter?" the bobby said. "Are you certain?"

"My late husband was a great fan of the fights." Mrs. Reynolds dabbed at her eyes with a handkerchief, as she always did when she mentioned Mr. Reynolds, though she never actually wept—Ellie wasn't sure if the eye-dabbing was an act, an affectation, or merely a habit held over from a time when her widowhood had been cause for genuine tears. "I saw Crippler fight three times at least, and there's no mistaking him—those black eyes, that great block of a chin, and that nose of his, broken so often it looks like a squashed plum—and our Miss Skyler here broke it for him again this morning I'd wager." She cackled. Apparently driving off housebreakers put her in a good mood. "A shame you couldn't have gone up against him in the ring, Miss!"

"We'll make inquiries," the bobby said. "I'm afraid this isn't the first complaint we've had about Crippen. He seems to have fallen in with bad companions."

Mrs. Reynolds sniffed. "He is a dirty cheat, you know. Let himself be beaten in a fight he should have won, to win money for rich men, and to fill his own pockets. Now he's reduced to menacing innocent women in their homes. You find him, sir, and I'll gladly go before the magistrate and point him out."

The constable said he'd make a point of keeping an eye on the building, attempted to tip his bell-shaped hat at them, and went on his way. Mrs. Reynolds looked Ellie up and down. "You'll have a cup of tea now," she declared.

Ellie forced herself to smile. "Really, no, I should check in at the office. I have some notes I need to turn into a story."

Her landlady sighed. "It doesn't seem quite right to me, a woman working at a newspaper. Doesn't seem like a woman's place. Making a home run smooth, that's what a woman should do."

With great effort, Ellie refrained from pointing out that Mrs. Reynolds was a fully independent woman who had just attempted to beat a man about the head with a frying pan—because in all likelihood her landlady would simply say that proved her point: driving out housebreakers made the home more pleasant, didn't it? Ellie did not want to argue with the woman, so she said, "Perhaps the right man will come along, and I can put away my pen."

Mrs. Reynolds scowled. "I didn't say *that*. You could still write in your spare moments, I dare say, if it makes you happy." She bustled off toward the kitchen, leaving Ellie a bit off-kilter, as usual after their interactions.

Her need to talk to Pimm was even more urgent now. She had to let him know Crippen had broken in to her home looking for "Jenkins." Crippen, or his employer, had obviously made the connection between Lord Pembroke's "assistant" and the man who'd escaped the brothel. They doubtless assumed that Pimm knew Bertram Oswald spent time in Value's brothel, too—and they might take steps to silence him on the subject. She couldn't let Pimm walk blithely around, unaware of the danger she'd put him in. She would see him at lunchtime, and tell all then.

Assuming she could avoid being assaulted by Value's thugs again in the meantime.

Pimm woke to see Freddy's face hovering only a few inches away from his own, and he startled as violently as if someone had thrown a pan of water into the bed. Freddy withdrew, grinning insouciantly. "So much for the vaunted Halliday perceptivity! I've been looming over you for minutes. You're fortunate I'm not a villain bearing a dagger."

Pimm merely groaned, until Freddy threw back the curtains, letting in torrents of sunlight, at which point Pimm shrieked and buried his head under the covers. "Freddy, you blackguard! Why must you torment me! First you leave me sleeping on the floor for half the night, then mere hours after I've crawled into a proper empty bed, you turn the sun's rays against me!" The bed shifted as Freddy sat beside him.

"A wife cannot wake her husband for breakfast?"

"I want to *sleep*, Freddy. I want to be like an oversaturated sponge, so full that water wells up at the slightest touch, but instead of water, I want to be saturated by *sleep*."

"It's nearly noon, old boy, and I told that delightful Ellie Skye we'd meet for lunch at one. I thought you might want to rinse your mouth out and change your shirt first."

Pimm lowered the blanket by inches, hoping to grow accustomed to the light by degrees. His head felt full of rubble and shattered glass. "Why did you invite her to lunch?"

"Because I found her incredibly charming. And also because I think *you* found her incredibly charming."

"This again, Freddy?"

She patted him on the shoulder. "You did a great service when you married me, Pimm. I know it seemed ideal at the time, a way to satisfy your family that you were settling down while helping me, too. But have you ever thought about what you've done to *yourself*? To your own prospects of true happiness?"

Trying for a light tone despite his crashing headache and the aridity of his tongue, Pimm said, "I daresay I've spared some poor girl a lot of misery."

Freddy frowned, a line appearing on her perfect forehead. "Don't talk rot, Pimm. We were at school together. I know the sort of poetry you like to read. And I knew Adelaide, and how you felt about her, before her unfortunate passing—but that was a long time ago, Pimm, a dozen years. Your heart has healed enough for love to blossom anew, I think. For all that you like to muck about with criminals and murderers, there's a soft soul inside you. You deserve to be happy, don't you think? Happier than liquor alone can make you, I mean."

Pimm swung his legs over the side of the bed and sat up, turning his back on Freddy. "Is this about Ellie Skye? I barely know the woman, Freddy, really—"

"Yes, and you won't *get* to know her if you think you *can't*. You have qualms about taking a mistress. Fine. There are other options."

"And what would become of you, if I pursued happiness with another—with a woman, Freddy?"

"There is such a thing as divorce, you know. It's been seven years since Parliament made it legal—"

Pimm shook his head. "Shall we brand you an adulterer, then? Or would you prefer to testify that *I* am an adulterer who dabbles in bestiality or bigamy as well? Because without those sorts of allegations, and proof to back them up, divorce is beyond our reach. Even then, I might not be allowed to remarry."

"There is already talk in Parliament of amending the Matrimonial Causes Act to be… rather less rigid, in light of the Constantine Affliction, and the social changes that illness has wrought."

"Oh, yes, I expect the law will be changed to allow a wife to divorce her husband for simple adultery, since adultery runs the risk of bringing a terrible disease into the home—but would that be better, if I were *just* an adulterer?

"Better than being an adulterer who cavorts with farm animals and his second wife? I daresay, yes."

Pimm snorted laughter. "Divorce is out of the question, Freddy. Be serious. Imagine the reaction from my family! I would be disinherited."

"So? You have a private income—your grandfather saw to that. You aren't dependent on the goodwill of your brother or mother. In fact, the freedom from their expectations would probably suit you."

Pimm frowned. "When did you become so cold, Freddy? My family may not understand me—or, for that matter, I, them—but they are not bad people, and I do love them."

"Mmmm. I forget you have the luxury of thinking well of your family." She sighed. "I suppose, if it comes to it, we could simply fake my death, and I could move to the Continent."

Pimm blinked, turning to look at his wife, and best friend. "That seems like a lot of trouble, doesn't it?"

"Love is *worth* a lot of trouble, Pimm. If you don't know that…" She shook her head. "You did once. Perhaps if we explained our… arrangement, to Ellie, she would understand, and we could work something out, without the necessity of divorce…" Noticing Pimm's expression, she snorted. "Oh, don't look so shocked, Pimm. People make arrangements all the time. Life is complicated."

"Perhaps in *France*," Pimm said. "But this is England. People would talk."

"You really must come to one of my salons some day, Pimm. Your eyes would be quite opened. *Talking* is half the fun."

"Do not tell Ellie—Miss Skye," Pimm said, "about your condition. Please. She's a *reporter*. That means she likes to learn secrets, and put them on the pages of a newspaper, and distribute them to anyone who can read, or who knows someone who can read the best bits aloud to them. She is not someone with whom you should share intimacies that are quite *that* intimate. And, blast it, as I said, I barely *know* her, you're concocting a love affair out of nothing—"

"If you aren't interested in Ellie for yourself, shall I introduce her to some of our eligible friends, then?" Freddy said. "Provide her with a bit more security in her life? Ellie and I chatted a bit this morning, and I learned that her family, though all dead, is respectable enough, solidly middle class. And she's not too old, for all that she seems to have resigned herself to spinsterhood. I could introduce her to Reggie Jolley, perhaps, or Edmund Thorpe?"

Pimm opened his mouth to speak, but couldn't quite bring himself to answer, and his headache returned with a terrible force. The thought of Ellie with either of those men affronted him in some deep way he could scarcely articulate. He finally managed, "Jolley, that ass, she's far too smart for him, and Thorpe is such a towering boor, I would never wish such a fate upon her, and—"

"As I thought," Freddy said, in an insufferable tone, but before Pimm could complain, she handed over a glass, and Pimm gulped from it gratefully.

He'd expected water, and there was water, but there was whiskey, too. He gulped it down even more rapidly once he realized, the warmth spreading through him, his headache receding.

"Good," Freddy said. "I hate to ply you with liquor, but this way you might look halfway human by lunchtime. And perhaps being in Miss Skyler's company when you *aren't* chasing a murderer will show you how delightful she is."

Pimm shook his head. "I *can't*, Freddy. If I don't go talk to Abel Value this morning, he'll send someone around, and I'd rather not have his people in my house again. I need to give him a... carefully edited... version of what happened last night. He will not be happy that I failed to bring the killer to him personally."

"Curses. Well, I won't break the date with Ellie, anyway—I could use another girlfriend."

Pimm looked at Freddy, alarmed. "Don't tell me *you* have designs on her?"

"Now, now, settle down. You know I am a paragon of discretion when I engage in such assignations. I don't think Ellie would be interested, anyway—one cannot always tell from such a short acquaintance, but I get no sense that she is interested in such... purely feminine pursuits. Doubtless the very suggestion would cause her to turn adorably red in the cheeks, though... No, no, I'll behave. You and I should never fight over a woman, it's unseemly. I feel more of a brotherly affection for her anyway. Or perhaps sisterly. I can't really tell any more. Perhaps you can join us for our picnic after, if Value doesn't murder you?"

The thought of seeing Miss Skye again did give a more pleasant dimension to the prospect of an otherwise wretched day. And Ellie had promised to tell him a story about Bertram Oswald, which interested him almost as much. "I will do my best."

"Do you want a pistol for your meeting? One of the air pistols I've modified, or even the revolver?"

Pimm considered. He didn't much like guns, and he had his electrified walking stick... "Yes," he said after a moment. "That might be best."

Services Most Unsatisfactory

This time the meeting took place in the back room of the Black Dog tavern, near Blackfriars Bridge. This was apparently a headquarters of sort for Value, who sat hunched over a small and cluttered desk, Big Ben looming behind, his head very nearly touching the ceiling. "Good morning, Mr. Value." Pimm seated himself in the rickety wooden chair opposite the desk. He inclined his head to the giant. "Ben."

"Morning, is it?" Value didn't look up from the mound of papers he scanned. "Afternoon, more like."

"I've always been terrible with time," Pimm said amiably. "I just wanted to let you know that your murderer has been unmasked."

Value looked up, removing his pince-nez glasses. "Ben told me about your adventures," Value said. "At least, the portion for which he was present. Adams was able to find some clue to the killer's identity on the new victim's person?"

"Indeed he was. I followed the evidence straight to the killer."

"Are you sure you found the right man?"

"Entirely sure. He confessed to me personally. And, as I had predicted, the killer was indeed a gentleman with an interest in your business."

"I need his *name*."

"Certainly. Thaddeus Worth."

Value was a man schooled at hiding his emotions, generally showing no more expression than a lizard on a rock, but he visibly flinched and paled. "There must be some mistake," he murmured. "Thad... Thad would never..."

Pimm brushed a bit of lint from the knee of his trousers and ordered his thoughts. Mix in truths with the lies, to make the lies seem more true... "Apparently his wife contracted the Constantine Affliction, and subsequently abandoned him. He held her departure against the prostitutes, I suppose, as he must have contracted the illness from one of them. Presumably it was one of your women—or else, he knew where to find your women, having once been involved in that part of your business. I understand he was a whoremaster. I can't say for certain why he left the dead women on your doorstep, but then, I suppose employees holding grudges against you is nothing new."

Value turned in his chair. "Ben. I need you to bring Thad—Mr. Worth— here, to me, as soon as you—"

"I'm afraid that won't be possible," Pimm said. "Mr. Worth has been taken into police custody."

Value stared at him through slit eyes. "What?"

"He confessed to murder—several murders—as I mentioned. It seemed prudent to call the police, in light of such information."

Value sighed. "How very droll, Lord Pembroke. You seek to spare him from my retribution? How noble. Of course, since my people made sure all the bodies vanished, there will be no evidence of his confessed crimes, and he will be dismissed as a madman, especially when a few of my people step forward to attest to his mental dissolution since his wife vanished—"

Pimm cleared his throat. "There is a body, actually. You heard about some excitement near the river last night? Police milling about? They discovered Worth's latest victim, exactly where he told them she could be found." Pimm spread his hands. "That should do for evidence, I daresay."

"Ben," Value said, through gritted teeth. "You told me you took the body to Adams."

"We did, sir. As for what Lord Pembroke did after that... I couldn't say. I reported straight to you afterward."

Value grunted. "I'd like to know how you contrived to have that body transported, Halliday. I may need to have a word with Adams."

Pimm shrugged. "Anything he did, he did at my request—and you *did* tell him to cooperate with me completely, so there's no point in blaming him." Pimm hesitated. "You threatened to tell people certain secrets of mine, Value, if I didn't find your murderer. While I realize I did not adhere to the letter of our agreement, I hope—"

Value snorted laughter. "I don't care about your sham marriage, Halliday, nor do I expect I'll have time to ruin your reputation, as I'll be rather too busy running for my *life*. Do you have any idea what you've done to me?"

"Running for your life? That might be overstating things, sir. I put a man with knowledge of your business into police custody, with a burning desire to trade information in exchange for his life. Yes, I'm afraid that might inconvenience you a bit, but unless he can implicate you personally in a murder, it hardly constitutes a danger to your life—"

Value laughed, hollowly. "You stupid man. I expected you to do something like this, you know, to bring in the police—I am not afraid for my *business* interests. There's no proof that I'm involved in illegal human prostitution, and what good is the word of a murderer anyway? But if I'd known it was Thad… that it was Mr. Worth… killing those girls, I would have handled things differently, I…" He shook his head. "Get out of here, Halliday. I have arrangements to make. Urgent ones."

Pimm frowned. "What can Worth possibly tell the police that would lead to your death? I never took you for the murdering sort, sir. At least, not in a firsthand way."

"I am not a killing man, as a rule—there are better ways to make your point, usually. But Worth knows other secrets, Halliday. And just the fact that he *might* tell those secrets puts my life in danger from people far more powerful than myself. If I turn up dead, know that you're responsible. But what do you care what happens to some old villain?"

"Mr. Value, I would not wish to see you murdered. To see your criminal enterprises stopped, of course, but not by means of your death. If there are powerful men arrayed against you, the police can protect you, in exchange for information—"

"You have no *idea* how wrong you are, Lord Pembroke. Please, be gone."

Thinking about Ellie's cryptic comments the night before, Pimm said,

"Is it… something to do with Bertram Oswald? Is he the powerful man—"

"Ben!" Value bellowed. "See the little Lord out, since he seems unable to comprehend a dismissal!"

Pimm rose, holding out his hands in a placating gesture, before Ben came for him. "I'll leave. But Mr. Value, do let me know if I can help you—"

"You've helped enough."

As Pimm left the tavern, passing the sad midday drunkards, he craved a drink even more desperately than usual. He'd started taking solace in the bottle seriously when Adelaide died, to dull the pain, and he'd never stopped—whiskey had become the obvious cure for all emotional upheaval, leveling things out nicely. But this was a new sort of upheaval. He had seldom, if ever, had the experience of becoming more mystified *after* solving a crime, and the experience didn't suit him. What was Value afraid of? What secret did Worth know, that could put Value's life in danger? Pimm didn't do well with mysteries. Fortunately, there were people he could ask.

The question was whether or not they would answer.

As Pimm walked, he noticed a disheveled black-haired man from the tavern following him at a discreet distance. Pimm took a few random turns down assorted streets, and even doubled back on his own trail, and the man continued to drift along in his wake. Had Value sent him? Or one of Value's mysterious "powerful men?"

Pimm ducked into an alley and crouched in a shadow behind a broken crate. After a few moments, the man following him entered as well, moving slowly. As he passed, Pimm jammed his walking stick between the man's legs at about ankle height and swung it forward, sweeping the thug off his feet. The man landed on the ground with a jarring thud and groaned. Pimm stood and pressed the metal ball of his cane against the young man's bulging adam's apple. "This cane is electrified," Pimm said, almost conversationally. "I can discharge the battery into your throat, but I'd hate to kill you before you answered a few questions. Why are you following me?"

"A man paid me," the fellow said, holding up his hands. "Didn't say why. Said I'm to see where you go and report back."

"Which man?"

"Dunno his name. Young, younger than you. Wore a nice suit."

"Mmm," Pimm said. That didn't sound like Value or Oswald, but it could have been one of their employees. Which made sense—neither one would hire a thug personally. "And where are you supposed to deliver this report?"

The man named a tavern, but not the Black Dog. Pimm considered his options. He could go with this man to the tavern, and confront whomever had hired him, but the odds were good that person would just be *another* thug acting on orders. And even if this man did lead him to Oswald, what good would that do? He didn't *know* anything about the man—at least, nothing more than any other casual newspaper reader did, and certainly nothing that would connect Oswald with Value. He needed more information. Pimm made a decision.

"I'd very much like for you to *stop* following me," he said. "How about, let's see… ten pounds? Would that suffice? You can go back to your paymaster and say I cunningly gave you the slip, how would that be?"

"I… suppose that would be all right," the man said, in the tone of someone who'd expected a kick and, in all defiance of reason, received a kiss instead.

"Good man," Pimm said. "I approve of the entrepreneurial spirit."

A Wrongful Termination

One of the bells Adam had connected to the doors leading to his laboratory rang, and he hurriedly whispered, "We'll talk later." He unscrewed a valve, cutting off the artificial air supply, then threw a dirty white cloth over the jar containing Margaret's brain, covering the brass speaking apparatus as well.

Adam made a point of appearing absorbed in work on an improved version of his battery when his visitor entered. "Mr. Oswald," he said, not looking up from his work. "It has been some weeks since you graced me with your company. What brings you here today?"

"You know I prefer 'Sir Bertram,' Adam," the scientist chastised.

"Ah, yes. Your knighthood. For services to the crown. I'd forgotten."

"You forget nothing, Adam. That's part of why you've been so valuable to me."

Adam did look up, now. His patron was dressed impeccably in a dove-gray waistcoat, and carried a cane made of some darkly gleaming metal—probably his own Oswaldium, an alloy lighter than glass and harder than steel, though when placed under sufficient strain, it had a brittleness that made it unsuitable for large-scale building projects. "*Have* been valuable? Don't I continue to be?"

Oswald picked up a pile of books from a wooden stool, glancing at their covers briefly, then placed them carefully on a wooden table next to a row of jars filled with preserved human eyes, sorted by color. He sat on the stool, placed the cane across his knees, and sighed. "I understand you met Lord Pembroke."

Adam inclined his head. "He is doing some work for Mr. Value, I understand. I was instructed to provide support in certain technical matters."

"You planted false evidence of a murder for him, didn't you?"

"I planted *true* evidence of a murder in a false location, to be more accurate. I know how much you value accuracy. Do you disapprove of my actions?"

"I am, generally, uninterested in your actions, apart from those that bear directly on my scientific projects. But do you know the name of the man you helped incriminate?"

Adam had to be careful here. As far as he knew, Oswald was unaware of Margaret's existence, and he preferred to keep her existence a secret. A speaking brain in a jar might be altogether too fascinating for a man of Oswald's intellectual leanings, and Adam wanted her all to himself. "Lord Pembroke may have mentioned the man's name. Thaddeus, I believe?"

"Worth, Adam. Thaddeus Worth. Do you happen to know someone *else* named Worth? Or someone who *used* to be named Worth?"

Adam frowned. "It is not such an uncommon name, but I assume you refer to the person we once knew as *Madam* Worth?"

"Yes," Oswald said. "Thaddeus Worth was her husband."

"Ah. I never knew that gentleman's given name. I can understand why you are… upset. I thought Thaddeus Worth had been paid handsomely for his silence?"

"That was the arrangement. And, true to his agreement, Mr. Worth did not tell anyone what truly became of his wife after her transformation—not in words. But he did murder women and leave them on the doorsteps of Value's clockwork brothels, which are really *my* clockwork brothels. But that, too, would have been fine—I begrudge no man his hobby, and murder is as good a way to pass the time as any—except Value, without consulting me, brought in Lord Pembroke to investigate. And Lord Pembroke, being a man of fine upstanding moral fiber, handed Mr. Worth over the police."

"Ah. And you are afraid Mr. Worth will tell the authorities about his wife, and thus about your connection to the Constantine Affliction?"

Oswald sniffed. "He won't have the opportunity. He'll be dead by nightfall. But his apprehension does indicate a troubling lack of forethought on the part of Mr. Value, doesn't it? Indeed, it makes me entirely reconsider our strategic alliance."

Adam sighed. "You mean to have Mr. Value killed, then. What impact will that have on my supply test subjects?"

"His assorted dead whores, you mean? Well, with Worth in custody—soon to be dead—your supply would at any rate once again be limited to those women dead of drink, or fevers, or tuberculosis, or misadventure. No more cleanly-suffocated girls, alas."

"Their deaths, whatever the cause, are tragedies, which I seek to redeem through science."

"Mmm. I've always felt I could talk to you, Adam. You hold the advancement of science in as high a regard as I do."

"Nonsense," Adam said. "I do not revere science, any more than I would revere a hammer. Science is a tool. Only the ends matter."

"Ah, yes. As you say. Any luck finding your true love among the dead women, then?"

Adam scowled behind his smooth mask. He did not intend to tell Oswald about Margaret's brain, though it was the first hopeful development he'd had in some time. "I continue to make incremental progress."

"You continue failing to achieve what your own creator accomplished, you mean," Oswald said, sniffing. "To bring dead flesh to life, endowed with a working mind. You have managed the first part, but not the second. Well, you are a *made* thing, of course. You can't be expected to make things on your *own*, any more than a steam engine is capable of independently creating more steam engines. That would make you a sort of self-replicating machine, wouldn't it? Seems a bit improbable."

"All biological life can be viewed as a series of self-replicating machines," Adam countered.

Oswald just shrugged, and that was when Adam began to worry. Oswald loved nothing more than a good argument, or an opportunity to demolish an opponent's malformed illogic, and if he was declining to engage, it must mean something dire was afoot. "Would you say we're friends, Adam?"

"Men like you and I do not have friends. Our work does not allow for such entanglements. But we are certainly colleagues."

"Good. Then we understand one another. I had high hopes for your program, you know. I really thought you might be able to help me solve my little problem with the Queen."

"The device works beautifully. The women who are resurrected on my table as ravenous beasts are transformed into docile creatures, biddable and easily led, with the insertion of a few wires and the severing of a few nerves."

"They are mindless," Oswald said, mouth twisted in disgust. "Good enough for Value to use in his secret brothels, catering to the more than usually depraved in a way few living girls could bear, but dead girls pretending to be alive are useless for my purposes. Mere puppets, without even the illusion of free will or agency. Why, my Air Loom—"

"Was entirely a failure," Adam said. "While my approach, at least, shows promise. I still say, given a living subject, I could perform the surgery successfully, making it possible to control the patient without destroying the personality. I just need—"

"Oh, well, I'll just bring the Queen here and we'll etherize her on your table. I'll let you put wires in her brain, why not? What could possibly go wrong?"

Adam shrugged. "You could contrive a means to bring me into the palace, unobserved, for the procedure. There are ways."

Oswald shook his head. "And if she should *die* during your surgery? Yes, you could replace her blood with your remarkable chemical slurry, and give her the semblance of life, but I dare say Lord Palmerston would notice a certain difference in her *affect* when she attempted to devour his nose at their first meeting, or stared at him glassy-eyed and doll-like. How many surgeries have you performed on the living?"

Adam frowned, lifted the bottom of his mask, and scratched an itch on his chin. "Do you mean… counting myself? Then, a great many. But the principles are the same, a living body and a dead one are not so different—"

"Spoken like a stitched-together corpse." Oswald rose from the chair. "No, Adam, I'm afraid I can no longer afford to fund your experiments. Or rather, of course I *could* afford to fund them, but I no longer wish to do so. I have a more promising solution to my difficulties, now."

"Your clockwork," Adam said, without bothering to conceal his scorn.

"Your little wind-up whores."

"Ah, Adam, they are so much more than that. The brothels were important, yes, to see if my clockwork creatures could be made human-seeming enough to satisfy a man, and to test the physical limitations of the devices. But I've gone much farther now. Did you know the latest models in the pleasure houses can dance, and play the harp, and recite poetry, and wield a riding crop? They can even follow selected verbal commands."

"I am sure they can do all those things, following a pre-set program, from which they cannot deviate. Where is the free will there?"

Oswald laughed. "My dear man—or should I say my dear semblance of a man—I do not require free will, only the *illusion* of free will. The brothels get my *previous* generation of clockwork women. Those models I am working on currently are able to perform actions of astonishing complexity. And so much of a Queen's life is rote, and ritual, and tradition—it is trivial to program a convincing simulacrum to do the things a Queen must do. With Prince Albert imprisoned, the Queen has few confidants, other than myself, who would notice any changes in her behavior. Simulating Lord Palmerston and other ministers will be more difficult, of course—damn this constitutional monarchy, things would be much simpler with an absolute ruler, only *one* person to replace—but I have confidence that I can surmount those problems as well. Controlling the Queen will give me greater access to the powers that truly rule England, and access is all a man like myself needs to achieve his goals."

Adam frowned. "But… what of the real Queen, then? Will you have her killed? Become a regicide?"

"Killing her would be problematic," Oswald said. "It is surprisingly difficult to entirely destroy a body, and getting her corpse out of the palace would be a devil of a job. But fear not. I have a plan. I always do. Alas, that plan does not involve you."

"I suppose that concludes our business, then," Adam said. He sighed. "It was a fruitful collaboration, Mr. Oswald. I am sorry we can be no further help to one another." He would have to sell the design for his battery after all, to raise the funds to continue his researches. Perhaps he should contact his solicitor to handle the arrangements…

"Oh, Adam. I see you misunderstand the situation. I am afraid that, in my initial enthusiasm about our collaboration, I shared too many confidences with you. Surely you understand that I cannot allow you to live, knowing all the secrets you do?"

Adam moved slightly toward the edge of the table, so he might dart around it. "I have no interest in your plans," he said. "Make the Queen and her ministers your slaves, and rule England through them—what does it matter to me?

Oswald clucked his tongue. "Do you truly presume my goals are to rule *England*? How… provincial. Seizing control of the country is merely the next step in a larger plan, a necessary precondition for a great experiment."

"Whatever your intentions, they are of no concern to me. I have only one interest, as you well know—creating a companion who I may love forever, throughout my possibly eternal life, and who will love me in return. I took your money, and turned my attention to researching mind control, in order to further those goals. In the absence of that money, you cease to interest me."

"You may be telling the truth," Oswald said. "But truth can change with circumstance. You are simply too large a risk, Adam. Value's indiscretion has made me more aware of the importance of keeping a tight leash on knowledge—at least, until my next great experiment is complete. I am on the cusp of important things, at a very delicate stage in my grand design, and it is important for me to… tidy up my affairs in order to move forward."

Adam rushed him, moving far more swiftly than Oswald could have anticipated. But Oswald already had a revolver in his hand, drawn from some inner recess of his coat, and he fired almost negligently into the center of Adam's body mass.

Adam had been shot once before, in the shoulder, many years ago—the gun fired by a man Adam had tried to help, who had been terrified by Adam's ferocious visage. That had been the beginning of a period of bitter disillusionment for Adam; a period that had never entirely ended. Now he was shot again, in the chest, this time, and the pain was worse than he remembered, but now, due to the strange cross-wirings in his brain, the pain also filled his mouth with the taste of fresh oranges, such as he'd tasted once in Spain. He twitched on the ground, staring up at the beams of the basement roof, with no memory even of falling. His entire torso was in agony, and he could not have said where, precisely, the bullet had penetrated his body.

Oswald stepped into view and peered down at him. "I considered dissecting you," he said. "But, ultimately, how interesting would it be? Flesh is so disgusting, anyway. Too many irregularities, and you would be more irregular than most, I imagine. I prefer gears and joints and struts and pivots to bone and muscles and nerves. Much cleaner." He aimed the pistol, and Adam knew that if Oswald fired into his brain, that would be the end—but Oswald instead crouched, and pressed the pistol directly over Adam's heart, and pulled the trigger.

The taste of oranges was overpowering, filling the world, at least until that world was dissolved into blackness.

A Picnic in the Park

Ellie reached for the knocker on the Lord Pembroke's door just as it swung inward. Winnie was there, beaming, her hair pinned up under a darling little hat, dressed in a pale yellow dress that seemed the very essence of springtime, and made Ellie feel terribly dowdy by comparison. Her best dress would be no match even for Winnie's worst, but Winnie exclaimed that she looked lovely anyway. She clutched Ellie's hands and pulled her into the house. "Come inside, come inside! I'm just finishing the preparations. I hope you're hungry. I have boiled eggs, cold roast chicken, some marvelous sweets…" She chattered happily as she led the way into the kitchen, where a large wicker hamper waited, filled with delectable things to eat. Ellie's stomach rumbled. She hadn't had anything all day, apart from a few shell-flecked bites of Winnie's breakfast and a stale roll at the newspaper office. A morning of fighting housebreakers and writing newspaper copy would make anyone ravenous.

"Is Lord Pembroke here?" Ellie asked, looking around.

"Oh, please, you *must* call him Pimm, everyone does. When you say Lord Pembroke I feel as if I should… curtsy, or something. It's not as if he's lordly in the least. He's just the younger son of a Marquess."

"Oh," Ellie said, faintly. "Is that all?"

Winnie chuckled. "I suppose it sounds impressive, but really, it just means one of his ancestors did something that pleased some monarch or another. Even Pimm's older brother has no greater personal achievement than successfully managing the family estates." She sighed. "I could do without the honorifics, myself. Do I look like a 'Lady Pembroke' to you?" Winnie picked up a yellow parasol from the table, frowned at it for a moment, then looked up at Ellie, blinking. "You'll want to know where he is, of course. Pimm I mean. He hopes to join us later, but alas, cannot be here now. He's out. Business, apparently, though you'd know more about that than I would, since you seem to be his partner in crime-solving these days."

"I'm terribly sorry, I don't mean to involve myself—" Ellie began, but stopped when Winnie threw back her head and laughed.

"Oh, dear, did I sound jealous? Please, be assured, I am anything but. Pimm has his interests, and I have mine, and while we are certainly bosom friends and great companions, we have our own lives. That whole notion of 'separate spheres,' you know, with the men out earning money, and the women running the house? It's a bit like that, but I have my tinkering, and my salons, and Pimm has his club and his crimes. Occasionally I aid him in his affairs, or he in mine, but, truly, we prefer things as we have them arranged. You need not fear you have usurped my position."

"I, ah, have never been married," Ellie admitted. "I suppose every marriage is different, in its way." Though the way Winnie airily described it, she and Pimm sounded more like friends who happened to live together than husband and wife.

"Some are more different than others," Winnie said dryly, and picked up the huge hamper as if it weighed nothing at all. "Come along, I told Pimm to hire us a cab, and it should be along soon. We keep our own carriage, you know, but Pimm's valet Ransome was our general man-of-all-work, driving us among his other duties, and since he's left us, we're simply bereft. We should interview potential replacements, but it's so *tedious*."

Ellie followed after Winnie—feeling a bit like she'd been swept along in a ship's wake—out the door, where a hansom cab waited. "Pimm prefers closed carriages," Winnie confided as the driver tipped his hat and lifted the picnic hamper into the cab's high seat. "He likes to peer out at people unobserved, I think. But on a spring day like this it's nice to be open to the sky, isn't it?"

Once Ellie and Winnie were seated, Winnie told the driver to take them to Hyde Park, somewhere nice under the trees, and he flipped the reins and set the horse to clopping along the cobblestones.

Winnie put her hand in Ellie's and smiled at her. "I feel that we shall be great friends, Ellie."

"I'd like that," Ellie said, and was surprised to find that she meant it. Winnie was rather above Ellie's own social station, but they were roughly of an age, and the woman's effusive warmth was contagious. "Winnie... how much do you know about Pimm's... business?"

"Oh, he tells me a lot. Not *everything*, I wager, but most."

"I'm sure if he keeps secrets it's only because he doesn't want to worry you—"

"Ha," Winnie said. "If he keeps secrets it's because he knows I'll disagree with how he's handling things." She glanced sidelong at Ellie. "I think you might have the wrong idea about me, Ellie. I am... not particularly genteel. There was even a minor scandal when Pimm and I were wed. As for my involvement in his work... you've seen his electrified walking stick in action, yes?"

Ellie nodded.

"I made that."

"You! You are an inventor?"

Winnie waved her hand. "More of a tinkerer, really. I confess, I seldom create entirely new things, but I have a knack for... combining the designs of others, and refining them, and finding uses the creators never intended. I have a workshop downstairs at home. In addition to the walking stick, I've built assorted other devices Pimm has sometimes found useful in his work. Are you surprised?"

"I suppose I imagined you... hosting formal teas," Ellie admitted. "And doing charitable work. Perhaps..."

"Shopping?" Winnie prompted, and smiled—though, to be honest, it was more a *grin*, broad and decidedly unfeminine. "Sometimes. But probably not shopping for the sorts of things you think. Consider me one of Pimm's operatives, if you like. I can tell you're worried about something, and that your disappointment over Pimm's absence isn't *entirely* due to the loss of his good company. What's on your mind?"

"I... it's complicated..." Ellie took a deep breath. "Promise me you will tell no one?"

"You have no *idea* how good I am at keeping secrets," Winnie said. She inclined her head toward the driver on his bench in front of them. "But perhaps save secrets for when we're better settled in the park?"

"A wise choice."

They rode in companionable silence until they approached the great park, when Winnie pointed and exclaimed. "What are they building over there?"

Ellie peered. "It looks like some kind of a stage... Oh, yes, of course, Bertram Oswald's Grand Exposition." Just saying the man's name, and remembering his cold eyes in the brothel, made her shiver. "It starts to-night, doesn't it? There's to be some sort of initial introduction at the park tonight, and then exhibits all weekend, a grand pavilion, and so on."

"Ah, yes, I read about the Exposition," Winnie said. "More modest than the Great Exhibition was, and more wholly devoted to Oswald's creations alone. He seems like a most arrogant man, though one cannot deny his scientific abilities."

Those abilities seemed likely to include the creation and servicing of clockwork whores, but bearing in mind the coachman who might be lis-tening, Ellie did not comment to that effect. Instead she pointed toward an immense pile of brassy metal tubes, all strange curves and arches, being fitted together by a group of workmen consulting printed plans. "What-ever could that be?"

"Something to change the world, no doubt," Winnie said. "Perhaps it boils a pot of tea at three hundred paces? Or makes a delicious hot dinner at the press of a button?"

"That would be a triumph of science," Ellie said, and they laughed.

The driver went around the park, away from the site of the Exposition, until Winnie directed him to stop near one of the gates and let them out. This end of the park was full of people strolling the paths, children playing, and other picnickers, but Winnie led them deeper, away from the sunnier well-traveled areas, so they could talk more freely. They spread a blanket and settled themselves beneath a tree, though it was a trifle cool in the shade. The hamper was ingeniously hinged, with multiple compartments, and Winnie set out china plates and silverware. "Tell me your secrets, dear," she said.

Ellie looked around to confirm their privacy, then took a deep breath. "Two days ago, in order to obtain a story for my newspaper, I disguised myself as a man—you've seen my costume—and gained entry into one of the, ah, houses of specialized tastes…"

"A clockwork brothel?" Winnie said, dishing out pieces of roast chicken. "Oh, how marvelous, I've always wondered what they were like."

"They are dreadful," Ellie said firmly. "Though my perception may have been colored by the fact that I was nearly killed. You see, I was taking an opportunity to look around, and… I walked in on Bertram Oswald. He seemed to be working on one of the machines. And he was unhappy with being seen."

Winnie let out a low whistle. "I can imagine why. Those houses may be technically legal, but Pimm says they're all run by criminals like Abel Value, and for the Queen's closest confidant to have dealings with a man like *that*… the consequences could be dire."

Ellie nodded, and explained how she'd fled the room, and the manner of her eventual escape from the brothel.

"That's dead clever," Winnie said appreciatively. "Men seldom see anything but the obvious and superficial. Nice to see that tendency used against them. But why haven't I read this on the front page of the *Argus*?"

"Oh, I wrote a bit of fluff about what the brothels are like just this afternoon, but made no mention of my… other adventures. Making accusations against Sir Bertram in print, without proof, hardly seemed prudent. And things are even worse than they seem. One of the men who hunted me in the brothel was present last night while I assisted Lord Pem—Pimm in his inquiries. He recognized me—or, rather, my disguise as Jenkins—and he must have been watching your house. He followed me out this morning." She told Winnie how Crippen had broken into her rooming house, and been chased away by her landlady.

"Oh, dear." Seeing Winnie frown was like watching a cloud drift across the sun. "You shouldn't have come over for lunch. You should have sent a letter with your regrets."

"What do you mean?"

"They saw Jenkins go into your house," Winnie said. "It's a rooming house, of course, so—"

"They have no reason to connect Jenkins with me, particularly," Ellie said—and then the light dawned. Or, more accurately, the darkness fell. She groaned. "Except shortly after sending Crippen off, I went to Lord Pembroke's house. They know Jenkins is connected to Pimm, and if they see you and I together, they will surmise that *I* know Pimm as well, and—"

"And that you know Jenkins. They will assume you were hiding him in your wardrobe, or something similar, when Crippen broke in. Which means Ellie Skye will go from being a complete non-entity to being a person who interests Sir Bertram very much. Moreover, as you are a journalist, they might concoct all sorts of conspiracy theories—that you and Jenkins intend to expose Abel Value, or Sir Bertram, with or without Pimm's involvement. And while Pimm is protected, to a certain extent, by his fame and his friends and family, you do not have quite so much armor." Winnie scraped the chicken off the plates and began putting the just-unpacked food away. "Walk away, Ellie. Go to your offices, somewhere with lots of people. I will let Pimm know the situation, and we will be in touch, and find a way to assure your safety until all this can be straightened out. Go, now."

Ellie nodded curtly, rose, and started to walk north… but paused. There were people watching them from beneath the nearby trees. She stepped back, and lowered herself again onto the blanket. "Winnie," she said. "Those women, watching us…"

"Mmm? Ellie, you should really—" She broke off. "There's something odd about them, isn't there? The way they're standing, so motionless…"

"I recognize that one," Ellie said, voice tight. "Delilah. I don't know if that's the name of the individual, or just of her… model."

Winnie swore, and it was a measure of how afraid Ellie was that she didn't even feel shocked by the profanity. "They're *clockwork*?" Winnie said. "But surely they're not sophisticated enough to…"

The clockwork women—there were six of them, rather overdressed for a day in the park, but they probably didn't have any clothing that wasn't meant for the bedroom or the ballroom—advanced from all directions, walking with what seemed to be very deliberate steps.

Winnie picked up her parasol and sighed. "I should have brought the parasol with an air-gun built into the handle. I was expecting a pleasant outing in the park. Not that a bullet hole would stop one of these things. Their movement is so *lifelike*, are you sure they're automatons? I think you're right that Oswald probably designed him, the man is a genius, whatever his other faults. I'd love to open one up and see how it works…"

"Winnie," Ellie said. "What do we *do*?"

"We can probably outrun them," Winnie said. "Their shoes are far less practical than ours. But I doubt they're here on their own. I presume they have a human operator, or at least an overseer. I suggest we make our way *quickly* to one of the more populous portions of the park." She stood, holding her parasol like a fencer's foil, and peered at the approaching automatons, who were now no more than a dozen yards away.

"Now, now, ladies. No need to run off." A young gentleman Ellie had never seen before sauntered out from between two trees. He had a cane in his hand, the end resting on his shoulder, and Ellie could easily imagine him swinging it like a cricket bat. He joined the artificial women, who now stood in a circle around Ellie and Winnie. All the clockwork figures were exactly the same height, Ellie realized, just a hair shorter than herself—and their faces were very nearly identical, too, apart from skin tone. The uniformity was eerie. "My employer would just like a word with you."

"Is this Crippen, Ellie?" Winnie asked.

"You wound me." The man pressed a hand to his chest. His mustache was black and neatly trimmed, his eyes blue and twinkling. "Crippen is a thug. He can't even follow someone without making a botch of it, apparently, so my employer sent me. My name is Ronald Carrington. I am the personal secretary of… well. Not Abel Value. Though he and I serve the same master, I suppose."

"You work for Oswald," Ellie said.

"I couldn't possibly comment, Miss *Skye*," he said, leaning hard on her pseudonym. "Your article about the families of those who've suffered the Constantine Affliction *moved* me, truly. Would you care to come with me now? My employer would love to speak with you about… oh, various matters."

"What makes you think we'll come quietly?" Winnie said.

He handed his cane to the automaton on his left, one with great masses of honey-blonde hair. She took the cane, a three-foot length of solid wood, in both hands, and snapped it as easily as Ellie would have broken a twig. "These devices are remarkable," Carrington said conversationally. "I have no *idea* why they were made so physically strong. That's not my area. But, the fact is, they are more than capable of subduing you, should you struggle. Now, let's just be civil—"

Winnie smashed him across the face with her parasol, and he squawked like a wounded pigeon and stumbled backward into one of the automatons, knocking her off her feet. They fell together in a tumble of limbs both flesh and artificial. "Run!" Winnie shouted. She hiked up her skirt and attempted to dodge between two of the other clockwork women. They seized her by the arms, and when she opened her mouth to scream, one of them covered her mouth with its dainty palm. Winnie bit down, but the automaton didn't react at all.

Feeling she was rather letting the side down, Ellie opened her mouth to shout for help, only to have one of the automatons grab her from behind and cover her mouth, too. Carrington stood up, wincing, and stroking his mustache back into place. "You loosened my teeth, Lady Pembroke. I knew you were of inferior breeding, but I never expected behavior so crass. Will you come peacefully, or shall I direct these fine examples of clockwork maidenhood to render you unconscious? Hmm? Oh, let her speak." He pointed to Ellie. The automaton removed its hand.

"I'd quite like to meet Mr. Oswald," Ellie said, surprised and pleased at how steady her own voice sounded. "Since he is the subject of a major article in tomorrow's paper. I should interview him for my follow-up story. 'Sir Bertram Responds to Allegations of Criminal Associations,' that sort of thing."

"I'm sure he'd be happy to answer all your questions," Carrington said. "He does love to talk. And you, Lady Pembroke?"

The automaton uncovered Winnie's mouth. "This is the part where I'm expected to say something like, wait until my husband finds out what you've done. And, it's true—Lord Pembroke can be ferocious when roused. But I'll let him concentrate on Oswald. *You*, Mr. Carrington, should be worrying about what I, personally, will do to you as retaliation for your actions."

"Now, now, Freddy," the man said, and smiled in a nastily insinuating way that Ellie didn't entirely understand. "That isn't very *ladylike*. Come along. We have a carriage waiting."

Pimm will find us, Ellie thought. *He knew we were going to the park, and he's good at following clues.* But as she was led away, she saw the clockwork automatons gathering up the picnic basket and the blanket, erasing every obvious sign of their presence and sudden departure.

Very well, then. If they could not expect outside salvation, they would have to save themselves.

A Man of Parts

Adam woke, and did not smell fire. Good. That meant Oswald hadn't attempted to burn the laboratory, which might have sealed Adam's fate. Such an action would have been profoundly ill-considered—the rooms were filled with explosive chemicals which would have burned uncontrollably, creating a conflagration that would surely have spread far and wide through the attached warehouses and other buildings, not to mention the tunnels. With Whitechapel already sealed off and uninhabitable, another great fire would have done away with most of the East End entirely—which many of London's upper class would have considered a small loss, probably. Adam had worried that Oswald would consider it an acceptable level of disaster in exchange for destroying all evidence of Adam's existence, but fortunately the scientist hadn't followed that course.

Adam dragged himself to a sitting position, pressing a hand to his chest. Blood oozed out weakly from the hole. The bullet lodged in his chest hurt abominably. He'd have to remove it.

Oswald had aimed for his heart, but Adam had taken the precaution of adding a second heart, in case his first one were ever damaged—humans had two kidneys, after all, which meant life could continue even if one failed, a redundancy that had always struck Adam as eminently sensible. Oswald had destroyed one heart, but the other was intact and still beating. Adam felt a bit dizzy and lightheaded, from the shock of his injury and the loss of blood. He tore the mask from his face and tossed it aside. Limping to his operating theater, he set up the array of mirrors he used when performing surgery on himself, and sat down on the hard table.

Adam had developed great control of his own bodily systems over the years. For the most part his autonomic system ticked on independently, but he could assert conscious control as necessary—that was how he was able to shut off all sensation from his injured leg and move with great speed when necessary, though it took a conscious effort. With concentration, he deadened the nerves in his chest, and, working with mirrors and harsh electric light, he cauterized a number of blood vessels and removed his now-ruined heart, dropping the shredded organ into a metal pan. The empty place in his chest made him melancholy, seeming entirely too symbolic, but he had neither time nor energy to do anything about that space right now. He settled for sewing himself up and bandaging the wound, tying yards of fabric around his chest. The lost blood was a problem. Adam was more robust than ordinary men, but even he could die if his body's vital fluids were sufficiently depleted. He had recently considered replacing his blood with the artificial substance he used for his reanimated cadavers, but was unsure of the long-term effects of such a transfusion, and so his heart still pumped ordinary human blood, though of a dozen intermingled types.

For now, he'd settle for eating lots of rare meat to replenish his lost iron. The hungering dead locked away in their chamber would have to go hungry today—he would feast on the kidneys and other offal he'd purchased for them from the stockyards.

After he'd eaten, and felt somewhat refreshed, he limped around his laboratory, to see what damage Oswald had done. Most of Adam's notes had been left behind—that was a blow, actually, to find that his research hadn't been worth stealing—but his prototype for the new battery was missing. Oswald was more comfortable with mechanical innovations anyway.

The door to the main tunnel, which led to the neighboring cellar, would not open, and was seemingly blocked from the other side. Adam wondered if Oswald had filled the opening with rubble or had it bricked up. The entry to the house above was also impassable, the trap door utterly immovable even for someone of Adam's considerable strength. More bricks?

"Sealed in like Fortunato," Adam murmured. "For the love of… God." Or so Oswald doubtless hoped. Why burn the laboratory when all access from the outside world could be sealed off? And that way, if Oswald ever had cause to return for Adam's research or equipment, he could bring a few men with pickaxes and do so. Several of Adam's other secret tunnels— including ones he would have sworn Oswald didn't know about—were also sealed, and all from the outside, suggesting that Oswald's attempted murder and successful entombment had not been hasty decisions, but carefully planned ones.

But Adam had learned long ago to make plans of his own, and secondary plans, and tertiary ones. In one corner of his laboratory, surrounded by other industrial detritus, there stood the huge, rusting boiler from what must have once been an immense steam engine. Adam put his shoulder against the boiler and pushed it aside, a feat no ordinary man could have accomplished on his own, and revealed another trap door. Once Adam satisfied himself that the door opened, and the way down the iron ladder was clear, he let the door fall closed again. Only then did he return to his work table and take the cloth off the apparatus that held Margaret's brain.

He reconnected the tubes that supplied air to the speaking tubes—then froze. In his haste when Oswald arrived, he had failed to disconnect the wires that connected Margaret's sensory apparatus. Which meant…

When he reactivated the speaking device, at first he thought it was malfunctioning—but then he realized the sound was simply inarticulate wailing. "Margaret," he said. "Margaret, are you all right?"

The wailing ceased. "Adam? Is that you?"

"Yes."

"I heard such terrible things! I thought I heard—a gunshot."

"Yes. My… visitor… fired on me, but as you can hear, I survived."

"Are you injured?"

Hearing such concern in the voice of a woman who'd lost her entire *body* was strangely heartening. "Not grievously. I will be fine. I am sorry you were frightened."

"Did he really mean the terrible things he said? That he hopes to… to do something awful to the Queen?"

"He is an evil man," Adam said. He did not, himself, believe in such concepts as "good" and "evil" in absolute terms, but a more nuanced explanation would be exhausting, and he was still very tired. "I am also sorry I did not attend to you immediately—I had to see to my own wounds, and make sure there was no further danger."

"Will he return?" Margaret asked.

Adam shook his head, then remembered she couldn't see, and smiled ruefully at his own foolishness. "I do not believe so. He has attempted to seal me inside my own laboratory, to make this place a grave, but fear not, there are still means to escape."

"This is not... a proper hospital, is it?" she said.

"No. No, Margaret. I am a physician, an expert in anatomy, but I do not work in a hospital. I had a private patron who funded my research."

"Mr. Value," Margaret said. "He was my employer, too, or he employed my employers. Is that why I was brought to you? Because you work for Mr. Value?"

"I had certain... business arrangements, with Mr. Value, and yes, that is why you were brought here—I sometimes tend to people injured in his employ. But, no, he was not my patron. Mr. Value and I shared the *same* patron, actually, a wealthy man with diverse interests in science and industry. He paid for the research that made it possible for me to save your life. Alas, he has withdrawn his support, as you heard. But I have other resources."

"Will I ever be able to see, again?" Margaret said. "To feel my arms and legs? Or am I to be blind and paralyzed forever?"

Adam pressed his cheek against the cool glass of the jar that held her brain. "I will do everything in my power to see you made whole again," Adam said, closing his eyes. "And my powers are considerable."

Conqueror's Words

Pimm went to Hyde Park, to all of Freddy's favorite picnic spots, but there was no sign of his wife or of Ellie. He tried to decide whether he should worry, but couldn't see any reason why he should. Oswald had taken an interest in Pimm, true, but there was no reason that interest would extend to Freddy or to Ellie—not as long as they didn't know Pimm's "assistant" Jenkins and Ellie were one and the same.

The two of them were probably just off… shopping, or something. That was enough cause for worry on its own. The thought of Ellie in Freddy's clutches was harrowing enough—Pimm's old friend had always possessed a streak of mischief as big as St. Paul's Cathedral, and Pimm shuddered to think how Ellie would react if Freddy tried to play matchmaker, or even made a few of her usual sly double-entendres. Turning into a woman certainly hadn't altered Freddy's sense of humor much, apart from adding a certain additional flavoring of bitterness, which was understandable.

Pimm stood aimlessly under a tree for a while, considering the recently-replenished flask in the pocket of his jacket. The temptation to sit under a tree drinking the afternoon away was a powerful one, but he felt he should do something more useful, if at all possible. Value's enigmatic statements and Ellie's own hints about Bertram Oswald's involvement with the old criminal hinted at some greater danger or conspiracy. He wanted to talk to Ellie, and find out what she knew, and—perhaps even better—what she suspected.

He could go home and wait for them to return, but he possessed sufficient self-knowledge to realize that he'd just end up profoundly drunk
if given unfettered access to his personal bar just now. He was anxious,
and uncertain, and those were states of mind the bottle cured... but only
temporarily. And while a spot of oblivion seemed a just reward for his
recent work—stopping a murderer, and sending one of London's major
criminals scampering off in fear for his life—there were too many other
mysteries to unravel first.

He paced around the tree, looking at the grass and trees and flowers and
the construction off in the distance, but really looking inward. All right,
Oswald, then. What did he know about the man? He'd become famous
a few years ago, just after Prince Albert was locked away for his adulter-
ous crimes against the Queen. He'd opened a factory building alchemical
lamps for domestic use and export, employing hundreds of skilled and
unskilled workers. That innovation was essentially what earned him his
knighthood, if Pimm recalled, and from that point onward, he'd become
an intimate confidant of the Queen's—though how he'd accomplished
that specifically was a bit of a mystery. (Pimm had met his monarch on
two occasions, both in the company of his esteemed older brother, but
even if he'd wanted to turn those formal introductions into a personal
relationship, he'd have no idea how to go about it.) Oswald had revived
the disgraced Royal Alchemical Society, which had disbanded decades
before after definitively failing to transmute base metals to gold or decant
the *elixir vitae*. He gave to charity. He constructed municipal hothouses
to grow vegetables and fruit in the winter. He had very little in the way
of a chin. And...

That was basically the sum total of Pimm's knowledge about the man.
If Oswald was truly involved with Value—if Sir Bertram was the powerful man Value feared—it would behoove Pimm to learn more about his
adversary. The time had come for a visit to Pimm's friend the professor.

He flagged down a cab, settling for one of the despised two-wheeled
open carts despite how dreadfully exposed they always left him feeling.
He directed the cab to King's College, an institution founded just a few
decades earlier to provide advanced education to the middle class and to
allow secular schooling for nonconformists of all stripes. Pimm, who had

attended Magdalen College at Oxford, looked upon the upstart King's with a certain amount of reflexive disdain, though he was in sympathy with the goals of its founding, and was immensely fond of a gentleman who worked in the school of applied sciences, with a specialty in alchemy.

The cab dropped him a short walk from the wing where Professor Conqueror kept his office. Pimm strolled along, marveling as always at the astonishing youth of the students walking and talking in little groups all about him. Had he ever been so young? He'd certainly never been so *earnest*, or serious about his schoolwork, but then, he'd had the family fortune to fall back on. Seriousness was not a necessity for him.

Once up the broad stone steps and into the musty hallways, he climbed a flight of stairs and proceeded down a narrow hall until he reached an office tucked away around a final corner. The door was open, and the office beyond was graced with overflowing bookshelves, a large dead plant in a pot, and a massive desk that must have dated back to the founding of Londinium, and seen hard use ever since.

Pimm rapped the doorframe with his knuckles, and Professor William Conqueror—oh, the teasing he must have suffered as a boy with a name like *that*!—raised one sausage-thick finger and continued peering at the pages of an immense book on the desk before him. "Just a minute, just a minute, I'm on the trail of a specious argument… ah ha!" He slammed the volume shut and looked at Pimm triumphantly. "Begs the question, doesn't it? He's got so many layers of postulates that it takes a bit to unsnarl, but the whole towering edifice rests on an unsupported and indefensible premise, as if I'm supposed to believe him just because he *asserts*—"

Professor Conqueror blinked. He was a big red-headed bear of a man, like something from an ancestral English nightmare of Viking raiders, with more beard than was good for him. "Pimm! If you're here hoping for more of my good brandy, I'm afraid you've wasted your time, because it has all mysteriously vanished."

"I've come for your brain, not your bottle," Pimm said, lifting a heap of books from a chair and setting them aside before seating himself in their place.

"Oh ho. Another mysterious crime scene reeking of strange chemicals? Did you bring a bottle of peculiar residues scraped from the palms of a corpse? I do so look forward to your little puzzles."

"I'm actually looking for information about a—well, I suppose you'd call him one of your colleagues. Bertram Oswald."

Conqueror leaned back in his chair as best he could, though there wasn't much room to do so. "Oswald, eh? I'm hardly an expert on the man, though we've met, of course, and I'm a member of the society he runs. Did you want to know anything in particular?"

"I don't know *what* I want to know," Pimm said honestly. "Why don't you tell me whatever you find most interesting?"

"Mmmm." Conqueror stroked his beard. "You puzzle me, Pimm. Oswald hardly seems like someone who'd run in any of your circles—neither criminal nor criminologist, and certainly not a gourmand or bon vivant."

"Do you really need an explanation for my interest?" Pimm said. "I dare say I could make up something plausible, if you'd like."

"Oh, no, don't bother prevaricating on my account, you know I prefer it when matters are kept on a firmly theoretical basis anyway. All right. Oswald. The first thing you should know is, he has the most brilliant scientific mind in England." Conqueror began to fill his pipe with his own blend of tobacco, which Pimm knew from bitter experience had a stench like rancid camel-hide. The professor said, meditatively, "Well, he may not be absolutely *the* greatest mind currently working in the sciences— there's a young English mathematician who published a treatise on the binomial theorem seven or eight years ago that is frankly astonishing, and caused quite a stir in Europe. They say he's working on a book about the dynamics of asteroids now, which I await keenly. He'll be someone to keep a close eye on, if he lives up to his early promise. One can never tell with these young—"

Pimm, who was accustomed to Conqueror's rather roundabout lecturing technique, provided a gentle nudge back toward the proper course: "You were saying about Oswald?"

"Ah, yes. Oswald is widely regarded as the most towering intellect to grace our nation since Newton. That said, precious little is known about him, or his family. He comes from money, I assume, or at least enough money to finance his own studies and experiments for many years. His first interest was in the biological sciences, and he spent some unspecified number of years abroad, in the jungles of Africa and South

America, collecting specimens. Apparently he discovered some quite ground-breaking things about frogs or lizards or some such, though I misremember the details—it's not my field. When he was not traveling, he lived in some great pile in the north someplace, where he had green-houses full of exotic plants and laboratories and workshops aplenty. At some point he took an interest in alchemy, and that's where his true genius blossomed. He studied the behavior of gases, and fluids, and plasma, and how to combine them. That's how he made his fortune, or at least, his current fortune—occasionally popping up from the realms of pure research to produce something with a practical application. Alchemical lamps, improved batteries, innovative magnetic medical devices, that sort of thing. And of course he designed the new contain-ment barriers and the dome erected a few years ago around the ruins of Whitechapel. His services to the country are legion, though I suspect they're incidental—he does whatever interests him, and occasionally those interests intersect with the needs of the people. He even took a medical degree, some years ago, having become interested in maladies of the human body, infectious diseases, and the like—that's how he first met the Queen, you know."

Pimm raised an eyebrow. "No. I hadn't heard?"

"He was studying the germ theory with Pasteur," Conqueror said. "Os-wald was instrumental in saving Prince Albert's life, in fact. Of course, it was Pasteur's innovations that made the difference, and say what you will about Oswald, he doesn't try to take credit for the achievements of others—but I gather the Queen was grateful for his assistance, and their friendship, ah, blossomed from there."

"And when Prince Albert's infidelity was revealed, when the Affliction transformed him into a woman, Oswald and the Queen became…. more intimate. Or so the rumors say."

Conqueror shrugged, puffing his foul pipe. "I am hardly intimate with the court, but I've heard the same rumors, yes. Oswald is by all accounts less interested in science now than in *society*, and having the Queen's ear can't hurt."

"What do you mean society? You don't mean… galas and things? Balls? Charities?" Pimm detested all such functions, except those which featured a well-stocked bar.

"No, no. I mean he wants to *improve* society. How many philosophers over the centuries have lamented the tendency of mankind toward evil, and laziness, and selfishness, and cruelty? How many men have dreamed of a better world, of societies that operated on sounder principles than 'take what you can and don't worry about the consequences'?"

"I would guess... easily eight or ten men," Pimm said. "Perhaps as many as a dozen."

"Ha," Conqueror said. "The difference between most philosophers and Sir Bertram is that the latter is a *practical* man. When he sees a problem, he becomes obsessed with solving it. And the little nagging voice that most of us have in our heads—the voice that might say, 'That's insurmountable,' or, 'It's more than one man can accomplish,' or, 'It's really none of my business anyway'—Oswald doesn't *have* that voice. He just... gets on with it."

"Mmmm," Pimm said. "One wonders what the voices in his head *do* say. So he's proposed reforms to the Queen, then?"

"Indeed. And she is amenable, at least to some of them, or so I hear."

"Of course she is," Pimm said. "She's always happy to support good ideas. She's been ceding power to her ministers for decades. It's really one of her more admirable qualities."

"A bit problematic for Oswald, though. If he had an absolute monarch as his confidante instead, he'd be able to put a lot more of his ideas into practice. I've been to a few of his fundraisers and lectures, mostly just for the *hors d'oeuvre*. Some of his notions are... fairly radical."

"Such as?"

"Sterilizing criminals."

"Oh. Is *that* all."

"The notion being that criminal behavior is an inherited trait, like hair or eye color. If criminals can't breed, they can't pass on those traits." Conqueror blew a few malformed smoke rings. "Of course, even if you grant Oswald's premise, the problem with sterilizing criminals is that, by the time they're caught, they've often bred already, sometimes quite often. So Oswald wants to catch them before their criminal tendencies manifest themselves."

"Seems a bit tricky," Pimm said, "since a criminal is defined as one who commits a *crime*. Catching a criminal before they commit a crime would be like catching a bird before it hatched. You can't do it. It's not a *bird* yet."

"But if you knew it was going to be a hideous terrible bird while it was still in the egg, you could always smash the egg," Conqueror said. "Not that Oswald suggests getting to these young criminals quite *that* early. He was a member of the Phrenological Society—"

"Phrenology? Isn't that, what, looking at bumps on a person's head to find out the nature of their character?" Pimm said. "Didn't that go out of fashion twenty years ago?"

"Oswald remains a proponent of the theory, in a way," Conqueror said. "Though he now believes you can observe fluctuations in an individual's personal magnetic field—using a device of his own invention, of course—to discern whether they have, say, musical aptitude, or an innate comprehension of spatial relationships, or deeply-buried murderous impulses. Scan children, and if they show undesirable traits…"

Pimm was aghast. "What? Make eunuchs of them?"

Conqueror shook his head. "No, he has some sort of chemical approach, I understand, to prevent reproduction."

"A chemical of his own invention, I don't doubt," Pimm said.

Conqueror nodded. "True, but then, who else would create such a thing? There's not a great deal of demand for nostrums that sterilize *children*. Oswald believes that through an aggressive program of early screening and intervention, we could eliminate criminal tendencies within a few generations."

Pimm, who would have been saddened by the extinction of criminals in the same way a lepidopterist would be saddened by the extinction of butterflies, frowned. "But what does 'criminal tendencies' even mean? All men have the capacity for criminal acts, if circumstances turn against them—consider the proverbial man who steals bread only to feed his starving family."

"I didn't say I agreed with his idea," Conqueror said. "Merely that Oswald espouses it. Frankly, I find it abhorrent. What if his bloody machine is wrong—even *once*? And no machine is perfect. Moreover, how long before he expands his definition of 'criminal' to apply to anyone who offends his personal sensibilities? To extend to… I'm sure he'd call them 'deviants'… of various stripes—political, personal, or otherwise?"

Pimm nodded. Conqueror was what one might call a "confirmed bach-elor," and while Pimm had made a point of never speculating on the man's personal proclivities or the reasons for his unmarried status, he'd occasionally wondered. "Very troubling."

"Indeed. But Oswald's ideas haven't gotten much traction—too many objections from too many groups, fortunately, and all the ministers look terribly askance at Oswald and his wild ideas, and wish the Queen would stop spending so much time with him. Oswald is entirely too willing to disrupt the status quo. But, fortunately, he is also… mercurial. He's already effectively abandoned his magnetic personality adjudicators. He's always leaping off on some new passion, leaving projects half-done once they cease to amuse him."

"Hmmm. Any idea about his latest interests?"

"I hear he's been bothering the astronomers lately," Conqueror said. "Turning his attention to the stars."

"At least he's not likely to do much damage up there," Pimm said.

Conqueror coughed. "You haven't heard the rumors about the *aurora anglais*, then?"

"What, the lights in the sky? Frankly, I've barely *seen* them."

"You tend to spend your evenings in well-lit rooms, as I recall, or in the bright streets of central London. In the country, with the sky unstained by the light of a thousand street lamps, the *aurora* are… rather more noticeable."

"It's just the Northern Lights, though." Pimm frowned. "I mean, you can see them in Scotland from time to time anyway, I've heard. They've just been… more common, lately, yes?"

"It's virtually unheard of to see the *aurora borealis* this far south," Con-queror said. "And every night for two months? Unprecedented. And those who have seen the *borealis* before say it's not the same, here—the colors are different. The patterns. The intensity of the lights."

"Where does Oswald come in?"

Conqueror glanced toward the door, as if just now noticing that it still stood open. Pimm stood, looked into the empty hall, and returned. "We're in private," he said, shutting the door behind him.

The old professor smiled tightly. "It's silly of me, it's just, Oswald has given a great deal of money to the college, especially to the Alchemy department—you know, we were calling it the Chemistry department when I started here, wanting to escape images of medieval men in star-patterned robes boiling beakers of lion's blood, but Oswald insisted the old name was best... Sorry, I've drifted again. Ah. Yes. It occurs to me that I shouldn't speak ill of someone who has so generously contributed to the institution where I am employed."

"You're saying you won't tell me?" Pimm said.

"Of course not! I just want to make sure I'm not overheard, and that you keep it in confidence." He leaned across the desk. "Oswald is an expert in many things, but magnetism is one of his longtime passions. There are many theories about the origin of the *aurora borealis*, but some hypothesize that it involves fluctuations in Earth's magnetic field. I've overheard some of the scholars from other departments wonder aloud, in a way that seems like a joke but isn't, quite, whether or not Oswald has embarked on another of his great experiments—if he's tried to manipulate the *Earth's* magnetic field, for some reason, and in the process... Well. Broken the sky."

"The Earth's magnetic field. That's important, is it? For compasses and things?"

"No one really knows how important the field is, Pimm, but..." Conqueror licked his lips. "Some think it is a sort of... suit of armor for the Earth, protecting us from the hellish radiations of the sun, and from even more dangerous bombardments from space. If the field were to fail... Dinosaurs were the dominant species on this planet, once. Not any more. We could become extinct ourselves."

"Surely not even *Oswald* would risk such a disruption?"

"If he thought the outcome might be *interesting*?" Conqueror said. "Then I think he might."

All of this was fascinating—and a bit terrifying—but it didn't give Pimm any idea at all of how Oswald might be involved with Value. "Does he have any interest in, ah... automatons?"

"Oswald? You might say so. He caused a minor scandal when he suggested that, in the wake of the Constantine Affliction, mechanical women could be created to serve the needs that men could no longer trust living women to fulfill." Conqueror shuddered. "Not long after, the first of the clockwork comfort houses opened. Someone must have heard his idea and seen the profit-making potential."

Ah ha. "Who *makes* the automatons, though?" Pimm said. "I've never seen them, but I've heard they're astonishingly lifelike."

Conqueror puffed thoughtfully. "You know, I've no idea. I would assume it's some mad tinkerer with a basement full of unmentionable items who seized the moment and sold his personal playthings to the brothel owners when the opportunity arose. But now that you mention it, there are *dozens* of the things, aren't there, which suggests a larger manufacturing operation... I truly don't know. You don't think it's *Oswald*, do you?"

Pimm shrugged. "Merely curious, that's all."

"He certainly has the technical expertise," Conqueror mused.

"And if he suggested the very idea himself.... from what you've told me he has a tendency to invent profitable solutions to problems he identifies himself."

"He hardly needs the money... but I suppose he might create such things if it *amused* him. Seems a bit crass. I can't imagine the Queen would approve."

"It would be quite a scandal," Pimm said. "Especially given the business partners one would need to thrive in such an undertaking."

"The sort of criminals one could identify *without* a magnetic personality adjudicator," Conqueror observed. "Well, well, well. I begin to understand why you came here to see me today."

"Whatever do you mean? I'm only here to visit an old friend. And I really should be going. But before I do—have you heard of a man named Adams? A scientist, working in private research?"

"I can't say I have. What's his field of study?"

"Ah. Human physiology, broadly, but more specifically... the persistence of personality after death, I suppose."

"Spiritualism," Conqueror said, dismissively. "Hardly a science. Wishful thinking and delusion, mainly."

"I've no doubt you're right," Pimm replied. He bid his friend good day, and set off across the campus, pondering. So Oswald was the inventor of the clockwork concubines, and he'd gone into business with Value. Of course, the man wouldn't want that connection to come out, and he would be averse to a scandal—but to the point of making Value fear for his life? *Someone* was overreacting there. Unless there was more to the relationship between the scientist and the crime lord. Something niggled at the back of Pimm's brain. Something about the Constantine Affliction…

He stopped in the shade of a flowering tree, and stared at nothing. Oswald had studied germ theory. Oswald liked grand social experiments. Oswald had saved Prince Albert's life and met the Queen in the process, and later, after Prince Albert was locked away as an adulterer, he'd become close to the Queen. The Queen could help him make *more* of his grand social experiments a reality. Oswald had invented clockwork automatons—unproven, but grant the premise—which had proven quite profitable for him, and were a direct response to the Constantine Affliction.

Why, only yesterday Pimm had suggested to Ellie that the Affliction might have been created intentionally as a tool of revolution or social disruption, though he'd later dismissed the idea as his own tendency to seek a culprit for every misfortune that afflicted the world—if there was a crime, it stood to reason there must be a criminal. Natural disasters and plagues were not crimes… but what if the Constantine Affliction wasn't natural? What if *that* was the secret Value knew? Discovering Oswald's connection to the brothels led inevitably to Value, after all, and that connection could be the true danger to Sir Bertram, far more than any scandal about his involvement with clockwork women. But why would Value know anything about a man-made plague? Oswald would hardly have confided something like that in such a man—

"Value," Pimm said, and closed his eyes. What was another word for Value?

Worth.

Pimm hurried toward the nearest street. He needed answers. But first, he needed a cab. And before that, a drink wouldn't be amiss. He patted the flask in his pocket, promising himself he'd only take one sip, or perhaps two. Sobriety was all well and good, but it could only take one so far.

Captivations

~⁓◦⊙◦⁓~

The ride was awkward, of course. Crammed in the back of a closed carriage with Carrington and two of his clockwork women, everyone jammed together uncomfortably close. In those narrow confines, Carrington chose to rely on a pistol pointed discreetly at Winnie's midsection to maintain order. Ellie was a bit offended to see that Winnie was apparently considered more of a threat, though based on their actions at the picnic, it was a reasonable assumption. They bumped along the cobbles for a bit in silence, but Ellie couldn't bear it, so she began to speak. "Mr. Carrington, is it? How did you come to work for Mr. Oswald?"

He shifted the pistol in her direction. "Don't speak, Miss Skye. I'm in no mood to be interviewed."

Winnie snorted. "Why shouldn't we talk? You won't shoot us. Not here and now, anyway. You're a *secretary*. You can't make decisions on your own. And Oswald wants to see us alive."

A muscle in Carrington's jaw twitched. "Fine. Chatter away, ladies. But do not expect answers from me."

"I keep notes, you know," Ellie said. "I *am* a reporter. I have written down my observations, and my suspicions. If something happens to me, and those notes are found, questions will be asked—"

Carrington chuckled. "Considering what will happen in this city soon, the disappearance of a troublesome lady reporter will hardly be a matter of concern."

"What do you mean?" Winnie demanded. "What's going to happen?"

"Why ask me?" Carrington said. "I'm just a *secretary*. Speak again, and I'll have the clockwork women press their hands over your mouths. Just take a moment to think about where those hands have been, and the *last* things they likely touched, before you decide whether to test me, hmm?"

Ellie shivered, but fell silent. She'd assumed Oswald's interest in her was meant solely to prevent her from revealing his connection to the clockwork brothels and criminals like Abel Value. But what if there was some deeper motive? What if Oswald was involved in something more serious than dabbling in clockwork whores? That alone would be embarrassing, certainly, but it wasn't *illegal*, and hardly seemed to justify a response that included kidnapping. Her reporter's instincts were not so much tingling now as screaming. There was a story here. A significant one. She was in an astonishingly good position to write that story. Assuming she lived long enough.

Pimm knocked on the door and stepped into Whistler's office. The policeman looked up from a heap of papers on his messy desk and frowned. His hair was disarrayed, and the dark shadows of exhaustion hollowed his eyes. "Pimm? How did you hear so quickly?"

A chill cut through the warmth of recently-imbibed brandy. "Hear what?"

Whistler sat back in his creaking chair and sighed a long exhalation. "Ah. I assumed… Our Mr. Worth, the lady-killer. He is no longer with us."

Pimm stared. "Did he—escape?"

Whistler shook his head. "Escaped mortal judgment, maybe. Dead in his cell when we checked on him this morning. We never even had the chance to interrogate him properly."

"Did he do himself in?" Pimm asked. Worth hadn't seemed to suffer from much in the way of a guilty conscience, and he'd certainly wanted desperately to go on living the night before, but sitting in a dark cell had a way of altering one's viewpoint. Pimm would have been disappointed at losing a potential witness against Value, if he hadn't known the old villain planned to run in fear for his life.

"No," Whistler said. "No sign of anything like that, he was just on the floor, cold. Could be a heart attack, I suppose."

Picking up on Whistler's doubtful tone, he said, "Or?"

"If I thought anyone had a reason," Whistler said carefully, "and that anyone had *access*, I might suspect poison."

"Not to impugn the honor of your jailers," Pimm said, "but someone with a sufficiently large purse could potentially buy access, don't you think?"

"Yes." Whistler's voice was as tired and grim as his expression. "You said Worth could give us evidence against Value. Do you think Value might have brought about the man's death?"

Pimm hesitated. He *didn't*, actually. Value had other worries, chiefly that Worth might reveal things about Value's real master, Bertram Oswald. But Pimm did not even remotely have enough evidence to bring up Oswald's name in the office of a London police inspector. "I suppose it's possible," Pimm said. This at least provided him with an opening to ask the question he'd actually come for. "What do we know about Abel Value, really?"

Whistler frowned. "I have his file here." He opened an envelope and spilled out a scant few documents. "There's precious little, really. He's never been arrested, though we've questioned him enough times. He claims to be a respectable businessman, and we know he owns a few taverns and, of course, the clockwork brothels, which are all kept scrupulously legal, absolutely free of human prostitutes. But we also know he still employs living women, on the streets, through a complex network of employees— know it, I say, but we cannot *prove* it. We suspect he's involved with smuggling, too, and various thefts, but he keeps himself above such activity personally, and we've yet to find a witness who'll testify against him. I shouldn't tell you this, but… Mr. Worth isn't the first suspicious death we've seen. You know about Martinson, of course, which *did* look like a suicide, but might not have been. We've also had people recant their sworn statements suddenly, only to be seen later wearing fine fur coats or smoking an altogether better class of cigar than before. Value is an *organized* criminal. He'll bribe when he can, and kill when he can't. He's not a bloodthirsty madman. He just sees people as either impediments or advantages in his business, and treats them as such, without regard for their humanity."

"That fits with my own knowledge of the man," Pimm said. "But where is he *from*? He must be in his late forties, at least. What did he do before becoming a criminal mastermind?"

Whistler shrugged. "No idea. We'd never heard of him before, oh, three years ago? He has made no public statements at all about his history, though his accent suggests he's a longtime Londoner. He seemed to appear fully formed, like a dark Athena burst from the head of a particularly thuggish Zeus."

"And he came on the scene just as the first cases of the Constantine Affliction were diagnosed," Pimm mused.

"Hmm? I suppose that's right, yes."

"What do we know about the late Mr. Worth's wife?"

Whistler frowned. "Do you mean can we reach her, to notify her about Mr. Worth's death? She vanished, you know, she was one of the earliest transformations we heard about, her husband came in raving about how his wife had become a man and run away."

"She was, in fact, the *very* first victim," Pimm said. "At least, the first ever reported. But what do we know about her before she ran off, I mean?"

"Mabel Worth," Whistler said. "She was notorious. Most of the criminal classes called her *Madam* Worth. She'd been a prostitute herself, in her youth, but when she got older she took up a management position. Ran a bawdy house of the very lowest repute in Southwark, while her husband oversaw a group of girls who worked out on the street. Nothing illegal about all that at the time, unsavory thought it might have been, but there were always rumors that the Worths would snatch young women visiting from the country off the street, dose them with laudanum, and press them into service. Madam Worth was by all accounts far more fearsome than her husband, known to thrash with a riding crop any customer who wasn't quick enough to pay his bill. A nasty piece of work, always with an eye on the bottom line, ruthless and pragmatic. By contrast, her husband was a bit of a mess, often arrested for public drunkenness, or for beating on his women openly in the street. Madam Worth was certainly the more dangerous of the two."

"And she turned into a man... and vanished... and, perhaps only weeks later, you first heard the name Abel Value? Mabel Worth vanishes, and *Abel Value* appears?"

Whistler stared at him, and, true to his name, let out a long, low whistle. "Pimm. That's quite a leap to make, based on a chance similarity of names."

"And a similarity of timing," Pimm said. "And of business interest. And of general personality. Madam Worth was a formidable woman in a world dominated by formidable men, yes? The type of woman who might see her transformation into a man not as a tragedy, or a terrible judgment from God, or a jape by the Devil—but as an *opportunity*?"

"It's a colorful theory," Whistler said. "And there's a certain pleasing symmetry to the idea. But Value had *money*, enough to set up and stock those clockwork brothels, and those aren't cheap. Madam Worth did well enough, I suppose, but she couldn't have made that kind of money."

"Perhaps she had investors," Pimm mused. "And her husband was living suspiciously well, wasn't he, for an out-of-work pimp? That suggests someone was paying for his lifestyle too, doesn't it?"

"Even if Madam Worth did become Abel Value, I'm not sure it changes anything. There's no law against having your sex changed by a *plague*, or changing your name, either. Value's crimes aren't any different if he began life as Madam Worth. It might change his status in the eyes of his fellow criminals, I suppose, if they found out he'd begun life as a woman, but legally speaking…"

"Oh, I know," Pimm said thoughtfully. "Though as I understand it, the rulings that have come down say that the sex you were at birth *remains* your sex, legally speaking, even after a transformation. I suppose that means, since women aren't sentenced to work the treadmill at Newgate Prison, Value might be spared *that* indignity if he is indeed Mabel Worth."

"Deucedly peculiar law, I've always thought," Whistler said. "The Affliction isn't even grounds for divorce—which means if a husband is transformed, two women can be married, or two men, if the wife changes. Though legally speaking I suppose they're still 'man' and 'wife.' No wonder so many change their names, run away, and try to pass."

"It's all down to inheritance laws," Pimm said, shrugging. "If an eldest daughter transformed into a man, she might inherit over her brothers, and a son transformed into a daughter might lose his inheritance. The rich have a certain amount of influence when it comes to making the laws, and they are loath to suffer change or disruption."

"All I inherited from my father was a pocketwatch," Whistler said. "But I suppose in a family like yours, it matters."

"I pray every day for the health of my elder brother," Pimm said, "so that it *won't* matter. Do I look like a Marquess to you?"

"No," Whistler said. "You have entirely too strong a chin."

Pimm rose. "Thanks for the information, old man. You've helped me satisfy my curiosity, at any rate. I suppose I might drop by Abel Value's office—at least, the last one I know about—and let him know of his husband's unfortunate demise."

"Assuming Worth *is* Value's late husband," Whistler said. "And assuming Value didn't actually order the man's murder himself."

"The wonderful thing about being an independent operator," Pimm said, "is that I can go merrily on my way fueled solely by assumptions, without your need for tedious minutiae like proof and evidence."

"And here I thought the wonderful thing about being independent was your freedom to be very nearly drunk by midday," Whistler said.

Pimm winced, and turned the wince into a smile. He'd tried to speak very clearly, slowly, and soberly—but overly-precise diction could reveal a drunkard just as well as slurring. "I don't know how you do it," Pimm said. "The kind of work you and I do, entirely sober? The mind rebels."

A Cage of One's Own

The carriage pulled in through the oversized doors of a warehouse, which closed after them, and then Ellie and Winnie were herded into the interior gloom. The space was echoing and vast, with birds fluttering in the rafters, and great heaps of twisted ironwork piled up at seemingly random intervals on the hard floor, along with large objects covered by sheets. Gray light filtered in through windows high up close to the ceiling, and a single alchemical lamp of the tall free-standing variety cast a pool of light in the dimness. "This way," Carrington said, prodding Ellie in the side with the tip of Winnie's parasol, herding them toward the light. "Into the cage."

Ellie drew up short, staring. The nearest pile of scrap metal resolved in her light-starved eyes into a great metal cage, of the sort seen at the zoological gardens at Regent's Park, suitable for confining ferocious lions or tigers or leopards. "You mean to *cage* us?"

"Would you prefer being tied up with ropes and chains?" Carrington said. "I could be persuaded to go that route instead. My employer wishes a captive audience, but he left the specific method of that captivity up to me."

"Tying them up might be best." Crippen emerged from the shadows—he was the one who'd shut the door after them, Ellie surmised—and cracked his knuckles. "You can't trust a woman, especially if she's got a frying pan or a flower vase near to hand."

"I will bow to your expertise in such matters." Carrington didn't bother to hide his sneer, obviously considering himself superior to Crippen. As if he wasn't someone's dog as well. "What say you, ladies?"

"The cage will do," Winnie said, in the tone of one consenting to be sold a new settee for the parlor. "It seems roomy enough." She strolled into the cage—the ceiling was just inches above the top of her head—and Ellie swallowed her trepidation and followed. Carrington swung the door shut and fitted an enormous iron key into the lock, turning it to produce a *clank* that seemed to ring in Ellie's ears with a distressing finality. "See to the horses, would you?" he called to Crippen, who grumbled and then set about leading the animals and the carriage away.

Carrington dragged a wooden chair close to the cage, near the lamp, and sat down, beaming at the women inside. Ellie stood with her back against the bars in the far corner, while Winnie lounged close to the front, elbow resting on a crossbar, one ankle crossed over the other, managing to look entirely at ease. Carrington glanced around, watched Crippen lead the horses off into the darkness, and returned his gaze to his captives. "I'm so sorry I don't have separate accommodations for the men and the women in your party," he said. "I know it's terribly uncivilized. You don't mind, do you, Freddy?"

"You are a cad, sir," Winnie said, in a tone that dripped with ice. She turned to Ellie. "I should tell you something, Ellie, if only to spoil Carrington's cruel fun, though I'm not sure why he's taken such an elemental dislike to me. It was only a glancing blow across the face with a parasol. I'm sure a man with a face as eminently slap-able as his has suffered worse. Ellie, I must confess—I was not born a woman. Until two years ago, I was a Frederick, not a Winifred."

"Oh, boo," Carrington said. "Spoilsport. I'd planned to draw that out a bit more, with many vicious remarks about your private parts. What will I do to pass the time now?"

Ellie blinked. "You... are a victim of the Constantine Affliction?"

"I'd never call myself a *victim* of anything," Winnie said, "but, yes, I contracted the illness. I was not always... cautious in my choice of intimate friends, I'm afraid."

Ellie had met people transformed by the Affliction before, but only in the course of researching her articles. She'd begun to think of Winnie as a friend, and to find out there was the mind and soul of a *man* in that body was a shock. She blurted out the first question that came to mind: "Does Pimm know?"

Winnie raised one elegant eyebrow. "Yes, of course. We've been best friends since we were boys. When I... changed... I knew my family would not be understanding about my new station in life. Far better for Freddy, who was always an unreliable chap, to take a long vacation in America without prior notice. Pimm offered to make an honest woman of me."

"But—but do you—" Ellie blushed.

"Oh, heavens, no!" Winnie said, and actually shuddered. "I know some people who are transformed find their, ah, preference of partners changed as well, but I feel no attraction to men, which is in some ways deucedly inconvenient. And even if I *did* want to be intimate with a man—with *Pimm*? Never. It would be incest, practically. No, dear, we are roommates alone, our marriage a fiction, almost entirely for my benefit."

"Then is Pimm... ah..."

"A mandrake?" Carrington said cheerfully. "An invert? A devotee of certain Greek philosophers? Yes, indeed, I've been curious about that myself—what *did* the two of you get up to together at school, Freddy, that made marriage seem such a natural progression in your relationship?"

Winnie ignored him, seemingly with ease. "No, dear," she said gently. "Pimm quite likes women, when he can tear himself away from his work long enough to notice the fairer sex."

"But to marry you... it means he can never marry anyone else..."

Winnie nodded. "That is, in fact, a source of great conflict between us. I refused his offer, initially, but Pimm has a strange conviction that he would make a terrible husband, and that our arrangement would spare some other woman the misery of his late nights working on cases—"

"Oh, please, the man's a drunk by most accounts," Carrington broke in. "Quite the detective when sober, of course, but how often is that? Though it's jolly good of him to recognize his weakness and want to spare a woman the shame. Anyway, your marriage isn't *legal*—you're still a man, Freddy, in the eyes of the world."

"Freddy is gone," Winnie said. "I am Winifred. Ask anyone."

"What does anyone know? We know the truth, and there are ways to prove it, as I'm sure you well know. A hair of yours, a hair from your old life, a dash of magnetic fluid, a sympathetic link established—we can prove Freddy and Winifred are one and the same." He shrugged. "Not that we'll bother. We have no reason to want to ruin Pimm, really. I just thought Miss Skye should know to look upon you with suspicion, Freddy. You were a rake when you were a man, and I understand you frequent salons with a keen eye for any followers of Sappho—"

"I do not recall asking you to speak with our guests," a voice said from the shadows.

Carrington flinched like a beaten dog at the sight of the onrushing boot. "I'm sorry, master."

"Your pettiness exhausts me, Mr. Carrington," the newcomer said, still in darkness, beyond the reach of the alchemical lamp's light. "Forgive him, ladies. He grew up impoverished, and has a profound bitterness toward those who ate regular meals as children. His nature and upbringing conspire to give him a nasty tongue, especially when speaking to his betters. Apologize, Mr. Carrington."

"You have my most profound apologies," Carrington said, in a tone that Ellie would have sworn was sincere, had she not known better.

"Is that you, Sir Bertram?" Ellie called.

"Indeed it is." He approached, a tall and well-attired man, holding a walking stick of some peculiar metal. He approached the bars, squinted, and then began to chuckle. "Oh, my," he said. "It is a pleasure to meet you again, Miss Skyler. Or, should I say, Mr. Jenkins?"

"What, they were *both* born men?" Carrington said in bewilderment.

A Note from the Underground

Pimm hurried up his front steps and through the door, hoping to find Freddy—and, dare he hope, Ellie?—inside, but the apartment was deserted. He sighed, and took the opportunity to refill the flask he'd emptied that morning. He was just putting the funnel away when a knock sounded at the door.

"Just a moment," he called, walking to the door. He opened it to reveal a filthy street boy of nine or ten standing uncomfortably on the steps, shifting his weight back and forth as if on the point of dashing away. "Are you 'alliday?" he mumbled.

"I am."

"Mr. Adams sent me with a message." The boy's eyes darted in all directions, as if expecting attack at any moment.

"Indeed? What message is that?"

"He said you'd give me a half-crown." Now the boy looked at him, directly and defiantly.

"Make it a half-sovereign." Pimm took a coin from his pocket and held it between his thumb and forefinger, out of the boy's reach. "The message?"

The boy chewed his lower lip in thought—apparently a nervous habit, to judge by the state of said lip. Then he dipped his head in a nod. "He says come see him straightaway. He has news about somebody named Mr. O. I'm to show you the way in."

"I think I know the way—" Pimm began.

The boy shook his head. "Not *this* way in, I don't think."

"That sounds ominous," Pimm said. The boy didn't answer, either because he didn't understand the remark, or didn't deem it worthy of comment. Pimm flipped the coin to him, and the boy snatched it from the air and made it disappear in an instant. "Lead on, my good man."

"It's a bastard of a walk," the boy said. "Can you hire us a cab? I never rode in one before, but you look like you could afford it."

The boy eventually led them to the same broken-down district Pimm had visited previously, but when Pimm suggested they approach the alleyway that led to Adams's laboratory, the boy shook his head. "It's all piled up with stones and rubbish," he said. "Two big men knocked down some posts with sledgehammers and a whole wall fell down. It's blocked up proper."

"Why?" Pimm said.

The boy shrugged with the simple eloquence of one who does not know, and does not particularly care to know. Instead he took Pimm through a warren of leaning buildings and narrow alleys, and finally to a small courtyard in back of several forbidding buildings, close enough to walled Whitechapel to smell the whiff of greenish alchemical vapor escaping from the vents in the dome.

The boy picked up a long wooden pole from a pile of rubbish, slotted it into a metal grate on the ground, and heaved the grate free, revealing a hole that was approximately the same circumference as Pimm himself, with a wooden ladder leading down. "I'll go first," the boy said, and descended as Pimm watched him vanish into the gloom.

This was too elaborate to be merely a ruse to rob him, Pimm decided, and chose to follow. As he descended, far enough down to make the light above fade to a distant circle, he wished he'd worn more practical clothing. He was dressed more for a business meeting than a spell of spelunking. At least he'd worn decent walking shoes. Though when he reached the bottom of the ladder, and stepped in something that softly squished, he wished he'd worn *less* decent shoes.

Light suddenly flared as the boy lit a lamp—not alchemical, just a bit of candle stuck in a tin dish with a wire handle. Pimm squinted at the old brickwork around them. "We started out crawling down into a drainpipe, but we've broken through to something deeper, haven't we? Was this a cellar?"

"Dunno," the boy said. "Mr. Adams says London is like a trash heap, with things piled on top of other things, but the other things are mostly just more London, from a long time ago."

"True enough," Pimm said, and followed the boy's flickering light through the darkness. They ducked through holes smashed through stone walls, crouched—Pimm did, anyway—through narrow tunnels with dirt ceilings, and finally, after so many turnings that Pimm lost all sense of his position in terms of surface geography, pushed open a roughly-cut wooden door and emerged into a corridor where electric lights were strung up on wires above. Broken bits of brick were scattered all over the ground, and a sledgehammer leaned against the wall, as if the entryway had just recently been smashed open. "Adams's laboratory?" Pimm said. "How remarkable!"

"I'll leave you to it then," the boy said, and disappeared back into the tunnel without further farewell, taking his light with him.

"Wait!" Pimm called, but the boy did not return. Pimm had tried to pay attention to all the turns they'd taken underground, but he didn't entirely trust himself to find his way back out again with a guide. He'd best find Adams. Perhaps the man could draw him a map back to the surface after he delivered whatever message he had.

Pimm checked his walking stick to make sure it seemed operational, and patted his pockets to confirm the presence of his pistol, along with one or two items of Freddy's invention he'd brought along in case Value proved to take disappointment violently. Adams had never threatened him, but a man who could remove a human brain so easily was probably not to be underestimated. "Adams?" Pimm called. "I received your summons."

"Down the hall, my lord," the hoarse voice called, and Pimm proceeded in the proper direction, ducking low to pass through what was less a doorway and more another ragged hole smashed through a wall. He emerged into the familiar main room of Adams's laboratory, though the slab was, blessedly, free of corpses today. Pimm glanced toward the brain in the jar, attached to its convoluted tubes and brass fixtures, and suppressed a shudder. Was the poor thing still *aware*? Did the woman not deserve the peace of death after her suffering?

Adams lurched into view from behind a shelf full of large clay pots, wires emerging from their lids. He seemed to be favoring his injured leg more than usual, dragging it after him, and when he turned his head, Pimm realized he'd dispensed with his mask.

Pimm stared, and Adams reached up, touched his face, and winced—at least, Pimm *thought* he winced. It was hard to tell. "Apologies," Adams said. "I will hide my face."

"No need, sir," Pimm said, controlling himself. "This is your home, and you certainly need not hide yourself here on my account."

"No, no. I would rather you listen to my words than be distracted by my figurement."

Surely he meant *disfigurement*, Pimm thought, but didn't say so. Adams retrieved his white mask from a long table and fastened it on, then sat on a stool, gesturing for Pimm to take a seat as well. "Thank you for coming," Adams said. "I was afraid you would not receive my summons before I departed."

"You're leaving the city, sir?" Pimm said.

Adams nodded. "I am no longer as welcome in this city as I once was."

Ah ha, Pimm thought. Value had said much the same thing. Was Oswald severing all ties with his less-than-savory associates? And did that severing involve things being *literally* severed? Like, say, jugular veins?

"The time has come for me to move on, once I make some… final arrangements. But I thought, before I left, I could pass on some information you might find interesting, in your capacity as a criminal investigator." Adams coughed, a terrible, rasping noise, and pressed his hand to his chest, as if suffering a pain there. "Ah. Though calling such acts merely *criminal* is an understatement. I refer to nothing less than treason."

Pimm leaned forward. "And who, may I ask, is the traitor?"

"You know I work for Abel Value. But, in truth, Value and I are *both* employees of another man—"

"Bertram Oswald."

Adams inclined his head. "Indeed. You are a keen investigator. What have you learned about Oswald?"

"I'm fairly certain he's involved with the clockwork brothels, and may be the creator of the mechanical courtesans himself."

"That is true," Adams said, and Pimm thought he detected a hint of amusement in the disfigured giant's voice. "That is scandalous, perhaps, but not criminal."

"And far from treasonous," Pimm agreed. "I have also wondered… with no proof at all, mind you, just something I've mused about… whether Sir Bertram may have been involved in the creation of the Constantine Affliction?"

"Ah, that certainly *would* be a crime, wouldn't it?" Adams said. "If you could find a statute that covered such a thing. Probably the deliberate creation and release of a plague could be considered akin to, oh, a mass poisoning? The difficulty would be in proving such an act. I know Oswald's laboratory and original samples were destroyed in a fire that was by no means accidental. Once the plague was loosed and proved suitably contagious, there was little need to maintain his facility to manufacture more. Which is not to say he doesn't have a few vials set aside against future needs. The toxin is quite effective when injected through a needle, or slipped into food or drink and ingested."

Pimm whistled. "Can it be possible? For a man to create a *plague*?"

"Nature does it," Adams said. "Without even *trying*, through a series of endless mindless iterations that don't even warrant the term 'trial and error.' If a man like Oswald turned his intellect toward the problem, of *course* he would find it tractable. He could never quite get the mortality rate as low as he liked, I'm afraid, and he never intended for people to die halfway through their transformations. He only wanted to change people, and to see what effect such transformations would have on society, but such a profound physical alteration could not be accomplished without occasional deaths."

"And he started with Mabel Worth as his first patient?"

"His first patient that survived, at any rate," Adams said. "Well done. You are a bright man." Pimm was annoyed that the huge anatomist sounded so surprised. "Imagine what you could accomplish if you did not allow liquor to dull your nerves. I do not know all the details, but I understand Oswald approached Mabel Worth and… offered to make a man out of her, and fund her expansion into greater criminal realms, in exchange for the use of her illicit connections. Mrs. Worth—soon Mr. Value—allowed Oswald to infect the prostitutes in his employ, spreading the disease throughout society. Though society has proven strangely intractable to the changes wrought by the Affliction. I think Oswald anticipated rather more social upheaval, perhaps a sudden universal realization that men and women *aren't* so different, genitalia and certain anatomical differences aside—that a mind, as it were, is a mind, and that one's sex does not necessarily define one's character."

"I am repulsed to find myself in agreement with Oswald on any point," Pimm said.

"Even lunatics can have good ideas on occasion," Adams said. "The problem with Oswald is, he does not understand *people*, not even remotely. He has some interesting insights about larger systems, but when it comes to individuals…" Adams shook his head. "He simply doesn't understand what motivates actual humans. He views everything intellectually, and whenever the world fails to behave rationally, it bewilders him. Oh, he knows people *have* feelings, or claim to, but he doesn't experience much in the way of emotion himself. Oswald has no true understanding regarding universal human motivations like spite, jealousy, anger, generosity, charity… or love."

"Speaking of love… Oswald infected Prince Albert with the Affliction, didn't he?"

"Ah." Adams clapped his hands together, slowly. "We now surpass the merely criminal and come ever closer to treason, do we not?

Other Plans

"That's a yes, then?" Pimm said.

"Our Queen was devoted to her Prince. Oswald hoped to gain her favor by helping to save the man's life—but when he succeeded, the Queen became ever more devoted to Albert, having realized how bereft his loss would have made her. She was favorably disposed toward Oswald, of course, but Oswald couldn't get close *enough* for his purposes. So, yes—he injected the man, using one of those cunning little rings said to be favored by the Borgias of Italy."

"Hollow, filled with poison, with a tiny needle on the underside," Pimm said.

"Indeed. A handshake, a barely-perceptible sting, and—the plague was passed on to the Prince Consort himself. Since it is well known that the *only* way anyone contracts the Constantine Affliction is by having sexual relations, the prince's denials of adultery were all in vain. Albert's death would have been preferable—so long as he died from something like the Affliction, to alienate the Queen's affection—but his transformation and subsequent imprisonment were good enough. Oswald took the opportunity to comfort the Queen in her time of sorrow and outrage. He can be quite charming, when he puts his mind to it, though he treats ingratiating himself with people like any other mechanical problem."

Pimm stood up and began to pace. "All right. But *why* poison Prince

Albert? Does Oswald want to be the Queen's consort himself? It's not as if the position includes much in the way of power, and she's shown no inclination to divorce Albert, anyway."

"Oswald *has* to get close to her," Adams said. "How else can he possibly be in a position to replace her?"

Pimm stopped walking, staring off into space. "Wait. Wait... No. I don't see it. Explain?"

Adams rose from his stool and began to sort tools on the long work table, placing some into a large leather satchel. "His *original* plan was merely to seize control of the Queen—to take over her mind, and force her to do his bidding. That was the goal of my project."

"What?" Pimm said.

"Oh, yes," Adams said. "Oswald is quite skilled at manipulating tiny bacteria, but he cannot equal my genius in dealing with the *human* body." He gestured to the brain, floating in its liquid. "You know I am very good with brains. Don't worry, Margaret cannot hear me—I disconnected her sensory apparatus, as there are things I plan to say I would rather she not overhear. Oswald's hope was that I could create a device that would enable him to control the Queen's mind. Alas, my results were not all that Oswald hoped. I was capable of making humans behave tractably, obeying instructions, but in the absence of guidance, they were docile, almost doll-like, without any spark of personality. That was not good enough for Oswald—he feared a Queen incapable of feeding herself without being told to do so might elicit some notice. But I thought the whole *point* of being Queen was that *others* had to feed you—"

Pimm reached into his pocket, touching one of Freddy's keen little devices. "You are saying you... *destroyed* the minds of people, in your experiments?"

Adams waved a hand. "Save your outrage, Lord Pembroke. I only experimented on the brains of dead whores. It's all very technical. I replace their blood with a special solution that restores a semblance of life, then perform the necessary surgeries on their brains, implanting a device based on recent magnetic innovations. You'd be amazed what a strong magnetic field can do to a brain, and thus to human behavior. Value returned the women I resurrected to their old lives as prostitutes, where a lack of initiative and complete obedience are admirable qualities. They aren't allowed on the streets, though—they serve in rather depraved secret brothels, I understand, but rest assured, they are beyond feeling pain or sadness or despair."

Pimm released the device, but his hands still trembled. "Even so. That is a desecration, Adams, it is *monstrous*—"

"I am a monster, sir," Adams said softly. "I have been called such my entire life, and see no reason to dispute it now." He stood unmoving for a moment, then shook his head and returned to sorting his tools. "I had hopes for better results if I could operate on the brain of a *living* person, to find a way to take control without destroying the personality, but Oswald… lost interest in my studies."

"I'm told he does that," Pimm said.

"Yes. He became more enamored with the concept of *replacing* the Queen than with merely controlling her."

"What do you mean, replacing her? With whom?" Pimm was thinking of certain melodramatic novels where kings discovered peasants who resembled them down to the last detail, allowing each to take the other's place.

"A clockwork replica, of course," Adams said. "Like the courtesans, but wrought in the Queen's image, and *much* more lifelike, as advanced a creation as Oswald is capable of producing."

Pimm gaped. His speculations had never taken him so far. "Good God, man, can you be serious?"

"He may have already replaced her." Adams spoke with a curious indifference, as if the situation did not concern him one way or another. He held up a tiny gearwheel, gazed at it in the light, grunted, and put it in the bag. "I am not privy to the details of his plan."

"But what would become of the *real* Queen?"

"Oswald did not share those plans with me, either, though he implied that he did not intend to kill her. I'm sure he does not want to risk someone finding her remains. Removing a corpse from the royal residence without arousing suspicion would be difficult. Though spiriting her out of the palace alive and whole would be difficult as well. Still, I'm sure Oswald's intellect is equal to the challenge."

"All right," Pimm said after a moment's thought. "Suppose all this is true. Again, I must ask, to what *end*? Why does Pimm want to replace the Queen, or control her mind? It's not as if she can give him the keys to the treasury, and from all accounts he doesn't want for money anyway. To have power, and rule by her side? Once the monarchs of England were absolute rulers, but those days have passed—the Queen herself helped make sure of that."

"As to his ultimate purpose, I don't care to speculate." Adams slammed his valise shut. "Oswald has hinted that he has some grand experiment in mind, something that involves large-scale construction and demolition in the city, the sort of things he needs influence in government to accomplish, but frankly I did not have much interest in his wild ideas, and never pressed him for details. Perhaps he means to replace the Prime Minister and other government officials with automatons as well? Certainly his clockwork Queen could summon them for a closed-door session. Oswald could gas them all into unconsciousness and replace them. He hasn't *told* me that's his plan, but it is the way his mind works. The Queen *does* give him access to the highest corridors of power. If he'd cultivated the friendship of some minister, say, they might have left government service before his plan could come to fruition—but the Queen is forever."

"Adams, if what you say is true, we have to stop him—"

"*You* have to stop him, sir. That is why I brought you here. To tell you what I know, and set you on your course. I wish you luck. As I said, I do not intend to remain here for long."

"Where are you going?"

"I have not yet decided," Adams said. "There are so many wonderful places for a honeymoon, are there not?"

Pimm blinked. "You are… to be wed?"

"I am." Adams seemed to be looking at him steadily, though with the mask, it was hard to be sure.

"My most heartfelt congratulations." Pimm's words emerged automatically. "May the two of you be very happy together."

"I am sure we shall be," Adams said, and, strangely, caressed the jar containing the dead prostitute's brain. "Assuming we can get far, far away from London. If you are successful in exposing Oswald, I am sure we will read about it in the newspapers, and if so, I may return. But Oswald has already tried to kill me once today. I do not wish to be here when he realizes he failed."

"He…. does not strike me as the kind of person who leaves things half-done," Pimm said. "How did he try to kill you?"

"He shot me in the heart," Adams said. "Fortunately, I have another. Now, if you'll excuse me, Lord Pembroke, I have *quite* a lot to do before I can leave the city."

"Ah." Pimm blinked, wondering if he'd misheard the man, and if he hadn't, wondering what that meant. "If you'll just… point me toward an exit?"

"Certainly," Adams said. "While, alas, many of my preferred points of egress have been rendered impassable, there are one or two tunnels still open to me, which lead on to other tunnels, and so on. Where in the city would you prefer to emerge?"

That, Pimm thought, was an excellent question. "Oswald himself will be easy to find—even if he isn't at home, his Grand Exposition is tonight, and I can find him there. But if I confronted him, he would just deny everything. What I need is *proof*—if not of his treason, than at least of his crimes, something I can give to my associates among the police. Do you have anything concrete linking Oswald to criminal acts?"

"I do not. Nor would my own sworn testimony do you much good, as, officially, I do not even exist. *My* involvement would bring more questions than answers, and I am not inclined to remain here so long in any case." He paused. "But you might talk to Mr. Value. He is a businessman, after all, and such men *do* tend to keep records. Value, especially, strikes me as the sort of prudent man who might make a point of keeping incriminating material on hand to serve as insurance in the case of a… falling out with his associates."

"Value is fleeing the city, too," Pimm said. "If he does have such insurance, he didn't believe it was equal to the task of keeping him safe—or simply knew it would serve to incriminate him as well. Still, if I can reach him before he leaves… Do any of your tunnels emerge near the Black Dog tavern, by Blackfriars Bridge?"

"My dear Lord Pembroke," Adams said, "my tunnels connect to the sewers, and the ruined cellars of fallen houses, and the ancient Roman viaducts from the days when this city was still called Londinium. If you are willing to walk far enough, my tunnels lead *everywhere*."

In the Employ of Great Men

"**M**y employees are so unobservant." Oswald sighed as he gazed at Ellie through the bars. "Put a false mustache on that love-ly face, Miss Skyler—or do you prefer your nom-de-plume, Skye?—and you are clearly the very image of our elusive Mr. Jenkins. You were in the brothel to write a story, I suppose?"

Ellie drew herself up straight. "Yes, sir. A secret look inside a scandalous house of clockwork ill repute."

"I'm sure it would have been a fascinating article," Oswald said, with seemingly real regret. "You are a fine writer. It is a shame that your in-quisitiveness led you to discover my presence at the brothel. Which, of course, has brought us to *this* point, as inevitably as rivers flow to the sea. Normally, I would have offered you a substantial sum of money to remain quiet about my involvement with the clockwork courtesans, but you hap-pened to discover my scandalous secret at an *incredibly* delicate time—a time when I can afford no hint of scandal, nor bear any special scrutiny at all. As for how you became involved with Lord Pembroke and his wife, and their investigations… I confess a certain degree of confusion on that point, but I suppose it does not matter." He turned and bowed to Winnie. "Lady Pembroke. I am sorry you had to become involved in this."

"It is easily remedied," Winnie said. "Set us free."

"Alas! Would that I could. But I feel it is best if the two of you remain my guests, for now, at least until I have the chance to alter your low opinion of me."

"Locking us up is certainly a good beginning," Winnie said. "You've made a marvelous first impression."

Oswald paid little attention to her. "I do not propose to detain you forever, even if you prove intractable. Just for a few days, probably, and at the very worst no more than a few weeks. By then, things will have progressed far enough that any wild allegations you make against me will be irrelevant."

"If we are gone for any amount of time, there will be inquiries," Winnie said.

Oswald waved a hand. "Oh, fear not—if a long imprisonment proves necessary, I will have you both replaced with clockwork replicas. They will not fool your closest friends, perhaps, but they will suffice to prove you are both alive and well."

"Pimm will *never* be fooled by such a device," Winnie said.

"Yes," Oswald said. "I know. I had him under observation too, of course, but he slipped his leash this morning. My people are looking for him, though, and I have no doubt he will be found soon. I'm sure he'll join us in due time. Just make yourselves comfortable. I'll see if we can manage more pleasant quarters for you soon." He turned away.

"Wait!" Ellie cried. "I don't understand—I thought you had questions for us?"

"Hmmm? Oh, I merely wanted to know how you were connected with Jenkins, and where I could find him, but since you *are* Jenkins, that is no longer relevant. I do wish to *tell* you some things, to explain myself, and make you see that opposition to me is synonymous with opposition to progress... but I want Lord Pembroke to hear my arguments as well, and I see no reason to repeat myself. Carrington, stay here while I.... attend to some other business."

"Going to check on the other prisoner?" Carrington said, and Oswald lashed out with his walking stick, cracking Carrington across the cheek and sending the man reeling.

"You are entirely too talkative, Mr. Carrington," Oswald said mildly, and walked off into the dark.

Carrington pressed his hand to his cheek and stared after Sir Bertram with an expression of ferocious hatred. "*I* talk too much?" he said darkly. "This from the great lecturer?"

"You have a most unpleasant employer," Winnie said.

"He is a brilliant man," Carrington said, cheeks flushing with embarrassment. "One must… make allowances for brilliant men."

"Must one?" Winnie said. "Pimm is brilliant, but if he beat me with a cane, I can't say I would make allowances for that. But then, I'm a very modern girl, after all. So there's another prisoner, eh?"

"Be quiet," Carrington said. "Women shouldn't speak—even false women like yourself."

"You should be nicer, Carrington," Ellie said. "If we're going to spend *weeks* together. What does your lord and master have in mind? What's his great experiment? Come, there's no harm in telling us, not if we're imprisoned anyway."

"It is Sir Bertram's tale to tell," Carrington said. "But let me just say… nothing will ever be the same. The promise of science is the complete transformation of the world. And that promise is soon to be fulfilled."

"And you are lucky enough to be beaten about the head by the man who will change the world?" Winnie said brightly. "How *proud* you must be!"

Pimm returned to the office behind the tavern, hoping to find Value still there, but the only inhabitant was Big Ben, who sat in Value's old chair, gazing up at the ceiling.

"Hello, m'lord," Ben said. "What brings you here?"

"I was hoping to speak to Mr. Value."

"He has departed for parts unspecified, sir. I do not think we'll be seeing him again."

"All right," Pimm said. "Do you have any loyalty to Bertram Oswald, Ben?"

"Never worked for the man," Ben said. "Mr. Value hired me personally. Wanted someone loyal to him, not paid out of Oswald's pocket, I think. Mr. Oswald made overtures to me from time to time, asked me to keep him informed about Mr. Value's actions, but I just took his money and told him lies. I'm not what you'd call a good man, necessarily, not in all respects, but I'm honorable in my way."

"Then perhaps you'd be willing to help me bring Mr. Oswald to justice?"

Ben pondered. "I try to stay as far away from justice as I can, as a rule, lest some of it get splashed on me, but I *am*, as it happens, looking for a new position in life, my previous employment having ended suddenly. What would you like me to do?"

"If Mr. Value has any paperwork linking him to Oswald—"

"Ah, no, sir, I'm afraid one of my recent duties was burning nearly every bit of recordkeeping Mr. Value kept. *Both* sets of books for all his legal businesses, and everything else as well. He converted as much as he could into ready cash and legged it, and didn't want to leave anything in the way of evidence behind. A prudent man, our Mr. Value."

Pimm nodded, disappointed but not surprised. "I need *some* kind of proof, something I can take to the authorities, that Oswald is involved in illegal activities. Just an *investigation* would be enough, really, once the police start looking I'm sure they'll find—"

"Perhaps there's something in the way of paperwork at Oswald's factory, sir," Ben said. "He orders parts from all over, so there must be records there."

Pimm frowned. "What factory is that?"

"The one where Oswald makes the clockwork whores," Ben said. "I went there once or twice with Mr. Value."

"Ah." Pimm smiled. "Yes, Ben. Yes, we should go there straightaway."

"At least give us the picnic basket, Carrington," Winnie demanded. "We're starving. You interrupted our lunch, as you may recall."

Carrington chuckled. He lifted the basket to his lap, opened it, removed a few of the choicer items for himself along with the plates, knives, and other silverware—even the spoons! He then placed the basket just outside the bars of the cage and returned to his chair. Winnie reached through the bars, opened the basket, and pulled out the remaining cold chicken and hard-boiled eggs, passing them over to Ellie. "We'll need water, too," Winnie said.

Carrington rolled his eyes and wandered off into the darkness. There was the sound of a pump being operated, and then he returned, carrying a sloshing bucket and two tin cups. He put the bucket outside the bars, and tossed the cups through them. "You may have noticed there's another bucket in the corner," Carrington said. "That should suffice for what happens *after* lunch. Tell me, Freddy, do you piss sitting down now, or do you still try to do it standing up? Old habits die hard, I should think."

"You are a thoroughly objectionable person, Mr. Carrington," Ellie said. "You should be ashamed."

"My master has taught me the folly of shame."

"And here I thought your nastiness was a natural trait, not an acquired one," Winnie said. "Don't worry, Ellie. We may have to relieve ourselves in a bucket, but Mr. Carrington will be the one charged with emptying our waste."

Carrington made a point of ignoring her, then opened a magazine on his knee and began to read, chuckling to himself.

Winnie sat back against the bars and ate her chicken. Ellie lowered herself beside her. "So," Winnie said quietly. "Do you despise me now, knowing me for what I truly am?"

"You are the victim of an illness," Ellie said, keeping her own voice low. "That hardly makes you despicable. And, I must say… you have adapted marvelously well to being a woman."

"I was fortunate," Winnie said, "having made the detailed study of women my entire life's purpose before my transformation." She grinned. "Pimm likes you, you know."

Ellie paused in her chewing for a moment, taken aback at the sudden change of subject, then continued, swallowed, and said, "I beg your pardon?"

"Pimm. I daresay he's *taken* with you. You made quite an impression on him."

"He… told you this?"

"He tells me everything. He thinks you are intelligent, formidable, and beautiful. Well, all right, he didn't say 'beautiful,' but I could tell by the *way* he said the other things. And, of course, by the evidence of my own eyes."

Ellie opened her mouth to object—*He is a married man*—and then realized the absurdity of that statement.

"I do not know what you think of *him*, but Pimm could use a good woman in his life—other than me. He's terribly unhappy, much of the time—whenever he isn't pursuing a case, really. He tries to bury the feelings in drink and social events and so on, but it's always there, a dark undercurrent. He cared very much for a young woman when he was young, not even twenty, and I don't think he's ever gotten over that. She was killed, you see, and her murderer was never found. I think that's why Pimm developed his interest in criminology, though of course he brushes off the suggestion as nonsense. He doesn't often like to talk about her, but I knew him back then, and he was devastated."

"I... did not know that," Ellie said, thinking of her own lost fiancé. "Winnie, are you suggesting that I might view Pimm... Lord Pembroke... romantically? Even if such a thing were true, given our current predicament this hardly seems the time—"

"Oh, we'll get out of this," Winnie said airily. "I have three plans for escape in mind already, and once Pimm realizes we're gone, he'll formulate twice as many to find us. You can't let little everyday problems like being kidnapped get in the way of truly important things, like love."

"I hardly know the man!" Ellie said.

"Oh, I know. All I wish to convey is... perhaps you should try to *get* to know him. Speaking as his wife, I'd just like you to know, I have no objection."

Ellie laughed bitterly. "And suppose we fell madly in love? What then? In the eyes of the world, he *is* married."

"I have already falsified my own death once," Winnie said. "I daresay it would be easier the second time. If love were to blossom between Pimm and *anyone* else, I would find a way to step aside. He is my best friend. He has denied himself happiness too long. I should never have let him marry me at all, but I was a bit desperate and frantic at the time, and it seemed quite the lifeline."

"Are you two talking about me?" Carrington called. "Speculating, perhaps, on the girth of my manhood?"

"He sickens me," Ellie said.

"Yes," Winnie agreed. "Two of my escape plans involve hitting him over the head with a bucket full of urine. The third is far less easy on him, you'll be pleased to know."

A Noteworthy Prisoner

~ⓔⓔⓖⓙ~

"**A**re you armed, Ben?" Pimm squinted at the squatting gray hulk of the warehouse, as menacing as a temple to dark gods in the late afternoon gloom. The sounds of activity on the London docks were audible but distant, like echoes from another world.

"I have a cosh," Ben said, patting his jacket pocket. "But my fists suffice, most often. Sometimes just the threat of them."

"I can see there are advantages in being a person of unusual size," Pimm said.

"Good and bad points, sir, like anything," Ben said philosophically. "Shall we creep around to the side entrance, then?"

Pimm let Ben lead the way, curving obliquely toward one side of the long warehouse. He was hopeful about the possibility of finding evidence of Oswald's perfidy. Ben said the man kept an office here, and liked to oversee the construction of his courtesans personally. Ben had seen Oswald writing in a ledger once, then putting the book away in his desk. Oh, it was possible the ledger was just a manifest of deliveries or something similarly non-incriminating, but Pimm felt the odds were good he might find something he could use. His head was fizzing like he'd had a bit too much champagne, which was odd, because he'd had barely enough of anything to drink, in his opinion—it must be the old thrill of the chase.

They crept, insofar as a man with a walking stick and another man the size of a draft horse could creep, along the graying wooden wall of the warehouse. "Here we are." Ben tested the latch on a small door, but it was locked. "It's all right, the frame's a bit warped," Ben said. "You can get in if you know the trick of it…" He grasped the door handle and pulled hard, opening a gap between the door and the frame almost big enough to slip one's fingers into. Ben grunted and strained, the muscles standing out in his neck, until finally the lock pulled far enough away from its groove for the door to pop open. Ben didn't even go stumbling backward when the door swung free.

"You've had some practice with this sort of thing, I see."

Ben shrugged. "You should see what I can do to a door with a short length of metal. I can get into all sorts of places, so long as you don't care if the door ever latches right again."

Pimm peered inside, but saw only gloom. "What awaits us in here?"

"It's partitioned up into rooms, like, with walls that only stretch partway to the ceiling," Ben said. "Oswald's office is in the back corner here. They build the courtesans up closer to the front. The rest of it's just filled with spare parts and all kinds of rubbish from the previous owners, broken bits of engines and things."

"Do you think anyone's here now?"

Ben shrugged. "Seems quiet."

"Yes. Into the breach, then." Pimm slipped into the dimness, Ben coming after him and pulling the door closed. They waited a moment for their eyes to adjust, and though the only light came from the high dusty windows, Pimm was soon able to see the shape of walls, heaps of what might have been equipment or trash, and a path trod in the dust on the floor. He set out along that path, feeling absurdly like Leatherstocking on the trail of some prey in the forest. A little room had been constructed against the back wall, a rectangular, windowed office raised up on a high platform, presumably to allow a supervisor to keep an eye on the workers toiling below. "Oswald's office," Ben said. The office was as dark as the rest of the warehouse, and Pimm and Ben made their way toward the stairs that led to its door.

A voice called to them from the darkness of the space under the platform. "You there!"

Pimm and Ben froze, and Pimm peered at what appeared to be a heap of stacked crates. Except there, on the bottom, partially covered by a tarp, was that... a box with vertical iron bars? Was it some kind of *cage*?

A figure in a white gown pressed itself to the bars and stretched out a hand. "You will release us at once," the man inside said, in a voice that brooked no disobedience.

"You stand guard," Pimm whispered to Ben. "Any prisoners of Oswald's are potential allies of ours."

Ben grunted and slipped off into the dark, while Pimm went to the heap of boxes, which were indeed supported at their lowest level by an immense iron cage that would have comfortably held a hippopotamus. He reached into his pocket and removed a tiny alchemical light the size of a pocketwatch, opening the lid to illuminate the cage and allow him to examine the cage's occupants—or, as it turned out, occupant, since as far as he could tell, the cage held only a single man. He was stout, middle-aged, and wearing a dirty dressing gown. His eyes were profoundly blue, his cheeks flecked with stubble and flushed red from either exertion or outrage (Pimm guessed the latter), his chin disappearing into jowls. He squinted in the light. "You are the youngest son of the Marquess of Bredon, are you not?"

Pimm frowned. "Sir, I am afraid you have the advantage of me—"

The man in the cage drew himself to his full height, and though that was no more than five feet, he somehow contrived to seem to be looking *down* at Pimm, from a position of breeding and status if not actual altitude. "You may *not* address your sovereign in such a casual tone."

"Sovereign?" Pimm said weakly.

"We are your Royal Majesty the Queen Victoria, Princess of Hanover, Saxe-Coburg and Gotha, Duchess of Saxony, Brunswick and Lunenburg. *You* may address us as 'Your Majesty.' We insist that you release us at once."

"Forgive me, Your Majesty," Pimm said weakly. "I did not recognize you."

Was this merely a madman, or, as Pimm feared, the Queen herself, altered by Oswald's terrible plague? That would certainly be *one* way to replace the Queen without murdering her: change her sex, and smuggle her out of the royal residence. The palace was full of middle-aged men going about inscrutable business—one more such would hardly be noticed, especially if drugged, say, or just weak and disoriented from the effects of the illness, and escorted out by a medical man like Oswald. Even if the victim broke free and ran through the halls, a man raving that he was the Queen of England would certainly be removed from the palace with all due haste. Oswald could have poisoned the Queen during one of their private moments, then simply unpacked her automaton doppelganger from a crate while the Queen underwent the transformation.

"We have been ill," Her Majesty said. "We have been *betrayed*. Set us free."

"I had no hand in your imprisonment, Your Majesty, and I do not have a key to this prison, but I will endeavor to find one forthwith." Freddy had a knack for picking locks, but Pimm had never been particularly good at such things—his hands tended to be slightly unsteady from either lack of drink or excess of drink, with only a brief window of perfect balance on any given day, and he'd never had the patience to overcome that handicap in the development of his housebreaking skills. Talking his way inside was generally simpler. "Perhaps there is a key in the office…"

"Pray go and apprehend Mr. Oswald," the Queen said. "He possesses the key. We will see him executed for his treason."

Pimm went still, and closed the lid of his lamp. He listened intently to the silent darkness, and then whispered, "Do you mean to say Sir Bertram is—"

"*Mr. Oswald*," the Queen said, making no effort to lower his voice. "We shall revoke his knighthood, of course."

"Yes, of course, Your Majesty, but do you mean he is *here*? In the warehouse? Now?"

"I am indeed, Lord Pembroke," a voice purred from the darkness behind him.

Pimm turned, reaching into his pocket for one of Freddy's weapons, but found himself staring into the barrel of a peculiar-looking gun—more a contraption of pipes and valves than a pistol. The dim shape holding the weapon must have been Oswald.

"Did you know my specialty, as a scientist?" Oswald said. His voice was strangely muffled, as if he wore some sort of mask.

"Pneumatic chemistry, I believe," Pimm replied.

"Very good," Oswald said. "That is, of course, the study of gases. I am *good* at gases." A mist began to pour from the barrel of the strange weapon, hissing as it came, and Pimm's head swam much as it did partway through a third bottle of champagne… and then his head seemed to float away entirely, drifting up, up, up into a warm and welcoming dark.

Our Heroes Reunited

"**J**ust toss him in with the others," Carrington said, and reappeared from the gloom followed by Crippen and one of the clockwork courtesans, who carried a limp, unmoving human figure between them.

"Pimm!" Ellie shouted, but he did not stir at her voice. Was he dead? The avalanche of feelings that idea set off inside her was more powerful than anything she'd felt since hearing her fiancé had died: a sensation of dark forces inside her gathering momentum, of titanic masses pressing unstoppably down upon her. She barely knew Pimm, but somehow the thought he might be dead seemed like the collapse of a pillar of the Earth.

"Oh, he's not hurt. Not seriously." Carrington twirled Pimm's clever walking stick inexpertly, then leaned it against his chair. He was carrying Pimm's coat over his arm, and he shook it out, checked the pocket, and drew out a pistol. "Just what I needed." He draped Pimm's coat over the back of his chair, then pointed the pistol at the cage. "Move back, Miss Skye, Freddy. No sudden lunges for freedom, all right?" They complied, and he advanced on the cage, then fitted a great iron key into the door and swung it open, never letting the pistol waver from Winnie.

Crippen grunted as he and the courtesan lowered Pimm to the ground and half-shoved, half-rolled him into the cage. Crippen groaned and stretched out his back. "Going to get the other one," he said. "Give us a hand."

"I must watch our prisoners," Carrington said. "I'm sure you can manage."

Crippen cursed him, then went back into the dark, followed by the automaton. They returned carrying an enormous unconscious man, and heaved him into the cage as well, his legs landing atop Pimm's chest. Carrington closed and locked the cage door, then went with Crippen off into the shadowy depths of the warehouse.

Ellie and Winnie rushed to the unconscious men, Winnie rolling the big man over so he no longer rested half on top of her husband. Ellie tended to Pimm, leaning to put her ear against his chest so she could listen to his heart. It was beating, and quite strongly. Pimm exhaled, and his breath was oddly sweet and chemical. Not quite ether, but perhaps he'd been drugged with some other substance that rendered him unconscious?

"Do you know this one?" Winnie prodded the giant of a man in the side, making him emit a vast snore.

"I do not," Ellie said. "But if our enemies have chosen to render him unconscious, he is in my good books already. Do you think we can wake Pimm?"

"He's a fairly light sleeper, unless he's very drunk, but who knows what substances they've pumped into him?" Winnie picked up Pimm's hand, then let it drop. She leaned toward his ear and shouted "Pimm!" but the only response was a faint moan and stirring. "He looks so peaceful when he sleeps, doesn't he?" Winnie said. "Like a baby hedgehog."

"Not the comparison I would have made," Ellie said. "But, yes, he does look relaxed." She realized she was clutching one of his hands very tightly, but chose not to release it.

"I can't abide it, either," Winnie said. She went to the bucket of drinking water, dipped in a tin cup, and brought the dripping freight back to Pimm. She dashed the contents into Pimm's face, and he gasped, bolted upright, and stared around, water streaming down his collar.

"Freddy!" he shouted. "How often have I told you, I do *not* like to be awakened in—" He stopped, peering at Ellie, then looking around, comprehension slowly filling his face. "Ah, yes, of course, I remember. Forgive me. Oswald exposed me to some horrid gas, I am still disoriented from its aftereffects."

"The principal things you should know," Ellie said, "are that we are locked in a cage, and Oswald intends to keep us here for some time."

"How beastly." Pimm ran a hand through his damp hair, and the gesture struck Ellie with the force of the best poetry. He was *alive*, disheveled and as trapped as she was, but alive, nonetheless. "Freddy, how do you rate our chances of escape?"

"Oh, quite good," Winnie said. "I was just waiting to see if Oswald captured you, really, so we wouldn't have to go to the trouble of rescuing you later. He told us he was searching for you. It seems he found you."

Pimm sniffed, then squeezed Ellie's hand—reminding her she was still holding it, which made her drop it immediately—and rose a bit unsteadily. "I'll have you know I came to this warehouse in the course of my inquiries, looking for proof of Oswald's crimes. I was *not* abducted—merely drugged and transported across a warehouse. At least, I assume this is the same warehouse. You won't believe what Ben and I—"

"This would be Ben?" Winnie patted the big man again, and he groaned, and rolled over on his side like a man in his own bed.

"Big Ben, to his enemies," Pimm said. "A former employee of Abel Value, who found himself abruptly sacked, and in need of a new position. I hired him to assist me. He suggested we might find evidence of Oswald's wrongdoing in this warehouse, and... here we are."

"One wonders if he'll consent to come in to work for you again tomorrow, given how well today has gone," Winnie said. "Should we wake him?"

"I shudder to think what Ben would do in an enclosed space if someone dashed cold water in his face," Pimm said.

Winnie sighed. "You have no sense of adventure. But do go on—did you discover anything interesting before Oswald detained you?"

Before Pimm could answer, they heard the click, click, click of Oswald's peculiar metal walking stick rapping on the floor. He returned to the circle of light cast by the alchemical lamp with Carrington on his heels, but Crippen was nowhere in sight. Oswald sat down on the chair and said, "Bring us tea, Carrington. Enough for everyone."

"Tea? But—"

"You will find everything you need in the office," Oswald said. "There is a gas ring, and cups, and pots, and so on. Biscuits." He made a shooing gesture. "Quickly, please. I will not have time to take a proper meal before the Exposition, and I am famished."

Carrington bowed and disappeared again into the dark. Oswald regarded the inhabitants of the cage silently for a while, then brushed an imperceptible speck from his knee. "I am not a murderer," Oswald said, looking up again, fixing his gaze on each of their faces in turn. "You should understand that. No more than a naturalist who pins butterflies to a board is a murderer. I am interested in truth. And, alas, sometimes, the living must join the dead in the service of that truth."

"Are we to die, then?" Pimm asked. "In your *service*?"

"That remains to be seen, Lord Pembroke. I would be so bold as to say it's entirely up to you."

A Life of Genius

swald nodded, as if pleased with himself for making an excellent point. "Let me say, first, that I do not wish to harm any of you. I do not even particularly wish to *detain* you, and certainly have no desire to kill you—though I will, if given no other choice." He frowned, as if they were children who'd disappointed him. "Admittedly, when I thought Miss Skyler was merely some middle-class barrister or merchant named Jenkins who'd stumbled on my secret business interests, I would have been content with a more… final solution to the problem of her existence. But now that I know her true identity, I confess I am actually a great admirer of her writing, and would like to see her prosper in the new world I plan to usher in. I want the same thing for you, Lord Pembroke—unlike most of the parasitic aristocrats who puff and strut their way through this city, wasting their pointless lives, you actually have a mind, though you bend it toward lesser pursuits than I might wish. And you, Winifred—surely *you* would prefer a world where you could be judged on the content of your character rather than the accident of your sex?"

"You must not know much about my character," Winnie said.

Oswald's eyes reminded Ellie of a crow's, looking at something fresh-killed in the street. "I prefer to make allies of my enemies, whenever possible. Do you think Abel Value was originally eager to work with me?

Of course not. But he—or she, at the time—wanted something, and I was able to grant her wish. The man you know as Adams was once a rival of sorts as well, but I took him into my confidence, and showed him I valued his contribution, and he soon became part of my great work. As I hope you will be. There is always room for intelligent, resourceful people in my organization."

"What great work do you mean, sir?" Ellie asked, in her best interested-journalist voice.

"I believe in the power of science, Miss Skyler. Do you?"

"I am as astonished as anyone by the recent advances in alchemy, steam engines, magnetism—"

"No!" Oswald slammed his cane down on the floor with a resounding bang. "You are speaking of *technology*, not science. Technology is the fruit of science—but science is the *tree*. Science is a way of understanding the world, Miss Skyler. One makes observations, extrapolates conclusions, carries out an experiment to prove or disprove the validity of those conclusions, and adjusts one's worldview as necessary. That process is what I believe in—not assumptions, not the base canard known as 'common sense,' not God, or the devil, or tradition, or faith, or religion, or all the collective institutionalized weaknesses known as human nature, or worse, human decency. Only the empirical matters to me." He stood up, his head bowed low. "But the world is a complicated place. Too complicated, truthfully—too chaotic. The key to any experiment is controlling the variables, you see. But how can I conduct truly vast experiments, studies aimed at laying bare the nature of society itself, when so many factors are outside my control? I have tried to conduct certain experiments anyway, despite those limitations, but always, outside forces tainted the purity of my efforts. The fire in Whitechapel, which still burns? Do you know what started it?"

"An illegal experiment in an alchemical workshop, as I understand it," Pimm said. From his tone, he could have been at a slightly boring dinner party, and not locked in a lion cage at all.

"Illegal? How could it be illegal? There were no *laws* governing the things I was doing."

Ellie stared. "It was… you? Your experiment? But how can that be? The fires began years before I was born. You were just a boy yourself, surely you're too young—"

"You are too kind," Oswald said. "I made it a point, early in my studies, to find a way to extend my lifespan. Not quite the fabled *elixir vitae*, it does not restore youth or grant immortality, but it arrests aging, if taken regularly. I am... rather older than I seem, and have reason to believe my longevity will exceed the vast lifespans attributed to certain Biblical patriarchs. I have been obliged to change my identity often over the years, going into seclusion and emerging later to pose as my own son, or nephew, or some other long-lost heir. I am the entirety of the Oswald line, stretching back for generations.

"Yes, the tragedy of Whitechapel was related to my work, though I am not to blame. I was attempting to unlock a source of power less filthy than coal, an energy that would enable me to run colossal engines of unimaginable power. To call my work then 'alchemy' is incorrect—it was something closer to geology, in this case. I discovered a strange crystal during my travels in the Amazon, a cave full of glowing purple formations. The local tribes used the shards of crystal as weapons—use one to tip a spear, and anyone stabbed would sicken and die. But hurl one of the shards at a stone with sufficient force... and the stone would explode, reduced to dust, and no plants would grow anywhere that dust fell, ever again. I realized there was enough energy locked in a single crystal to level a mountain, if properly released... and I conceived of a method to control and harness that power, releasing a far greater force of energy than merely tossing a shard at a rock could ever do. I gathered a few crystals, packed them carefully, and transported them to London. I chose to make my lab in a filthy block of Whitechapel, because I knew accidents were possible, and if there were an explosion... well, I could hardly risk blowing up the West End, could I?

"I was careful, oh, so very careful... but I could not personally craft every vessel and every tool. I hired a man to make me a containment box from lead. For reasons I will never know, he did not use pure lead—he adulterated it with some other metal. And why? To do it more cheaply, and keep a few coins for himself? Because he simply had the other materials close to hand? Who knows? But he deviated from my exacting specifications, and when I finally cracked open the secret heart of a crystal to release the energies inside... the forces I unleashed were not contained.

The vessel cracked. I was wearing protective garb, of course—one does learn to be careful—but my assistants were not so lucky. The strange energies I released had a deleterious effect on the human body. Sores appeared on their faces, and their hands, and, I presume, all over their bodies. They bled from their eyes, and screamed, and flailed. Of course, their frantic actions and the force from the broken crystal led to an accident in the lab, a terrible fire, chemicals reacting terribly, numerous explosions which caused nearly my entire stockpile of crystals to erupt, and…" He gestured vaguely northward. "The disaster began. Some of those chemical reactions are still ongoing, and may not cease for decades or centuries. I managed to keep my name out of the affair. When those first stray dogs came crawling out of the remains of Whitechapel, so horribly changed, and everyone realized how deadly the region had become, I saw a way to turn disaster into opportunity. The crown commissioned a company I owned to build walls to contain the area. I have been improving the barriers ever since, most recently with the addition of the dome, and have made many remarkable discoveries in the realm of materials science in the process. I was *very* careful with the construction of that wall over the years. I let it be known that any craftsman caught supplying materials of poor quality would be left *inside* the walls." His tone throughout this tale was mild, and it seemed the recitation of an anecdote drained of all emotional power by time, or the simple indifference of the teller.

"Your experiments killed *hundreds*!" Ellie cried.

Oswald frowned. "I killed no one. Thousands died, in fact, counting those who lived near the walls and succumbed to strange illnesses later, but their deaths can be laid at the feet of the man who gave me *tin* when I asked for lead. Human error, you see—*that* is the problem. My next course of experiments were meant to eliminate human error. I constructed a device called the Air Loom, which acted to send certain waves and emanations through the air toward specific targets. The purpose of the device was to correct the behavior of unreliable people—"

"Mind control, you mean?" Pimm said. Then, apologetically, "I only wish to be sure I understand."

Oswald harrumphed. "I suppose you could call it that—but is training a dog 'mind control'? A well-trained dog is happier and more useful than a feral stray, I am sure you would agree, and its owner is happier, too.

I thought I could induce men to behave better, that is all. The Loom had certain shortcomings—it was necessary to douse subjects in a volatile magnetic fluid before the Loom would affect them, which was difficult to do surreptitiously, and when activated, the Loom did not alter the workings of their brains in quite the way I'd predicted."

"Did the people explode?" Winnie asked. "Burst into flame? Only I seem to recall stories of spontaneous human combustion…"

"No, no," Oswald said. "That was an unrelated matter. The Loom failed in different ways. Its emanations could affect the fluids in the brain, but instead of altering thoughts, they caused terrible pain and discomfort, and my test subjects either took their own lives, fled the country, or were committed to Bedlam. I had to retire the Loom, though I still think of it fondly—it was a beautiful device. I believe in beauty, you know. I just don't see beauty in the same things that most people do. The failure of the Loom made me realize I did not understand enough about the human brain to achieve sufficiently precise effects. That is when I retained the services of the man you know as Mr. Adams, Lord Pembroke. He has a keen understanding of all elements of physiognomy—within his limited field of expertise, he far surpasses even my own knowledge, and he has a tremendous grasp of electricity and chemistry as well. We worked together for a time to create a device that would enable us to control human minds…" Oswald sighed. "It could have worked beautifully. Alas, it required brain surgery, which is difficult to do in secret. We recently chose to part ways, and pursue our own efforts separately."

"And here I heard you shot him in the heart," Pimm said. Ellie looked at him in alarm.

"Hmm," Oswald said. "You *are* a detective, aren't you? Yes, it's true. If it gives you consolation, you should know Adams was not truly a man, but a stitched-together amalgam of several corpses, the monstrous reanimated creation of a brilliant natural philosopher, now himself long dead. I did not so much kill Adams as… deactivate him. He had ceased to be useful, and a useless tool may be reasonably discarded."

"From anyone else, that would sound like a threat," Winnie said. "But do you know, I don't even think he *meant* it that way."

Oswald waited patiently for Winnie to finish, then went on. "In the past few years my focus has altered, away from changing individuals to addressing problems with the system—with society itself, which is part of why most individuals are so dreadful. One of the greatest problems with our culture is the fact that men and women are treated so drastically differently, their spheres of life so rigorously separated. The class of 'humans' is complex enough without adding further arbitrary divisions—men and women are the same, in the aggregate, apart from certain secondary sexual characteristics that do not interest me overmuch. The apparent differences in their abilities are, it seems to me, largely determined by cultural prejudices, excepting generalizations regarding muscle mass and, of course, reproductive ability."

"You may be right," Ellie said. "I have certainly grown weary of men telling me no woman can write as well as a man."

Oswald positively beamed. "You see? We are in agreement. I knew we would find grounds to make common cause. I decided it might be useful to destroy those notions about the essential fundamental differences between men and women, and so I spent several years studying certain frogs, lizards, and fish, and learning about the transmission of various infectious diseases, and—"

"Yes, I was going to mention," Pimm said. "Sir Bertram here is responsible for creating and releasing the Constantine Affliction."

The Burden of Vision

After a long moment of shocked silence, Winnie said, "All this time I've been cursing God for giving me the Constantine Affliction, when I should have been cursing you."

Oswald sighed. "Your inconvenience is irrelevant when compared to the greater good, Winifred. And the Constantine Affliction is a foolish name. I was disappointed to see you perpetuate the term in your articles, Miss Skyler. I call it the Great Transformer, in my journals."

Journals! Ellie thought. Journals meant *evidence*.

Oswald went on, pacing in front of the cage. "Though it is true that an ambassador from Constantinople was among the first to contract the illness, when I introduced it into a certain brothel. Though he—or she—was not the original carrier."

"What did you think would happen when you engineered this catastrophe?" Ellie said. "What was your prediction, your *hypothesis*?"

"Chaos, of course. But I expected—I still expect—that eventually having men transform into women, and women into men, while retaining their same essential minds and faculties, would make people realize how ridiculous and arbitrary the division into male and female 'spheres' truly is. I would class that experiment as…. ongoing, rather than a failure. One of the advantages of having an extended life is the ability to engage in long-term social experiments like this one. Of course, one must occupy oneself while awaiting the results. Hence my interest in the clockwork courtesans—"

"That plague killed more people than it transformed," Ellie interrupted. "Were all those deaths a worthwhile price to pay for your experiment?"

Oswald frowned. "What is this obsession with life and death? Life is not precious, Miss Skyler. Leave a filthy puddle of water alone in a beam of sunlight, and it will teem with life in a few days or weeks. Oh, some lives are more worthy than others, certain individuals more valuable than the rest of the milling hordes—I myself, and the three of you perhaps, and even Abel Value, in his grim and simple way. But if some must die in order to further my researches, what of it? Some of my colleagues study fruit flies. Such flies are wonderful subjects, because they breed rapidly, and their lives are very short, so they churn through new generations at a prodigious rate. Introduce a new variable into a colony of fruit flies, and one can watch the consequences propagate swiftly. Humans are, compared to my own likely lifespan, scarcely more than flies themselves. And anyway, killing off a few people is the humane thing to do."

"Your powers of rationalization are astounding," Pimm said.

"Oh, don't be naive, Lord Pembroke. There are too many people alive now. Do you have any idea how many human beings teem on this earth? One and a quarter *billion*." He shuddered. "Such a number is scarcely comprehensible by the human mind!"

"The fact that you can't comprehend their number doesn't mean any of them deserve to die," Pimm said.

"What does deserving have to do with it? They never earned the right to live, so I do not require them to earn the right to die. Have you read the writings of the Reverend Malthus? He pointed out decades ago that population growth is exponential, while the growth of the world's food supply is merely arithmetical." He sighed. "I can see by your expressions that you are all functionally innumerate. What I mean is, population grows by leaps and bounds, while our ability to produce food plods along at a rather more modest pace. Malthus predicted that, sooner rather than later, the population will far outstrip our capacity to *feed* that population. Thinning out the horde is actually merciful, like hunting deer to keep their numbers in check—otherwise, they will overpopulate and starve to death."

"But we shall not starve today," Carrington said, returning with a tray of tea. "I found some frosted biscuits, they're marvelous."

Oswald seemed peeved at the interruption. He took his own tea cup and told Carrington to put the tray where "our guests" could reach it. With exaggerated care, the secretary placed the tray on the ground and then used Pimm's walking stick to push it slowly closer to the bars.

"Whatever are you doing?" Oswald demanded.

"I wouldn't put it past Freddy to hurl hot tea into my face in an attempt to escape," Carrington said.

"The thought had crossed my mind," Winnie admitted. "Not to help us escape, of course, that's obviously ridiculous, but just for my own amusement." She reached through the bars and poured tea for herself, Ellie, and Pimm, while Oswald tapped his walking stick impatiently—some property of its odd metallic composition made it ring unpleasantly against the floor.

"Carrington," the eminent scientist snapped. "Take tea to our other prisoner, and stay with him. He's a bit overwrought. You should calm him down."

"Of course, master." Carrington bowed so obsequiously it seemed an obvious mockery, then disappeared into the shadows again.

"I suppose it never occurred to you," Pimm said, after taking a sip of his tea, "to use your intellect to find new ways to *feed* the starving?"

"What do you mean? *Farming*? That is hardly one of my interests, Lord Pembroke. Moreover, a smaller population makes it easier to track variables in my experiments. I am disappointed in this reaction, I must say. Mr. Value comprehended the obvious wisdom of my arguments immediately, and Mr. Adams shared my interest in exploring the full range of human potential. You are a journalist, Miss Skyler—surely you value truth above all else? Let us tear away the shroud of nature's mysteries, then. Let us lay the truths of the world bare."

"If you advocate truth in all things, then you won't mind me quoting you in my paper?" she said.

Oswald chuckled. "Newspapers. Yes. You are an insightful writer, Miss Skyler, and that insight is wasted on your readers. I could stand in a field and expound on the principles of pneumatic chemistry to a herd of bleating sheep, but that act would neither aid me, nor enrich the sheep. The same must be said for telling the truth to the inhabitants of this city.

They would not understand. They would try to stop me. But, certainly, print what you like... when you have your freedom. Which, of course, is entirely at my discretion. Even if you succeeded in smearing my good name, I would likely weather the storm. I have influential friends."

"Ah, yes," Pimm said. "You sit at the right hand of the Queen."

"Rather closer than that, old boy." Oswald winked, and Ellie shuddered. "My experiments—the ones people actually appreciate, the development of the alchemical lamps and magnetic field manipulators to improve health, and so on—were enough to bring me to Her Majesty's attention, so that my name was not entirely unknown to her. She was still quite fond of her husband Prince Albert in those days, and when he miraculously survived his fever—thanks to some of my own advances in germ theory, though I let Pasteur take all the credit, as the original insight was his own—her interest in me grew into friendship and affection. Unfortunately, in the wake of his illness, the Queen's devotion to Prince Albert only grew. I understand that almost losing someone you love makes you appreciate them more."

Ellie thought of Pimm being carried into the warehouse unconscious, how she'd assumed he was dead, and how her heart had transformed into shards of glass in her chest at that moment. Oswald was mad, but he was not always wrong.

"He poisoned the prince, incidentally," Pimm said. "I gather he's building up to that revelation, but really, this lecture could go on all night. It's not always true that criminals secretly long to confess, but the criminals that consider themselves clever *do* like to hold forth."

Oswald smiled thinly. "You are an industrious detective, Lord Pembroke. I would worry about your allegations, if I believed I had left any evidence of wrongdoing behind. Yes, I infected the prince with my Great Transformer. Initially I hoped he would die in the change, but in retrospect, it is better that he simply transformed. Even given evidence of his adultery, his death might have brought on too much emotion in the Queen—at the very least, she would have been compelled to go into mourning, which is quite a tedious affair all around. Fortunately, the prince lived, and became a woman, ugly and horse-faced. The Queen will not let his name be mentioned in her presence. His declarations of innocence, though true, were of course disbelieved. The whole endeavor was quite neatly arranged, and

I was there to comfort Her Majesty in her time of trouble. We have been incredibly close ever since."

"Oh?" Pimm said. "Is that why you poisoned *her* with the Affliction and locked her in a cage?"

Oswald scowled as Winnie and Ellie gasped. "I'd wondered whether or not you had ascertained the identity of my other guest. I thought it wise to gas you unconscious as soon as I discovered your presence. Perhaps I should have asked."

"You have the *Queen* imprisoned here?" Winnie said.

"He'd be the king, now, I suppose," Oswald said. "Or does he remain the queen regardless? I'm sure there's an answer in some book of courtly protocol somewhere, but I don't care—he still calls himself my 'Queen,' for whatever his opinion is worth. The transformation was regrettable but necessary. I'm afraid that even when I exercised my full influence, marshaled my best arguments, and entreated the Queen as a friend, she proved… intractable… when it came to assisting me in my latest grand design. I'd had hopes for controlling her mind, but when that line of inquiry proved fruitless, I turned to another approach."

"How does turning her into a *man* help you?" Ellie demanded.

"The clockwork courtesans," Pimm said. "He made a mechanical double for the Queen. An imitation."

Oswald bared his teeth. "You know more than I expected, Lord Pembroke. Wherever do you get your information?"

"Like Miss Skye, I am not at liberty to divulge my sources," Pimm said.

"But she could use *you* as a source, I suppose," Oswald said. "And print all this in her newspaper, intended as a slanderous character assassination—"

"You mean libelous." Ellie could not resist the chance to puncture this pompous ass's self-congratulatory tone. "False charges in writing are libel—false charges when spoken are slander." She gave him a gentle smile. "It is a common mistake. And, of course, none of these charges are *false*."

"I bow to your superior knowledge on the subject of libel," Oswald said, and he *did* bow, in a very courtly way. If Ellie had annoyed him, he didn't show it. "I admire your precision when it comes to language, Miss Skyler, and apologize for my own shortcomings. So, yes—you could print libelous nonsense. But why take that course? Why try to destroy me, when you could aid me in my great work instead? Everything I have prepared for is in readiness, now. This country is on the cusp of greatness."

Oswald stepped closer to the cage. "We have come now to the point of decision. I am a reasonable man. I will offer you two paths of action: you may remain imprisoned for the next few days or weeks, or you may join me in my great work."

"What great work is that, again?" Pimm said. "I'm afraid you've been rather vague on that point."

"Ah, but you find my lecture interminable enough as it is. Wouldn't you agree that I've rattled on enough already? Suffice to say my new project makes my past experiments seem pedestrian and unambitious. My great work will help me bring the population of this planet down to a manageable level, and furnish me with a perfect experimental chamber to create an ideal society. Agree to join me, and, after certain tests of loyalty have been passed, I will happily share all my plans with you."

"What would our compensation be?" Ellie said.

Pimm started to say something—or to swear, possibly—but went silent when Oswald chuckled. "I will give you whatever you want, Miss Skye. And, yes, once my experiment is concluded, such an outrageous promise *will* be in my power to fulfill—I could give you your own *country* to rule, if you wished it. So tell me. What do you desire?"

"I… Only to pursue the truth, and to write, and to have a happy life."

"Hmm. That is simple enough, though a bit vague. We'll have to nail down the particulars later. Winifred?"

"Give me back my life," Winnie said. "Make it so you never inflicted this disease upon me."

"A difficult problem, but not impossible," Oswald said. "I could perhaps reverse your condition, at least. After surviving the Great Transformer, one develops an immunity to the disease, but I could create a new strain, I suppose…"

"Oh, piss off," Winnie said wearily.

Oswald sighed. "What about you, Lord Pembroke? What do *you* want most in this world?"

"Another drink, generally," Pimm said. "You have nothing to offer me, sir."

"Nonsense. Everyone wants something. Value wanted wealth and power, and I provided them—he is a child, essentially, though a very cunning child, and he does love his toys. Mr. Adams wanted... well, love, actually. Soppy romantic notions were a peculiar blind spot in his otherwise highly-developed worldview. I tried to help him find the perfect love he sought, but I fear he never did. Everyone has a price, my friends, and I am a man with a profoundly full purse. Just let me know what I need to pay." He turned away.

"There is a third option," Pimm said.

"Eh?" Oswald was consulting a pocketwatch, and suddenly paying them very little attention.

"You said we could join you, or we could remain imprisoned, but there's something else we could do. We could *oppose* you."

"Ah." He snapped the watch shut and put it away. "Yes, I suppose you could, assuming you could escape. Though that option might just as well be reformulated as, 'We could die, for no particular reason.' If you wish to die, do let me know. It can be arranged with trivial ease. But I have hope for you all. To have learned as much about my plans as you did demonstrates impressive intellectual development. I have uses for people of your talents. Don't waste your abilities on a silly grudge. There are more important things in the heavens and Earth." He yawned. "I must prepare for the Exposition tonight. The great work begins. Do you wish to assist me, or remain trapped?"

"Of *course* we'll help you," Winnie said. "Your argument has swayed me completely."

"Indeed," Ellie said. "I look forward to helping disseminate your insights to the masses."

"Naturally. We are entirely devoted to your cause. Only let us out—" and here Pimm smiled, showing all his teeth—"and we will be pleased to show you the *full* extent of that devotion."

"You all disappoint me terribly," Oswald said, and seemed as saddened as any parent who sees his children behave in a dangerous and stupid fashion. "But perhaps some time in captivity will alter your viewpoints. Forgive me. I have preparations to make. I trust you will excuse my rudeness if I depart? I'll be sure to visit you in future days, as time allows— though I expect I will be *quite* busy after tonight. Society won't reorder itself, you know." He gave them a little bow, turned smartly on his heel, and marched off into the darkness.

They watched him disappear. "We really should leave soon," Pimm said. "I think we've stayed here quite long enough, and there's the other prisoner to think about."

"You want to free the Queen?" Winnie said.

"Do you propose that we leave her in a cage here?" Pimm said.

"A fair point."

"Now, Winifred, darling—"

"Oh, call me Freddy," she said. "Carrington already told Ellie the truth about me."

For the first time since she'd known him, Ellie saw Pimm look totally at a loss, his mouth agape. He glanced sidelong at Ellie. "Ah... you know? About... her?"

"I do," she said. "And I can see the fear on your face. But I have no intention of making a sensational story out of your marriage. I consider Winnie a friend, and have only the utmost respect for you. I do not feel compelled to *divulge* every secret I uncover, Pimm—it is enough for me, sometimes, to discover the truth for myself alone. Nor am I troubled by the revelation on its own terms. Winnie may have begun life as a man, but that makes no difference—her soul is still the same."

"That's a relief," Pimm said. "Though it's rare to hear anyone attribute the possession of a soul to my wife. All right, then, Freddy—how quickly can you get us out of this cage?"

"Ten minutes," Winnie said. "Perhaps five, if you can prevent yourself from prattling at me while I work."

"Let's hope I can get Big Ben awake in that time," Pimm said, looking at his snoring comrade doubtfully.

"You mean to say you can circumvent the lock?" Ellie said.

"Of course," Winnie said. "The lock on this cage is meant to keep *lions* captive, not creatures with thumbs and cunning small tools." She reached up to her hair and began pulling out fine wires and rods, to Ellie's astonishment.

"You've got lockpicks in your *hair*?"

"A woman needs a hobby," Winnie said. "And you never know when you might find a nice lock to practice on."

"But why didn't you free us before?"

"Carrington was sitting there watching, mainly," Winnie said. "We didn't have time then, but for now, they seem to have left us unguarded. And I *was* curious to see whether they would capture Pimm or not. I made a small wager with myself, and in consequence, I now owe myself a sovereign."

"And she accuses *me* of prattling," Pimm said.

"Silence," Winnie commanded, and knelt by the cage door to commence her work.

Love Life

This was to be the culmination of his long life's work, and while Adam was annoyed to rely so heavily on the advancements of the loathsome Bertram Oswald, the end result would surely be satisfying enough to overcome his distaste.

The automaton on the table had been modified considerably from its original design. Oswald had consulted with Adam about the anatomy of his mechanical women early on—little did Adam know then how the success of the clockwork courtesans would lead to his own brush with death—and there were several partially-complete models stored around the laboratory. Adam had combined the best features of those mechanical women into a single harmonious form.

The parallel with the way Adam himself had been constructed, stitched together from pieces of corpses, was not lost on him, but while Adam was a patchwork creature of skewed proportions and inelegant seams, the clockwork body he'd created for his true love was perfection—mostly because Oswald was a great believer in uniformity and interchangeability of parts, while natural human bodies showed an astonishing range of variation even within the parameters of ostensibly "normal" physiognomy.

The heads of Oswald's standard models didn't contain much other than tubing for suction and speech—and rudimentary speech at that—plus some gears to run the eyes and facial muscles. With some rearrangement, there was ample room in the mechanical skull for a human brain. Connecting that brain in such a way that it could control the mechanical body was a rather different question, but in a way, it was a problem Adam had already solved: the delicate spiderweb of wires he used to transform ravenous flesh-eating corpses into docile submissives could be altered to act as an interface between mind and machine, without the magnetic mind-manipulators. This resurrection would have a mind of her own.

Adam carefully removed Margaret's brain from its vat, disconnecting the leads, and placed it in the open skull of the clockwork courtesan on his table. He carefully attached the tubes that would circulate his artificial blood around the brain, keeping it fed and oxygenated, then attached the metal spiderweb that would allow her control of her body. These eyes were better than human eyes, capable of seeing spectrums invisible to ordinary mortals, and the hearing and senses of smell were likewise advanced. While the sense of taste was non-existent, he could address that problem in the future. Adam and his beloved could embark on a life of eternal self-improvement, literally making one another better people.

If Adam had known how to do so, he would have given Margaret his own synesthesia, to let her taste the cross-connections in the sensory universe—but without dissecting his own brain, he wouldn't know how to replicate the effect. Still, being able to see magnetic fields and into the infrared and ultraviolet spectrums would help her understand *something* of his own unusual perceptions.

Mutual understanding was very important, in love.

For he *did* love her, and as he worked on integrating her living brain into her clockwork body, peace and happiness suffused his entire being. Since bringing her brain to life, he had spent hours speaking with Margaret, and she was a funny, quick, witty woman, driven to a life of prostitution by desperate circumstance rather than stupidity or low character. For her part, Margaret was delighted by Adam's company, and understandably grateful for his efforts to restore her to a normal life. Oh, he hadn't been *entirely* honest with her about her circumstances or his plans, but he'd told her that she'd been attacked, her body damaged terribly, and that he had a bold plan to give her back her sight and other lost senses, and to make her stronger and more beautiful than ever before.

And now was the time.

He stood back to survey her body. She was dressed in a simple linen shift, which Adam had sewn himself. (He was an excellent tailor, with cloth as well as flesh.) Her face was peaceful and composed, her lips succulent, her cheeks eternally touched with a fetching hint of blush, the lashes of her closed eyes long and lovely. And her body... well. Oswald knew his work well, and Adam had improved upon it. She was perfect, a statue of a goddess, brought to a semblance of life—and with a real human brain, possessed by a real human mind, brought to *true* life.

"Arise," Adam murmured, and triggered the device in his hand that activated the spiderweb in her brain.

Margaret gasped, drawing a deep breath—not strictly necessary for life, but it did remarkable things to her bosom—and sat up, opening her eyes. She did not look much at all as she had in life, apart from the red hair and the cream complexion, but she was in every respect more lovely than before, and the animation of her soul in the body made it even more astonishingly lovely.

"I can see!" she shouted, holding up her hands in front of her. "The light, it... it is so much *richer* than the light I remember, and I can smell, oh, everything, nothing blends together, I can detect every strand of scent, and I *feel*—" She turned her perfect head to look at Adam—and flinched away, crying out in alarm, nearly sliding off the table in the violence of her reaction.

"Do not be alarmed," Adam said from behind his mask. "I know I am... fearsome."

She reached out and took his hand, running her finger across the stitching where his fingers—all with flesh of different colors, and none quite proportional in their lengths—were attached to his hands. "Were you in an accident, Adam?"

"No, my darling." He closed his hand on hers. There could be no lies between them, not now. "I was made, you see. Created, by a man, many long years ago, sewn together from broken pieces to make a whole. And I *am* whole, where it counts, in my mind, in my soul—in my heart." Only one heart, at the moment. He'd have to rectify that when he had a chance.

She nodded, apparently having no difficulty believing him—she was intelligent, but not well-educated, and while someone with scientific knowledge might have found the story of Adam's creation difficult to believe, she had grown up surrounded by the wonders wrought by Oswald and his ilk, and did not appear to doubt his story at all.

"You should see yourself, Margaret. I hope you will be pleased. Let me bring you a glass." He fetched a highly-polished sheet of metal, the closest thing he had to a mirror—he still had a tendency to smash any mirrors in his vicinity, when the dark moods took him—and let her hold it up to her face.

"Oh, Adam, I… I can't believe it. You have given me a whole new *face!*"

"A whole new body," Adam said.

Margaret lowered the glass, frowning. "What do you mean? This is not my own body, repaired?"

"You were beyond repair, my sweet, your body broken—but your mind was whole. I saved you. I gave you a new form."

"Am I made… as you were?" She examined her face more intently in the glass, as if looking for scars, seams, inelegant joinings.

"Oh, no," Adams said. "I am a far better creator than my *own* maker was. No, your form is not fearsome, but beautiful, and you are not sewn from broken bodies, but made from only the most modern materials. You will not age, Margaret. You will not grow sick. You will be this beautiful forever. And we will be together, just as we discussed." He laced his fingers into hers.

"Can I stand?"

"Of course." He helped her down from the table, and she tottered a little, then found her balance. She looked around the low-ceilinged, cluttered workshop, frowning. "This place is so cramped, so dank, Adam. This is where you work your miracles?"

"It is indeed. But we need not stay here, my darling—I have money put away, and we may go anywhere. Where have you always wanted to go? Paris? Rome? Someplace warm. Someplace with lights. Some place where we may love, and be loved, and be in love—"

She touched his cheek, though he could not feel it, through the mask. "May I see your face, Adam?" Her voice was low, a whisper, and he could not read her tone, though her voice looked like swirls of dark ink dispersing into the air.

"I… I fear…"

"I must see your face," she said gently.

"Of course." He removed the mask, keeping his own eyes squeezed tightly shut, but nevertheless, he heard her sudden gasp, felt her hand tear away from his. "I know it is frightening," he said. "I was not beautiful to begin with, and my skin suffered terrible frostbite some years ago when I was in the Arctic, and there was also a fire, but—" He opened his eyes. Margaret was standing several feet away, and had a hand to her mouth in horror.

Adam's first memory was of his own creator, looking upon him in horror at the monstrous thing he had wrought, and though Margaret and Victor could not have been more different, their expressions were almost the same.

He took a step toward her.

Margaret backed away farther, faster than he advanced. "Adam, I… Forgive me. I will always cherish you as a friend, and as my savior, but I fear… I cannot be your… your…"

"Wife," he whispered. "When you were ill, in the darkness, we spoke of marriage, of eternity together—"

"Yes, of course, but I was *ill*, and frightened, and the only thing in the world was your *voice*, and now that you have changed me, transformed me in this way, it seems unwise to rush into such an arrangement. I—I am simply overwhelmed, and—"

"I know I am fearsome to look upon, Margaret, but truly, I am the same man you loved before." He tried to stand still, to keep from frightening her further, but his need for her drove him to take another step, even though, as he knew she would, Margaret took a corresponding step backward. "The man you talked with for all those hours, sharing your dreams, your fears, your history."

"I know, I know that in my *mind*, but your face, the *size* of you… I do not wish to offend you, but in truth, you frighten me, Adam. And to tell me my body is not human, that *your* body is not human, it is all too strange, too much for my mind to cope with at once, and my every instinct tells me to run away—" With a visible effort, she straightened her spine, standing her ground. "I will not flee, because I know you are a gentle and wise soul, and in time I will grow used to your appearance, but even so, marriage… we barely know one another, you do not truly know *me*, and—"

Adam opened and closed his enormous, scarred hands. "You are beautiful, inside, and I have made your body match that inner beauty. That is all I need know. You are… exquisite. I have made you so. And in time, as you said, you will become accustomed to my appearance, you will grow to care for me, and love will blossom—"

"You will always have my gratitude," she said, lowering her head. "And my friendship. You have given me a new life, Adam. A fresh start. I owe you so much, but I cannot—"

Everything was collapsing. Just as everything always did. He felt the familiar dark storm rising within him, and did not try to resist it. The darkness was his birthright. It was his only inheritance.

Adam dashed a row of beakers from his table, and they shattered on the floor, spraying glass. Margaret wailed in alarm, and a dark part of Adam was happy to hear her cry of fear. It was only natural to want to cause pain to the one who had caused you pain, after all. It was only *human*. "You rutted with men in alleys," Adam said, his voice soft and low as he stalked toward her. "Filthy men, stinking of rum, ignorant men, beneath contempt, you let them spill their diseased seed into you—but you will not touch *me*? *I* disgust you?"

"Adam, I do not mean to—"

"You were a *whore!*" he shouted, spraying spittle into her face, making her flinch. "I took your dead brain and put it in the body of a goddess! I am your *creator*, your *maker*, and you dare to disobey *me*—" He reached out, not sure what he meant to do, but knowing it would be violent.

"Did you never dare to disobey your own creator?" she whispered. "Did the fact that he created you mean you had to be his slave?"

Adam froze, his arms extended before him. He began to tremble, and the wound in his leg ached.

"Leave here," he whispered. "Run, Margaret. There are tunnels, behind you, with your new senses you should be able to sense the flow of air, and follow the passageways to the surface. You must go *now*, before… before I… I cannot always help myself…"

She must have heard something in his voice, because she did not attempt to calm him, to change his mind, or even to say goodbye. She ran.

He sat down deliberately on the floor of his laboratory, held his face in his hands, and sobbed. This filthy world. He had become that which he despised—a creator, possessive of his creation, determined to make it do his bidding. Love had been in his grasp, and had escaped. Or else he was a fool, and there had never been love at all, only a desperate woman, grateful to have her life saved, responding warmly to the only voice she heard. And what had he done? Called her a whore—a truth, but not a kind one. Nearly attacked her. Driven her away.

He was a monster. This world had *made* him a monster. He should never have come to London, never taken Oswald's money, never listened to Oswald's promises, never pursued his desire to create a mate for himself.

If love was lost to him, then what did he have to live for? What emotion was strongest in him, apart from the desire for love? What desire could guide him *now*?

Pressing his hand against his heart, the one Oswald's bullet had stopped, the question was answered. His name was Adam. He knew he would never find love.

Now all he wanted was revenge.

Adam went to the room where he kept the ravenous, feral dead women he thought of as his honor guard. They strained against their chains, but they did not attack him, and so he had no need to activate the small magnetic device that he used to guide them: their rudimentary minds had come to associate him with food, after all, the only kindness they cared about. They were devoted to him, at least.

Adam walked into their midst. "Come," he said. "I will feed you. I will feed you fresh meat. I will feed you the brain and liver and heart of the most brilliant man in London."

In Dark Places

Ever since awakening in the cage, Pimm had wanted to pull Ellie to him and bury his face in her hair, so glad was he to find her unharmed. During Oswald's grandiose soliloquy, he'd been more interested in looking at her profile than in hearing the old man's mad secrets. Now that they had a quiet moment, he considered taking her hand, and telling her that being gassed and awakening with his head in her lap had altered his viewpoint on certain significant subjects… but he settled for pouring Ellie another cup of tea while Freddy worked at picking the lock, muttering and wiggling her tools. Big Ben was awake now, sitting in one corner with a teacup seeming thimble-sized in his huge hand, keeping watch in case Carrington or Crippen or Oswald himself should return. They could be out in the gloom, observing, Pimm supposed, but none of them seemed like the types to sit quietly and watch.

"I'm sorry I missed the picnic," Pimm murmured to Ellie.

"Yes, then we could have all three been abducted all at once," Ellie said. "That would have saved a great deal of time." She glanced at Freddy, then leaned in toward Pimm—making his heart trill a bit—and said, "Why did you marry her?"

Ah. "Well, she was in a dreadful predicament, of course. She needed help, and I was in a position to give it. Freddy's family was never particularly patient or understanding, and they would not have tolerated

225

the shame. And back then, especially, Freddy was entirely incapable of making a living on his—her—own. Taking on a new identity was an obvious necessity, and I had the contacts to make that possible. I might have merely given her money to set up her own household, but an unmarried woman of obvious means living alone would have been a target for fortune-seeking suitors, and never had a moment's peace. And obviously I couldn't have a young lady living in my house *without* marrying her. It just… seemed to make sense, and to solve both our problems—my problem being a family that had grown increasingly insistent that I marry *someone* and settle down."

"But… to close yourself off to the chance of every marrying for *love*…"

Those of Pimm's class seldom married for love, or only for love, but that was hardly worth mentioning. "I suppose it never seemed right, to attach myself to a woman, given the way I live—chasing criminals. And, to be frank, drinking more than anyone else seems to think I should. My parents kept pressing these sweet society girls on me, you know, their friends' younger daughters—who seemed to grow younger every year—and I was afraid my family would wear me down, that eventually I would marry one of them just to make them stop, and subsequently make the poor thing miserable. A girl who loves dancing at balls and doing needlework and going horseback riding and playing the harpsichord… life with me would be an unrelenting horror for such a person. Marrying Freddy saved some poor girl from just such a fate." He made an effort, and met Ellie's eyes: so blue, so focused. "I confess, I did not anticipate meeting another woman whose personality seemed a rather better fit than, ah…"

"But you are married," Ellie said.

"Yes," Pimm said miserably.

"How very complicated this new world is," Ellie said. She took his hand. "But we must be willing to change with the times. The world is no longer conventional, after all. Perhaps we have no choice but to become somewhat unconventional ourselves."

"Are you saying…"

"I am saying, if we do not die here, or in the near future, then you and I should dine together. But this time, I will not be wearing a false mustache and a waistcoat. That is *all* I am saying, for now. But I am saying it most emphatically."

"Seeing you two leaning together like that does my heart good," Freddy called, "but we should really be on our way." She grinned and pushed open the cage door, which hardly squealed at all since she'd dripped a little olive oil from the picnic basket into the hinges.

"We can't flee immediately," Pimm said. "There is another lock for you to pick, Freddy."

"The Queen, yes. I can scarcely credit it. Seems she should be immune to the terrors of the flesh, somehow." Freddy slipped her lockpicks back into her hair, wrinkling her nose. "The picks are dirty from the lock now. I really must get some dresses with pockets. The absence of pockets in women's clothing is part of a systematic attempt to oppress women, did you know that, Ellie? You should write a story on it."

Once they were out of the cage, Pimm picked his coat up from the chair and patted the pockets. "The pistol is gone—Carrington must have kept it—but everything else is here. And, of course, I have my walking stick." He snatched the latter up from the floor. Shading his eyes against the alchemical lamp, he peered into the dark. "Do you think it's a trap? I can't believe they left us entirely unguarded."

Ben snorted. "Oswald doesn't know what he's doing, nor that Carrington neither, not when it comes to holding prisoners. Without Value to advise them on the practical end of being a criminal, they're lost. Of course they'd trust a lock on a cage door to keep us in. But we should move away from the lamp. It only it makes us a target, you see."

"I'm not sure where I'm going," Pimm said, setting off into the darkness in the direction Carrington had gone when he left to fetch the tea. "Do you know which way the office is from here, Ben?"

"'fraid not. I was in no state to pay attention when they dragged us over."

"Ah, well, how big can this warehouse be?" Pimm said.

"Oh, you should know better," Freddy complained. "You've just tripled the size of the building by saying that, you know."

"I do recall Mr. Value telling me this was originally three warehouses that got all joined up together," Ben said. "So we may have a bit of a walk ahead of us."

They moved carefully in the gloom—the light from the high windows was fading as the afternoon wore on—skirting around heaps of old machinery and patches of floor slick with grease. They discovered a dozen of the clock-work women, standing stock-still in rows as regimented as any group of toy soldiers, their eyes blank, unwound and undirected, eerie sentinels in the dark.

Not far from the grove of courtesans they encountered a tall partition dividing up the space, walked around the wall, and found Oswald's clock-work factory. Alchemical lamps dangled from beams overhead, illuminating abandoned work surfaces scattered with tools. Great shelves held bins filled with what looked for all the world like severed body parts: arms, legs, torsos, feet, hands. Pimm and the others drifted around the space, marveling at the horror of it all, the eyeless bald heads of women arrayed in a row on a high shelf, with a line of wigs draped on stands beside them. "I wish I had an artist here," Ellie said. "An engraving of *this* would be a striking accompaniment to the newspaper story I will inevitably write, and I fear a mere description won't do the scene justice."

Ben picked up a large box of eyeballs, all different colors, and rattled it around. "Gruesome, innit?" he said. "But I *have* been to this part of the warehouse before, when I visited with Mr. Value, and I believe I know how to get to the office from here."

"By all means, lead on," Pimm said. Ben guided them through a low door, into another cavernous space—this one occupied chiefly by the sound of dripping water—and on a roundabout path among splintered crates and broken machinery until Pimm saw the outline of a door off in the distance.

"That's where we came in," Ben whispered. "The office is just over—"

"Shh," Ellie said. "There's someone moving around over there."

They all peered toward the office on its raised platform some hundred yards away. The windows of the office were now lit by the steady light of an alchemical lamp, and a shape moved inside. After a moment the door banged open and Carrington stepped out, whistling, and walked down the steps.

"You must release us at once!" a querulous voice called, but Carrington didn't slow his stride, shouting, "Shut up, you old baggage!" over his shoulder as he descended. Pimm gestured to his friends, and they all faded back, ducking behind a stack of crates.

When Carrington passed by their hiding place, Pimm stepped out, jammed the metal ball at the tip of his walking stick into the man's side, and depressed the button that released the stored charge. Carrington shuddered and collapsed into a twitching heap.

"Could I kick him?" Freddy said. "Just a little?"

"We should question him," Ellie said. "He may know more about Oswald's 'great work,' and what he has planned for the Exposition tonight."

"Fine, fine." Pimm knelt, removed his pistol from Carrington's pocket, and rose. "Ben, bring him along, will you? But first we'd better free…"

"The old baggage?" Freddy said.

"Show some respect for your sovereign, Freddy." He led them—Ben carrying Carrington over his shoulder like a sack of beans—toward the cage. "Your Majesty!" Pimm called. "My friends and I will free you shortly."

"See that you do," the man in the cage called.

"Your Majesty," Freddy said, dropping a curtsy as she removed the lockpicks from her hair. "If my Lord husband will be good enough to lend me his portable light, I will endeavor to free you."

Pimm passed over his pocketwatch-sized alchemical light, then looked at Ellie, and followed her gaze up the stairs to the office. "You want to go through Oswald's papers, don't you?" Pimm said.

"It is my heart's most fervent desire," she said.

That's what a man likes to hear, Pimm thought wryly, but said, "I was hoping to find some true evidence of his perfidy myself." He gestured for Ellie to go up the stairs, then followed, watching Ellie lift her skirts and rush with girlish enthusiasm up the steps and through the door.

The office, when Pimm reached it, was nothing particularly exciting: a desk with neatly stacked papers arrayed upon it, shelves crammed with binders and books, and a wall of pigeonholes filled with rolled papers. While Ellie methodically sorted through the contents of the pigeonholes, Pimm sat down at the desk and opened up the bottom drawer. A small bottle of brandy, half-full, rested inside, along with a single glass, and he smiled. Ah, there was *his* heart's most fervent desire. Or second most fervent, anyway. He poured himself a glass—Ellie looked over and frowned, but didn't say anything, so he chose to construe that as permission, if not approval—and drank it down fast. The cresting wave of an approaching headache receded, and he poured another measure of brandy to sip more slowly.

"There is ample evidence here tying Oswald to the clockwork courtesans," Ellie said. "Bills of lading, invoices, work orders, all with his signature. But there's no crime there, and certainly no *treason*. I'm sure the Queen in the cage will be happy to see justice done… assuming anyone believes she is who she claims. I'm not entirely sure *I* believe it, but that may just be my native skepticism."

"The man down there hardly *looks* like the Queen," Pimm said, "and I'm sure Bedlam has a patient or two who claim to be some monarch or another, with little evidence to support the assertion."

"Surely there are ways, scientifically, to prove or disprove that she is who she claims…" Ellie said doubtfully.

"There are indeed," Pimm said. "Getting anyone to bother to do the tests may be a different matter. Incontrovertible documentary evidence of Oswald's wrongdoing would be helpful." Pimm sorted through the drawers in the desk, but didn't find much of interest… until he noticed that the bottom of one drawer seemed perhaps two inches higher than it should have been.

"Something hidden here," he said. "People think they're being so *clever* with hiding places like this, and I suppose it is clever in a way, but everyone is clever in the same *way*, which makes it predictable, and predictable is sometimes functionally identical to stupid." Pimm rummaged in the desk's top drawer until he found a metal letter opener. Ellie watched as he jammed the edge of the letter opener into the crack around the false bottom and levered it up, revealing a small space beneath. A long book bound in red leather rested inside. Pimm lifted out the ledger and flipped it open to a random point, revealing lines of cramped writing in brown ink.

"A cipher," Pimm said after a moment.

"Sort of," Ellie said. She ran her finger along a line of prose from right to left. "It's mirror writing, you see? Every letter is backwards, and every word and sentence written back-to-front. It's how Leonardo da Vinci wrote in his own journals."

"I'm sure the comparison to Leonardo was not lost on our Sir Bertram," Pimm said. "He tends to place himself in the company of geniuses. Indeed, one gets the sense he considers Newton and Galileo tiresome amateurs."

"This would be easier to read if we had a mirror," Ellie said, "but this section seems to be about the disaster in Whitechapel, do you see? And the date, here, it fits, and more prattling about purple crystals."

They flipped farther along in the journal, and this time it was Pimm who stabbed the journal with his finger. "Here, the 'Great Transformer,' that's the Constantine Affliction. Look, he writes all about it, here's Mabel Worth's name—" He rubbed his eyes. "My eyes are not made to read backwards. Reading forwards is quite enough of an effort for me most of the time."

"This is proof positive of his criminality," Ellie said. "With luck, he's written something about his plans to poison and replace the Queen…"

Pimm nodded. "I hope so. That would help see the prisoner downstairs recognized as the monarch again. Assuming we can keep her from striding into the palace and demanding her full honors immediately…"

"We are not foolish, Lord Pembroke," the Queen said sternly, standing in the doorway of the office. "We realize there will be some resistance, but we have trusted friends at court who will not be fooled by a mere change in our appearance—and there *are* things only the monarch and a few others in the realm know, by which we may prove our claim. We are confident that our position will be restored… if we can reach those who need to be convinced."

"The prime minister and the rest of the cabinet will likely be at the Exposition tonight," Freddy said from behind the monarch. "Along with whomever Oswald has standing in for the Queen. Sir Bertram—forgive me, Your Majesty, *Mister* Oswald—will be there too. We should pay the Exposition a visit, don't you think?"

"Oh, yes," Pimm said. "But first, let us speak with Mr. Carrington, and see what he can tell us about Mr. Oswald's plans."

A Mouthful of Blood

T hey bound Carrington to his own chair in front of the cage where they'd been imprisoned, next to the alchemical lamp. Ellie had no desire to see anyone tortured, but if she had to see awful things happen to *someone*, Carrington was an acceptable choice.

Pimm sat down on another chair they'd brought from the office, in front of the prisoner, but some distance away. He nodded at Ben, who dumped a bucket of water on Carrington's head.

Carrington gasped, staring around him, then sighed as the water trickled down his face. "Good heavens. Did my master just walk off and leave you lot unguarded? I suppose he sent Crippen away, too, or took him along to the Exposition. The man is brilliant, of course, but he just isn't *practical*. He knew *he* wouldn't be able to escape from the cage, so he assumed you wouldn't either."

"I was just remarking on that fact," Ben said. "Seems a shame for all your plans to be undone over something so foolish."

Carrington chuckled. "My dear huge brute, you have no idea about our plans. They are not so easily disrupted."

"Speaking of those plans," Pimm said. "I find I have a few questions on the subject."

"Oh, I'm sure you do. Oswald was so *coy*, wasn't he, about his ultimate goals? How maddening it must be, to be so ignorant, so eternally under-informed!" He noticed the Queen for the first time. "Oh, you let our friend Victor—it's Victor now, isn't it? What else could it be?—out of his cage. He's a bit bossy, but it's just his little way."

"Please pay attention to me," Pimm said. "I have questions. You will answer them."

"I can't see why I should," Carrington said. "You hardly seem like the torturing type, Lord Pembroke, you'll forgive me for saying so. You're entirely too good-hearted. Why, I doubt you'd even set your great ox of a bodyguard there on me—"

"Oh, he won't torture you," Freddy said, from behind Carrington, bending down to speak right in his ear. Ellie was gratified to see the secretary's smirk slip a fraction. "Pimm will take Her Majesty, and Miss Skye, and even Big Ben there, and they'll go for a little stroll around the property. That way, the two of us will have some private time together. The peculiar thing is, I don't even *care* what you have to say, and even a torrent of true confessions wouldn't induce me to *stop* what I plan to do with you. Really, the only way to avoid such a tête-à-tête with me would be—"

"All right!" Carrington said. "I was only winding you lot up, anyway. I don't mind telling you what my master has planned. Why should it matter? You could tell a cow in the stockyards it was about to be slaughtered, but the foreknowledge wouldn't change its fate."

"Then tell us," Pimm said. "And quickly, please."

"A drink of water wouldn't go amiss. I gave *you* lot that courtesy, when you were caged, and confessing one's sins is *such* thirsty work—"

Ellie brought Pimm a cup, and he held it to Carrington's lips, while the man sipped. Carrington smacked his lips appreciatively. "Ah, glorious, glorious. All right. Tell you quickly, you say, but there is some necessary context, of course, isn't there always? You recall the Crystal Palace, I'm sure, erected for the Great Exhibition?"

"Of course," Ellie said.

"There you have it. The great glass enclosure made quite an impression on my master—nearly a million square feet, covered in a great construction of cast-iron and glass, simply *tons* of material, but the whole effect lighter than air! My master was born in a hut made of *mud*, much longer ago than you would credit or he likes to admit, and seeing construction on such a scale always has a powerful effect on him—"

"*Quickly*," Pimm reminded him.

"Your soul lacks poetry," Carrington said. "But, briefly then: Oswald wishes to enclose all of London, and much of the outlying agricultural areas, in a construction similar to that of the Crystal Palace, though made with more advanced materials. His aim is to make the entire city a sort of greenhouse. Or, more properly, an experimental chamber, one where Sir Bertram himself controls all entries and exits. He envisions an entirely closed system—except when it suits him to open it, to allow imports of food and such, I suppose. The city would become a test site where my master could finally control all the variables, including the climate, the weather, and all other factors he can possibly influence. And, oh, the things he plans to do in that chamber. Introducing transformative potions into the water supply. Chemically castrating criminals. Improving—or dampening—the minds of certain... elements of society. He has toyed with the notion of creating a plague that would transform everyone into true hermaphrodites, partly to finally erase what he perceives as a foolish belief in the difference between the sexes, and partly to create a test population that was more biologically uniform, yet still be capable of breeding. I don't like that idea—making us all partly female would just make us all partly *weak*—but I know Sir Bertram won't believe in the folly of such measures until he has experimental proof. My master would, of course, institute selective breeding programs as well, and why not? If a prize pig can be bred, why not a prize *human*? That's why he wants you lot alive— he thinks you're fine specimens, intelligent and young and fertile, and he hates to waste decent breeding stock. I daresay Sir Bertram's scientific approach to creating perfect humans would be more successful than the similar ad hoc attempts made by, say, royal families." He bared his teeth at the Queen. "We'll have rather less in the way of bulging eyes, vanishing chins, and anemia, I daresay, under *his* breeding program. Fewer marriages between first cousins, too."

The Queen drew herself up, but Freddy murmured in her ear, and Her Majesty settled down, though her glare was poisonous.

"That's madness," Ellie said. "Who would stand for such a construction, even with a puppet impostor of the Queen lending her support? Even if Oswald managed to replace the entire cabinet with automatons, or all of Parliament, the people would rise up in the face of such madness!"

"At the very least, the people would pilfer all the building materials in the night," Winnie said, "and nothing would ever be successfully constructed."

"Ah, but the dome will be *beloved* by the people," Carrington said. "And why not? It will be their only protection against the horrible monsters from the void."

The others frowned, but Ellie understood immediately. "Oswald plans to manufacture a threat, doesn't he? Some sort of terrible outside peril to frighten the populace into accepting drastic actions in the name of protection?"

"Precisely," Carrington said. "You've heard of the terrible tentacled things that dwell now in the river? They are... escapees... from his early experiments along those lines. And they are only *babies*. When he unleashes the full-sized creatures on the city, and proves himself the only man capable of protecting us from their ravenous man-eating intentions? With the false Queen supporting him wholeheartedly, crying out for swift action? Of *course* the people will support a vast building project to keep us safe, and Parliament will pass the New Enclosure Act with all due haste. The legislation has already been drawn up, and awaits only the right moment for introduction. Oswald means to employ nearly every able-bodied man in London to help construct the enclosure, at amazingly generous wages, which will also ensure the project's popularity. Such payments will exhaust Oswald's personal fortune and perhaps even the royal treasury, too, but what of it? One of his first acts once the enclosure is sealed will be to abolish money and personal property." Carrington leaned forward, straining against his ropes. His eyes glimmered with the passion of the true fanatic. "And the marvelous part is, the people *still* won't rebel, because they will see the tentacles appearing in the sky, lashing against the newly-built dome, the monsters terrorizing the countryside, and they will hear tales of the beasts laying waste to the remainder of the British Isles... and, perhaps, even the world beyond. They will learn to *love* the dome."

"These monsters are more clockwork, I suppose?" Pimm said. "Controlled remotely, like this automaton of the Queen?"

Carrington began to laugh—to *giggle*, really. "Oh, no. They are real. Very real. Have you ever peered through a microscope at a bit of slimy pond water, Lord Pembroke?"

"I have not had that pleasure."

"I have," Freddy said. "The water teems with life—strange creatures, with limbs like hairs, flailing flagella, tiny beasts that devour one another."

"Oh, yes," Carrington said. "Sir Bertram made similar observations, and he began to wonder, if there is such a *micro* world, a place of whirling ferocity beneath our notice, its denizens ignorant of our very existence— was it possible that there was a *larger* world, inhabited by creatures so much vaster than ourselves that they, too, were effectively invisible to us? Creatures who would view *us* much as we view amoebae through a magnifying lens? He began to investigate the idea, building exploratory apparatus that, frankly, far exceed my technical understanding. And he *found* them, out there beyond the stars—in the same way *we* are beyond a drop of pond water under a microscope. The next step was to call the attention of those creatures. His first experiment… did not go well, and its aftereffects are still visible to any who care to look, though none recognize their import."

"The *aurora anglais*," Ellie said.

"He broke the sky," Carrington said, almost dreamily. "That setback only energized him, though, and he later learned the secret to opening portals to that distant realm, and observing the creatures therein. Apparently just as all matter is an illusion composed mostly of empty space, all *scale* is just a matter of perception too, and those vast creatures can be brought down to a… more manageable size. Small enough to enter our world, in fact."

"And these creatures are monsters?" Ellie said.

"Oh, they might seem so to our eyes. They are inhuman, certainly. Vast, in their own world. Sir Bertram says we can perceive only a small part of their bodies, that portion which intrudes into our gross physical world. He thinks *all* the manifestations he's witnessed of these creatures may be segments of a single vast entity, and that the individual 'creatures' only appear to have independence because we cannot comprehend the connections between them—much as an ant might think a man's middle toe and the same man's eyeball were unrelated objects. These creatures inhabit other dimensions, ones we cannot perceive, he says…" Carrington sighed. "He says a great many things, restating wisdom long known to adherents of certain secret religions, transforming the poetry of faith into terribly dry scientific terminology. I confess, it took some effort to guide Sir Bertram toward the desired outcome. He was reluctant, at first, despite my urgings. He was afraid he would be unable to control the creatures if he allowed them entry to our world. But I convinced him nothing was beyond his power."

Ellie's stomach roiled. "Speak plainly, sir. Why did you try to influence Oswald to undertake this course of action?"

"Some people have known of the existence of these creatures for years. For *centuries*. My own family belongs to a sect devoted to bringing about the coming of these creatures, and we have been about our work for generations. Oswald is not the first to discover their existence. Certain standing stones in the countryside were erected in order to open passageways for them, brief portals that appear only during rare astronomical alignments. Sometimes the portals open in the deep sea, and a few of these old gods—for, understand me, they *are* as gods to us—slip through, and dwell for years in the deeps. They are the source of most tales of sea serpents, you see, though they cannot live long in our world. Not as our world is *now*, that is—but they could make certain changes, and transform our Earth into a habitation more hospitable to them... if rather less so for us. But Sir Bertram truly *is* a genius, at least by human standards, and he has developed the means to create more stable portals, which may be opened at will, and which can allow larger intrusions. Once the old gods can reach into our world whenever they wish, they can send in a few of their numbers—or their *fingers*—to subdue mankind, and then alter our world to suit their own purposes. After that they can arrive en masse, having cleared their new home of vermin—much as a human might level a forest and burn out a mound of ants and exterminate a colony of rats in order to build a new house on clean ground. Their world is *full*, you see, they are crammed together there like lengths of firewood stacked for the winter, and they wish to come *here*, where they may stretch their terrible limbs."

"I have heard of such cults," Ellie said. "Fools wearing robes, drinking blood and chanting incomprehensible syllables under bridges, all while gazing dumbly up at the stars."

"Call us fools if you like," Carrington said equably. "Our gods are on the verge of arrival—I daresay I can withstand a few more days of your contempt. Oswald thinks he knows how to control the creatures, because I led him to believe that, and contrived situations where he could influence their behavior, using knowledge passed down through my family. But when Oswald opens a portal tonight to frighten the populace, he will find his techniques fail, and he will be devoured along with the rest. Consuming hundreds is just how our gods say *hello*. Fear not. His great dome will never be built."

"I confess some confusion as to why you would choose to worship such creatures," Pimm said, remarkably calmly, Ellie thought. "The Church of England only wants me to *tithe*, but you willingly serve a church that requires you to be devoured?"

"Oh, our gods will need servants, but even their servants will be as *kings* to the rest of humanity," Carrington said. "The transformation of our world—our *universe*—into a suitable habitation for their kind will not be accomplished quickly, and they will require local assistance. Those of us so favored will be raised high, to rule among the others of our kind."

"To rule as head dog in a pack of pets, you mean," Winnie said.

"Just so," Carrington said. "But everyone is *someone's* dog. At least I shall have the most powerful masters." He began to chew on his lower lip, drawing blood, and Ellie wondered if he'd gone suddenly mad.

"We will accept no threat to our sovereignty!" the Queen thundered.

"I wouldn't worry, Your Majesty," Pimm said. "As Miss Skyler says, these are the prattlings of known cultists and lunatics, and there is no truth or substance to them—"

Carrington spat a mouthful of blood onto the floor. "There," he said, blood running down his chin. "It seems like magic, I know, but it's not—the area has been primed already, this is where Oswald did his first experiments. The cages where we locked you up were used to house the first creatures that... came through. That bit of blood on the floor just serves to call their attention, just as blood in the open ocean can draw the attention of sharks." A strange humming sound filled the air, accompanied by a smell like burning lavender, and a change in pressure, like the sudden onset of a storm, but even swifter and more profound.

"Prepare to meet your new masters," Carrington said. "And, shortly after, to meet your maker." He cackled as the air around them tore itself apart.

An Uncouth Beast

Pimm grabbed Ellie by the hand and dragged her away. His hair was standing on end, floating about his head in a cloud, and Ellie thought her own hair must be doing the same. Ben roared and stumbled toward Carrington, then staggered back as what seemed to be a net of lightning wove itself around the man as he laughed on. Once they drew away from the chair, the air pressure seemed to return to normal, with the frenzy of sparks and strange odors seemingly confined to a circle some ten feet across, not quite centered on their captive. Even the terrible, head-filling humming noise was diminished once they stepped away from that circle. Carrington's mad laughter, alas, was just as loud as ever. "What is *happening*?" Ben cried, looking about him, perhaps trying to find an enemy he could actually fight.

"I fear exactly this is exactly what Carrington promised," Pimm answered, one hand in his pocket, doubtless touching some weapon or another. Ellie wished fiercely for pockets of her own, and pistols to put in them. "Some beast is being summoned, or revealed, or translated to this world."

Winnie had leapt away from the chair as soon as Carrington spat blood on the floor, and now prowled around the edge of the disturbance, her head darting this way and that, tearing tarps off of piles of crates, prodding piles of metal with Pimm's spent walking stick.

"Freddy!" Pimm called. "What are you doing, and can we help?"

"There must be machinery!" she called. "Projectors, or engines, or *something*, the blood may have triggered this, but all this chaos is coming from *somewhere*—Ah ha!" She shoved aside a few loose boards and tore away a dropcloth to reveal a surprisingly delicate contraption the approximate dimensions of a hatrack, made of curved brass metal, glass tubes, and odd crystalline protrusions—though the crystals were not purple, fortunately, only milky white. Up close, the thing buzzed like a beehive, a sound that made the small hairs on the back of Ellie's neck seem to vibrate. "Smash it up!" she shouted, and Ben, clearly aware that such destruction was his metier, picked up a length of broken wood and proceeded to lay about the contraption, shattering crystals and warping metal, making a terrible racket. The buzzing hum first stuttered, then lowered in pitch, then ceased entirely.

Winnie grinned savagely at Carrington. "There, you see? It's far more difficult to *build* things than it is to destroy them."

Carrington chuckled. His hair still stood on end, giving him the appearance of a demented dandelion. "Well done. You closed the door. Of course, you also destroyed the magnetic containment field. Not all cages are made of iron bars, you see—after certain ugly incidents following the initial summonings, Sir Bertram invented a sort of magnetic pentacle to hold the beasts in place, better than iron can. Anyway, you were too late. I am reminded of a certain proverb about closing a barn door after the horse has already—"

Something lashed out from the darkness, a slick shadow that moved with the blurring speed of a hummingbird's wings, and Carrington's head vanished in a burst of red, like a tomato struck by a bullet. They all stared as the headless body slumped to one side in the chair, but remained held upright by the ropes. Off in the dark, something moved across the floor, making a sound like fish flopping in the bottom of a boat, and the squelch of boots in mud, and the patter of rain on a roof, and the mewl of a gravely-injured kitten—and other sounds beside.

Pimm edged behind a stack of crates, beyond the limits of the pool of light, and gestured for the others to join him. They did, though the Queen came slowly, and with exaggerated dignity. "I think—" Pimm began, and the shadow lashed out again, smashing one of the crates into flying splinters. They all hunched and huddled, behind what remained of the barrier of crates, waiting silently, but the thing did not attack again.

"I don't know if it sees us," Ellie whispered. "But it seems to *hear* us."

"Can we kill it?" Ben asked, his own voice hoarse and low.

"The things in the Thames have been killed," Ellie said. "By guns and bludgeons and axes. My paper ran an engraving of one, or part of one—the creature came apart in the water like a rotten cabbage when the boatmen tried to pull it out, and all that remained was a bit of ragged tentacle. If they are truly the same sort of creatures, then yes, this one is mortal."

"Hunting it would be easier if we could see," Pimm whispered.

"It's a shame you didn't bring the monocle I made you," Winnie said.

Pimm looked at her blankly, then closed his eyes for a moment. He patted his vest pocket. "Ah. I do. I have it here."

Winnie rolled her eyes. "It might have done you some good earlier, don't you think?"

"You are right, as always, dear wife." He screwed the lens—tinted strangely green, Ellie noted—over his right eye, closed his left eye, and peered around the edge of the crates. He drew his head back, face pale. "It's... bigger than the things in the Thames. The size of an elephant, easily."

"What does that lens do?" Ellie asked.

"Lets me see in the dark," Pimm said. "One of Freddy's inventions, some chemical trapped between two pieces of glass. Remarkable, really. Though it makes everything a sort of ghastly green color."

"Our fighting men could make great use of such a device," the Queen said.

"I suppose I have to hunt the beast, don't I?" Pimm said. "Heavens. I hunt *criminals*, of course, but in practice, that usually means I just point out their whereabouts to the police."

"I will assist you," Ben said. "I can distract the thing, at least."

"You may all assist me—excepting of course Your Majesty," Pimm said. He reached into his pocket and removed a handkerchief, unwrapping it to reveal a pair of rounded, off-white objects that might have been bird's eggs. "Freddy, would you mind showing Ellie and Ben how these work?"

"Oh, how lovely," Winnie said. "You brought my favorite things." She held up one of the eggs. "This, my friends, is a pocket distraction. The

alchemical fluids that light our lamps are quite stable, but with a few….
alterations… they can be made more volatile. I've sealed a bit of the altered fluid inside these hollow clay balls. Simply throw them against a
hard surface with sufficient force to smash them apart—it takes a bit of
effort, I didn't want them breaking in Pimm's pockets so they're fairly
thick—and you will be rewarded by a *most* unpleasant burst of noise and
light." She grinned. "I call them 'bangers and flash.'"

"I'll go *this* way," Pimm said, pointing left, "and you lot go *that* way, and
fling the bangers at the wall, get the beastie's attention."

"And what will you do?" Ellie asked.

"Shoot it," Pimm said. "And if that fails, Ben can beat it to death with
that length of wood he found. Seems straightforward enough, eh?"

Ellie put a hand on his arm. "Pimm. *Do* be careful."

"Oh, well," Pimm said. "If you insist." He reached over to squeeze her
hand, then slipped off into the dark, Ben following.

"Shall we?" Winnie said, and passed over one of the bangers.

"I am supposed to report the news," Ellie said. "Not *become* it."

"Ah, but there's no better vantage point than the thick of things," Winnie said.

Ellie had once shared that perspective, but she was reconsidering now.
Give her a high place with an unobstructed view rather than a spot at the
center of a melee any time. But Pimm was going to face a monster, so the
least she could do was make some noise. At least she couldn't *see* the thing.
Hearing it was bad enough.

Hearing it was bad enough, Pimm thought, but seeing the monster was
even worse, especially with it rendered in the horror-show green tint the
monocle lent all things that passed before it. He'd told the others the beast
was as big as an elephant, and that was true, but it didn't *look* much like an
elephant. It looked like a quivering mass of chicken fat shot through with
dark structures like the branches of a tree—some sort of skeleton, perhaps,
or nerves, or blood vessels, or something without analogue in the animal
kingdom. The monster had no discernible eyes—or even a head, for that
matter. Tentacles, or things that looked enough like tentacles to justify

the name, sprouted from the mass at irregular intervals, waving like reeds whipped by inconstant winds. Worst of all was the fact that the monster looked *blurry*—Pimm could not focus on the beast, and continually had the sense that it possessed more limbs, more *mass*, tucked somewhere just out of sight, hidden around a corner that didn't actually exist. The thing moved with a ghastly sort of undulation, leaving grotesque smears across the floor. Oddly enough, the beast had no discernible odor. Pimm supposed there must be some scientific explanation for that. Oswald could probably explain it. Pimm would be sure to ask him just before the man was hung for treason. Or perhaps Oswald would be beheaded. That was traditional, and if it was good enough for Carrington....

Pimm heard the *crack* of breaking porcelain and shut his eyes just before a blindingly bright flash of light burned the world orange even through his squeezed-tight eyelids. Ben, who hadn't been prepared for that level of brightness, cried out in the dark behind Pimm. Even more disorienting than the light was the noise, the sound of a thundercrack resounding in the confined space. The beast made no sound—a scream would have been nice, some indication that it had been discomforted—but when Pimm opened his eye, he saw the creature lashing its tentacles wildly and smashing its bulk repeatedly into a pillar, clearly frenzied or disoriented by the noise. Pimm raised his pistol and fired, but he may as well have shot at a muddy embankment for all the impact it made. The beast paid no attention to the assault at all.

Pimm began to wonder if the men who'd "killed" this creature's smaller cousins in the Thames had actually killed them at all, or merely hacked off pieces, leaving the rest of the beasts to submerge, still alive. Perhaps losing a tentacle for one of these creatures was no more traumatic than a man losing a fingernail or a lock of hair.

"What do we do?" Ben said, or at least, Pimm thought that was what he said—the ringing in his ears made it difficult to be sure.

"I don't know," he tried to say, and then the beast turned on him, lashing out with its pseudopods. The only reason Pimm and Ben weren't struck down was because the beast's limbs smashed into one of the warehouse's support pillars first. They stumbled backward, ducking behind another contraption of metal and crystals and brass. Pimm cast around desperately for something he could use as a weapon. Fire? He had his flask, and while it would be a shame to waste its inflammable, intoxicating contents on an assault, perhaps he could improvise some sort of incendiary bomb—

Something flashed in his vision, on the far side of the creature—a long streak that looked like a spear, piercing the creature's side. The beast stiffened, went entirely still—tentacles sticking up at strange angles—and then shuddered, its flesh rippling like the windblown surface of a lake, until it slumped. Its body began to collapse into itself like a melting snowman, and now there *was* a smell, of burnt meat and acidic chemicals.

Pimm rose, looked at Ben, shrugged, and made his way around the deliquescing mass of the great beast. Ellie and Freddy stood near the alchemical lamp and the remains of Carrington, chatting as amiably as if they were at a dinner party. "What did you *do*?" Pimm asked, his voice probably entirely too loud due to the ringing that continued in his ears.

"It was Ellie's idea," Freddy said.

"Oh, no," Ellie said, blushing. "I only said I wished you had not discharged your cane—I wondered if an electric jolt might have an effect against such a creature. I know electricity can cause muscles to contract, to jerk, to spasm—and this thing seems nothing *but* a muscle."

"But I *did* discharge my cane," Pimm said.

Freddy nodded, then beckoned and led him to a third engine like the one Ben had destroyed. "Yes, but there's other electricity in the world, darling. These things are rigged to run on batteries—more sophisticated batteries than any I've ever seen, I must say." Pimm squinted, noting what looked like a metal urn, remarkably similar to the vessels he'd seen lining shelves in Adams's workshop. "With a little tinkering, a great expanse of wire, and a bit of effort, I turned a length of broken metal into a harpoon. We attached the wire to the metal, let Ellie fling the spear, and once our weapon was firmly seated in the creature's side—like sticking a finger in a pudding—I threw the switch." She gestured, and Pimm saw the twisted filaments extending from the engine toward the monster's corpse. "I expended the battery's entire charge and ruined the engine, but I can't say I mind."

"Lucky thing he had more than one of these engines around," Pimm said, thumping the side of the device.

"Oh, he needs at least three," Freddy said. "The engines connect with one another, you see. One engine is nothing, just a point in space. Two engines connected, well, what good is that? With two points all you can make is a *line*. How are terrible otherworldly monsters supposed to enter our universe through a *line*? But with three points, you can make a triangle, and while that is not the traditional shape for a door, it proves sufficient to create a field these things can pass through. Assuming the engines are strong enough, you could move them farther and farther away from one another, and make a very *large* triangle… and, thus, let through very large beasts."

"Carrington said these apparatus were smaller than the ones Oswald planned to use tonight," Ellie said.

"We have to get to the Exposition," Pimm said.

"We do," Freddy said. "I think I saw one of these engines, you know, being set up for the event. I had no idea what it was—something magnetic, I would have guessed, some new technology Oswald had created to show off to his admirers. But Pimm… the device was far larger than this one. I don't know where the other engines at the Exposition are positioned, what the dimensions of his portal are going to be… but it wouldn't surprise me if he intends to turn all of Hyde Park into a door for these creatures to pass through."

An Orderly Departure

꧁ꕥ꧂

"You threw the spear, eh?" Pimm said, falling into stride with Ellie as they walked out of the warehouse. The Queen, of course, led their procession, with Ben at her right hand—she'd apparently decided to adopt him as bodyguard, to the man's obvious discomfort. He had his hands full lugging two of the batteries salvaged from the other arcane engines, too. Winnie had plans for them, apparently. She came along behind, seemingly lost in her own thoughts, probably mentally crafting devices of electric mayhem. "Well done," Pimm said. "I suspected you had marvelously dangerous qualities from the first moment I met you."

Ellie thought, not for the first time, how unfair it was that one could not suppress a blush. "Winnie insisted her aim was horrible, so I agreed to give it a try. It was no great challenge—the creature was as broad as a barn, and it had blundered close enough to the light for me to see its shape looming there."

"I shall resist the urge to call you Queequeg," he said.

Winnie laughed behind them. "You certainly know how to flatter a girl, Pimm!"

But Ellie brightened at the remark. "You've read Mr. Melville's *The Whale*, then?"

Pimm coughed. "Well. Freddy brought it home, really. She has a passion

246

for novels. I read *parts*. And only from the first volume. I confess the portions devoted to the particulars of sailing were only slightly less tedious for
me than those passages devoted to theological musings."

Ellie nodded. "I commented on the author's longwindedness on the
former subject in the review I penned for the *Argus*, but nevertheless, it is
a worthy volume, with much of value regarding the subject of unhealthy
fixations. You should never resist the opportunity to learn something new,
I think. Pray give the story another look. We could discuss the text."

"Just tell me if the mad captain ever caught his great fish?"

"I will not satisfy your curiosity. You'll simply have to read it yourself."

They emerged into the fading day, all squinting against the fog-dimmed
sun. "Finding a cab in this neighborhood will be difficult," Pimm said.

"Carrington brought us in a carriage," Winnie said. "That horrible Crippen took the horses away somewhere. Oswald came separately––perhaps
the carriage that carried us is still here?"

"I know where they keep the horses and such," Ben said. "Around back
here."

They tramped around the perimeter of the warehouse, until they found
a disreputable set of stalls, and the poor horses, still hitched up to the
carriage. Ben looked around and pronounced the area deserted. "Will this
conveyance suit Your Majesty?" Pimm said. "I'm afraid we will all have to
ride together."

"It will have to do," the Queen said, and sniffed.

Pimm opened the door of the carriage, then backed suddenly away.
"Ben," he whispered, and Ellie stepped forward to peer into the coach.

"Crippler" Crippen was seated inside, leaning against one wall of the
coach, quite asleep, a thread of drool running down his chin.

"Ah," Ben said. "Allow me." He put down the batteries, reached into the
carriage, grabbed the ex-fighter by the ankles, and jerked him out of the
carriage in a single motion. The back of Crippen's head banged the seat,
then the carriage floor, then the step, then the ground. Crippen squawked
and waved his arms, until Pimm cocked his pistol and pointed it down
at the man.

"Aw, Ben," Crippen said, rubbing his head and looking up at the giant
holding his ankles. "What's all this then?"

"I've gone over to the other side, Crip," Ben said. "I'll have to tie you up, I'm afraid. Will you give us any trouble?"

Crippen sighed. "Even on my best day I never faced more than *one* man at a time in the ring, and never a fellow with a pistol." He looked hopefully at Pimm. "Am I to understand you're hiring help, sir? Sir Bertram pays me quite handsome, but I'm open to other offers—"

"I am afraid I have no positions in need of filling just now," Pimm said. "We'll just bind you and prop you in the stable, all right?"

"Just promise to send someone 'round to get me later, Ben," Crippen said. "It's been terrible cold nights, lately."

Ben glanced at Pimm, who nodded. "Consider it done," Ben said, and commenced to bind his old associate with a length of coarse rope he found dangling over the side of one stall.

Ellie drew Pimm aside. "That man attacked me with a knife. I understand we hope to avoid further violence, but to simply set him free—"

Pimm blinked. "Ah, no. I will indeed send someone to get him—but that someone will be a policeman. Probably best if we don't mention that to *him*, though."

Ellie laughed, relieved. "I should never have doubted you."

"Oh, no. It's always wise to doubt me. There's no better way to avoid disappointment."

Ellie had never expected to ride in a carriage with a Queen, and the experience was not what she might have imagined. The Queen was a querulous, portly man, after all, though undeniably regal. Winnie and Ellie sat across from Her Majesty, while Pimm sat up top with Ben, who was driving the horses across the city toward Pimm's home. The opening ceremony at the Exposition was due to start in Hyde Park near sundown—some of the effects were meant to be more spectacular in the dark, or so the handbills promoting the event had promised.

Ellie worried they wouldn't make it there before Oswald set his plan in action, but Winnie insisted they stop by her home first—"Unless you'd like to fight Oswald's monsters with a walking stick and a pistol?" When they arrived, Winnie opened the carriage door herself—the Queen tutted—and climbed out, where Pimm was already waiting with the batteries. "This will take me a bit of time to prepare," Winnie said. "You should go on to the park without me. Look for the devices, the ones made of brass and crystal, and smash them up. Destroying even one of them should be enough to prevent Oswald from opening his portal. With luck, you can stop the monsters from coming through at all. And if not… I'll be along with weapons."

"More harpoons?" Ellie said.

"Oh, I think I can do better than that. Remember the horrible engine we saw being assembled? Look for me in its vicinity. I'll be there as quick as I can."

"Perhaps Your Majesty would consent to stay at my home?" Pimm said, leaning into the coach. "There is no reason for you to go rushing into danger—"

"We are meant to *be* at this exhibition," the Queen said, chins quivering with suppressed fury. "We intend to be in attendance, and to denounce whatever imposter presumes to take our *place*."

Pimm closed his eyes briefly, which Ellie had already learned was a sign that he was attempting to calm himself down. He opened his eyes, smiled, and nodded. "Of course, Your Majesty. Your presence would be an honor."

"Don't allow yourself to be eaten before I arrive," Winnie said, and patted Pimm on the cheek before hurrying to her front door, batteries held under her arms.

"Once more into the breach," Pimm said, and shut the carriage door.

"I suppose I shall have to give him a knighthood, assuming he survives," the Queen murmured, apparently to herself, or so Ellie gathered from the fact that she said "I" instead of "We."

Forearmed

Hyde Park was jammed with bodies. Ellie had observed often that Londoners were fond of anything that promised spectacle at no charge, and the handbills promoting the Exposition had been exceptionally lurid for what was, after all, described as a display of "the newest scientific advancements in electricity, magnetism, and alchemy." Such a thing might suggest dry lectures, but the handbill was festooned with engravings featuring lightning bolts, a levitating man, and, for no reason Ellie had been able to discern, an elephant with enormous curving tusks.

A portion of the park along the northern bank of the Serpentine had been transformed for the exhibition. The area was lit by hundreds of alchemical lights strung along ropes and hung atop towering wooden poles, and a large stage had been erected, filled with tantalizing-looking mechanical apparatuses, some visible even from the back of the crowd: something like a huge orrery, but featuring a strange configuration of planets, with twin suns at the center; an enormous engine topped with a huge horn, stylized to resemble the bell of a flower; a huge cannon pointed skyward, its barrel embellished with dozens of tubes curving in baroque profusion; a glass-walled tank as tall as a man, full of faintly-glowing pink liquid; and other remarkable devices and displays of uncertain purpose. Oswald wasn't visible yet, nor the false Queen, and the special seats set up to one side of the stage for the Prime Minister and other high officials were only about a quarter occupied—apparently most of the great men of London had better things to do than attend Oswald's celebration of his own accomplishments.

"I'll work my way around toward the river," Pimm said, all but shouting in Ellie's ear to overcome the steady din of the crowd, which conversed, complained, commiserated, attempted to sell one another boiled sweets and ham sandwiches and gingerbread-nuts and Persian sherbet, speculated about what sights the Exposition might present, and bellowed angrily at the inevitable pickpockets. "I think that tower must be one of the engines." He pointed to a dim construction that towered over the crowd on the river side of the stage. "You should check on the far side of the stage!"

Pimm moved away before Ellie could object—or point out that the engine she and Winnie had seen constructed was *on* the far side of the stage, not over by the Serpentine. She was left with Ben and the Queen, both of whom looked a little sick, doubtless for different reasons—the Queen probably because she had not been so close to the milling shouting stinking press of her subjects in years, if ever, and Ben because he was taking his position as her bodyguard seriously, and looking around at the hundreds of potential threats to the royal personage, who was, after all, barefoot in a dirty dressing gown.

"I'm going to go search this way!" Ellie shouted, and Ben nodded glumly as she set off toward the north-west. She was fairly certain the construction Winnie had noted before their aborted picnic was in that direction, though with the landscape so changed by the Exposition's construction and the crowd, it was hard to be sure of its precise location. Ellie heard the Queen shout, "We wish to be closer to the stage!" and gave a shudder. A man the size of Ben could get the Queen through the crowd, no doubt, assuming he didn't give himself a heart attack worrying about Her Majesty in the process.

Ellie wished she had a walking stick, or at least Winnie's parasol, to help clear a path. As it was, she had to walk to the far edge of the crowd, where the press of bodies was not so overpowering, in order to work her way around the edge, making a slow loop toward the place where Winnie had noticed that peculiar building project. She could just see it, now, a spire raised above the heads of the crowd, more than twice the height of a man—

"Welcome to the Grand Exposition!" boomed the voice of God. The audience fell silent, apart from a few shrieks of alarm. For a moment, Ellie thought the crowd would break and run, like a herd of deer startled by the snarl of a predator, but the vast voice chuckled and spoke again. "Do not be alarmed! The voice you hear belongs to me, Bertram Oswald, not to some terrifying behemoth. This miraculous amplification—this extraordinary *loudness*, to put it in simpler terms—is the work of one of the many inventions I intend to reveal tonight. I have toiled long in my workshop, my laboratory, and my studio to create a cavalcade of wonders that will dazzle the mind and enrich the soul!"

Ellie stood on tiptoe, and could just make out a figure dressed in a white suit standing at the edge of the stage, holding some small device trailing a long wire up to his mouth as he spoke. Ellie looked away and wove her way through the crowd, past people staring raptly at the figure on the stage. Someone who could talk *that* loudly could command a lot of attention. Fortunately, Ellie knew from recent experience that Oswald secretly longed to be a stage actor—or, at least, loved the opportunity to deliver long speeches. He could probably be counted on to expound on his own greatness at some length before attempting to unleash hideous creatures from beyond the sky.

If they could just stop the *immediate* threat the man posed, Pimm could contact his fellows in the police force, perhaps even exploit his family connections to secure a meeting with members of Parliament or ranking ministers, and present their evidence against Oswald—let him be damned by his own journals. They would also, of course, have to present the Queen. Ellie wasn't entirely sure how that meeting would go... but she knew it would be the makings of a phenomenal article, no matter what.

She finally reached the base of the tower, not too terribly far from the right-hand side of the stage... and her hopes fell. Amazingly, no one was leaning against the tower, or trying to dismantle it in hopes of selling the pieces, and as she drew nearer, she understood why. The smaller engine in the warehouse had emitted an unpleasant buzz, but this thing was *vastly* more powerful. The sound was not any louder, not really, but it seemed to make her bones vibrate at terrible frequencies, and her stomach churned abominably when she drew near. She could bear the discomfort in order to smash the thing apart... but that was impossible.

The engine in the warehouse had been smaller, and it had also been un-protected. *This* device was secured in a cylindrical cage of black wrought iron, the metal worked in an elaborate astronomical design featuring comets, shooting stars, planets, suns, and the moon in all its phases. Inside the metal cage, she could see crystals twinkling, and the glint of brass. Very pretty, and also very *secure*. The whole must have been erected by a crew of men working with ropes and pulleys. The tower wasn't that large in diameter—she couldn't have reached her arms around it, but Big Ben could have, just—but it was quite tall, at least fifteen feet high. Ellie leaned her shoulder against the tower and pushed, hoping perhaps its height and relative slenderness would make it unbalanced and easy to topple. But push as she might, it didn't even sway. Too securely seated in the earth. Perhaps with half a dozen more people shoving, it would shift, but Ellie couldn't hope to knock it down on her own. Oswald's voice droned on in the background as she pondered and fretted, and Ellie knew she would be hearing his prattlings in her nightmares later.

She hesitated, unsure what to do next. Work her way back around the crowd and find Pimm? Look for the Queen and Ben? If Oswald saw *them*, he would be furious, but he wouldn't be able to do much about it while running his Exposition. She backed away from the horrible humming of the engine, because it was hard enough to think without that buzzing in her head.

A moment later a carriage drew to a stop on the street bordering the northern end of the park. Ellie squinted and saw a woman climbing out of the carriage, without even waiting for the coachman to open the door, and knew it must be Winnie. Ellie lifted her skirts and ran through the grass toward her friend. Winnie was directing the coachman to lift some items out of the carriage, but she glanced around and saw Ellie, and gave a wave. "Come here!" she shouted. "I can't carry all this myself!"

Ellie reached the cab and looked at the items now piled on the ground with just as much bewilderment as the blinking young coachman. The batteries looted from the warehouse were there, but with leather straps attached to them now, alongside a pair of fencing rapiers trailing long wires from their hilts. "Winnie, what *are* these?"

"Weapons, my dear. You'll have to stop being Queequeg, though. How do you fancy being d'Artagnan?"

"Wasn't he beaten horribly with sticks by an old man and his companions?"

"I was thinking more of his formidable displays of swordsmanship," Winnie said. "Try to avoid old men with sticks, would be my advice."

"I don't know how to use a sword," Ellie said.

Winnie glanced at the coachman, who looked predictably aghast at this exchange, then handed him a few coins. He turned back to his horses, muttering.

"And you were experienced with harpoons prior to this afternoon? I don't expect you to win any duels, Ellie dear. If you encounter one of those monsters, just jab in the sword, like a needle into a pincushion. The electricity will do the rest."

"Electricity?" Ellie said, though it was obvious, really, now that she thought of it.

"Naturally. We've seen the effectiveness of a little bottled lightning against these creatures." Winnie attached the wires dangling from one rapier to a pair of bolts on top of one of the urns, then slipped her arms through the battery's straps, settling the device firmly on her back. She held up the rapier attached the battery, depressed a button on the wooden hilt, and a spark sizzled at the sword's tip. "Be sure not to touch the metal with your bare hands, all right? These swords can do worse than slice you open." She whipped the rapier through the air and grinned. "Don't you just love the smell of electricity in the evening?"

An Unanticipated Arrival

Pimm thumped his fist against the metal cage surrounding the engine near the river and swore. There was no knocking *that* thing down, not without a team of drafthorses and some stout chains, or at the very least a few strong men who wouldn't mind rocking the iron tower back and forth until it worked loose from the earth. He moved away from the engine, out of range of that hideous buzz that made his bowels all watery, and considered his next move.

Dash it, he might have to confront Oswald on the stage. A public denunciation could be marvelously effective, and it would be a pleasure to interrupt Oswald's prattling, but the assault could go badly if the man had guards on hand. Still, if breaking the towers wasn't possible, the only way to stop the carnage to come was to interrupt the Exposition before Oswald could unleash the beasts from beyond.

He started to make his way toward the stage, where Oswald was talking about the wonders he planned to display: "I make no claim that my Grand Exposition will be the equal of the Great Exhibition, that marvel organized by the sadly disgraced Prince Albert. Nevertheless, when you consider that all the creations to be featured at this Exposition came from the mind of a single man, I hope you will be suitably impressed. But I could not have created these wonders without the support, in every sense, of my dearest friend, who has deigned to bestow her favor upon this humble subject, and to join us tonight. May I present your Queen, Victoria Regina!"

The audience knew when they were meant to applaud, and they did, thunderously, as Queen Victoria—or a convincing imitation—stepped toward the front of the stage, dressed in an elaborate white gown, a crown of gold upon her brow. Pimm spotted the guards, now, who had emerged when the Queen did, standing discreetly back on the stage. Oswald whipped a cloth off a shrouded object to reveal a high-backed throne, decorated with the same astronomical symbols as the cage that surrounded the engine, though in gilt rather than black iron.

The Queen waved to the crowd—no more mechanically than she did at any other public appearance, Pimm noted—and then seated herself on the throne and looked toward Oswald, presumably with an expression of rapt attentiveness and expectation, though from this distance, her face was a mere blur. The presence of a false Queen on the throne rather spoiled Pimm's plan to rush the stage, though—her guards would seize him before he could even begin an oratorical denunciation.

"With Her Majesty's permission, I will continue," Oswald thundered through his loudspeaker. "I have created marvels, my friends, yes, to improve your lives and fill your days with pleasure, but I feel I must take this opportunity to warn you of certain dangers I have discerned in my recent study of the skies. Look above you, my friends, and behold the strange lights the press have dubbed the *aurora anglais.*" Most of the crowd obediently tilted their heads backward, and Pimm did, as well. Dusk was upon them now, and the sky was lit with the jewel-toned threads of the aurora, shifting and shimmering above. "These atmospheric anomalies may be heralds of some greater danger," Oswald said solemnly. "I have, with my great telescope, observed strange movements upon the surface of the planet Mars. I fear the mysterious denizens of that red planet are engaged in some vast building project, much as our own nation might build a fleet during war time. Could the changes we've seen in our sky be some part of some alien plan? Are these lights a misguided attempt to communicate? Or some strange preparation for their arrival on our shores?"

The crowd murmured in alarm—and some in healthy disbelief, Pimm noted, resisting the urge to shout "Balderdash!" himself.

Oswald nodded as he paced back and forth on the stage, like a minister warming to his sermon. "Oh, yes. There is life beyond our sky, strange life. And you will be disturbed to hear… these creatures have visited us before, in isolated ones and twos, not unlike scouts for an invading force. I know. Because I have *captured* them." He gestured toward the back of the stage, and a bright alchemical light shone down on a pair of men who wheeled a huge glass-walled tank toward the front of the stage.

Many in the crowd screamed. Several ladies fainted. There was great agitation among the few government officials present in their special raised seating area. "Do not fear!" Oswald shouted, and his booming voice was so powerful that, remarkably, the crowd seemed to obey—at least that portion of the crowd that retained consciousness. "The creature is safely contained."

The creature was broadly similar to the one Pimm had fought at the warehouse, though rather smaller, the size of a cow instead of an elephant. It was a sickly yellowish color, and in addition to tentacles it sported bony protrusions like the beaks of raptors. The creature slapped its tentacles against the glass walls of its tank in a frenzy, trying to attack everything at once—Oswald's huge voice must have driven it mad, seeming to come from every direction. Oswald thumped his fist on the side of the tank. "I have developed methods to kill the creatures, though they are fearfully resilient—"

Someone in the crowd shouted something, though the only word Pimm caught was "river." Oswald seemed to hear it too. He nodded. "Yes! Yes, the strange creatures sighted in recent months in the Thames are almost certainly further scouts from Mars, the vanguard of a force of exploration… or invasion. My colleagues urged me to keep these discoveries secret, or at most to do a private presentation for certain members of the Royal Society. But I believe—and your Queen supported my belief—that the people of our great empire deserve to understand the dangers that face us. We have the power of technology at our disposal, and we can protect our city from any threat, no matter how terrible. Most of the wonders I have to unveil tonight are weapons capable of destroying these beasts—or even controlling them, to turn the invaders into weapons for our side. If these creatures from the stars *do* attempt to invade our shores, they'll find we're more than a match for a bunch of wriggling beasts. God save the Queen, and God save England!"

The crowd cheered, though a bit uncertainly, and who could blame them? Oswald was not a great orator, and the subject matter was disorienting in the extreme. The people had come expecting to see lightning and levitating men, and instead they were presented with a monster in a jar and wild stories of invasion from a neighboring planet. Perhaps Oswald overestimated how easily it would be to manipulate the people of London with fear—

One of Oswald's stagehands led out a goat on a tether. "But I do not wish to mislead you," Oswald said. "These creatures are ferocious. They are driven into a killing frenzy by the scent of fresh blood. In order to protect yourselves, you must understand the extent of the threat before you. Allow me to demonstrate." The stagehand offered Oswald a cane, and Pimm frowned. Did the man intend to bludgeon the goat to death and feed its corpse to the thing in the tank? That was showmanship, of a sort, Pimm supposed...

But the stick was a sword-cane. Oswald drew the blade and tossed the scabbard aside. Before Pimm could shout "No!"—not that it would have helped—Oswald had brought the sword down cleanly across the animal's neck, sending a jet of blood across the stage, and the goat's head rolling into the crowd.

The creature in the tank *was* in a frenzy, though not noticeably more so than it had been a moment ago. A terrible buzzing hum began, far louder than the similar noise back at the warehouse. Wind began to whip across the park, blowing Oswald's jacket around him wildly. He raised his arms overhead and bellowed, a shout loud enough to overwhelm the screams of the people in the park, most of whom were now trying to stampede away. "Do not be afraid!" Oswald shouted. "This is the sort of atmospheric disturbance that heralds the arrival of these creatures. Perhaps they have come to seek the return of this prisoner! But no matter. We shall show them our might! We shall drive them back! We shall—"

Pimm watched in fascinated horror as a slit appeared in the sky over the stage, as if the twilight air was a bit of cloth being rent asunder. The space beyond the tear was a ghastly sort of blackish purple... and then a pale green tentacle unfurled from the slit, wriggling down like a root questing into the Earth. Oswald didn't see the tentacle, and the people pointing and shouting made no impression on him—he probably assumed they were still pointing at the beast in the tank beside him on the stage, which had gone strangely calm, as if awaiting rescue.

The tentacle—which was easily fifty feet long now, thick as a tree trunk near the slit, but tapering to the diameter of a child's arm at the end—reached down and wrapped itself around Oswald, trapping his arms against his body. The scientist dropped the device that amplified his voice when the thing seized him, but his scream as the tentacle lifted him into the air was loud enough for anyone to hear. He struggled, but he was no match for the tentacle's strength, of course. The terrible pseudopod withdrew into the tear in the sky, taking Oswald with it, and the sound of his screams ended abruptly.

A shower of red pattered down from the hole in the sky—a rain of blood in miniature—and spattered the false Queen, who sat watching these events with all the equanimity one would expect from a machine. Her guards attempted to get the false Queen to rise, to hurry her away to safety, but they found her immovable—the automatons had metal bones, and were far stronger and heavier than mere humans, Pimm supposed. The mechanical Queen showed no inclination to do anything but sit in her throne and watch the madness overtake the park.

Pimm had hoped that Oswald's death would be the end of the horror, but of course, the creatures had no intention of passing up the appeal of an open door. Whether Carrington's claims about the goals and motivations of the creatures were true or not, they were undeniably a grave danger.

As Pimm watched, three of the elephant-sized creatures precipitated out of the air before the stage, materializing like a vile fog. They were each different from the others: one appeared as half a dozen globular sacs, like oversized fish eggs, joined by spokes of bone, and he watched in horror as it rolled over an injured woman and somehow absorbed her into one of the translucent orbs of its body. Pimm could see the woman trapped inside the globe, pounding her fists against the membranous sac, mouth open in a scream he could not hear.

Another was like a great black pudding made of mouths. He'd read something once about how the angels of the Mohammedan were terrifying creatures, each having seventy thousand faces, and each face with seventy thousand mouths, and each mouth with seventy thousand tongues. This creature was not quite so blessed with excess mouths, but it had easily several hundred, lined with tiny triangular teeth, and long, narrow, tonguelike protrusions emerged from each mouth by the dozens, lashing about wildly, wrapping around any fleeing people they encountered, and dragging them toward the waiting, drooling maws.

The third beast resembled a snail out of its shell, but where a snail had only two eyestalks, this one had dozens, and while some of the stalks were topped with eyes, others were topped with pincers, or serrated mandibles, or shapes like fleshy flowers, or oozing orifices of uncertain purpose. As it slithered along the ground, it left a smear of thick, clear ooze behind that made the grass turn black and smoke.

Most of the crowd had rushed away from the stage before the things appeared, but those who'd been knocked down or injured in the stampede were easy prey for the creatures. And still the horrible engine at Pimm's back hummed. How long would the portal remain open? How many more creatures would arrive? Just looking at them was enough to make Pimm's mind reel, and he wished desperately for a drink. Ten drinks. All the drinks. But he had to act… somehow.

Ellie obviously hadn't been able to disable an engine, either—but had she made it to safety? Was Ben protecting the Queen? And where was Freddy? Had she brought weapons? Pimm could surely use a weapon now.

He crouched and began to hurry across the park, on a path tangential to the marauding monsters, thinking of finding his fellows, but he stopped when he glimpsed a group of figures approaching from the direction of the river. There was something familiar about the way the one in the lead moved, favoring one leg, and the man towered over the other people crowding behind him— "Adams?" Pimm said to himself. It was unmistakably the giant anatomist, with a crowd of milling figures at his back. Pimm rushed toward the man, hoping his keen mind might have some insight into how to destroy the engines, or fight the beasts. "Adams!"

The giant looked toward him, face hidden behind his white mask, and held up a hand in greeting. The people behind him staggered to a halt, and as Pimm got closer, he slowed his approach. They were women, he thought, but bald, and dressed in rags, and their faces were animated snarls, all teeth and drool and snapping ferocity. "Adams?" Pimm said weakly.

"Lord Pembroke," Adams said. "What a pleasant surprise. I came here to destroy Sir Bertram's Exposition by perpetrating acts of horrendous violence against the spectators… but I see my presence is hardly necessary. Sir Bertram certainly did make a *lot* of plans, didn't he? I had no idea he planned to summon monsters such as these. They make me feel positively human myself, by comparison."

"Adams!" Pimm cried. "Listen to me. These monsters were part of a plot by Oswald, to frighten the city into obeying him, but he couldn't *control* the beasts. Now he's been killed, and the whole city is in danger—"

"Yes," Adams said. "I see that you are right. But, I am compelled to ask… what does any of that have to do with *me*?"

Pimm gaped at him, and after a moment, Adams shrugged, turned, and began to trudge back toward the Serpentine, his hissing, spitting bodyguards following along after him.

Vanquishing Swords

"It serves him right," Winnie said, gazing up at the torn piece of the sky where Oswald had vanished. "But what a dreadful way to go." They were still near the iron-wrapped engine, out of the path of the general stampede, and as they watched, several recognizable men from the government leapt down from their raised seats and raced past the women as fast as their portly physiques would allow. The red-faced, sweating, terrified men looked like caricatures of themselves in *Punch*, Ellie thought.

"There are more creatures, Winnie." Ellie gestured with her rapier, careful not to depress the button that would send electricity coursing through the blade. "Two… no, three. They are *ghastly*."

"And there are many more to come, I don't doubt it." Winnie sighed and lashed her rapier a few times. "I hope Pimm is concentrating on how to sabotage the engines, because I can't see how we can accomplish much. But we can do something about the beasts… if we have the courage."

"I think it is less courage, and more simple necessity. If we do not confront the monsters, who will?" Ellie thought of her fiancé—she could barely remember his face, anymore—of the way he'd been crushed by a machine in the shape of an elephant. Now she would face something the size of an elephant, but of a rather stranger shape. "Winnie," Ellie began, "if we should die, I wish you first to know, in the short time we have been

262

acquainted, you have become a great—"

"No, no." Winnie shook her head fiercely, blonde ringlets bouncing. "Changing from a man to a woman has largely upended all my old views about the differences between the sexes, but when facing battle, I think it's best to go with something a bit more stirring, a bit less soppy, so let me quote a great poet who happened to be a man: 'From this day to the ending of the world, we in it shall be remembered—we few, we happy few, we band of sisters; for she today that sheds her blood with me shall be my sister.'"

"I don't think that's *quite* as the bard wrote it," Ellie said.

Winnie tightened the straps on her battery. "He used to wear a dress and pretend to be a girl on stage, didn't he? He can cope with a certain degree of infidelity to his original pronouns. Well, sister? Shall we?"

"Cry havoc, then," Ellie said, "and let slip the dogs of war."

"You mean bitches, surely." Winnie grinned, and together, they went striding toward the nearest of the beasts, swords crackling and sparking in their hands.

Winnie looped to the right, and Ellie to the left, as the great snail-thing extended its hideous stalks toward her. Ellie brought her rapier down in a looping arc, severing the nearest stalk, and the creature drew in *all* its questing stalks, like a turtle withdrawing its limbs into a shell. She danced forward, extending her arm, and jabbed the tip of the rapier into the thing's slick gray side, then depressed the switch in the sword's handle. The sword vibrated in her hand, making her flesh tingle, and the creature's stalks burst forth again, smoke issuing from the ends, as its whole hideous body quivered like a bowl of jelly.

Ellie turned off her sword and, glancing down, saw one human leg sticking out from underneath the monster, its foot clad in a ragged boot. The stink of sizzling, rotten meat assailed her nostrils. She considered whether or not to vomit—doing so might make her stomach feel better, at least briefly—but in the end had no time. The great globular monster was lurching in their direction, heaving itself forward on its grotesque arrangement of sacs, and Winnie was already darting toward it, slashing at the egglike globes. Great torrents of clear fluid poured out of the holes she made, and the people the thing had consumed slid out of the openings, too, some coughing wetly and trembling, most already dead.

Ellie joined her, trying to free those who'd been absorbed, until finally the beast was a limping mass of broken spheres, and then she electrified it, and sent it to sizzling death.

Winnie whooped and joined her, hair matted with sweat, eyes bright and alive, cheeks hectic and red. "They don't stand a chance!" she shouted. "At least, until the batteries run out!"

But as they paused to catch their breath, two more creatures appeared, seeming to emerge from shadows—but there were no shadows. One was a mass of twisting tubes, or perhaps a nest of living red snakes, its body in constant squirming motion, while the other was like an immense yellow jellyfish, ringed by tentacles that branched and bifurcated into flailing lashes like a score of cat-o-nine-tails. More shapes shimmered in the air, monsters about to achieve immanence.

"Pimm had better kill the engines soon," Winnie said grimly, and before Ellie could respond, she moved to fight these new monsters.

"You must help me!" Pimm cried, pursuing Adams. "If not for me, then for England!"

"I am not an Englishman," Adams replied.

"For the sake of human decency, then!"

"I am not human," Adams said.

That took Pimm aback, but he soldiered on. "Then, damn it, Adams, help me for *love!*"

Adams paused in his journey toward the river, tilting his head, then turned and regarded Pimm. "Love? You speak to me of love?"

"Yes, damn you! The woman I love is back there in that *melee*, somewhere, Adams. You told me that love was the only thing you cared about, so I ask you, as one man to another—and I don't care if you're human or a troll or a god from Olympus, you are still a man—will you help me save the woman I love?"

Adams stared at him for a moment. "I would have to be Hephaestus, I suppose," he said at length. "Of all the gods of Olympus, I mean. I have the limp, and I'm fairly good at working metal. And Hephaestus was married to Aphrodite, the goddess of love. But *you*, Lord Pembroke, do *not* love the woman to whom you are married, and do not try to tell me otherwise—"

"You mean you don't know?" Pimm said. "My wife is really my oldest and dearest friend, Freddy. He was transformed into a woman by the Constantine Affliction, so he changed his name to Winifred and I married her so she wouldn't be cast out on the street, friendless and alone. I thought you *knew*, Abel Value was blackmailing me on the subject, you're the one who did the tests proving Winnie and Freddy were one and the same—"

Adams nodded slowly. "The hair samples? Ah. No, I was merely asked to do the test. I was not told why, nor given the identity of the subject. Value did not share his plans with me—we were not intimates. Who, then, is this woman you profess to love, Lord Pembroke?"

The conversation was maddening, and surreal, with the screams and sounds of violence Pimm could hear not so far behind them. "Her name is Ellie," Pimm said. "Ellie Skye. She is a journalist. She is brave. She is… she is… dash it, she's the writer, not me. I do not have her eloquence— which is one of the reasons I love her."

"You love a woman you cannot marry," Adams said, as if musing to himself. "Because you have chosen to wed another. It is a doomed and unrequited love. I see. Yes. All right, Lord Pembroke. I will help you. What would you have me do?"

Pimm felt dizzy with relief. "That device there, in the cage of iron, we have to destroy it, or those monsters will continue to materialize."

"Mmm. Very well. And the beasts themselves, I suppose, must be dealt with."

"Electricity has proven effective—" Pimm began.

Adams waved that away. "I have, alas, left my batteries at home. But these poor souls I brought with me, meant to ruin Oswald, have a taste for flesh, and they are not particular about the origin of that flesh. Nor do they feel pain. Those beasts appear to be flesh, strange though that flesh may be. I am sure the beasts will serve to slake the appetite of my honor guard." Adams took a small square device from his coat pocket and began twisting dials.

The horde of ragged creatures at his back streamed forward, rushing past Pimm, carrying with them their eye-watering stink of raw meat and blood and unwashed skin. Pimm watched as they attacked a roiling mass of red serpents near the stage. It unfurled some of its tentacular body to smash them away, but the honor guard rose again, relentless, and began to bite and tear at the tentacles, clawing their way toward the main body, which they seemed bent on consuming. Pimm frowned. There were other figures on the grass, dashing around one of the new monsters—was that *Freddy*? With a *sword*?

"They were dead when they were brought to me," Adams said, forcing Pimm to return his attention to him. "I had hoped to restore them to true life, but I failed. I *always* failed. Except once."

"The brain in the jar, you mean?" Pimm said. "Margaret?"

Adams nodded. "Yes. I saved her mind, and I gave her a new body, strong and beautiful. But I frightened her. She ran away."

"I'm terribly sorry to hear that, Adams." Pimm wanted to shout at him, to tell him they had to smash the engine—yet another creature had appeared, not far from the river, looking like nothing so much as a length of intestine the size of an omnibus, undulating toward them. But Pimm sensed this was a delicate moment, and held his tongue.

"Love, eh?" Adams said dolefully. "The only thing worth living for. Even doomed love. All right. I failed to take my revenge on Oswald personally, but smashing up his engines might satisfy my urge. Show me that which you need destroyed. I am a better destroyer than a creator, and I should embrace that fact."

Pimm raced along the river away from the new beast, Adams moving surprisingly quickly alongside him. The giant's limp never went *away*, but it didn't seem to hinder his forward progress at all. Soon they reached the base of the horrible tower.

Adams considered the engine. "Yes, all right, I can tear it down."

"Don't we need a team of horses, or a few more men, or—"

"No, no, I have it well in hand." Adams stepped closer to the tower, standing at the base, tilting his head. "That buzzing…"

"Yes, abominable, isn't it?" Pimm said. "It makes my very bones vibrate."

"Oh, I find it quite pleasant, myself. The harmonics of a universe just on the edge of shattering. The sound tastes like a sweet and sticky pudding. How marvelous. I hate to destroy the source of such a sensation. Ah well." Adams set his shoulder against the tower, braced his feet against the ground, and shoved.

"I tried that," Pimm said, "it's no use. I know you're taller and stronger than me, but—"

Adams grunted, braced himself again, and continued pushing. Was the tower beginning to *list* toward the river? Surely not. No one could be that strong, no one could possibly—

The tower definitely moved, and as it began to topple, momentum and gravity took over, doing their part, and Adams stepped back as the iron and the machinery inside fell, one end smashing into the waters of the Serpentine. The crystals inside shattered noisily, and the buzzing stopped. The unnatural wind whipping across the park ceased as well, and the park was still again, but for the monsters and those fighting them.

Pimm could hear the grunting of the dead women—they were gathered around a fallen behemoth like dogs on a carcass, squabbling over mouthfuls—and then, clear as a bell, Ellie shouting, "Have at you now!" A monster like a great jellyfish writhed and then went still, and… yes, that was Ellie and Freddy, wielding Pimm's old fencing swords, leaping about beyond the monster's carcass!

"Your lady's voice?" Adams said, and smiled. "I think she and your wife have the other monsters well in hand." He twisted at the device in his hand, and the dead women slumped and fell over, collapsing into the corpse of the thing they'd gutted. "Please see they get decent burials, would you, Lord Pembroke? A decent burial is so important. I've had dozens, myself, every one a comfort."

"How did you perform such a feat?" Pimm said, looking down at the toppled tower. "You…" He wanted to ask: What are you?

Adams seemed to sense that. "I am but a poor and patchwork thing, Lord Pembroke. Neither troll nor Olympian—though my maker fancied himself a sort of modern Prometheus. I am merely in possession of a great many muscles—far more than I started with. I tend to add more whenever I begin to feel helpless and out of control. And my bones are reinforced with metal, here and there, to help bear the strain. My blood… is not like your blood. I am strong. Though I have no other good qualities, it cannot be denied that I am strong." He looked toward the river, where the last of the beasts, the intestine-thing, surged forward blindly.

The creatures weren't so dangerous, Pimm thought, as long as there weren't too many, and if they couldn't catch you by surprise. But the monster that had reached through the tear in the sky to seize Oswald had been larger, doubtless the size of an ocean-going vessel, and if that had made its way to the Earth… Pimm shuddered. "You don't want to capture that monster or anything, do you? For study?"

"Hmm? Oh, no. I wanted to kill something today. Toppling that tower only whetted my appetite for devastation. I shall sate myself on this beast." The giant limped toward the monster, and when he drew close, the thing lashed out at him with half a dozen slimy protuberances, jointed like the legs of a crab, emerging from the slickness of its hide. Adams seized the closest limb, and, to Pimm's astonishment, tore it right off, like a man ripping a drumstick from a chicken. He flung the limb toward the river, and then reached out to tear off another.

"Pimm!" Winnie shouted. "Pimm, come quick, the Queen!"

The Queen! How had he forgotten about her?

Quite easily, actually, considering everything that had happened—but since they *weren't* all going to die, it seemed, matters like the safety of the rightful monarch seemed to matter again. Pimm hurried across the park, stepping around the bodies of the more unfortunate visitors to the Exposition—though fewer bodies than there would have been in the long run, if Oswald had succeeded in his plan—and the dead women and the beasts, the latter already dissolving into slime and ooze and jelly.

Ellie and Freddy were dirt-smudged paragons amongst the corpses, wielding terrible swords, majestic as angels of vengeance. He wanted nothing more than to sweep Ellie up in his arms—but there was the matter of her sword, which appeared to be electrified. And, of course, the Queen—

Affairs of State

"I couldn't stop her," Ben said, staring down at a cup of tea in his huge hands. They were all—Ben, Pimm, Winnie, and Ellie—seated together in a beautifully-appointed room, with trays of biscuits and hot strong tea, but they were still too energized from events at the park—and anxious about the future—to relax. "We hid under the stage when the monsters appeared, you know, the Queen and me, but when it seemed like things had settled down, Her Majesty said it was time to take charge. I tried to hold her back, but only with words of course, I didn't dare lay hands on her. She climbed up on the stage, and I went with her. A couple of the guards had stayed with that false Queen, brave lads they were, so I felt a bit bad when the Queen told me to make them move aside. So I did—they were ready to fight monsters from the sky but not me, I suppose. I didn't hurt them much, just knocked them down. I turned back and the Queen..."

"We saw that part," Ellie said, holding her own cup. There were guards waiting discreetly outside the closed doors, while various cabinet ministers and other officials and the Queen herself tried to untangle just what had happened, and what it all meant, and where to go from here. Ellie was glad she didn't have a seat in those councils. She'd done quite enough thinking lately.

"Queen Victoria, wielding a sword," Winnie said. "The sight of her in full ferocity made me rethink my uncharitable feelings about the monarchy."

"It was a lucky thing Oswald left his sword cane on the stage," Pimm said. "Or Her Majesty would have been forced to tear the head off that automaton with her bare hands."

"I believe she would have done it, too," Ben said. "She didn't like how it looked a bit. Said it was nothing like her. Far too jowly, she said."

When the guards had risen from their beating, and realized the now-headless monarch on the throne was a machine—oozing oil and sprouting broken springs—they were at a loss. Their confusion only intensified when the middle-aged man in a dressing gown began shouting at them imperiously that *he* was Queen Victoria, and that her cabinet must be assembled at *once*.

But they'd done it, by God, run off and returned with all the available authorities on Earth or in heaven, it seemed.

And now here they were, the saviors of the empire, some hours later, having been fed only tea and biscuits, waiting to see if they'd be given medals or tried for treason.

Ellie wanted her bed. She suspected Pimm wanted a drink.

The door opened. A man with a ginger mustache and twinkling eyes stepped in. "Hello, you lot," he said.

"Jonathan," Pimm said. "You know my wife. This is Eleanor Skyler, the journalist, and Ben, ah—"

"Drummond," Ben supplied.

"Ben Drummond. This is detective Jonathan Whistler, a police inspector. So, Jonathan? What's it to be? Are we bound for the Tower of London?"

"It seems the mad old man you brought back from the park really *is* the Queen," Whistler said, perching on the arm of a chair that was, at a conservative guess, three hundred years old. "The head of the Royal Society did a test comparing a strand of her hair to a few strands taken from the Queen's brush, the same way we can link the hair of a murderer to a sample found at a crime scene. The eminent scientist in question says he has proved the Queen's identity definitively—to his own satisfaction, at least." Whistler took a flask from his pocket and passed it to Pimm, who opened it and filled his cup with amber liquid, then took a deep drink. Ellie felt a flash of irritation, and was then irritated with *herself* for being irritated—surely the man deserved a drink? But then, he probably usually deserved a drink, and by all accounts, he took all the drinks he deserved and then some.

"So, no, no Tower for you," Whistler went on. "Only a few of the lords think you were part of some vast conspiracy to overthrow the throne, and they're the sort who always think the worst of everyone, because that's what *they* would do. The general consensus seems to be that you saved the city, so, well done. It was fortunate you brought along Oswald's journal—it verified everything you claimed, and a great deal more besides."

"What will happen with the Queen?" Ellie asked. "I mean, will she *continue* to be Queen? Or... Monarch, anyway?"

Whistler raised an eyebrow. "I'm just a policeman, Miss. That sort of thing is well beyond the scope of my duties, fortunately. A secretary of my acquaintance told me a few things when he slipped out of the cabinet's closed session, and I thought I'd pass the information along, as a courtesy to Pimm. If pressed, I would guess the country's leading scientists will make a deeper study of the Affliction, since we can hardly treat it like a shameful secret anymore—once your Queen suffers from an illness, it tends to become a priority. Legally, I understand the Queen is still the Queen, unless they decide she's a King instead. Either way, she's clear that she intends to continue ruling, with Prince Albert at her side. He's been set free from the Tower, and cleared of all wrongdoing. Good news all around, eh? Apart from, ah, transformative plagues."

"And what of Adams?" Pimm said.

Whistler shook his head. "No sign of your mystery man, Pimm. You're sure he exists? We did find one of those beasts, with all its tentacles torn off, and a hole punched right in its—forgive me, ladies, I forget myself. But of our fifth hero, no sign. From what you told me about his criminal entanglements, he may have wanted to avoid attention."

Ellie yawned. "When do you think we'll be permitted to go home and sleep?"

"Ah," Whistler said, and smiled. "Not quite yet. My friend the secretary was sent to fetch you, but I said I'd run that errand for him. I'm told the Queen wants to see you."

"Why?" Pimm said.

"I think it's best you find out for yourself."

"I dub thee knight," the Queen said, touching Ellie on first one shoulder with her sword, and then the other. The officials gathered behind them in the opulent chamber muttered, and Ellie's head spun as she stared at the Queen's shoes.

Women were not *knighted*. A woman could be made a *dame*, but not a knight. And yet: Sir Eleanor! The Queen had refused to brook any argument in this matter, and had insisted on knighting them *all*, in the old style, with a sword.

Ellie rose from the knighting stool, and barely heard the words as the Queen invested her with her knightly orders. Then the Queen moved on to Winnie, dubbing her Sir Winifred. Since Winnie had begun life as a man, perhaps that honor made more sense, but…

Pimm and Ben had been knighted already, and stood off to one side of the chamber, looking as dazed as Ellie felt. She joined them as the Queen completed the ceremony, then handed the sword to a waiting official. "We feel most secure," the Queen said, glaring at the men clustered together in the back of the chamber, "with defenders such as these to protect our realm."

The room was silent, but then someone began to applaud. Ellie recognized the horse-faced woman clapping her hands as Prince Albert, now restored to the position of prince consort—or perhaps princess consort? Who could say? If Ellie could be a knight…

With Albert leading the applause, the others joined in, some with what seemed to be genuine enthusiasm. Ellie recognized members of Parliament, cabinet ministers, and other assorted dignitaries, some of them familiar from the flight at Hyde Park, all brought together to deal with the crisis of monsters from another world—a crisis which was, more or less, finished by the time they arrived.

The crowd came forward to congratulate the new knights. A man with enormous whiskers greeted Winnie as "Lady Pembroke," and earned an icy stare. "I think you'll find you mean 'Sir Winifred,'" she said coolly, and the man fell over himself apologizing.

Somehow, in all the milling of people, Pimm managed to take Ellie by the elbow and lead her away to a pair of chairs in a corner, where they sat, knees just touching, half hidden behind an enormous leafy plant in a pot. "You've got quite a story to write, I suppose," he said. "A firsthand account of the madness in the park. When I saw you wielding that sparking sword! I should *not* have been surprised, I know, but I was. You never stop surprising me, Ellie."

Writing. The newspaper! How could such mundane matters still exist? "Heavens. I suppose I do have to go to work again, don't I? Somehow I don't think I'll ever be able to convey the experience properly, but I'll have to try."

"Alas, the knighthood does not bring with it a guaranteed income for life," Pimm said. "You will need to go on living by your pen. And we readers are all the luckier for your necessity."

"It occurs to me," Ellie said, "to wonder what poor Ben will do? Now that he's Sir Ben he can hardly carry on being a street tough. How will his old friends treat him now?"

"It's not entirely fitting for his new station," Pimm said. "But I was thinking of inviting him to join my household. He was in service, actually, as a boy, before circumstances conspired to send him to London to seek his fortune. And I am in desperate need of a valet. Of course, I'll have to call him something like captain of the guard, to avoid offending his knightly dignity, but I can hardly think of a better man to have at my back."

"So you shall all live together, in that lovely house," Ellie said. "You, and Winnie, and Ben."

Pimm cleared his throat. "I, ah. Ellie. I wish... well, that is to say..."

"I know," Ellie said. "It is complicated. Do you know what Winnie said to me, after we electrocuted the last of those monsters? She said we'd ruined everything. If Oswald's plan had gone off, things would have changed, all of *society* would have changed, all the old rules would have fallen by the wayside, and you and I, we could have..."

Pimm took her hand. "Our Queen is now a man, but is still somehow a Queen. We have driven off monsters brought from a place stranger than the stars. You have been made a *knight*. I would say things *are* changing. I know nothing is simple, but... perhaps we can cope with things that are complicated?"

"I—"

Winnie appeared. She was holding a glass of champagne, acquired from who knows where. "Ellie! There you are. I have a proposal for you. How would you like to help me write a book?"

Ellie blinked. "What do you mean?"

"I mean I'm a fine storyteller, but I've never been good at getting the *words* to line up on paper, as it were. I want you to help me turn my life story into something people would actually care to read. We'll skim over my undistinguished youth, I think, devote a chapter to my Affliction, another to my subsequent despair, another to my peculiar arrangement with Pimm, another to my frequenting of salons and gatherings of artists, with perhaps a hint of scandal, subtly done, and for the climax, of course, my heroic actions in saving Queens, slaying horrible monsters, and etc.—"

"Winnie, you can't be serious!" Ellie said.

"No, never," Winnie said. "But I *can* be notorious, and give lectures, and become very rich from the fame, in my own right. But we have to be quick, Ellie dear, because the Queen's transformation is going to make changing into the opposite sex a *cause célèbre*, and will doubtless bring the Afflicted out in droves to tell their own stories. But *I* have the best story, I'm sure. What do you say?"

"But… what about your marriage to Pimm? If you tell the truth—"

"I daresay the marriage will be revealed as a sham," Winnie said. "It shall be stricken from the books, I'd think. The Queen has promised to exert her influence to smooth over any little… technical difficulties with the Church." She put one hand on Pimm's shoulder, but smiled down at Ellie. "Poor Pimm! He looks as if he's been hit in the forehead with a hammer. See, my lord? I told you I'd think of something. But it seems there's no need to fake my own death to set you free. I can live my own true life instead. And if I've misjudged the public and people are too disapproving, that's fine—I'll just move to Paris. Someone might as well use that vast tunnel they're digging under the channel."

She knelt and threw her arms around Pimm's and Ellie's necks, dragging them down from their chairs to the floor in a three-way embrace. "You had better treat this woman properly, Pimm. She and I have been in battle together. She is my sister in arms."

"I, ah—" Pimm stammered.

"Oh, dear," Winnie said. "I'll have the most difficult decision of my *life* ahead of me!"

Pimm and Ellie drew back, exchanged a glance, and then frowned at Winnie together. "You will?" Ellie said.

"What decision is that?" Pimm said.

"Whether I should be the maid of honor at your wedding," Winnie said, "Or best man!"

The Music of Flowers

With Oswald dead, Adam had no particular reason to flee the city. He had no particular reason to *stay*, either, but habit sent him back to the tunnel near the Serpentine after he finished beating the monster to death. He slipped into a fetid hole in the ground and plodded along a dark tunnel, the ichor of a fell beast drying on his fists. Killing the monster had left him feeling curiously hollow. He wanted to create life, and to kindle love, but he was only skilled at murder, and destruction.

After a time, he reached his workshop. He flung his mask to the floor, where it cracked in two, and then he stretched out on his own operating table, closing his eyes. He never slept, and did not own a bed, but he was so terribly weary, now. He envied mortals their capacity for rest.

A hand brushed his forehead, and his eyes shot open. He grabbed the wrist hard enough to crush bone, but the person who'd touched him did not cry out. She simply gazed down at him, then stroked his cheek with her other hand.

"Margaret," he whispered. "You... what are you doing here?"

"You must promise you will try not to frighten me again," Margaret said. "Do not shout, or smash things, when we disagree. Can you promise?"

"I... of course. I promise."

"I, myself, can make no promises," she said. "But you saved my life, and as I ran through the tunnels, I thought back on our talks, when I was lost in the dark. I thought of your voice. You are fearsome to look upon, Adam. You know that. And you may be capable of fearsome acts as well. But you have a gentle heart. I believe that. A heart that is capable of love."

Adam closed his eyes. He held her cool hand in his own. "Oh, Margaret."

"You said you thought we might visit someplace warm. I… have always wanted to see Spain."

"We will go to Cordoba," Adam said, and opened his eyes to look upon her beautiful, perfect face. The perfect thing he had made, given life by a beautiful soul *no* man could have created. "In the spring. When the scent of orange blossoms fills the air. That smell… it smells like the chiming of church bells, Margaret."

"I look forward hearing them," she said.

THE END

Acknowledgments

Thanks to the writers of some of my favorite detective novels, without whom I wouldn't have invented Pimm—he came to life as a thought experiment, one part Sayers-ish nobleman detective, one part functional alcoholic PI with a troubled past. Ellie Skye is a slightly ahistorical homage to the great journalist Nellie Bly (the novel is set in the year of Bly's birth). I wouldn't have written this book without the formative influence of K.W. Jeter's *Infernal Devices* and *The Anubis Gates* by Tim Powers, which introduced me at an impressionable age to the joys of the gonzo-historical novel. I owe a similar debt to the wonderfully weird English mysteries of John Dickson Carr. (The debts I owe to Mary Shelley, Virginia Woolf, Arthur Conan Doyle, and some others are likely more apparent from the text.)

Thanks to Jess Nevins, our field's leading expert on fictional histories, for providing details for some of my little meta-fictional Easter eggs; and to Shannon Page for heroic acts of copyediting.

A complete bibliography of research materials would be exceedingly long and likely of minimal interest, but I owe special debts to *Murray's Modern London* (1860), Henry Mayhew's *London Labour and the London Poor,* Dickens's *Dictionary of London*, and Edward Stanton's astonishingly detailed 1863 map of London (which spent much of the past year spread out across nearly the entirety of my office floor).

My gratitude to Jeremy Lassen at Night Shade for acquiring this book; to Ross Lockhart for his editing; and to my agent Ginger Clark, for handling practical matters so I could concentrate on the impractical ones.

And, of course, the utmost thanks to my wife and son for their tolerance and patience with me over many months of writing, muttering to myself, and wandering around the library for entirely too long at a time.